Time was running out

The streets became a blur of artificial light, people and moving buildings. No time now to make a proper recce. They had seen enough; all they had to do was to get out.

But Ryan had no idea where they were headed. He could only trust Jak's instinct.

The albino youth cut across more streets, this time firing to left and right, the Colt Python clearing a path before him. Some of the ville dwellers were alert enough to react when the recce party burst past them, drawing their blasters, but the blistering return fire was enough to drive them to cover.

And now, after seeing the vid broadcasts as they took flight, Ryan and the others had no illusions that they could proceed without being noticed.

Their only hope was to reach the exit tunnel and escape down the sewer. And it was nowhere in sight.

JAMES AXLER

DEATHLANDS®

Strontium Swamp

A GOLD EAGLE BOOK FROM
W⊕RLDWIDE®

TORONTO • NEW YORK • LONDON
AMSTERDAM • PARIS • SYDNEY • HAMBURG
STOCKHOLM • ATHENS • TOKYO • MILAN
MADRID • WARSAW • BUDAPEST • AUCKLAND

First edition June 2006

ISBN 0-373-62584-7

STRONTIUM SWAMP

Printed in U.S.A.

Dictators ride to and fro upon tigers which
they dare not dismount. And the tigers
are getting hungry.

—Winston Churchill,
1874–1965

THE DEATHLANDS SAGA

This world is their legacy, a world born in the violent nuclear spasm of 2001 that was the bitter outcome of a struggle for global dominance.

There is no real escape from this shockscape where life always hangs in the balance, vulnerable to newly demonic nature, barbarism, lawlessness.

But they are the warrior survivalists, and they endure—in the way of the lion, the hawk and the tiger, true to nature's heart despite its ruination.

Ryan Cawdor: The privileged son of an East Coast baron. Acquainted with betrayal from a tender age, he is a master of the hard realities.

Krysty Wroth: Harmony ville's own Titian-haired beauty, a woman with the strength of tempered steel. Her premonitions and Gaia powers have been fostered by her Mother Sonja.

J. B. Dix, the Armorer: Weapons master and Ryan's close ally, he, too, honed his skills traversing the Deathlands with the legendary Trader.

Doctor Theophilus Tanner: Torn from his family and a gentler life in 1896, Doc has been thrown into a future he couldn't have imagined.

Dr. Mildred Wyeth: Her father was killed by the Ku Klux Klan, but her fate is not much lighter. Restored from predark cryogenic suspension, she brings twentieth-century healing skills to a nightmare.

Jak Lauren: A true child of the wastelands, reared on adversity, loss and danger, the albino teenager is a fierce fighter and loyal friend.

Dean Cawdor: Ryan's young son by Sharona accepts the only world he knows, and yet he is the seedling bearing the promise of tomorrow.

In a world where all was lost, they are humanity's last hope....

Chapter One

Ryan Cawdor curled up into a fetal ball, trying to gain some respite from the sand that lashed at his skin, scouring into every crevice, biting through the material of his clothes, the exposed parts of his body raw with the sharp winds that blew the grit against him. The more he tried to cover the exposed flesh, the harder the sands ripped into the few inches of skin that he couldn't cover. What the sand didn't scour, the rain did. The howling winds of the storm carried with them a chem-loaded rain that hit hard with each drop, the soft acids within the water making exposed skin soapy and easy to peel back. Like a rubbery solution that eased away from flesh under pressure, the chem rain began to break down any exposed area. Ryan struggled to cover as much of his skin as possible.

The storm had come upon the companions quickly, and in the flat landscape there was nowhere to hide. As the dusk bled slowly into night, the wind from nowhere had whipped up across the expanse of sand, lifting clouds of the vicious, stinging particles and the bludgeoning raindrops that had eaten into the companions with little warning.

In the confusion and the darkness, they had been separated, despite their desire to stick close together. With no landmarks and no outcrops to provide even the barest minimum of shelter, they had stumbled blind into the storm, losing sight of one another. With nothing to identify their position, they were now completely alone.

Ryan tried to protect his body as much as possible from the buffeting of the storm, burrowing into the loose surface of the desert floor, taking the itching, shifting sands as a lesser problem than the stinging clouds of the storm and the eviscerating rain. Hoping it would soon pass. These storms had never, in his experience, lasted that long. But there was always a first time. Mebbe this would be it, mebbe this would take forever to blow itself out, scourging the skin from his flesh as it proceeded, leaving him nothing but a mess of bleeding flesh, the nerve endings rubbed raw by the insistent grains of sand.

Every fiber and muscle ached as he tried to hunker down lower into the sand, forming a barrier between himself and the storm.

It hadn't started like this. A few hours earlier, it had been different…

WAKING from a jump, the hammering in Ryan Cawdor's head felt as if every single atom in his body had been ripped apart and then put back together again with sledgehammer force—which it had, but why did it have to feel that way every time? Why the fireblasted hell couldn't he get used to the jumps in the mat-trans? The companions had made enough of these jumps for their bodies to acclimatize by now, surely?

Getting to his feet, checking almost unconsciously that everything was there, and somehow he hadn't lost a leg or and arm in the jump, Ryan took a look around the chamber. The armaglass was a smoky gray tinged with electric blue. It was semiopaque and he could see the faint outline of the anteroom beyond, thanks to a dim light. It was empty, which was a good thing; and it seemed to be in one piece, which was another. The random nature of the comp-controlled jumps every time the chamber door shut meant that it was always a gamble: one day they could end up in a chamber where the redoubt had been flooded, or the redoubt had collapsed, so that the chamber trapped them in a mass of compacted rock with no way out. The only consoling thought was that this hadn't happened so far, and that the old tech would probably screw up under such conditions, meaning that the chamber wasn't in working order and could not materialize them...hopefully.

There were still a few tendrils of white mist around the circular disks that were geometrically arranged on the chamber floor. So he had come 'round quickly after the jump. He wondered how the others had fared.

J. B. Dix was breathing heavily, slumped on the floor, his hand still unconsciously gripping the stock of his mini-Uzi. His fedora had fallen over his face, masking his features, and his body had the awkward, splayed posture of a man yet to come 'round. Next to him, Mildred Wyeth was sitting against the chamber wall, her head back, her plaits hanging down her back. She was moaning softly, her eyes flickering behind the still-closed lids. Slowly, she was beginning to surface from the rigors of the journey. She coughed as something caught in her throat, bringing her up faster as she fought the choking, her eyes suddenly wide but still not focusing.

Ryan's attention was taken by the sounds behind him. Whirling, and instantly regretting it as his head spun, he saw that Krysty Wroth was coming to her feet. Her long fur coat was draped across her shoulders, and she hugged it tight to herself as she shivered, her lips twisting into a wry grin as his eye met hers.

"Never get used to that, eh, lover?" she said in a cracked, dry voice.

Ryan shook his head gently, not trusting his own parched throat. He marveled at the way in which Krysty was able to shake off the rigors of the jump. She looked a whole lot better than he felt as she turned her attention to Doc Tanner, who had been lying at her side. He was mumbling to himself, twitching convulsively, his brow beaded with sweat. Doc had suffered more than any of them could ever know from the rigors of the mat-trans. He had been trawled through time as well as space, and the resultant physical strains had made him weak. Every time they made a jump, it seemed as if it could be the last one for the old man. How much longer before his body ceased to fight the demands placed upon it and gave in? Certainly, his wandering mind sometimes had a tenuous grasp upon reality.

While Krysty tried to make Doc comfortable, Ryan turned his attention to Jak Lauren. The albino youth was tough and wiry, pound for pound perhaps the strongest among them. Yet he was the one most affected by the jump. He was still unconscious, and Ryan turned him onto his side so that he wouldn't choke, for the first thing that Jak did on coming around, without fail, was to vomit copiously.

By the time that Jak stirred, and wretched his guts onto the floor of the chamber, the others were all conscious and beginning to return to their normal selves. Soon, they were ready to tackle the redoubt beyond the chamber door, waiting only for Jak to fully recover.

Once conscious, and once he had spewed, Jak's progress was always rapid.

Their tactic was always the same: move swiftly but carefully, advancing, securing an area and then moving on until they were into the corridors of the redoubt, and knew whether there was any immediate danger.

In this instance, they were safe. The redoubt was empty, with little sign that it had been disturbed since the nuke-caust that had rendered all of these old military posts obsolete.

HOWLING AROUND HIM, the storm ate into Ryan, sapping both his strength and also his will. The iron-hard resolve that had kept him going in these situations was draining under the assault of the storm, the pain of the sands flaying at him, and the cold that was riven into his bones with the winds and every heavy drop of chem rain. Tiredness crept over him like a warming blanket, tugging at his mind and begging him to give in to the desire to fall into a sleep—a sleep from which he would never wake. He knew the first signs of hypothermia and knew that to give in to the desire to sleep now would be the first step in his own chilling. The bone-freezing cold of the desert night was intensified by the bone-shattering winds, and he had to fight to stay awake, to keep moving, no matter how little, to keep the circulation going around his body.

If only he wasn't so tired. If only they had been able to rest up in the redoubt.

But it hadn't been possible…

THE REDOUBT HAD BEEN empty for a long time, and the old tech powering the comp systems had been in a long-spiraling state of decay. Gradually the machinery and plant that powered the redoubt had begun to break down. And as one piece fell into decay the effect spread to another part, making it malfunction, so the gradual decline of the redoubt began.

As the companions searched the redoubt, the extent of the shutdown became clear. Corridors were swathed in gloom where the lighting had failed. The elevators were stuck, failing to respond to the call button. Sec doors had closed as the key circuits had fused, causing them to fall and jam. It was only because the companions had used the redoubts for so long, and knew that within the circuits lay a manual override that they were able to get the doors raised. Not that it led to anything. The darkened corridors beyond told their own mute stories.

The biggest immediate problem was that there was no running water. They had been hoping that, at the least, they would be able to shower. But the only water that could be found was the bottled variety kept in the kitchen areas. The pump for the water recycler and tank had long since ceased to function, and the only way to access the tank would be to try to break into it. Even then, given that the system had failed, all that would await them would be the contents of a stale and stagnant tank.

Further exploration revealed that dried foods and self-heats were still intact, but anything that had been kept in cold storage had spoiled as this system, too, had succumbed to the ravages of entropy. At least they would be able to stock up on water and self-heats to take with them into the outside world. For any chance of staying to rest within the redoubt, even without the luxury of bathing, was to be lost to them.

"Notice anything?" Mildred had asked as they explored the redoubt.

"Hard to breathe," Jak murmured. "Sweat, too…"

"Yeah, exactly—only we haven't been working our asses off, and it isn't too hot," Mildred replied.

Ryan agreed. "Figured the air was stale in here. It smelled kind of musty when we first came out of the chamber, and it's not been getting any fresher."

"Right," Mildred said firmly. "Which can only mean one thing, right Ryan?"

Ryan looked up at the blank ceiling of the redoubt tunnel, as though it would give him an answer other the one which he feared. But there was only one real option here. "Cooling and recycling for the air is as fucked as the water. We're breathing it in, and it isn't going anywhere. If we don't get out of here real soon, then there isn't going to be any air left."

"That's assuming we can get the main door open," Krysty murmured.

"We'll take that one when we come to it," Ryan muttered. "Best to get what we can and get up there as soon as possible. J.B., you and Doc take the armory, see if there's anything we can use in there. Jak, Krysty, you go back and gather as much water and self-heats as you can.

Mildred, I'll go with you and see what's in the infirmary.
We try to do this as quickly as we can, and then get the
hell out."

"Remember, hurrying is going to make it worse," Mildred counseled before they split up. "Take it easy, and
make every move count. Try to conserve the air by not
breathing so hard. Quick, but not so quick you get shorter
of breath than this air makes you, okay? And let's keep
talking to a minimum."

J.B. shot her a look that told her he felt that last sentence had been a waste of words in itself, stating the obvious. She grinned back at him before they went their
separate ways, keen to loot the redoubt of any resources
while they still had the air to keep them alive.

Moving swiftly and silently, with no need for words
now that they knew what they were doing, they soon had
their tasks completed. For Jak and Krysty, to return to the
kitchen area and gather up the water and self-heats was a
simple task, and they were soon on their way to the main
corridor leading out into the outside world.

For the other two pairs, things were not so clear-cut. The
redoubts had all been planned and built along similar lines,
which made finding their way around a relatively easy task.
However, some were larger and deeper than others, and in
some the positions of some of the storage and working areas
had been altered to accommodate the specific purpose of that
redoubt. So although each pair knew where it should head
to find the infirmary and the armory, they couldn't be sure
if each should be where they suspected until they reached
them. And if the locations had been changed, then it would
take up valuable time to find the alternative placement.

So it was with some trepidation that each pair arrived at its intended location. Thankfully, this redoubt was of a standard layout and they had found their target at the first attempt. Mildred and Ryan cleared the infirmary of any supplies that might be of use, the one-eyed warrior packing bandages and dressings while Mildred went through the drugs cabinet to find pills that might still be potent and of some use to them. They both moved swiftly and efficiently. Eventually, Mildred finished rifling the drug supplies and nodded to Ryan, who returned the gesture. They made their way toward the exit.

On another level, Doc and J.B. had found the redoubt armory, which was mostly intact. The Armorer scanned the racks of blasters on the walls and helped Doc to open a few crates that held ammo. Doc knew which boxes of loose ammo and magazines for SMGs fitted the requirements of the companions' weapons, so J.B. left him to this while he scoured the armory for grens and plas ex with which the replenish the stocks kept within the canvas bag he carried.

When both men had completed their tasks, they exchanged looks and then began to make their way out of the armory and toward the exit.

The six companions converged when they neared the main corridor, which led to the exit sec door. They had to take the emergency stairs between levels where the elevator was the only means of access between levels. Some redoubts were ramped all the way through, others had only elevators between some or all of the levels. It depended on the purpose for which the particular redoubt had been built.

In this instance, the redoubt was a relatively small installation that would have carried a military complement of no more than one hundred, and had no wags or troop carriers stashed in its depths. So a consistent ramp hadn't been necessary, and the companions were left to make their way up the emergency stairs.

The darkness became filled with bright lights that flickered and raced only in their own skulls as the poor air made them light-headed with the lack of oxygen. It said much about the staleness of the air on the stairwell that the atmosphere on reaching the exit onto the main corridor seemed sweeter.

Each of them gulped down lungfuls of the stale air, sucking the oxygen from it to compensate for the burning in their lungs. But the comparative sweetness was dangerously deceptive. There was still very little oxygen in this part of the redoubt and all they succeeded in doing was filling their systems with yet more carbon dioxide.

Every step was now an effort, like swimming through sludge, as they made their way along the corridor toward the sec door that led to the outside. The corridor seemed to lengthen like an optical illusion, the door zooming away into the distance as molten lead filled their limbs.

If the sec door refused to open, then there was no knowing how they would get out. There was no guarantee that the main door had a manual override, though most did. But even if there was one, there was no knowing if they had the strength—any of them—to operate it before the final darkness descended.

The interior lighting was still working in that area of the redoubt, and they moved under neon strip lighting that seemed to move away at speed toward the silent and imposing exit door.

Maybe that was a good sign. Maybe the electricity was working in this section.

Jak took the initiative. Unlike the others, his wiry frame dictated a lesser capacity for oxygen, and his shallow breathing gave him an edge over the others. Measuring every pace so that he didn't waste energy, draw in any more of a breath than was necessary, he hurried to the keypad that triggered the main sec door lock. Lagging behind, the others watched as though from a great distance, willing him to reach the door, willing the system to still be operable.

Narrowing his eyes to focus as the extra effort and the poor quality of air made his vision swim before him, he carefully tapped in the numbers and waited. There was no lever to press.

It seemed like forever, but could have been only a second or two, slowed only by the failing circuitry to respond immediately. The door creaked and moaned, and lifted slowly, air rushing in from beneath the ever-widening gap as the differing volumes on each side attracted the outside atmosphere.

And the sand.

There was a desert outside the redoubt, and one that had filled the small enclave that housed the redoubt entrance. Most of the redoubts had either been built into outcrops or in small valleys to mask the entrance in those predark times. The corridors from the main door leading into the complex itself was usually on an incline, built so that the gradient was hardly noticeable. But still there: it had made the struggle toward the exit door from the emergency stairwell that bit harder, that much closer to a gradual fade from consciousness.

But now they gulped greedily at the fresh air that came in through the opening door. The light outside, and the heat that flooded in, suggested that it was the middle of the day. The sand spilled down the incline, trails of grain snaking around their feet, around their hands and knees as they sank down, thankful that they were now able to breathe freely.

It took Krysty a little while to realize what was happening. Unlike the others, who were either unable to focus or had their eyes closed, concentrating on drinking in the fresh air, the Titian-haired beauty was looking down and could see the sand build up around her hands, planted on the floor of the corridor, flowing and growing so that it covered her knuckles, then the backs of her hands, burying them up to the wrist and flowing around her calves and thighs, pulling at her as she tried to free them.

She yelled, wordless, and after the lack of air it came out as a dry, hushed croak, but it was enough to make the others look up.

The entrance to the redoubt had to have been buried in a sand dune, and the opening of the door had set up a movement in the sands that were drawing them into the tunnel, down the slope, flowing at speed. There was sky visible above the sand, but also a vast wall of the almost liquid grains that were slowly sweeping toward them, growing with momentum as the mass began to move.

Marshaling what strength he could, the lactic acids in his muscles that hadn't dispersed easily with the decreasing oxygen making his limbs feel like they were filled with molten metal, Ryan got to his feet, pulling himself free of the sand so that it only flowed around his calves. He could feel the growing strength of it as the momentum of the fall built. Unless the companions moved quickly, the sea of sand would sweep them all back into the redoubt, crushing them against one of the closed interior sec doors, suffocating them before they had a chance to break free.

J.B. and Mildred were also on their feet, the black woman casting her eyes around for Doc. His frail physique meant that he had suffered the most from lack of oxygen and was the most vulnerable right now. She grunted as she located him. He was still on all fours, looking down, barely aware that the sea of sand was burying him, now up to his elbows and halfway up his thighs. If he didn't move quickly, it would cover him and start to smother the life from him.

Jak, recovering quicker than the others, had taken in what was happening and used the flow of the sand to save energy that was only just returning, surfing the sand back to where the others were moving, almost in slow motion. The wiry albino joined Mildred, and they tugged Doc free of the sand, hauling him to his feet. He grunted and whispered to himself, wordless mutterings that were masked by his inability to speak through a parched throat. His eyes were staring and vacant. Whatever Doc was seeing, it wasn't the corridor before him.

Jak and Mildred began to haul themselves out of the sand, struggling to move their still-leaden limbs against the flow, hampered by Doc's near deadweight. As they moved forward, Ryan and J.B. stepped in to help, joined by Krysty when they reached the point at which she stood. The six companions formed a chain, uniting their strength—failing as it was—to fight against the flow of the sand to try to reach the yellow-tinged sky that lay at the top of the spilling wall.

It was like swimming in a swamp: the current of the sand wanted to pull them back into the redoubt, but they fought against it, even though their limbs ached and their lungs, still fighting to make up oxygen deficit, felt like bursting.

With every fiber screaming for them to stop, to just give in and let the sand sweep them down into its warm and welcoming depths, they crested the wave that flowed from the peak of the wall, struggling until they were past the top and pulling themselves over sand that was barely moving.

The world swum around them, stars and lights flickering inside their skulls, their lungs screaming for more air. It was only now that they were on the outside, away from the fetid air of the redoubt, that Mildred realized why it had been such a struggle. Out here, the air was little better. It was foul and hot, the sun heating up the chem clouds that made the sky so yellow. Just to breathe normally, a person had to try twice as hard against the atmosphere.

Looking around at her five companions, Mildred could see that Doc was almost unconscious and the other four were barely able to move. Come to that, she felt herself teetering on the brink of unconsciousness. She looked up at the sky, squinting into the intense light. It was impossible to see beyond the covering of clouds, but she figured that it was the middle of the day. If they succumbed to unconsciousness now, they could dehydrate and risk exposure and sunstroke. She lifted her head and looked around. Now that they were out of the valley in which the redoubt entrance was housed, she could see why the wall of sand had tried to cave in upon them.

The surrounding area was a flat desert, with no peaks or valleys, and no scrub that she could see through the chem-assisted heat haze. The entire area was flat and covered with sands. At some time, the area could have been arable, but the intense buffeting of the chem storms had left the area a wasteland of desert, all features of the land covered by layers of sand. That had to have been what had happened to the redoubt entrance. Once in a valley, the dip had been filled by the sand, and in opening the door they had done nothing more than allow the sea of grains to shift once more.

As she tried to focus on the area where the redoubt entrance had been, and where the sands were already settling into their new pattern, she found darkness creeping into the corner of her vision. Alarmed, she battled against it, looked for the others. Doc was down, Jak was trying to get to his feet but stumbling and falling once more. She couldn't locate J.B., he had to be behind her somewhere. She caught a flash of Krysty's hair as the woman tried to stay awake, shaking her mane before her head slumped once more. Where was Ryan? He had to be behind her somewhere, too...

The blackness closed in, blotting out all else.

RYAN FELT THAT he had to black out all else and concentrate on keeping awake. The howling wind swept through him, chilling him to the marrow, and he felt the heavy splash of the rain on his back and sides, could almost feel the acids eating through his clothes. He burrowed deeper into the sand, feeling the exposed areas buffeted less and less, but always mindful of the new danger. If he should accidentally breathe the sand, clogging his nostrils and lungs with the sharp grains, then all this would be for nothing. He was still weakened, and didn't know how much he could fight against that implacable enemy. The sand around him was still, protected him from the worst of the storm, but held its own dangers.

It was important he stay triple red, yet everything in him wanted to curl up and go to sleep.

If he did, he would close his eye forever.

There was no way of telling how long it lasted. Only that each second could have been an hour, and each hour a day. It was all as one: the winds, the sand, the rain...

But gradually he became aware of a lessening in the winds and the rain, the sand stung his skin less often. He didn't dare relax, in case his body give in and sink into a fatal unconsciousness. If anything, he redoubled his efforts to stay alert, to try to determine what was going on around him.

Even after he was sure, he waited a little longer. Gradually, Ryan disinterred himself from his sandy tomb and, every muscle and tendon creaking, rose unsteadily to his feet.

The sky above was clear, the stars twinkling peacefully above as though the previous hours had never occurred.

The storm was over.

MILDRED FELT LIKE a dog turd that had been left on the sidewalk to dry out for an eternity. The heat was still burning, but nowhere near as intense as it had been before. She opened her eyes and immediately screwed them tight again. She had been lying on her back and the light was too bright to take. She rolled over, feeling the hot sand against her face, and opened her eyes again. After adjusting, she tentatively raised herself onto all fours. Once she felt steady, she groped for some of the bottled water they had rescued from the redoubt and distributed among themselves. It was tepid and unpleasant, but it was liquid, and it helped rehydrate her. She was slick with sweat, yet the military OD green jacket she wore had covered her skin and saved her from too much direct exposure to the sun.

But what of the others?

Mildred slowly raised herself to her feet and looked around. Jak was sitting up, drinking. Like her, he looked as though he had only just regained consciousness. He managed a weak grin and slowly rose. Ryan and Krysty seemed to be coming around slowly, and J.B. appeared by her side as though from nowhere.

"Doc's not so good," he said simply, guiding her to where the old man lay. He had less covering than the rest of them, and so had suffered most from being unconscious under the harsh sun. Mildred settled herself beside him. His skin was burned and flaky, and there was froth flecked at the corners of his mouth. He was mumbling incoherently to himself.

While J.B. lifted his head, she used some of the water to wet his lips and gums, then pried away the dry skin of his mouth where it stuck to his teeth and gums. He reacted to this, and she risked pouring a little of the liquid into his mouth. He choked at first, but soon began to swallow.

While J.B. continued to feed Doc the water, Mildred fumbled in her jacket pockets for salt tablets. She had been able to replenish her supply from the redoubt its infirmary. Doc would be in dire need of these after being so long exposed to the sun.

By the time Doc had recovered enough to realize where he was, Krysty, Ryan and Jak had joined Mildred and J.B., clustered around the old man.

Doc managed a weak grin. "Always the liability, I fear," he whispered through chapped lips. "If I were a horse, then the knacker would be a necessity. And if I were a carpenter—"

"Shut up, you old fool," Mildred interrupted. "You're in no fit state to be talking sense, let alone the drivel you always come out with. You need to drink some more, for a start."

Doc agreed, taking a water bottle from her.

Ryan had been surveying the area while they stood over Doc, and he didn't like what he saw. Stretching in every direction was nothing but sand. It was an almost entirely flat landscape, only the occasional undulation of a dune to break the monotony. The sand covered everything so completely that even now he couldn't be too sure where the redoubt entrance had been situated.

J.B. joined him. "Doesn't look so good, does it?"

Ryan shook his head. "Nothing but this fireblasted desert, and no way of getting back to make a jump."

"Which direction gives us the best chance?"

Ryan shrugged. "Your guess is as good as mine. Just looks like sand, as far as you can see. Figure the best thing to do is form into pairs and fan out, see how much territory we can survey." He looked up at the sky. "Hard to tell with this cloud, but I reckon we've got a couple of hours before sundown."

"Only plan that makes sense," J.B. stated. "But one of us should go solo. I can't see Doc being up to it," he murmured, indicating the prone figure.

Ryan shook his head. "Mebbe a good thing. Doc can be our anchor. Gives us somewhere to head back to."

"My dear boy, you are too kind—making an asset from my infirmity," Doc wheezed. "But, I suppose, if it is all I can do, it is, at least, something."

The five companions used their baggage to form a sunbreak around Doc, offering him at least some shading from the sun, angling it to shield him from the angle of its descent. That angle also gave them some kind of compass point from which to try to determine their location. But their first task was to see if they could find shelter before the night fell.

Ryan trekked alone, while Jak accompanied Krysty and J.B. marched with Mildred. The plan was simple, but backbreaking. Taking a different position, they were each to fan out from the point of their location to see if they could sight anything other than sand on the horizon.

Simple, and also soul-destroying, for it soon became apparent that they could march for hours and see nothing but sand stretching out before them, rolling in dunes and broken only by the occasional patch of grass or scrub. As they marched outward, so the sand pulled at their calves, each step an effort to drag their boots from the grip of the sand, sapping what little reserves of energy they had.

It was nearing twilight when they converged once more

on where Doc lay. The old man had used the time well, taking more water and resting, and was now almost back to normal. It was little consolation, however, when they compared their lack of sightings.

"It would appear," Doc said with a glimmer of a smile after listening to them, "that we are caught between a rock and a hard place, except that there are no rocks and the sand is far too soft."

"Wish I could see the funny side, Doc," Ryan muttered. "We've got little option other than to pick a direction at random and keep marching, or try to find the redoubt and force our way on for another jump—and that's always assuming we could dig our way in, which I doubt."

"So it's just the marching, then," Mildred said wryly. "Pick a direction—any direction."

"How about thataway," J.B. said, pointing to his left. "Or mebbe not...'cause I think that's where trouble's coming."

Before he even finished, they knew he was right. A mistral wind was reaching them, tendrils of sand picked up in the light breeze that was getting stronger with each second. The chem clouds had gathered densely in the twilight, and the air became damp as chem rain started to drizzle. The speed at which it gathered was phenomenal.

"Fuck it! Try to get some cover. It's coming down too fast!" Ryan yelled as the first fat, heavy drops of rain began to splatter them and the tendrils of sand became sharp bullwhips of grain, lashing against them.

Within minutes, as they tried to dig a trench into the sand, the storm had risen to a pitch where the sand and the rain made it impossible to see in front of them and the gathering clouds turned twilight into darkest night.

They could no longer see one another.

As the sands were whipped up by the storm, it became hard to even tell where the ground began and ended.

Chapter Two

Ryan Cawdor shuddered and groaned as he raised himself slowly, painfully, from the tomb of sand he had made for himself. Every part of his body was in pain, and parts of his skin felt as though they would slither from his flesh at the slightest touch. He was thankful that there had been no open wounds for the rain to run into, which would have been too painful to contemplate.

He looked around, trying to locate the others, there was no sign of them. No sign of any other life at all. And no sign of the storm, which had blown over as quickly as it had arrived. The sky above was clear, the stars illuminating the dark, the crescent moon casting a pale light over the sands, which now seemed as calm as they had before the storm hit, as flat and undulating, and showed no relation to the whirling clouds of flaying grit that had battered him just a short time before.

They were also completely unrecognizable as the sands on which he had stood before the storm. Although there had been no real landmarks by which to judge, the shape of the dunes had become familiar as they had recced the area. Now, the landscape was unrecognizable, the sands whipped into new contours by the currents of the mistrals and gales of the chem storm. Ryan could be in the same place as before, or he could have been swept along in the tide of the sand, landing miles from where he began. He had no way of knowing. He hadn't felt as though he had been moving, and yet the sands had been shifting around him. Where would his movement begin and the sands end? Or vice versa?

"Fireblast and fuck it," he murmured to himself, sinking to his haunches. He was tired beyond belief, every muscle ached, and his head felt as though it had been pounded by a thousand hammers: a legacy of dehydration and salt loss as much as the storm.

He was alone, with no sign of his companions. The quiet of the night was eerie and unearthly. If he could get past the pounding in his skull, the sound of blood hammering in his ears, then there was nothing beyond. He couldn't remember the last time he'd heard the sounds of silence…if ever.

It meant that the slightest sound would register, however, so Ryan's body tensed, and he whirled around as quickly as his protesting muscles would allow when he heard the whispering of shifting sands from somewhere over his left shoulder.

WHEN THE STORM HIT, Mildred's first thought was not for herself, but for Doc Tanner. For all that she would argue with, and insult the older man, she was aware that he was the most vulnerable of them at this moment. And more than that, she shared with Doc something that none of the others could ever truly understand. Neither of them belonged to this time; they had been thrown into the Deathlands by freaks of chance and designs of evil, both taken from their own times in differing ways and made exiles against their wills. It wasn't something they ever spoke of, but Mildred knew that if Doc bought the farm, she would feel just that bit more alone in a way that could never be truly explained.

Doc had been raised on one elbow when the storm hit, and before the first heavy drops of rain hit him, Mildred had thrown herself down to cover him.

"Madam, contain yourself," Doc yelled in bewildered tones. "I am not that much of an invalid that I need to be treated this way."

"Shut up and dig, you old fool, as deep as you can," Mildred replied, her eyes flashing at him.

"That's more like it," he countered in a milder tone, as he turned to join her in digging into the sand. "I fail to see that this will be of much practical use to us, but I suppose it is all we can do," he continued, raising his voice above the rapidly growing winds.

"Save your breath for when you need it," Mildred snapped back.

J.B. stumbled on them by chance. Blinded by the flying sand, trying to shield his face from the rain as it suddenly roared from the heavens, he turned and stumbled over the backpacks they had earlier set up to act as a sunbreak for Doc, falling into the hollow trench that Mildred and Doc were digging for themselves.

"Nice of you to drop in, John," Mildred yelled, unable to prevent herself cracking the gag despite the situation.

"No time to be funny," J.B. snapped sourly. "Lost the others. Dig and use these to cover us," he yelled as tersely as possibly, pulling one of his canvas bags over the top of them as they scrabbled in the sand.

It was hard to tell exactly what was happening in the narrow trench, but all three of them used their backs to try to reinforce a sand wall, giving themselves a small, clear area of breathing space in the middle. The bags were dragged over the top of them to form a makeshift roof, not as stable as any of them would like, but nonetheless temporarily effective. At least it prevented the sand overhead from burying them, as they became aware of the weight increasing with the buildup of sand on top of their makeshift shelter. It was stiflingly hot, and sand still moved around their bodies. No one would say, but it occurred to all of them that they could possibly be making their own burial ground.

As they seemed to fall deeper into the sand, it became difficult to tell when—or if—the storm subsided.

KRYSTY AND JAK HAD stumbled blindly into each other as the storm began to hit, each searching for the other, and for the rest of their companions. With no place to hide, and no time to move, the storm had taken all of them unaware. Jak cursed himself for not realizing the changes in the air before the others. His instincts dulled just that little too far by the rigors of the day.

Wordlessly, unwilling to waste energy in the middle of such a crisis, and unable to make herself heard above the roar of the storm, Krysty clutched at Jak, pulling him to her as they stumbled and fell. Feeling the acid rain hit her skin, her air coiled tightly to her neck and scalp as the danger increased, Krysty shrugged out of her long fur coat and draped it over herself and Jak, hoping that the chem rain would pass over before enough had fallen to eat through the fur and hide of the coat. They dug themselves into the sands, constantly fighting the shifts that threatened to overwhelm and bury them, rather than provide protection. The coat, just about covering the pair of them where it had been spread out, acted as a buffer between their prone bodies and the raging wind, sand and rain above. It grew heavier as the shifting surface began to cover them, and their arms ached from trying to hold it up just enough to give them some kind of cover without it smothering them.

It was a question of playing odds. Would the storm subside before their muscles finally gave out under the strain?

THE WHISPERING SANDS came from over his shoulder. Ryan whirled and scanned the dunes behind him, the light just good enough for him to be able to see any movement, the sand acting as a reflector to the crescent moon.

About 150 yards away there was a shifting on the surface, as though a bank of sand was rising up out of the mass. Ryan began to walk toward it, unable to move at a faster pace because of the way his feet sank into the loose sand, up to and beyond his ankles.

The sand wall dissolved in a cloud of scattering grains as two figures emerged from behind a blanket of fur, shaking off the sand that had sought to entomb them.

"Krysty, Jak," Ryan yelled, his voice sounding strangely alien and harsh in the silence of the night.

"Ryan, what fuck that?" Jak grinned, relieved to see at least one other of their companions was still alive—come to that, glad that he had managed to survive the storm.

"Weirdest shit I've seen for a long time," Ryan replied, shaking his head. "Come and gone, just like that."

"Just like us, almost," Krysty put in, pulling the coat around herself to keep out the chill of the desert night. "Gaia, you look like shit, lover," she continued, noting how Ryan's exposed areas of skin had been blasted raw by the sand and the chem rain.

"Thanks for pointing that out," he said wryly. "Feels like it, too. Just about managed to keep covered long enough to stop the worst, I guess. Lucky to make it out."

"Yeah. Mebbe only ones," Jak mused, looking around and flexing his aching limbs, trying to get the cramp out of them.

"If we did it, Mildred and J.B. must have. Mebbe they're with Doc," Krysty suggested, hardly daring to voice the opinion that Doc was the least likely to have made it on his own.

"Bastard thing of it is, where would they be?" Ryan asked, scanning the bland and unremitting wastes of the desert.

"You end up there," Jak mused, indicating the disturbed sands where Ryan had dug himself out, "And us here," he continued, indicating their own patch of desert. "Figure same radius others. Mebbe spread out, search."

Ryan agreed. "It's all we can do, I guess."

The friends began to spread out and search in an arc, moving in wider spirals from their beginning. In truth, no one knew exactly what they were looking for. The lanes of the desert had been altered then smoothed by the storm, so unless their friends were attempting to dig out—assum-

ing even that they were alive—then there was no way of
knowing where they lay. Or even if they were together, or
had been separated.

Tired and aching, the search was a struggle. Tired legs
tried to deal with the sucking sands that made each step a
chore; eyes stung by wind, rain and sand, aching from the
same tiredness that beset their limbs, tried to focus on the
flat landscape, searching for something…anything.

It was Jak who stumbled on them. His left combat boot
hit the harder surface of the backpacks that were being
used as a roof for the trench. Expecting his foot to sink into
the sand as before, he was surprised when he hit a harder
surface, and an uneven one that made his ankle buckle beneath him.

"Ryan, Krysty…" he yelled, waving and beckoning to
them in the wan light of the moon.

As they made their way over, battling the sapping desert floor to move as swiftly as possible, Jak began to dig.
Eighteen inches of sand had gathered in some places, but
only six or seven in others, as the bags revealed themselves
to have been steepled on either side of the trench. As he
burrowed into the sand, clearing as much as possible on
his own, he became aware of some movement beneath the
makeshift roof. The angle of the steepling changed as
someone stirred beneath the cover.

Relieved that whoever was under there was still alive,
Jak redoubled his efforts, and he had made good headway
by the time he was joined by Krysty and Ryan, who immediately fell to their knees and helped him to dig. They
cleared the backpacks of the sand that had buried them,
and made an indent into the area around it.

"Think they're okay under there?" Krysty asked anxiously as they continued to dig.

"Mebbe. Whoever it is, at least they're moving," Ryan grunted as he worked.

The makeshift roof was cleared, and the three companions hurried to clear it away from the trench beneath, making room for whoever was underneath to come out.

"Thank Gaia," Krysty breathed as the last piece was removed and she saw J.B., Mildred and Doc lying huddled together. Doc was unconscious once more, but still breathing. Mildred was struggling to stay awake, her breathing labored and her eyes flickering, trying hard to focus. J.B. was the most aware, and it was the Armorer who had been trying to move the roofing from beneath as he heard the others dig and felt the weight upon them decrease.

"Thought you'd never get here," he croaked hoarsely, barely able to speak.

A hot, fetid air had escaped from the narrow trench as they had uncovered it. The air within was almost all that the trio had been able to breathe, the thick layers of sand gathering on top of the roofing making it hard for any other air to filter through. As a result, the heat had been unbearable, and the air had quickly grown foul. On top of their earlier problems with bad air in the redoubt, this had a bad effect on Doc, and the old man had passed out quickly. Mildred and J.B. had tried to keep their breathing as shallow as possible, but had still used the air quickly. If they hadn't been found, it would have been time for them all to buy the farm. The lack of oxygen combined with the weight of the sand pressing on them would have made it impossible for them to dig themselves out.

Ryan held out an arm, which J.B. took, helping to haul himself out of the trench. He collapsed on the sand beside the one-eyed warrior, gasping for breath as he fought to get some relatively fresh air back into his lungs. Jak plunged into the trench, into the gap that the Armorer had left, and lifted Mildred. As the fresher air of the desert night hit her, she began to stir, and Krysty was able to help her out. Mildred fell to the sands as the Armorer had, doubled over as she began to retch and puke.

Doc was harder to lift out. He was a deadweight, and the companions were exhausted from what they had already endured. It took some time for Krysty and Jak, assisted by Ryan, to lift the old man out and lay him on the sands.

Mildred came over to check him almost immediately.

"You okay to do this?" Krysty asked her.

Mildred fixed her with a stare, then shook her head to clear it as the stare became glassy. "I'm not totally there yet, but it's enough to see this old buzzard is okay," she replied.

Doc's vital signs were good. He had passed out from the continuing lack of oxygen. Mildred hoped that the combined effects of the past few hours hadn't caused any lasting damage. Hell, right then she felt as though she'd lost a few brain cells herself, let alone someone like Doc, who acted occasionally as if he didn't have any to spare.

Muttering to himself, lost in some private dream or nightmare, Doc began to surface. He opened his eyes and took in what was around. Remarkably, and with that facility that only Doc had to buck the odds, he seemed to be completely lucid almost immediately.

"By the Three Kennedys, what a day this has been," he remarked mildly. "Any more like that in a hurry, and I fear it shall see the last of me."

"That's not the first time you've said that, Doc," Ryan stated.

"And I fear it shall not be that last," Doc mused. "But we carry on, my dear Ryan, because we have to… The option is too fearful to contemplate."

"Yeah, talk shit, you okay," Jak commented.

Krysty had been surveying the surrounding desert while Mildred tended to Doc, and Ryan joined her.

"Not good, is it?" he murmured to her. "Nothing for as far as the eye can see, and nothing we can use as shelter. The only good thing, as far I can reckon, is that we're completely alone."

She shook her head slowly, and he noticed that her hair was waving independently of her sway, the sentient red tresses flicking like an irritated cat's tail, gathering close to her head instead of flowing free. "There's something, lover. I dunno what it is, and I dunno where it comes from, but there's something out there that we really need to beware of."

"But what? It's like a vast fucking graveyard out there, a killing field with nothing left alive, everything chilled…" Ryan was bewildered. It wasn't that he didn't trust her mutie sense. How much trouble had it saved them in the past? How many imminent dangers had it alerted them to? But what could be out there in this emptiness was something that was beyond him.

"Wish I could tell you," she muttered, drawing closer to him. "All I know is that it's there, whatever it is…"

CHECKING THAT DOC WAS returning to normal, Ryan organized a camp for the night, setting watches and putting
himself and Jak on first watch. They had no materials
with which to build a fire, so those that were sleeping huddled together for warmth in the freezing desert night,
warming themselves with some of the self-heats they had
taken from the redoubt. The cans, with their thermal reactions that were triggered by the act of opening, always
tasted foul. But taste wasn't an issue. It was nutrition, and
it was warming. That was all that mattered. They had no
time or option to be fussy about the additive-soaked fla-
vors of the ancient food.

Despite the cold and the foul food, the four who were
able to sleep soon found themselves falling into slumber,
the rigors of the day and night catching up with them.

It left Ryan and Jak alone with the darkness and the
void of the desert.

"What chances getting past this?" Jak asked softly,
after some time. He had been squatting on his haunches,
still and silent, surveying the night around him. Ryan had
kept his peace, unwilling to break the incredible concentration of the albino mutie. Now he pondered an answer.

"You tell me," he said finally. "No way to make a jump,
no telling how far this stretches, and which direction to
take."

"Tell you one thing…no, two… We now in southeast,
and not alone."

Ryan looked at Jak, puzzled. "How the fireblasted hell
do you know that?"

Jak pointed up at the stars. "Know sky. Not quite same,

but not that different. We head out for west in morning, then sooner or later hit swamps and water."

"How far?" Ryan asked. He trusted Jak implicitly, and felt a sense of relief that was soon quashed.

"Dunno. Not seen this desert before." Jak shrugged. "Mebbe a day, mebbe two, mebbe more."

"Have we got enough water and food to last?" Ryan asked. They had used a lot of the water to counter the effects of dehydration after their ordeal leaving the redoubt. There were few bottles left, and already he had known that it would be necessary to ration them. But now? Then something else occurred to him, and he continued. "What do you mean, we're not on our own?"

Jak grinned. In the moonlight his red eyes glowed and his teeth glinted, the predator in him becoming all too clear.

"Never alone in desert. Come out at night, but driven down by storm. Can hear them, getting nearer. Just wait."

Ryan frowned, but didn't push Jak for further explanation. Instead he hunkered down next to the albino and decided to wait. He didn't have to wait for long.

As the two men crouched, still and silent, their breathing slow and moving into sync with each other, the silence only broken by the snufflings of those sleeping behind them, Ryan became aware of another sound that began to creep into his head, from beyond the limits of normal hearing. At first he thought it was nothing more than the sound of his own nervous system, amplified by the intense silence, then he realized that this was what Jak had been hearing for a long time with his sharpened sense, heightened by years of hunting.

It was a whispering, gentle hissing that grew louder by almost imperceptible degrees until it was clearly audible without his having even been aware of it impinging on his hearing. It was like the whispering of the sands as they moved, but accentuated by more movement within, as though there were several currents moving beneath the surface, making it whisper in different tones, until it built up into an overlap of harmonics that produced strangely shimmering and unsettling sounds.

Ryan inclined his head toward Jak. The albino met his monocular gaze with a vulpine grin that grew ever wider.

The one-eyed warrior was on the verge of blurting out the question. What the hell was this? His answer came to him with a sudden surprise.

Spumes of sand shot up into the night, dunes rose and fell with the disturbances, and suddenly the pale desert floor was filled with dark shapes moving at speeds varying from a crawl to a scuttle.

"Always life, even in desert," Jak whispered softly.

As Ryan's eyes adjusted to the shapes, he could see that there were lizards, spiders, beetles and even a few skinny mammals that looked a little like hybrids between cats and rabbits. The shapes moved over and across one another, starting to engage in combat as some sought to use the others for food.

It was a battle that occurred every night, with some emerging winners and some never even realizing they were losers as their lives were snuffed out. Ryan realized that the creatures were moving in the direction of the camp, and whirled to look behind him. There were none to their rear, just an empty expanse of sound.

"What the hell is going on?" he yelled at Jak, the chatter of the creatures, shrieks of those that were buying the farm, rising to a louder and louder level.

Jak indicated the sand around them and gestured to the rear. "Figure we're uphill, sand deeper where they nest. Mebbe telling us where there's water—"

"That's if they're not headed for us because we're a strange scent," Ryan countered. He turned to the sleeping companions, but could see that the noise had penetrated their rest and they were beginning to waken.

"Ryan, what— Dark night! What the fuck is that?" J.B. yelled, sleep driven from his brain by the shock of the sight that greeted him.

"That's trouble," Ryan snapped. "Triple red, people. We need to get moving, and fast."

"Should take some out," Jak commented. "Food what short of."

"Yeah, and mebbe that's how they see us," Ryan told the albino youth. "They're not much on their own, but there's thousands of the fuckers, and we're not a hundred percent."

Jak shrugged. "Yeah, guess so." He pointed beyond where the initial mass of creatures had come from. In the distance, the sands were exploding as more nests of lizards, spiders, beetles and small mammals were stirring after the temporary hibernations caused by the storm.

"Oh my Lord, I never did like spiders, and I really don't want a crash course in getting used to them now," Mildred cracked as she helped Doc to his feet.

"'Pon my soul, it's almost biblical," the old man breathed as he took in the sight that greeted him. "The plagues came down upon the deserts and—"

"Yeah, some other time, Doc, or else you're gonna be a lizard's next meal," Krysty snapped, cutting him off in midflow. "Why the hell are they all coming this way?"

"Mebbe we're uphill, and they come up this way to search for food and water," J.B. said as he gathered his bags.

"Make more sense if we were downhill," Mildred snapped. "Could be they're all down there because it's easier to make burrows. Maybe this moves more with the storms."

"It doesn't matter," Ryan yelled. "Wake up, people, triple red. We need to outrun these little bastards before they overwhelm us. Just try to keep one step ahead of them."

The companions wasted no more words on speculation, but instead devoted their energy to outrunning the mass of desert life that was closing on them.

Which wasn't as easy as they could have hoped. They were still exhausted, having had no real chance to rest, and the sand was of an erratic depth and consistency, in some places being loose and clinging, in others relatively hard and compacted. For every step forward that seemed to buy them time and distance, there was another where a step meant sinking halfway up to the calf in the clinging sand, tugging insistently at them as they had to tug insistently to free themselves.

Looking over his shoulder, Ryan could see that the creatures were gaining on them. He couldn't tell if they were on an uphill gradient: certainly, the struggle suggested this, but with their fatigue and the erratic depths of the desert floor to impede them, it was almost impossible to tell. Doc was exhausted, and was already falling behind, despite the efforts of Mildred and J.B. to assist him.

Then the worst thing that could happen in the circumstances occured—as Doc freed his left leg and took another step, J.B. moved over slightly to the old man's left, took one step forward, and was swallowed up to the waist in a sudden cave-in. The sand, acting as a top crust at this point, was delicately balanced over a series of tunnels, and the Armorer had put his foot on a weak spot.

He yelled in surprise and pain as his heel hit something hard and the jarring traveled up into his hip. Obviously, there was some kind of rock shelf under this part of the desert, and that was what he hit...but it wasn't all.

His yells grew as he was surrounded by a squealing, yelping mass of fur and teeth that scrabbled to get free of the collapse, using his body as purchase for their scrambled escape.

"Oh my God," Mildred breathed, stunned into a standstill by what was unfolding before her. Even as she muttered those words, the creatures were swarming over the desert floor, scuttling around and over her feet, some of them being pitched up to cling for safety on her calves and thighs as the mass exodus caused fighting among the fleeing rodents.

For that's what they were—rats, with slick black fur and red pinpoint eyes, large teeth and sharp claws threatening in their mass.

Suddenly, the reason for the insects, lizards and other small mammals to be heading in this direction became clear, as did the reason that this area had previously been deserted. The companions now found themselves caught in a territorial war, a struggle for supremacy between the rats and the other life-forms that inhabited the desert wastes. It may even have been a nightly occurrence: the rats raiding the nests of the lizards and reptiles for eggs, the insects falling prey to them, as did the other mammals, which would be vulnerable attacked en masse. On the other hand, there was the exodus of these creatures toward the rats' warrens, still fighting one another but somehow united by a survival instinct that told them to band together against a common enemy.

Their warren violated by the unfortunate step of the Armorer, the rats had fled in panic and were now charging headlong toward their foes, regardless of who was in the way. They swarmed over Doc, the mass of them catching him around the calves and shins, making his knees buckle under their force. He thrashed at them with his silver lion's-head cane, figuring that he could beat them off more effectively using it as a club than drawing the blade contained within.

The old man was wavering dangerously. If he went down, the rats would engulf him and he would be in danger of buying the farm under a hail of angry, disease-ridden rodents. Ryan, Jak and Krysty moved back toward where Doc struggled, and Mildred was trying desperately to help J.B. out of the hole made by his fall. She wasn't helped by the fact that the sand had closed around the hole as soon as the rats had freed themselves, the grains pouring into the opening like water, trapping J.B. up to the thighs in its elusive, slippery grip, still pouring in so that it would cover him up to the waist, the weight of it sealing him in, trapping his legs under the surface, and preventing him from moving.

Some of the rats had reached where the mammals, lizards and insects were swarming over the sand, and a skirmish had commenced between them. The night air was filled with squeals, howls and screams of pain as the rats hit their foes like a furry wall, lashing and biting at anything that came near.

A rustling roar from behind them, the air rent with more squeals, made Ryan turn around. He swore softly at the sight that greeted his eye: there were more rats, those still left in the other parts of the warren, that were now breaking surface, spreading like a sentient carpet over the surface of the sand. They swarmed toward the companions, and the one-eyed warrior knew that this was going to be a rough ride.

The lizards and reptiles, with their toughened hides, were coping well with the attacks of the rats, their tails flicking and breaking the spines of the furry marauders, their tongues wrapping around the creatures and wringing the air from them as the bites of the rodents failed to penetrate the toughened lizard skin. And yet some of the rodents were making their own progress. Masses of them could chill a lizard by swarming over it, the sheer mass of bites getting through the hide, making the creature turn so that its soft underbelly was exposed, an easier target for the razor-sharp teeth.

The insects, although smaller and easily swallowed or crushed by the weight of the rats en masse, had their own weapons to offer: venom from their shells or from their mouths and pincers pierced the rats' flesh, penetrated into their bloodstreams and made them scream in the agony of being chilled.

While thc battle raged just feet from where they were standing, the companions faced their own fight. The rats that had swarmed out of the other sections of the warren were upon them, the sheer weight of the rodents moving around and beneath them making it hard to keep a steady footing, which was particularly important for Mildred and Jak, who were trying to help J.B. out of the sand, where he was now buried up to the waste. It was almost impossible to try to dig him out, as the sand was covered with rats that—although they had no interest in the Armorer, and had a mind only to join the battle below—were only too willing to lash out at any hands that tried to move them and scoop the sand. In their haste, they were climbing over J.B.'s torso, swarming over his neck and head and almost obscuring him from view.

Ryan and Krysty reached Doc and helped the old man steady himself as he swiped at the rats with his cane. Together, the three of them began to move toward where Jak and Mildred labored.

Ryan drew his panga from its thigh sheath, and he and Doc—who had by now unsheathed the Toledo steel blade contained within the cane—set about carving some space around the area where J.B. was trapped. While they did this, Krysty joined Mildred and Jak in helping to dig the Armorer out of the hole. They still had to fend off the occasional rodent, but the vast majority were now engaged in the struggle for survival just below them, and those that still lingered were, for the most part, deflected by the blows of Ryan and Doc.

"Oh for a pipe to blow," Doc grunted between sweeps of the sword.

"What?" Ryan asked, bewildered.

"A long story, and one I shall—" he grunted as another rat became history "—tell you when it becomes more provident. Though it could hardly be more appropriate."

J.B. struggled out of the sand pit, cursing and shaking himself, still feeling the rats scurrying over him. He turned to look at the carnage that was to his rear and stopped dead, silenced by the battle that was still raging.

The companions watched, spectators who were glad to be no longer caught in the middle, as the fight continued. The small mammals were no match for the rats, and most of them were either chilled or retreating, but the match between the lizards and insects on one side, and the rodents on the other, was evenly balanced. Both had their weaknesses, but their strengths contrasted and evened up the fight. It was awesome to witness the struggle for desert supremacy.

The struggle was brought to an end only when the sun began to rise. The knowledge that the day would soon become unbearably hot sent them fleeing back to their lairs, determined to make the shade before they began to fry. The ultimate battle for supremacy could wait until another night. Ryan wondered how often this had been played and replayed.

The rats swarmed around the companions but seemed to ignore them, heading only for their warren, carrying the carrion from the battlefield with them to add to their supplies of food deep underground. Receding into the distance, the lizards and reptiles were doing the same. Nothing was to be wasted in this harsh environment.

As suddenly as it began, it was ended. The desert was

silent once more, with only the disturbance of the sand and some patches of blood and fur to mark the battle. Even those would soon vanish with the shifting of the sands during the day and with the coming of the next storms.

"Not much chance of resting now that the sun's coming up," Ryan stated. "And I don't know about you, but I don't want another night like that if I can help it. I say we press on."

As he expected, there was no opposition to this plan. He told J.B. of Jak's comments about their location and the best direction to strike out. The Armorer took his mini-sextant from out of his canvas bag and took a reading.

"Yeah, if we go thataway," he said, pointing west, "then we should hit where Jak thinks. I just wish I could say how long it'll take."

"It'll take as long as it takes," Ryan said, "and we've got no other choice. As long as we can get the hell away from here."

It was a comment that needed no argument after the rigors of the night. Wearily they formed into a line, with Ryan at lead and J.B. covering the rear, and began to march—slowly, achingly—toward whatever destiny next had in store for them.

Chapter Three

"Three days and nights. Let us hope that it does not extend to forty days in the wilderness." Doc sighed in a distracted manner as he rose from sleep and took in the new morning around them.

"If you keep being that cheerful, I might just put you out of your misery," Mildred told him with a sour tone. "Anyway, when the hell did you get so damn religious?"

Doc smiled beatifically. "One was always brought up with the good book, even when Mr. Darwin made certain parts of it seem a little like a fable."

"Two suns, two argument same. Shut up," Jak ranted as he took a sip of water then grimaced before taking a chunk out of the lizard they had cooked the night before. "Boring."

Certainly, something had happened to Doc in the time between coming out of the jump and the current morning. Perhaps it had been the states of delirium followed by the storm, or perhaps it had been some jump-induced dream of which he had said nothing. Either way, he had been spouting in a religious vein ever since they'd begun their trek across the desert. For Mildred, daughter of a preacher in the predark world, this was irritating for some reason she couldn't comprehend.

After the attack on their first night out of the redoubt, and after J.B. had secured a direction from his minisextant, they had started to march. Pacing was difficult. It was an unknown distance balanced against their lack of water and salt tablets, and the sparseness of their diet. The fact that there was water and life present in the desert was a given—the events of that night had proved it. However, locating the obviously deep springs and trapping some of the wildlife was another matter entirely.

The heat under the chem clouds, trapping and magnifying the intensity of the heat, set the pace for them. Regardless of any intent, to go any faster would have been to consciously buy the farm. If not right now, then a little way down the line. It would have used their water and salt resources too quickly.

So they had kept the pace steady and set up camp for the night as the darkness fell, settling in against the freezing temperatures of a desert night. Away from the storm-ravaged area, the wildlife had been less intent on a power struggle and had emerged slowly, with more caution and with less obvious hostility.

That made it easy for Jak to trap a few lizards and small mammals that strayed away from the safety of the pack. At the same time, the albino hunter observed their patterns of movement, attempting to divine where the water table came up through the sand, and rock beneath, to be close enough to the surface for the companions to attempt a dig.

He wasn't so successful. The layers of sand kept the wells and springs of the desert running deep. However, a brief search did reveal more signs of scrub and plant life than before.

Meanwhile, J.B. and Ryan rigged their own device to try to squeeze a little water from the unwelcoming desert. Using some plastic wrap that had been on some of the materials taken from the redoubt, they built small hammocks that collected the dew in their centers. The resulting water was brackish, but at least it showed that they could attempt to prolong their survival in this manner.

Mildred and Krysty collected some of the scrub as they marched each day. It was few and far between, and mostly tinder-dry. Although not encouraging for the presence of water, it did signify that there was something present, and at the end of each day it meant that they had enough to build a fire that could keep burning—small, but bright— through the night, offering warmth and a warning to any wildlife that may be too bold.

It also meant that they could cook the small mammals and lizards that Jak had caught. These were tough, stringy and none too tasty, but compared to the self-heats that were the only other option, they were like manna from heaven. It also meant that they could preserve the self-heats for a real emergency, and the salty meat enabled them to cut back a little on the consumption of the salt tablets, another commodity they might have to retain for an emergency.

It took only two days for the companions to settle into a routine, and by the third day it seemed as though they had been marching forever. It was partly because their bodies were beginning to adjust to the conditions and the rules of consumption imposed upon them by the environment, and partly because they had no time scale they could work to, and so lived totally in the moment.

Jak finished chewing on a piece of lizard meat and choked it down. It was tough, with little taste, but at least it didn't have the chem taste of the self-heats.

"Mebbe not have argument much longer," he said, referring to the exchange between Doc and Mildred.

Ryan looked at him sharply. "Why's that?"

Jak shrugged. "More life. Last night they move less wary, less searching. Like they know food and water okay. And look at that—" he gestured toward some scrub in the distance "—even from here see more green."

"Mebbe we haven't got too far to go, then," Ryan said with the ghost of a smile. The thought that they may be within striking distance of a more hospitable terrain was heartening, but he didn't want to get his hopes—or those of his companions—up too much before discovering the actuality.

J.B. looked up at the early morning sun. In the area they had now reached, there was less of the heavy, yellow chem-cloud cover, and the blue sky shone through. As the sun rose, the heat would undoubtedly beat down on them, but it would be an easier heat to deal with as the lack of cloud cover would mean less intensity and magnification.

In itself, the lessening of the chem clouds bespoke of leaving the worst of the desert behind them.

"Y'know, Jak might just be right," the Armorer said.

So it was with a refreshed and renewed spirit that they set off once more. Packing up their camp and starting to move to the west, there was a spring in their pace that they had to fight hard to control: too much energy expended too quickly would be of no help to them if the prize was farther than they thought.

IT WAS PAST MIDDAY when the breakthrough happened. There had been an increase in the amount of scrub, and just before the sun reached its peak Jak had stopped them with a gesture, pointing up into the clear blue. There, soaring in an arc against the blue, was a dark shape with a long wing-span. It was the first bird they had seen since leaving the redoubt, and an indication that taller plants and trees lay somewhere close to hand.

It gave them a lift to see this, and they continued with a greater sense of optimism and purpose, as well as an increasing awareness—more life meant more risk of danger and attack.

The edge of the desert was delineated in a strange way. They had seen many bizarre land formations in their travels, but this was one of the oddest. For some time it had seemed to them that they were moving uphill once more, the sand lifting up before them in a series of dunes that grew higher. Although the sand here was harder packed and firmer underfoot than the treacherous grains they had first encountered, the gradient was enough to pull at their calf muscles. It was an effort to keep up the pace, so they slowed slightly to make the ascent easier.

The summit was on them before they knew it; and a strange, bizarre sight greeted them. As they stood on the peak of the dunes, they were aware that the land fell away for a couple of hundred yards then leveled, so that it was higher than the level of the desert floor behind them. This land was lush and covered in vegetation and scrub, with copses of trees peppered around, forming small woods. The air carried with it the scents of animal and plant life, and similar sounds could be heard at the edge of their hearing. There was a faint tang of ozone in the breeze, suggesting that they were nearer the coastline Jak remembered than they had realized.

Ryan looked back at the desert behind them. It stretched away as far as he could see on every side. But the dunes on which they stood also seemed to carry on out of view to the left and right. It was as though the disturbance of the land after the nukecaust had caused this area of the Deathlands to drop down and form a valley, one in which the chem clouds had been sucked in and trapped, perpetually hanging over the lands within. This had magnified the effects of the elements and converted this area into an arid desert at a rapid rate, evolving into the sandy wastelands in a fraction of the time it should otherwise have taken.

Ryan realized that the redoubt had pitched them into the middle of a trap, and it was only by dogged persistence that they had escaped. How many others had wandered into the desert at some point and never reemerged?

Turning back to the fertile lands beyond, he breathed a sigh of relief. Whatever trouble they got into from here on in, at least it wouldn't be for starvation or thirst.

"Reckon we're near the coast now?" Krysty asked.

Ryan shrugged. "Figure we're closer than we were before. There's only one way to find out. Triple red from here on in, people," he added, shrugging the Steyr off his shoulder and checking to make sure it was ready to fire. "There's no knowing what we may come up against now."

The rest of the companions followed suit, checking that their weapons were ready for rapid response, then falling into line behind the one-eyed man as he set off for the interior. Jak followed directly in Ryan's wake, with Krysty and Doc taking the middle positions, Mildred and J.B. at the rear, with the Armorer taking the last place, covering their backs.

The woodlands and scrub grew dense rapidly, and before half an hour passed, they had to start hacking a path through the thickets, watching for the tangles of roots that crossed the floor of the woods, laying treacherous traps for the unwary.

Ryan wanted them to be as unobtrusive as possible, but this was hard when the very density of the woodlands made progress impossible without some kind of noise. The thick grasses and tall plant life also made it possible for someone with a good vantage point to be able to track their progress. It was far from ideal, and Ryan was aware of the additional problem. The very noise of their progress made it hard for them to hear anyone who may be advancing on them.

The deeper they went, the darker it became as the sky overhead was shielded by a canopy of green. The sounds of birds flying between the trees and the rustling of animals and reptiles moving in the upper branches also took their attention. Most of the wildlife seemed far more wary of them than they were of it. Despite the sounds, a glimpse of anything living was a rarity. From those few examples that did occasionally come into view, it seemed that the resident wildlife of the woodlands was small and nonthreatening.

The humidity grew even as the glare of the sun vanished, and the companions became aware of the sweat that ran off their foreheads and down their backs, gathering in uncomfortable pools at the base of the spine. Some were more afflicted than others, but gradually all of them shed at least one layer of clothing, opting to wrap it around them rather than swathe themselves. The humidity and sweat was an irritation, and made them all edgy. Even though it was better than the killing sun of the desert, it had its own dangers, making them prone to be trigger happy, something none of them wanted to be. A needless shot could alert far more danger than the sounds of movement in the undergrowth. There were no signs of human life at the moment, but as they neared the coast, chances were that they would hit a ville or habitation of some kind. No one liked a group of strangers descending on them unannounced, so the companions needed to be on triple-red alert.

"Fireblast," Ryan hissed as his panga half sliced and half bludgeoned more plant life from his path. "This seems more trouble than all that sand."

"I think on the whole I'd rather have this," Mildred answered, even though the one-eyed man hadn't really been asking anyone's opinion. "At least we can get some food and water in here, and at least we're going the right way."

"Mebbe, but I'm getting sick of this undergrowth. It's thicker than flies on a twelve-times-a-night gaudy slut," Ryan returned.

"Never fear, friend Ryan. It is said that when we come from the desert we shall find both revelation and salvation," Doc replied beatifically.

"What's with the revelation and salvation?" Krysty asked. "You sound like some kind of old-time preacher, like the ones that Mother Sonja used to tell us stories of back in Harmony."

Doc looked blank for a second, as though he was scanning his mind for some kind of clue. Eventually he gave up and shrugged. "Truly, my dear lady, I have no notion of from whence these notions have sprung—nor, indeed, if they wish to disperse in some manner or to continue. I only know that they are flashing into the forefront of my consciousness with such a strength that I feel compelled to give tongue to them. I wonder," he continued in slightly awestruck tone, as though to himself, "if they will continue, or indeed if they are some part of my mind that is trying to tell me something?"

"Trying to tell you that you're a crazy old bastard," Mildred muttered. "I really wish you'd give it a rest with the biblical shit, Doc. Reminds me too much of my own childhood."

There was something about her tone that would brook no argument, but Doc was so lost in his own thoughts that this completely passed him by, and he asked in a naive manner, "Really, my dear Doctor? Why, pray tell, would that be?"

Mildred rolled her eyes and considered telling Doc where he could shove his questions, but was stopped by Jak.

"Shut up—no stupe shit," Jak whispered, staying them with a raised hand.

Ryan stopped and turned to the albino, questioning him with a raised eyebrow. The others also stopped behind Jak, waiting to see what he had to say. Each of them listened, but couldn't, at first, pick out what had alerted the albino hunter's finely tuned instincts.

Jak pulled on his camou jacket with a smooth, silent motion, wrapping the material around him so that he had easy access to the leaf-bladed throwing knives hidden within the body of the jacket. As he did so, the others strained to catch what had taken Jak's attention.

Each sound within the woodlands became more than just a part of the overall tapestry. As they listened, each sound became distinct to the point where they could isolate and identify it as bird or animal…except for something that sounded like themselves, crashing through the undergrowth. Quieter, perhaps, as mere people who were more used to the layout of the woods, and could pick their way through the thickets with greater ease. But not enough to conceal their presence.

If they were tracking the companions, then they would know that they had been spotted, as they would have heard the cessation of activity. But if they were making their own way regardless of anyone else in the woodlands, then they wouldn't know that they had been heard.

Either way, they were headed straight toward where the companions were gathered.

Ryan turned in the direction of the oncoming group and planned his defense. He had to move swiftly, as they were getting nearer with every second. He looked at the companions, blasters in hand, and grinned wryly. Plan their defense? In this situation, his people would probably be able to second guess whatever he was about to say.

With just an exchange of glances, the companions sprang into action. Jak took a standing jump at an overhanging tree and pulled himself into the lower limbs, finding his balance and scaling it with ease until he was in the upper reaches. He scanned the area visible from the top, taking care to keep himself concealed. About a mile away he could see a small inlet from the sea beyond, and the signs of a village—too small to really be called a ville— that had settled there. Coming toward the companions from an oblique angle to the village were four men and a woman. They were dressed raggedly, and although they moved with a degree of care, they looked haggard, and their movements were made audible by a weariness that made them careless. They carried swords and machetes, with revolvers stuffed into their waistbands. From the careless manner in which they were carried, Jak guessed that the five were unused to blasters.

Quickly climbing down the tree, Jak rapped out what he had seen. The party of five was only a couple of minutes away from them now, and Ryan directed his friends into defensive positions in the undergrowth.

"We want to let them pass if possible. If there's a settlement, last thing we want is to piss off the people there by chilling some of their own."

"Not look like after us," Jak added.

Without further discussion the companions moved into position. Ryan and J.B. had blades in the shape of their panga and Tekna knife, respectively. For Jak, the leaf-bladed knives were almost a part of his person. And Doc withdrew the sword from within the silver lion's-head cane. The blade was made of the finest Toledo steel, honed to razor sharpness, and despite their continuing travels the old man took care to keep it polished and sharp.

Mildred and Krysty, who never habitually carried blades, took a leaf-bladed knife each from Jak. They both weighed the blades in their palms, getting the balance of the delicate but deadly knife.

Now armed for silent combat, they took up position. Jak and the Armorer ascended into nearby trees, giving them a good position of both the view on the ground beneath, and also of the path of their enemy.

For the other four, it wasn't quite as simple. With no clear-cut path for the approaching enemy to pursue, the grounded companions had to guess the least likely areas to be traversed. Ryan took a thick clump of shrub that had a prickly leaf as his base, figuring no one in their right mind would want to cut through it. Mildred and Krysty both opted for dense clusters of tree and shrub growth that they had to squeeze into. These weren't impassable, but anyone in a hurry would opt for an easier path. Doc chose to conceal himself in the bole of tree that had been hollowed out by insects.

Once in cover, all they could do was wait, the sounds of the villagers growing louder as they neared. It was obvious that they were trying to keep the noise down, but were unsuccessful. Snatches of urgently whispered exchanges came drifting through the undergrowth.

"...heard it, I'm sure..."

"...better be something big—too long since the last time..."

"...you don't shut the fuck up it'll..."

This last was from the woman, hissed in an irritated tone. The group was obviously on edge and hunting some kind of animal. Up in his tree, Jak grinned to himself. Whatever these people were, they were no hunters. There had been little sign of large animals so far in the woodlands, and the noises they had been tracking were obviously the sounds made by the companions.

The positive thing in this was that the hunters were so poor that they would probably walk right past the hidden companions without even knowing they were there.

Or at least, they would have done if not for Doc.

For some time, Doc had been aware that the bole of the tree wasn't the best place for him to have secreted himself. As he heard the hunting party approach, he also heard the small tickings and scratchings of the insects that had eaten out the hollow bole of the tree. They had been silent when he had first entered, and so he had assumed that the tree had long since been vacated. Now he knew that he was wrong, and that the insects had merely been dormant. His disturbing their space had awakened them, and now they were intent on seeing what had invaded their domain.

His skin began to itch. Whether the insects were really starting to crawl on him, or whether it was a matter of his imagination going into overdrive, was in a sense immaterial. All that mattered was that the sensation was driving him mad. He tried to keep his resolve as he heard the enemy slash its way through the woodlands, getting closer, but all he could feel were thousands upon thousands of tiny insect feet crawling over his skin, tiny teeth nipping at his flesh, injecting his bloodstream with who knew what kinds of venom.

Doc fought the panic rising within him, knowing that to burst out of the hollow tree yelling would be to blow any kind of cover the companions had. If these hunters could pass by without a fight, then it would be the better to approach the coastal village. Yes, Doc knew all this, but only with the rational side of his mind. The irrational side, that which had been accentuated by the rigors of being trawled through time twice, being tortured by Cort Strasser, being the weakest and the most prone to injury and infection, that side of his mind was sometimes the stronger.

"Dark night, I don't believe it," J.B. whispered from his perch. One moment, all had been quiet and secure as the five-strong hunting party made their way past the companions, clueless as to how close they actually were to their quarry. The next, the peace of the woodlands was disturbed by the sound of Doc Tanner, yelling and screaming like a soul possessed, leaping from the bole of the tree, waving his sword above his head, treating his finely tuned blade like a broadsword. J.B. couldn't make out what the hell Doc was yelling, but it sounded like something to do with insects.

The Armorer had no time to think about this and puzzle over it. Like the others, he knew that any chance of escaping hand-to-hand combat had now disappeared, and they had to silence the hunting party as quickly as possible.

Ironically, given that it was his eruption that had spurred the fight, Doc's violent entry into the fray gave the companions the upper hand. The hunting party, who had almost passed unknowing through the area where the companions were concealed, were stunned by the sudden apparition before them.

That moment of indecision gave the others all the time they needed. J.B. slid down from the trees, Ryan emerged through the shrub and Mildred and Krysty came out of hiding.

The shock on the faces of the hunting party showed how little they had been aware of their opponents. It would have been a swift and clean chill for the companions, if not for the crazed Doc. Screaming, and swinging wildly with his sword, he teetered off balance and fell toward J.B., the blade swishing down so close to the Armorer that it nicked his shoulder, ripping the cloth of his shirt as he tried to move out of the way. He cursed, and as Doc flew past him he lashed out at the old man. He didn't want to injure Doc, but with the old man floundering as a loose cannon, the best thing would be to put him out of action, and quick. He caught Doc a glancing blow and the scholar fell to the forest floor with a grunt as the impact drove the air from his lungs. Without thinking, he rolled and pulled the LeMat percussion pistol from his belt.

Wild-eyed, barely seeing, he pointed it at J.B., who froze. If Doc discharged the shot chamber, there was no way that he would be able to get out of the way of the hot metal in time. Was this how it was to end? At the hands of a friend, albeit one who was temporarily mad?

Doc, in a crazed world of his own imaginings, had no idea that it had been J.B. he had inadvertently attacked, and who had been defending himself. In his head, the insects and the hunting party were confused in such a manner as to make everything that touched him a potential enemy. By instinct he had drawn the LeMat and aimed at the indistinct blur that had thrown him to the ground. But now, as he focused and his finger began to tighten on the trigger, the world around him swung into an equal focus.

"By the Three Kennedys!" he exclaimed, realizing that he was about to blow J.B. into pieces. "John Barrymore!" he yelled, jerking his arm up at the last moment so that the round of shot was discharged harmlessly into the air, ripping the overhanging foliage to shreds and chilling a few birds, but coming nowhere near harming the Armorer.

J.B. blanched, felt the blood drain from his face. It was so close that he could hear his heart thumping in his chest, his head prickle and feel faint as lights exploded around him and the deafening roar of the LeMat shut out everything else.

For a moment, everyone else in the gathering had been silent, all mute witness to the drama unfolding. The explosion of the LeMat seemed to galvanize them into action. With a yell, the woman in the hunting party threw herself at Ryan, wielding her knife in an amateurish, overhand action. It was easy for the one-eyed warrior to sidestep her clumsy attack and club her to the ground with the hilt of the panga.

The off-hand manner in which he did this, and the fact that he didn't seem to take her attack seriously enough to chill her, only seemed to enrage the four men all the more. With a volley of screams, they launched themselves at their prey.

The companions couldn't afford to take chances. Given time, they might have tried to overpower the hunters and find out about their village. They needed food and shelter, perhaps a boat to take them across the inlet. Chilling five of the inhabitants wasn't the best way to show peaceful intent. However, with the noise of Doc's pistol likely to attract more attention, and all of it hostile, it became an imperative to free themselves from the hunting party. Especially as these five had made it clear their intent was to take no prisoners.

The four men were faced by Mildred, Krysty and Jak. Each carried a blade, but the one facing Jak looked suddenly uncertain as he caught the cold gleam in the eyes of the albino hunter and paused midflight to try to draw his ancient revolver. It caught him in a no-man's-land of indecision, and area where he could expect to be shown no mercy.

With a slow, almost lazy gait, Jak stepped toward the man, feinting with one arm and using the other to pull a precise, tight arc that took in the attacker's right-hand side. This was the side holding the knife, and it dropped from nerveless fingers as the leaf-bladed knife sliced cleanly through the flesh of his lower arm and wrist, blood dribbling and spurting from the wound, severed nerves causing his fingers to open. The villager looked at his suddenly lifeless fingers, hanging loose and open, all intent of grabbing his revolver with his left hand forgotten. Not that he had much time to stand and stare, as the continuing arc carved up the side of his head, splitting the flesh from jaw to hairline, before a flick of Jak's wrist took the blade down again, the point burrowing into his exposed neck—opened to a clean blow by the instinctive jerking back of his head as the flesh was carved—and, with a gentle pirouette of the blade, severing the carotid artery so that the man's lifeblood pumped out, hissing and steaming across the surrounding foliage.

Mildred and Krysty had three men opposing them, and with the extra player it should have been simple for the hunters to take down the women. However, they showed their lack of experience in such matters by rushing blindly for their opponents.

Krysty sidestepped and tripped one of the hunters, whose impetus carried him into an uncontrolled tumble, his flailing arms catching the man next to him and throwing him off balance. As the first hunter careened out of range, Krysty stepped in close to the unbalanced man and drove her blade up under the rib cage, catching a lung and puncturing it before pulling back, using the heel of her free hand to pummel the attacker's head back, pushing him back off her blade. His punctured lung began to fill with blood, starting to drown him. But before he had a chance to make a last, dying lunge, Krysty wheeled and kicked out, her leg coming up to his head height, the heel of her silver-tipped cowboy boot catching him at the temple, sending him backward, unconscious before he hit the ground, his last drowning moments lost in darkness.

Mildred was less extravagant with her attacker. Partly because this hunter had a little more awareness than the others, and stayed his rush just enough to jerk back and avoid the full thrust of her attack, the knife scoring his chest, cutting through his shirt, but not stopping him. As Mildred attempted to pull back, he closed in on her. She could feel his hot breath, smell the fear in his sweat, see it in his eyes, as he attempted to pin her back against a tree with one arm and drive his knife into her eye with the other. She could almost see the point grow larger in her right eye, her own knife arm pinned across her body.

She had only one chance. She jerked her knee savagely upward, catching him in the groin. It didn't fully land in the soft sac of his balls, but it was close enough to make him yelp in pain and loose his grip on her. It also deflected his arm enough for her to move her head, one of her plaits pinned to the tree by the point of his blade.

Mildred pushed him back a couple of steps, enough for her to bring her arm back and step forward, slicing across him with the razor-sharp, leaf-bladed knife, cutting his face from the corner of his eye across his nose and top lip, a flap of flesh falling bloodily free. He screamed and instinctively clapped a hand to where his eyeball was bleeding white goo down his opened cheek, dropping his own knife. Ignoring the pull of her plait as she tugged it free of the knife and the tree, Mildred wasted no time in following up on her initial attack, driving the knife up to the hilt into his chest. He gasped and coughed blood over her hand and arm, looking bewildered and astonished as he slumped toward her. She moved back, tugging at the knife to free it as he fell onto her. She cursed and let go of the knife, in case he fell and pinned her underneath.

Meanwhile, Ryan was making short shrift of the careening hunter, who had lost his balance and fallen at the feet of the one-eyed man. He looked up into the ice-blue orb, knowing that his time had come to buy the farm. It was almost too easy for Ryan, and he felt a twinge of regret as he sliced through the man's neck with the panga, almost severing his head from his body with the force of the blow, taking off three fingers from the man's hand where he, at the last, tried to protect himself from the chilling blow.

A growling sound to his rear made Ryan suddenly spin. The woman had regained consciousness in time to see her compatriots routed, and was determined to try to take one of the companions with her if she had to buy the farm. With a manic cry she launched herself toward Ryan, her blade held high above her head.

It was an incredibly stupid and unskilled thing for her to do, and only reinforced the one-eyed man's opinion that these weren't habitual fighters. Although she was in close proximity to Ryan, her stance left her body completely open, and one thrust from the panga was enough to impale her, the light of fury dying in her eyes to be replaced by bemusement as she dropped her blade from fingers rendered nerveless by her sudden demise.

"Fireblast, what a stupe fuckup," Ryan swore as he pulled out the blood-slicked blade. "There's no way we can approach the village now, and they'll be after us."

"Ryan, I—" Doc began, but the one-eyed man cut him short.

"Don't have to explain, Doc. Shit happens. You okay, J.B.?"

The Armorer was still shaking his head to clear it from his near-chilled experience. "Guess so—guess I'll have to be."

Ryan checked the others. They were covered in blood, but otherwise unharmed.

"Shit," he cursed loudly. "We really didn't need that. Let's get moving away from here."

"Yeah, triple quick," Jak added, inclining his head. "Can hear more, coming fast."

Chapter Four

"This way. Keep the noise low and keep triple red," Ryan said in an urgent whisper, straining to hear the noise that had alerted Jak. A questioning glance brought an answer from the albino hunter.

"'Bout five minutes away, moving fast. There," Jak added, indicating a direction away to the left.

Ryan nodded and continued to move to the right. He hoped that there was only one party coming out to investigate the blasterfire.

"Ryan, I recce then report," Jak continued. "Go that way, I scout ahead."

The one-eyed man was wary. He would prefer to keep his people together, and Jak moving about could draw friendly fire unless they held back. And if they did, it might be on a foe rather than a friend. But the albino youth had the ability to move almost silently, and there were other problems. They couldn't go back, as this would drive them back into the desert. They had to forge ahead and somehow skirt around the village and the pursuing war parties. The only way it seemed that they could do this was if they had prior knowledge of their opponents whereabouts.

Jak was the obvious choice.

All that went through Ryan's head in a flash before he nodded at Jak. "Yeah, do it," he said simply.

The albino hunter grinned briefly, then melted into the undergrowth, only the slightest rustling of foliage marking his passing.

Ryan turned his attention to his chosen direction. "Keep those blasters ready, and stick close," he ordered as he took the panga in hand and began to clear a path through the woods. Behind him, each of the companions kept an impassive silence, faces set, and lost in their own thoughts as they followed him.

JAK MOVED SILENTLY through the woods, circumventing the source of the noise. He didn't want to cross the path of the group that was beating its way toward the scene of combat, and he figured that the best way to observe them would be to move around and in behind, where they would least expect anyone.

The albino youth paused and listened intently. He could pick out at least half a dozen sets of footfalls, perhaps more. It was hard to tell in the crashing of the undergrowth. He tried to pick out how many voices were exchanging whispered and urgent messages. The words were indistinguishable among the other sounds, but he could hear at least four different voices, no more. So at least two weren't talking. He reckoned there were probably six in the chasing pack. Not too bad as odds went.

The war party crashing through the jungle was causing a major disturbance among the wildlife. Birds and animals were making noise, alarmed by the intruders and still agitated in the aftermath of Doc's LeMat discharging

among them. The treetops were rustling and moving as
birds, squirrels and other small mammals hopped from
limb to limb, tree to tree, moving in a blind panic.

It could be just the cover he needed. Jak scrutinized the
canopy of tree cover with a practiced eye. The limbs on
each tree were strong, and they seemed to hang close together. It would be easy to leap those that were a little
apart; the others he could just crawl across. Jak's vulpine
grin spread across his scarred visage—the hunter in pursuit of the hunters.

Jak scaled the nearest tree, moving smoothly up the
gnarled trunk, which gave him a multiplicity of easy foot
and handholds. Once up into the lower limbs, he edged
out, carefully testing the weight. He was able to move with
ease along them, and he was soon scudding across the canopy of leaf cover, using the sounds of the disturbed bird
and animal life to mask his progress.

In a matter of a few minutes, he was just to the rear of
the hunting party. Circling them widely enough to escape
detection, but close enough to get the members in sight
quickly, he settled onto a limb as they stumbled across the
scene of combat.

Still, as though he were now a part of the tree rather
than an alien presence on the limb, Jak sat and watched
while the hunting party were stopped in its tracks at the
sight of the carnage. There were six of them, as he had
guessed, two women and four men. Two of the men
were weatherbeaten and looked old, although they still
moved easily and without the stiffness he would expect
from age. The other two were younger, one of them
nursing a large gut, but otherwise looking strong. The

women were both young, with long, muscular limbs. One of them had large breasts that bounced as she moved, made more obvious by the belt of ammo that was slung in a diagonal across her chest. She carried a remade AK-47, which failed to account for the belt, as it was fed by a magazine. The other woman, however, was carrying what looked to Jak like a Sharps, which would necessitate the belt. But why wasn't she carrying it?

No matter, except that perhaps it told of this party being unused to combat. Certainly, Jak would have put the village down as a fishing community, with little need for much blaster use when they were this isolated. They were also unused to seeing the results of battle. This much was obvious from the way the young man with the pendulous belly turned away and hurled the contents of his stomach onto the grass. The woman with the Sharps went over to comfort him while the others just looked, dumbfounded.

"Shit, must be an army," the other woman whispered.

"Or just good," one of the old men commented. "Too fucking good, I figure."

"Good or not, we owe them for this," the other young man snarled. "They thought they were only chasing game. They weren't expecting this."

The two older men exchanged glances. The one who had spoken previously said quietly, "They should have been expecting anything. So should we."

The other man moved in the direction that the companions had forged their path. He studied the undergrowth. "Moved this way," he said thoughtfully. "Figure that they're moving out to the west and trying to get around the side of the village, which means that they'll move right into the regular scouts."

The younger man grinned. There was something in it that spoke of the smell of vengeance in his nostrils. "Serve them right. Take them alive and make them suffer... Hey, Leroy, you hear that?" he asked suddenly. "Up there somewhere..."

"Only the birds, Tyne, only the birds," the old man replied, following the younger man's gaze. "What we want is over thataway."

Indeed he was correct. Jak had already vacated his vantage point and was speeding through the upper reaches of the trees, on his way to meet up with the companions. He had only heard the one group moving through the woods, but if the regular sec patrol they spoke of would cross paths over to the west, then there was no way that he would have been able to detect them. And there was little chance that the others would to know they were there until it was too late.

At the back of his mind, it struck him that the hunting party, and those they had chilled, had been dressed like people from a ville that was poor. The clothes were threadbare and well worn. They'd need something hardier as a predominantly fishing ville. And why the hell were they hunting game when they were supposed to get most of their food from the seas? It was starting to look as though the companions had walked straight into someone else's crisis. But right now, that was unimportant. It could wait until they were in the clear, past all possible attack.

Behind him, he could hear the hunting party start to follow the trail left by the companions. He would be able to outrun them easily and reach Ryan and his people before the hunters, but would he be able to reach them before they crossed paths with the sec patrol?

A FEW MILES AWAY to the west, Ryan and the rest of the companions were moving through the woodlands at a rapid pace. The idea was to put as much ground between them and the scene of combat in as quick a time as possible. The farther they were from the scene, the harder it would be for the pursuing party to catch them, for there was no doubt in Ryan's mind that the trail would be easy enough to follow. It was virtually impossible for five people to cut their way through the undergrowth without leaving a trace of their passing. So speed was their best weapon.

They couldn't know that the faster they went, the longer it took Jak to reach them, the more they were hacking their way into a trap.

They continued, regardless. They couldn't hear the distant approach of another party, the noise of their own progress obscuring the distance.

JAK HAD NEVER MOVED SO FAST, and with so little caution. There was no point. He had left the hunting party far behind, and knew that the only other sec party in the woodlands was to the west.

His red eyes were unblinking, every nerve ending screaming, the blood pumping at a bursting rate as he pushed his muscles, springing from branch to branch, sometimes landing on the toes of his combat boots and trusting his arms to carry the bulk of his weight on an overhead limb. Once or twice his feet had slipped on guano or moss that had gathered on a limb, and his arms felt as though they would be wrenched from his shoulders as his feet flailed into empty air, slipping off their perch, the momentum increasing his weight at these moments.

But his luck held, and he carried on his way, making time and ground as fast as was humanly possible.

The trouble was, he needed to be more than human.

"I WOULD HATE TO BREAK SILENCE at such a moment, my dear Ryan, but I feel I must," Doc blurted suddenly, his previously purposeful stride faltering as he stumbled, turning his head to the rear. He was second from last in the line, with J.B. bringing up guard position.

"Doc, this is no time—" Ryan began, but J.B. cut him short.

"Doc's not bullshitting," he snapped. "Wait—listen…"

Ryan, Mildred and Krysty stopped.

"Fireblast! Who the hell is that?" Ryan hissed.

"Doesn't matter. Whoever they are, they're nearly on us," J.B. snapped, bringing his Uzi up to level.

Ryan couldn't believe they'd been so slack as to miss the oncoming sound of another hunting party. It couldn't be the one they were avoiding, as these had to be some distance behind. It had to be another who had guessed their path and cut them off, for these sounds were coming from in front of them.

There was a rustling in the trees behind them. The one-eyed warrior looked up, but could see nothing: the noise continued past them. He looked at his people. They seemed as bemused by this as he was himself.

Before any of them had the chance to say a word, the rustling continued and Jak appeared before them, springing down from the trees.

"Different party. Five. Handblasters and blowpipes," he said without preamble. "Only minute, mebbe two, and coming right for us."

Ryan swore and gestured to his people to adopt defensive positions in whatever cover they could find.

Using shrubs and clumps of trees to locate themselves in areas less likely to be hacked through, they settled in quickly. Jak was the only one to use the treetops, as he was the only companion swift enough to make it in the time they had.

Or at least, that was how it should have been. But as they waited, tension extending each second into hours, it became apparent that something was wrong. There was little sound from the woods beyond, and the five-man hunting party failed to appear.

Up in the branches, Jak scanned the area around. He cursed to himself, slowing his breathing and focusing on every slight sound or movement. The sec party had been able to locate the companions from the noise they had been making, and had opted to split up to encircle their enemy. They knew the area and were hiding themselves well. Even Jak was having trouble locating them.

So what chance did the others stand, mired on the ground?

MILDRED WAS HUDDLED close to the bole of a tree, her Czech ZKR pistol raised, barrel skyward, ready to aim in any direction, at the slightest sound. She was scanning the surrounding area intently, but could see nothing. There was no movement, no sound, no indication of anything that could pose a threat.

That was when she heard it—a rattle and a hollow sound, like someone had kicked a stone against a tree. She pulled the ZKR down so that it was leveled, then turned toward the source of the noise.

As she turned, she felt a pricking in the side of her neck, like an insect bite. She slapped at it and felt the protruding dart.

Dammit—she knew immediately that the noise had been a decoy and she had fallen for it, leaving herself open to a shot from the side. She opened her mouth to call a warning, but it felt as though her chest was tight and her vocal cords had seized up. She felt her balance fail, and as she fell forward, the world spun briefly before blacking out.

JAK HEARD MILDRED FALL, whirled and saw her hit the ground. He also caught the flicker of movement as the sec man came out of hiding, moving over to check Mildred's condition.

The albino youth took this as a chance to move in on the sec man, swinging across the limbs that were intertwined above the ground, noiselessly slipping lower so that he was able to launch himself downward from behind, hoping to take the man out without giving him a chance to use the blowpipe.

He should have known. Even as he fell, he realized that the sec man had been leaning over Mildred for far too long just to check on her. He'd known Jak was up in the trees somewhere, and was waiting for him to make the first move. The sec man began a half turn as the albino plummeted earthward, moving his body to meet the full impact.

Jak was holding a knife and hoped to get the blade into position for a chilling blow as he landed. He got in one thrust, but the sec man managed to parry it with an arm, taking a slice out of his bicep, but preventing the knife from being anything other than a painful irritation. At the same time, he raised his other arm, opening his clenched fist to slap Jak on the side of the head with his open palm.

The albino reeled back. It shouldn't have been a blow to cause that, being light compared to the punishment Jak had taken in the past. And yet there was something about it. Realizing—but too late—Jak raised his hand to the side of his head, using his fingers to probe where the after-shock of the slap was still tingling.

He could feel the small dart. It was almost flat to his temple, the point of it having only just punctured the skin. He cursed and pulled it out, throwing it to one side. Maybe he had caught it in time, maybe it hadn't released any of its toxin into his bloodstream as it hadn't been driven in. Even as he reeled back, he knew he was hoping where there was no hope. The sec man stood in front of him, legs apart, in a stance that was wary and ready to spring: but he didn't see Jak as posing a problem now.

Blinking, feeling himself grow numb and his vision clouding and becoming distant, Jak knew that he was done for. If this was a lethal toxin, then he was a chilled piece of meat. If not, then he could only hope that he would have a chance to fight back when he came around.

That was the last thought running through his head before the dark curtain fell.

J.B. WAS SWEATING. The Armorer's patience had already been stretched far too thin by Doc, let alone a wait for an enemy that refused to show. Every sound, every movement of wildlife put him on a hair trigger, just one ounce of pressure away from ripping it to shred with a burst from the Uzi.

When it came, though, it was as if all that pressure slipped away and he locked into a calmer, cooler frame of mind.

It was to his right, behind a clump of flowering shrub, the large purple blooms of which gave a good expanse with which to hide. Too good. There was no way he could tell if there was anyone there. To spray 'n' pray would be a spectacularly futile act, as it would do little except betray his position and invite attack.

There was only one thing he could do if he wanted to avoid being trapped in this position. He had to take the initiative. Using all the skills he had picked up during decades of simply staying alive, J.B. moved out from his position, keeping low and using whatever cover he could, moving toward the shrub. He paused at every new piece of cover, ready to fire if there was any indication that he had been spotted. All he could hear each time was the sound of his own shallow breathing, all he could feel was each drop of sweat running down his brow, down his back.

He made the distance between last cover and the shrub, going into a roll to come up to the rear of the purple blooms, Uzi raised to see off any opposition.

The space behind the shrub, which he felt sure harbored the enemy, and from which it would have been impossible to move without betraying position, was empty. J.B. frowned, for a moment nonplussed. It was only when he heard the faintest movement behind him that he realized he had been fooled by someone who knew the woods much better than he ever could. He had only half turned when he felt the prick of the dart in the back of his neck. Before he had completed a 180, the world spun on its axis and started to darken.

KRYSTY KNEW THERE WAS danger here. Her doomie sense was telling her, so strong that it was making her feel sick to the pit of her stomach. But that was good. She remembered Mother Sonja explaining to her that this gift was to preserve life, to give due warning of when the darkness of death was to descend.

It was just a pity that it wouldn't tell her from where it was choosing to make an appearance.

She shifted uncomfortably. She felt that she was in good cover, but there was something about the nagging insistence of her mutie sense that told her she was wrong, and if she didn't get the hell out then it would be too late.

She grasped her .38 Smith & Wesson in both hands, eyes never ceasing to scan the surrounding area. It was too quiet, as though the chattering wildlife they had previously disturbed knew that there was more trouble and had evacuated the area.

Every fiber of her body was screaming for her to move. She could see nothing, hear nothing around her to suggest she was in danger, but she could ignore it no longer. She identified another patch of cover she could move to. It wouldn't be too hard to remain hidden while she moved.

As she edged out, she realized why her senses had been screaming at her. One of the enemy party rose up out of tree and shrub cover, directly in front of her, waiting patiently for her to show herself, knowing she was there. Krysty leveled her blaster and squeezed off a round.

It went high and wide, her aim ruined by the dart that caught her in the forehead, the impact making her jerk at the last. She steadied her hand for a second round, but couldn't stop the world from spinning.

"FUCK IT," Mildred cursed, the words escaping her lips before she had a chance to stop them. Then she cursed herself for making noise and giving away her position. Her heart was racing, thumping so heavily against her rib cage that she thought it was going to break through. There was no way that she would usually be so stupid as to jump like a frightened rabbit at one blaster shot in the silence, but the lack of rest and continuous physical and mental stress since landing from the jump had left her strung out in a way she couldn't remember.

Breathing deeply, trying to keep it together, she closed her eyes for a second and counted to ten. She could hear nothing except the light rustle of a gentle breeze around the woods, so she felt okay about keeping her eyes closed for—

Shit, she shouldn't let her grip slip in this way. She heard a faint increase in the rustling and the crackling of ferns under a tread that, no matter how light, was still enough to register.

Mildred opened her eyes and found herself staring at a man who stood with a blowpipe, almost unable to believe that it had been this easy.

Before she had even got the Czech ZKR leveled to snap off a shot, the dart struck her cheek, making her start and slap her hand to her face. It had to be a toxin on the dart, but was it fatal or merely temporary?

As the world faded, it occurred to her that it would be a stupid way to buy the farm. After all she had endured, to lose her life because of one small panic attack.

RYAN HEARD THE SHOT at the same time as Mildred, and kept his attention fixed on the direction from which it had emanated. There was no follow-up, and nothing else to indicate any kind of action. The shot had been a pistol shot, and its timbre indicated that it came from Krysty. Unless it was a random shot, then the lack of follow-up meant that she was in trouble.

Ryan didn't want to betray his own position, but he couldn't in all conscience leave her to it. Dammit, he was sure J.B. was moving over there to give assistance anyway. And the fact was that they were in a stalemate, and someone had to do something to break it.

The one-eyed man had never been afraid of taking chances. It was the only way he'd managed to stay alive for so long. All risks were calculated; some were just more so than others.

Slipping from cover, Ryan made his way through the undergrowth to where he had heard the shot. Although he was looking for Krysty, it wasn't long before he could see Mildred, slumped on the turf. He couldn't tell if she was breathing. She was in the open, and he would have to break cover. If she was down, then what the hell had happened to Krysty after she had fired that lone round?

He paused, checking the surrounding area. It was deathly quiet. If there was anyone waiting, they were damned good. The fact that he seemed to be the only one of his people to respond was worrying, but that could wait.

Shouldering the Steyr and drawing the SIG-Sauer as it would be more maneuverable in the circumstances, Ryan recced around him one more time before taking a deep breath and moving out into the open.

Mildred was facedown. He turned her over.

Ryan heard movement behind him. Working on pure instinct and adrenaline, he rolled away from Mildred and in the opposite direction to the sound, snapping off a shot from the SIG-Sauer to give himself some kind of covering fire.

But even as he was midroll, he heard more movement, this time in front of him. He couldn't stop, couldn't adjust himself... He felt the snicking of a dart as it hit him, didn't feel it as it was in the numbed scar tissue on his cheek. With his good eye he caught a glimpse of a woman half hidden by the leaves, a blowpipe in her mouth. He kept rolling, now unable to stop himself as the world began to lurch beneath his still moving, now rubbery and uncontrollable body.

As he began to black out, he heard a man say, "Lord, thought we'd never get that bastard. Fuckin' fine shot, Jude. Let's—"

And then the dark.

THEY WERE TRUSSED like hogs and carried to the ville.

The two hunting parties met, the sec patrol calling the other with a series of bird and animal calls that were used as a code. The party that had followed the first combat were already on the trail of the companions, and hadn't far to go before they met with the sec patrol.

A brief description of the carnage they had seen made the sec patrol sorry that they hadn't chilled the bastards.

"No, save them for Erik. He'll have plans for them, I'm sure," said the hunter with the bullet belt. She was still consoling the fat man, who was visibly shaken even now by what he had seen previously.

"Easy for you to say, Collette. Your sister wasn't among the chilled," he commented bitterly.

"All the more reason for you to keep your hate," she answered. "Think they'll get off lightly? Erik needs something like this to help the catch. You wait and see," she added in reply to his bewildered stare. "First we got to get this scum back to Ewelltown."

The inert and trussed enemy loaded onto poles they cut from the surrounding trees, the two hunting parties shouldered their burdens and made their way along long-trodden paths to the small fishing village.

Ewelltown was hardly large enough to be called a ville. A series of timber huts and shacks, with a few buildings constructed from the remains of old houses or from recycled brick and concrete, it could have numbered no more than a couple hundred inhabitants. Despite their seeming isolation, they were of a relatively healthy stock, with evidence of a wide gene pool. The lack of interbreeding was due to the nature of the village's subsistence. They relied on fishing the bay in which they sat, and the waters beyond out into the reaches of the seas surrounding the swamplands that lay across the bay.

Isolated by land due to the dense woods and the desert that sat beyond, they were able to trade via the waters, and the influx of other fishers and traders by sea gave them the opportunity to escape the inbreeding that had degenerated so many other small, isolated communities.

However, they were now poverty-stricken, more so than ever before. The fishing stocks had dried up in recent months, which left them no basic diet beyond the small amount of crops they could raise on land reclaimed from the woods and whatever fruits they could take from those very woods. Unfortunately, the toxic nature of some of the soil meant that much of the fruit was inedible, and also accounted for the sparsity of land they could use for farming.

That had never been a problem, as the rich fishing stocks had left them plenty to trade with those who came in on ships from around the swamps and the sea beyond. Until now, when a school of predators—unseen, but running deep and occasionally ripping nets—had started to drain the stocks.

Now there was little jack, little trade and little food, which was why a previously uninterested people had taken to hunting small game in the woods…and why they had stumbled across the companions and been found so wanting in combat. They were fishers, not hunters, and not sec…and now they would be avenged.

Word had spread to the village by the time that the hunters arrived with their trussed captives, still unconscious from the effects of the darts. Families were out to meet them as they took them past the dwellings, and down to the docks, where the wooden boardwalks extended out to the docking for the fishing ships, lying idle where there was little for them to do.

But perhaps not for long.

"…THINK THEY MAY BE COMING around soon… some of 'em, at any rate."

The voice was strong and assertive, the sound of a big man who was used to being obeyed. That was the impression Krysty had as she stirred, rising back to the surface. She tentatively opened an eye, peering at the painful light. She flexed her arms and found them almost numb. Her legs were the same. As she gained better use of her faculties, she figured that she was tied—a little more than securely—and that she was on her back, which would explain the light being so strong, if nothing else.

More and more she opened her eyes, gradually adjusting to the light. She discovered that she was right. She was trussed and bound to a pole that had been laid horizontally on some kind of perch. Moving her head—and neck movement was about all the secure binding gave her—she could see that she was on the end of a row: the rest of the row comprised five other poles, on which were placed Ryan, J.B., Mildred, Doc and Jak, all of them as securely bound as herself. They were all facing the sun. There was little else she could see except some wood, some water and a whole bunch of angry-looking people. The air smelled of ozone, fish and hate.

"Hell, looks like they're coming around—the redhead sure is." The voice was female and harsh. Straining, Krysty could see that it was a woman with a string of bullets slung across a generous chest. She had a fat man beside her, and his eyes bored into Krysty's as they met. He would have chilled her—and the rest of them—as soon as look, if he could.

No question that they were fish food. To assume anything else after the five chilled they had left behind would be triple stupe.

But why this? Why not just chill them and have done with it?

A face loomed over her. It was thin, hatchetlike and sparsely covered with gray hair. Weathered and lined, the eyes were cobalt-blue. Could have been a kind face, a good face under any other circumstances. But not now. Krysty was a little surprised when he spoke and the voice issuing forth was the one she had identified as that of a leader when she was coming consciousness. Somehow, the voice and face didn't fit. No reason why they should. Shit, her mind was still cloudy, still wandering.

"Well, looks like they're all ready," the voice said as the face disappeared, presumably examining all the others. "Guess you should know what's gonna happen to you and why. I'll tell you what. You're good fighters, and mebbe another time things would have been different. I know there are plenty here who are pissed at what you did, but a fight's a fight, and you have to risk buying the farm. Trouble is, if we weren't so desperate for food, then none of us would have been out there. But those who are chilled have left family behind, and they want vengeance. Fair enough. And mebbe it gives us a chance to get rid of two problems at the same time."

Krysty opened her mouth, tried to speak. She was surprised that the others had remained silent, then discovered why: no sound would issue from vocal cords that were still paralysed by the toxin from the dart. She tried to move her fingers and toes and found that they wouldn't respond. So feeling was returning, but only gradually.

Meanwhile, Erik continued. He hadn't even bothered to tell them his name, or where they were. He didn't have to, he had other matters on his mind.

"We're a fishing village, and you can't fish much when you've got some nuke-shittin' big bastards eating all your catch. So we need to lure them up near the surface where we can chill them, and let things get back to normal. Best way that I can figure to do that is give them some bait. Give them something good and big to feed on, and make sure you get some blood in the water to give them the scent. But what could we use?

"Seems to me that you've given us the answer. All we've got to do is get you ready, then haul you out. This way those who loved the lost get to extract some personal vengeance and make you suffer, then see you get chilled while we solve the problem that's starving us.

"It's perfect. Oh, by the way, don't try to struggle, because you can't. Shit on those darts is real good. Comes off the bark of one of those trees out there, and a dart usually paralyzes for three hours. You've had just over one and a half, so you should be ready to thrash about and spread that blood in the spume just about the time we're making bait of you.

"See, it works out just fine…"

So they were to be used as bait for whatever was out in the bay. That was bad enough. Maybe they would have a chance if the toxin wore off, maybe they could try to get free of their bonds before the predators had a chance to take a chunk of them, maybe… But what was this about those who had lost getting a chance to take revenge?

"Okay, you can have at them—but don't do too much damage. We want them alive, remember," Erik said in an offhand manner.

Krysty twisted her head and wished she hadn't been able to see the sight that greeted her. A clutch of villagers was moving toward the immobile and helpless companions. Each of them carried something that gleamed in the sunlight of late afternoon.

Each of the villagers carried a sharpened paring knife, of the kind used for gutting their catch.

Only this time their catch was human.

Chapter Five

An old childhood ditty ran through Mildred's head repeatedly, and she wondered at the capacity for the human mind to try to find distraction at times of distress. It was an old couplet, a song from when she was still an intern. Something that guy Rob who was in her path class used to play in his car all the time. Some kind of long-hair shit when she was listening to Rick James. She hadn't thought of it in years, except that it made a lot of sense all of a sudden, some piece of junk hidden in the recess of her memory and coming out now that it was appropriate—now that it had some kind of function to fulfill.

Part of her mind was rambling through this, and the other part was that silent scream itself, pain and terror with no outlet as her paralyzed voice could not give vent.

It was the same for all of them. Lying prone and defenseless, they had been unable to do anything to prevent the villagers taking revenge on them whilst preparing them for the fishing expedition. The inhabitants of Ewelltown had clustered around the six poles, using the paring knives to slice through their clothes. Not reducing them to ribbons, but making small cuts and tears, almost with an air of precision. The cuts were designed to break the skin, slicing across the surface to open wide cuts that were shallow, and gently ooze blood in small trickles that began to stain the cut material, soaking into it before starting to leak out.

The cuts were maddeningly painful. Taking the very nerve endings at the surface of the skin, they were sharp and insistent pains that wouldn't have been disabling, but were halfway between the pain of a deep cut and an itch, doing little more but inspire the desire to scratch—something they were unable to do, leaving them half insane with the insistent torture of the cuts.

While the villagers worked on them, the old man Leroy and the woman Collette, who had been among the villagers bringing in the companions, had gathered together their outer clothes, backpacks and the bag in which J.B. carried their ammo and explosives. They hadn't bothered to check the contents, not caring what the bags contained. They had another concern.

"Erik, a word," Leroy murmured, pulling his chief away from the area where the cutting—almost ritual in nature, so calm were the villagers in taking their revenge—was occurring. As the hatchet-faced elder of Ewelltown walked away, anyone stumbling upon the scene would have assumed that another catch was being calmly gutted, so perfunctory was the way in which the cutting was taking place. The companions were obscured to outside view by the crowd clustered around them, their invisibility lending the scene an everyday air.

Leroy said nothing as he led the elder to the collection of outer clothes and bags. "Their things," he said. "What shall we do with them?"

"Does it matter?"

Collette shrugged. "Not sure. Me 'n' Leroy been talking about it. They seemed to come from out of nowhere, and they ain't part of no convoy that's trying to get past the desert. But mebbe there are others looking for them, and mebbe those others wouldn't take too kindly to our chilling them in such a manner—never mind that they took some of ours."

Erik chewed that over and nodded slowly. "Good point. Guess you're right about that. We should get rid of them where they can't be found. Weight them down and dump them overboard after we've got rid of these fuckers and the big fish."

Leroy and Collette assented, and Erik walked back to where the companions were being bloodied for bait.

"They ready yet?" he asked in an almost offhand manner.

One of the villagers turned to him. "Hard to tell when they can't scream."

Erik screwed up his face in thought. "Tell you what. Leave them be about now. We don't want them so far gone that they don't move about in the water. The more they thrash, the more they'll churn up that blood smell and attract our little problem."

The villagers grinned crookedly. "That'll be good to see."

Under the direction of the village elder, the villagers stepped back, their knives disappearing as soon as they'd appeared. The companions were left lying on their poles, breathing as heavily as the paralyzing effects of the toxin would allow, still unable to utter any sound.

Twelve of the villagers, two per pole, took hold of them

and removed them from the perch, walking down the dock to where a fishing boat lay at anchor. There were several such boats moored around the bay, but this one had been tied up for a specific purpose. There were six lines running from it, made of a thickly woven hemp.

The poles, with their bloody cargo, were dropped roughly onto the dock, and six metal rings were driven into the head of each pole with sledgehammers. The insistent ringing impact of the hammering made the heads of each one of the companions ring, aching until it felt as if each blow was directly into their cortex. Not that the villagers cared. They couldn't see if it was causing discomfort, and would only welcome it if they knew.

Once this was done, and the rings tested for strength, the ropes from the fishing boat were passed, one through each ring, and securely tied.

Now the boat was ready to cast off. The crew made ready, and within ten minutes had untied the vessel, ready to sail out into the bay, watched by the silent villagers.

The rope payed out as the boat pulled away from the dock, taking up the slack. Each of the companions was aware of this, could see the coil of each rope as it decreased until the lines were pulled tight, and yet none could say a word or move a muscle. All they could do was try to brace themselves for the moment when the ropes would pull tight and the poles would begin to move.

When it happened, it wasn't a sudden jerk, as might have been expected. Instead, as the boat was still building up a head of sail, the combined weight of the poles stopped them moving suddenly. The ropes stretched and creaked as the momentum of the vessel started to overcome their inertia. Slowly, they began to move, scraping across the dock, banging over the uneven boards, shaking every bone in their bodies. And then they reached the point where there was no wood beneath them.

For one moment each of them seemed to hang in the air, free of the dock but not yet falling. To those villagers watching from on the dock, it seemed to be only a blink of the eye before they fell into the waters of the bay, but for each of the companions as they hung helplessly in the void, it was a moment that stretched forever as they prepared themselves as best as they could for hitting the water below.

There was barely time to tense muscles that moved, ignoring the pain that slithered across their cut skins like a living creature, and to draw a deep breath, filling their lungs as best as possible, before the warmth of the day and the lightness of air was replaced by the cold of the water and the heaviness of the liquid around them. The sudden cold and the hard impact of hitting the surface at speed was almost enough to drive the conserved air from their lungs, allowing the cold water of the bay to seep in. It moved around their bodies, making the cuts neither better nor worse, the pain merely different.

Doc spluttered, losing air and trying to replace it, his body working independently of his brain, drawing water into his lungs that made him cough, the cold fluid in his throat and nostrils. Ryan and J.B. held it together better, losing some air with the impact, but restraining the urge to suck in more when it would only be water.

Krysty and Mildred both felt the strength begin to return to their limbs, feeling seeping back, in some strange way spurred by the sudden shock of cold. They managed to keep most of the air in their lungs, both controlling their respiration, starting to flex and move muscles that were cramped by the sudden cold but nonetheless beginning to respond.

Jak fared best of them all. The albino was wiry and tough, and had spent many years learning the arts of hunting, including the ability to stay immobile, almost without breathing, for hours on end while waiting for his prey to come into view. Right now, that ability to keep breathing contained, and to conserve oxygen, was the most useful. Perhaps because he had absorbed less toxin, plucking the dart quickly from him; or perhaps because his constitution was better able to cope with its effects, Jak was now beginning to regain full use of his muscles and limbs.

The poles didn't remain under the water for the whole time. They broke surface then dipped again, giving the companions a brief snatch of time in which to gasp in air before the water closed over them once more. The fishing boat began to gather speed as the wind took its sails, and the pilot guided it out of the bay and into the salt waters beyond.

The poles on which the six companions were trussed twisted and turned with the movement of the boat and the flow of the current as the sea met the fresh water of the bay, which in itself was at the mouth of a river. The poles turned in spirals as they bobbed up and down on the surface.

The salt water hit them, increasing as they moved out from the bay, the salt seeping into the cuts, mingling with the blood and irritating nerve ends that were already ragged and sore from the fresh water.

And yet, in some way, the pain galvanized them, made them fight harder. Independently of one another, the same thought went through each of their minds—there was no way that they were going to have come this far to be chilled by a bunch of fish, fish that were now beginning to mill around them. There was no indication that the big game for which they were bait was anywhere near, but in the waters where the salt and fresh mixed uneasily, small schools of other predatory fish were attracted by the trail of blood that mixed in the spume of their wake and floated down into the depths as the waters settled. Following this trail, the small fish were catching up with them, nibbling at their flesh, the sharp pains of razor-teeth contrasting with the irritation of the cuts, the attacks opening up the cuts so that there was a larger trail of blood in their wake. Each of them bucked against the fish, trying to shake them off, but it was almost impossible as they were so securely tied to the poles.

They were saved by the fact that the boat hauled them rapidly out beyond the range of the fresh water, driving the small fish back into their own environment.

As they moved through the water, and the use of their muscles and limbs began to return, they each fought to loosen themselves from their bonds. It was far from easy, as the knots on the ropes securing them were tight and the rope itself was made slick from the water. Fingers with feeling just returning to them were slow, clumsy, and felt twice their usual size.

Jak was the first to free himself. He used his control over his own muscles, and the water swelling the fibers of the rope, to flex and expand the space he took up within the confines of his bonds, forcing the sodden rope to pull tighter against him until it reached the point where it felt as though he had taken the bonds to their limit and they were threatening to cut into his already sore and bloody skin. Then he relaxed, breathed out, and his body became smaller—almost unnoticeably so, but just enough to give him the fraction of an inch he needed to slip one arm free. With this done, there was more space within the bonds for him to move. He was able to free his other arm. From there, it was a relatively easy task to maneuver his body in such a way that he was able to pick at the bonds that bound his legs and feet to the pole, loosening them enough to slip free. Not that this was as simple as it sounded. The boat had picked up pace as it moved into the sea, the winds outside the confines of the bay catching the carefully drawn sails so that the vessel was speeding toward its destination. That meant that the poles in tow were moving at a rapid rate, taking a bruising buffeting from the currents in which they moved.

Once he was free, Jak's main problem was to keep hold of the pole. The force of the water was such that every twist, turn and bump threatened to throw him off, making it hard for him to make any more progress once he had freed himself.

Ryan and J.B. were also using similar tactics to free themselves. The Armorer struck lucky in that the rope binding him was frayed in one small portion, and the action of the water combined with his attempts to free himself caused it to give way. The rope, its tension now broken, fell away behind him into the water, and the sudden freedom and its subsequent momentum nearly pitched him out behind the pole. He swore heavily to himself and managed to keep a grip, turning himself around so that he was able to grasp the slippery pole and work his way up toward the hook and the length of rope that was holding it to the boat.

Soon, Ryan, J.B. and Jak were in a position where they were able to see one another over the ride of the surf. Looking up at the boat, they could see that the crew was paying little attention to the progress of their captives, They had taken it as an absolute that the six people tied to the poles would be unable to move, and so concentrated their attention on piloting the vessel to the area where their target predators were known to swim.

This gave the companions a chance. It was going to be hard, but it was all they had. Each would have to climb the slippery, flailing rope that linked them to the boat, hoping that they wouldn't be spotted during their progress—if they were, then they were easy targets—and that they would then be able to overpower the crew. However many may be aboard.

The ropes and poles were close enough for them to be able to see one another clearly, but not enough to exchange words—even in a shout—over the roar of the water.

Krysty and Mildred had also freed themselves in a similar manner, and they could be seen. But there was no sign of Doc. A feeling of unease spread among the five. Ryan, Jak and J.B. indicated with hand signals that they would try to scale the ropes connecting them to the boat. Mildred and Krysty, who were the closest to the pole on which Doc was still secured, signaled their intent to try to free the old man.

It was a close call as to which of the groups had the harder task. The ropes were pulled tight to the boat as they towed the poles, but with the changes in weight as the companions moved off the staves, this tautness may alter. To be thrown from the rope if it bucked too heavily would almost certainly mean buying the farm. That was if the crew didn't spot them and fire on them.

But Mildred and Krysty had to leap from their own ropes to the one attaching Doc to the boat—in Mildred's case, that meant crossing two ropes, as she was farther away from Doc than the redhead. Each jump would mean risking falling short and crashing into the sea, with the chance of the poles following behind slamming into her and knocking her unconscious... something that would almost certainly mean buying the farm.

What else could they do? If Doc had come around and was having trouble freeing himself from his bonds, then he needed assistance. Even more so if the toxin had been more effective on him than the others, and he was still paralyzed. The longer he remained at the mercy of the sea, the greater the chances of him breathing in salt water and drowning, the greater the chances of the predators for which they were intended as bait attacking him as they neared the target area.

The thought that Doc may already be nothing more than fish food had crossed the minds of both women, but neither would give it any countenance. They hadn't come this far to just leave Doc to his fate on the chance that it may already be too late.

Not while there was still hope. It was the same reason that Ryan, Jak and J.B. were risking climbing up to the boat. Not until the last breath had been dragged scream-ing from their lungs would any of them consider giving in to fate.

Krysty and Mildred exchanged glances, and the phy-sician gave the briefest of nods. Her companion nodded back and turned to face the rope and pole carrying Doc. It was moving at speed, and also veering from left to right in an erratic pattern dictated by the currents it crossed. Kir-sty pulled herself up to the top of her own pole, wrapping the rope around her hand to anchor herself as she tried to gain a foothold on the slippery wood, hauling herself up from a lying position until she was on one knee, then planting her feet on the wood. Her muscles protested at the strain of keeping balance and adjusting to an uncom-fortable crouch as she settled into a stance where she had both feet on the pole, and could still keep her hand se-cured.

Her sentient hair, sensing that this was a moment of tri-ple-red danger, was gathered close to her scalp, wrapping its tendrils so protectively around her neck that she felt as though it might inadvertently choke her. She ignored it and watched as her intended target swam in and out of range. She was trying to judge the rhythm of its movement, to gauge the best moment for a leap from pole to pole. But the pole moved erratically and she'd just have to rely on blind instinct.

She unwrapped her hand from the rope, so that only her balance was keeping her on the pole, and tried to clear her mind completely. She remembered those far-off days when she was a child, growing up in Harmony. Mother Sonja and Uncle Tyas McCann, the two people who had

meant more to her than the world then, had always told
her that the power of Gaia ran through her, and that even
if she didn't call upon it, all she had to do was trust in it.
The Earth Mother would guide her.

Mildred would have called it following your gut, and
watching Krysty from behind, she could see the change
come over her as the Titian-haired woman let her instincts
flow. From a tentative crouch, she seemed to suddenly
grow more fluid and graceful, body tensing lightly before
she leaped into space.

Krysty herself hardly knew that she had jumped, only
that she had blanked her mind and let her body take over.
Suddenly she was sailing through the air between the two
poles, feeling the splashes of surf against her exposed
skin, the salt tingling in her still open cuts.

She hit the pole heavily, the wood thudding into her rib
cage as she wrapped her arms around the pole, the air
driven from her stomach and lungs by the sudden impact,
the wood coming at her with a sudden force as it changed
direction in the current. She could feel it under her; she
had made it. But little else registered for a moment as she
fought to get the air back into her lungs, gasping heavily
and coughing as some salt water went down her throat.
She was aware of something softer than the wood beneath
her legs, and realized that she had partly landed on Doc.

Even in the middle of the surf, clinging for grim life to
the pole, it occurred to her that it would be ironic if she'd
tried to save him and only broken his neck on her landing.

No time to think about it. Taking air deep into her
lungs, feeling the oxygen pump into her brain, she moved

up, using the ring driven into the top of the pole as a hand-hold while she maneuvered. She wanted to get a better look at Doc before she started trying to free him, and also leave room for Mildred to make her way across.

"Lord, if I get out of this, remind me to try to find somewhere to lead a nice quiet life…" Mildred muttered to herself as she saw Krysty land. Now it was her turn to make the first leap onto Krysty's now empty pole.

Problem was, the lack of weight meant that the damn thing was waving around with an even wilder arc in the crosscurrents behind the boat.

Mildred blew air out and shook her head, took a deep breath and just jumped.

The pole moved toward her as she was in midair. It was like slow motion, as though time had slowed to allow her to see everything clearly everything like the piece of wood being caught in another swell and being whipped away from the arc of her trajectory, leaving her with only water to fall into.

She snaked out an arm without thinking about it, and her hand closed around the rope securing the pole to the boat. As she hit the water, the weight and momentum dragged her hand down the rope, the burn making her yell and take in a mouthful of salt water. Coughing and sputtering, ignoring the burning in her chest and the burning on her hand, she flung out her other arm and got a stronger grip, hauling herself toward the empty pole, which she clung to with a sense of relief.

Dammit, this was only the first jump; she still had to reach Doc and Krysty.

Looking across as she steadied herself, she could see

that Krysty had started to check the old man for signs of
life, and also try to free him from his bonds. There was
little time for her to waste. She shot a glance toward the
boat: so far they had been lucky. No one on the deck had
given them a second glance while the vessel was moving
into the target area waters, but sooner or later they were
duty-bound to check the bait. What would they say when
they saw Ryan, Jak and J.B. inching their way up the
ropes toward the back of the vessel, ignoring the buffeting of the sea and staying focused only on their progress?

Shit, if they were making progress—and they were just
over halfway to the stern of the boat—then she sure as hell
should move herself.

Mildred steadied herself and made ready to jump again.
This one may prove a little easier, as the extra weight
Krysty's presence had brought to Doc's pole meant that
it was no longer moving so wildly and erratically in the
water. It was reacting less to the current, and the arc of
movement was smaller. There was a good chance that she
could make this jump with ease.

Mildred blinked twice, didn't think and jumped. She
aimed for the very top of the pole, hoping to catch the
metal ring for a handhold. She'd managed to judge that
right, and she wrapped her fingers around the metal, feeling the wrench on her shoulder as her momentum tried to
carry her past the pole and into the churning sea beyond.
For, at the last, she had overestimated the movement of
the pole in the water, and her jump had almost taken her
past it.

Cursing incomprehensibly, she flailed with her free
hand to gain another hold and felt fingers like iron clamp

around her flailing forearm, hauling her onto the pole where she nestled up against Doc. Looking up, she could see that Krysty's eyes were glowing with a strength that she was drawing from something other than herself. It wasn't the power of Gaia that Mildred had seen her draw on in the past, with devastating effect both to her opponents and herself, but rather it seemed to be some kind of reserve within herself.

Hell, I must have some of that somewhere down inside myself, Mildred thought, her resolve hardening. If she needed any other encouragement, the sight of Doc gave it to her. The old man was deathly pale, his skin almost whiter than his mane of hair that was plastered to his skull. His eyes were open, but were staring without focus, the whites only showing as they rolled up into his head, seeing only some vision that was within and nothing of the outside world.

First they had to get Doc free, then they had to bring him around enough to climb up to the boat under his own steam. The first would be relatively easy, even though she and Krysty had nothing but their broken-nailed and bleeding fingers with which to unpick the salt-swollen, slippery knots. It was the second that may prove to impossible, for once Doc was gone, there was no knowing when he would come back...or even *if,* for every time might be the last.

Without speaking, the two women worked on the old man's bonds as he lay against the pole, moaning and muttering to himself, lost in some strange world of his own imaginings. They picked at the knots, sometimes only with one hand each as they gripped the pole and those lines still secured to protect themselves from the buffeting of the ways. It was an irony that their being on the pole made it easier to work on the knots. The drag of the extra weight on this pole had significantly cut down on the amount of movement in the water.

Dark shapes moved through the water around the poles, large enough for their wake to cut across the wake of the boat and cause another crosscurrent. As Mildred looked up, one of the shapes broke surface briefly, tiny cold eyes and rows of razor-sharp teeth showing in a wide mouth, tiny specks of foam covering the blunted snout.

It was like no shark she could ever remember seeing in the years before the nukecaust: larger, maybe thirty to forty feet in length, and about half that in width and breadth. It was bulkier, less streamlined. It probably ate enough sea life to feed an average ville every day; they had to find an area, strip it of its marine life, then move on. No wonder the fishing village had been desperate, their stock depleted by this beast, and... She tried to count the shapes as they moved around the boat and the poles, scenting the blood. She reckoned on at least a dozen, perhaps as many as twenty. They moved so fast it was impossible to tell.

All she knew now was that they had to redouble their efforts and get themselves—and Doc—out of the ocean. If the sharks didn't get them, then the villagers would. They were the intended prey of these beasts. How long before the crew took a look over the stern of the boat to see if the sharks had taken their bait, only to find the bait was biting back?

While Mildred and Krysty worked at Doc's bonds, Ryan, Jak and J.B. were slowly inching their way toward the boat's stern. They concentrated on going hand-over-hand, palms raw. Each movement was like white-hot needles into their palms as their body weight pulled them toward the water. For Ryan, as the heaviest, it was the worst, but the one-eyed man gritted, biting his cheek until he could taste the same blood in his mouth that ran down to his wrists.

The ropes swung wildly as the lightened poles were tossed around freely in the crosscurrents behind the boat, threatening with each move to throw the companions off and into the water if their grip slackened for a moment. They hung beneath the ropes, moving hand-over-hand with their ankles wrapped around the rope to secure them, the rope burning their already raw ankles and calves as they moved upward.

Their progress seemed interminably slow, but was fast enough for them to each be at least halfway up to the stern when the sharks began to circle the boat. Ryan caught sight of one of the dark, massive shapes from the corner of his eye as he weathered a sudden tug and swing at the rope. He cursed, as he knew that it would bring the crew to the side of the boat, and all three of them were currently in a vulnerable position. He couldn't get a good look at the other two—wouldn't want to, as to twist his body to try to catch sight of them would be to risk losing his own grip or impede his own progress—but figured that they wouldn't be that much ahead of him, if at all.

In fact, Jak was making rapid progress. The albino hunter had focused the immense strength of his will into ascending the rope with the minimum of effort and the maximum of speed. Ignoring the pain from his hands and calves, and concentrating instead on breathing steadily, timing each movement of his hands and legs to work to the rhythm of his breathing, he was moving toward the mooring of the rope on the rail running around the vessel's stern. He didn't look up, neither did he look down. It didn't matter, he could do nothing to affect what may go on above or below. All he could do was get up that rope and leave the rest to fate.

On the deck of the boat, the eight-man crew that had been chosen by Erik to pilot and man the vessel on its journey was relaxing before it had to tackle its enemy. Two women—one of them Collette, who had been in the hunting party—and six men were on board. They were at the prow, armed with remade Heckler & Koch MP-5s, flare guns and scavenged air-pressure harpoons. They had no idea if the SMGs would be any use against the creatures, knew that the flares would be explosively effective if they hit at close range, and trusted their fisher skills to use the harpoons when the creatures came in range.

They were watching the waters ahead, apprehension churning in their guts. They were hunter-gatherers, not warriors, and a predator like the school of sharks that had devastated their fishing stocks was an enemy that they had no experience tackling. All were hoping that the bait they dragged in their wake would attract the school, and as they saw the dark shapes move in the water, and start to cluster at the wake of the boat's backwash, they snapped out of their relaxation and primed their weapons.

The companions' belongings and blasters, weighted and ready to be dumped overboard as per the orders of Erik, sat neglected in the corner. There had been too much to consider on the way out. In much the same way, the crew hadn't thought to check what was happening to the bait they trailed behind them. If they gave it any thought at all, it was merely to wonder if they would still be alive when the predators came in to take them. If they were, then their thrashing in the waters would stir up the bloodlust of the school and attract them all to the one area for a cleaner chill from the fishermen. And besides, to still be alive when the sharks began to eat them would be a suitable fate for those who had chilled people from their village so mercilessly.

So when they saw the school of predators approach and begin to circle the vessel, when they had primed their weapons, when they had steeled themselves for the battle, when they turned to the stern of the vessel...

When they did all of these things, the last sight they expected to greet them was the wraithlike vision of Jak Lauren, dripping wet, hair clinging to his skull in tendrils, white scarred skin covered in a film of blood from still open wounds, blood that also stained his clothes and trickled down his arms and over his hands, which hung free at his sides. He was breathing heavily but steadily, and stood slightly forward, resting on the balls of his feet, poised to spring. His eyes blazed like malevolent hot coals, boring into those who faced him, the fury in them making them flinch.

He was one against eight, and unarmed, but he had surprise on his side. And he had the ice-cold heart of vengeance. They might try to chill him, but all he had to do was hold them until Ryan and J.B. reached the stern, as he was sure they would.

For a second, nothing happened. Jak faced the eight-strong crew and they were too stunned to react. If Jak could make his first move count, then he would have the initiative.

Like an unholy avenging angel, Jak sprang forward into the midst of the crew. Fortunately for him, they had been clustered together in the center of the deck, about to allocate sections of rail from which to fire. He took advantage of that, knowing that as long as they were in a cluster, he could take down more than one with a single impact.

Jak was small, but strong. He got a lot of lift from his leg muscles, and his momentum over the short distance was enough to send the eight-man crew flying in all directions. Blasters and harpoons scattered across the deck as the unprepared fishermen found themselves in the middle of a whirlwind. Although he had no weapons—his knives were in his jacket, along with his Colt Python—he had his hands and feet. Despite the cuts and ragged rawness of his flesh, he was still wearing his combat boots, and his fingers and palms were hard ridges of muscle, sinew and skin that had been honed over years of fighting and hunting. Ally that to the intense anger and red mist of hate that he felt for the people who had treated himself and his friends in such a manner, and it was little contest.

Outnumbered, he first struck out at those who were still armed—two men with flare guns. One of them brought his weapon up to fire directly into Jak's face, but found his arm snapped as the albino youth gripped his wrist like an iron band and twisted it back. He yelled a high-pitched scream of shock more than pain, and before the note had left his open mouth he found himself pitched into the other flare holder. A woman of about forty, she had the flare gun grasped in both hands and aimed at Jak. When she squeezed the trigger, Jak swung his first opponent around so that his body was between them. The flare exploded with a dull, loud "whump," splattering the ribs and waist of the fisherman as it hit him. He made no sound this time, as he had no lungs left from which to expel air. The woman slumped to the deck, in shock over the fact that she had just chilled one of her own.

But this was no time for reflection.

Jak was already on to his next target: Collette, whom he recognized from the woodlands, was bending to retrieve an MP-5 that lay on the deck, where it had fallen in the confusion. Jak noticed that she was still wearing that stupe bullet belt across her chest. He noticed this as he took a flying kick at her, the sole of his combat boot crunching into the side of her head, knocking her jaw and temple toward an acute angle. She grunted, feeling her vertebrae shatter at the base of her neck as they failed to take the strain of being twisted with such sudden violence. She felt little more as the lights dimmed on her world, the MP-5 clattering to the deck once more from her nerveless fingers.

Two down, one out of action...but the other five had scattered across the deck, leaving him vulnerable whichever option he chose to take.

Or perhaps not. Without registering it on his always impassive face, Jak noted that Ryan and J.B. had reached the rail and were hauling themselves over. As the five crew members were facing him, they hadn't spotted the companions. Jak launched himself off to the left, to tackle a fat man with a harpoon gun. This took their attention away from the section of the stern where Ryan and J.B. had arrived.

Jak didn't see what happened next. He relied on his friends to get it right while he took on his man. Like a stupe, the fisherman waved the harpoon gun as though he wanted to use it like a club. Perhaps, in the back of his mind, he wanted to save the harpoon for their original target, not realizing that he would never get the chance to use it this way unless he dealt with Jak.

The albino teen stepped in toward the man, ducking under his swing with ease. The movement left the fisherman's torso open and undefended. It was almost too easy as Jak hit him in the chest with the heel of his hand, shocking the heart. The fisherman gasped for breath, trying to suck air into lungs that didn't want to work. It distracted him some more and left him open to a blow to the throat, straight fingers, hard like rock, that caved in the cartilage around his windpipe and made a mess of the artery and veins that fed his brain.

While he attended to his prey, Jak also drew the attention of the other crew members. There were four in all, ranged in a semicircle around the middle of the deck. Jak had deliberately chosen the one isolated man to attack because of his position. If the fishermen had been fighters, they may have questioned this strange tactic… But they had little combat experience and didn't think to look at the deck to their rear.

With a quick exchange of glances, Ryan and J.B. divided the four into pairs, electing which two to take out.

Both were exhausted, but they were driven by adrenaline and the will to survive.

As the crew members prepared to fire on Jak with MP-5's and harpoon guns, they hesitated, not wanting to risk taking out their own man. It was a hesitation that was to cost them dearly. Ryan and J.B. both attacked at the same moment, choosing to tackle a crew member wielding an MP-5. Neither man expected the attack, and as they were grabbed around their throats, the blasters were jerked up into the air, the chattering of blaster fire audible over the roar of the ocean.

Both J.B. and Ryan used the men they were tackling as shields, turning so that their immediate opponents formed a barrier between themselves and the two free crew members. As they choked the life from their struggling, flailing opponents, they made sure that the free men—one of whom carried a harpoon, the other an MP-5—couldn't get a clear shot at them. As his opponent began to lose consciousness, becoming more of a deadweight, Ryan felt him slump into him, and he reached around to take the SMG as it began to slip from his grasp. Before his human shield had a chance to completely fall free, Ryan already had the SMG raised and rattled off a burst before the crew member opposite him had a chance to open fire. The one-eyed warrior's burst stitched a ragged, bloody line across the crewman's torso, running from his waist up to his neck, which exploded in a gout of blood where the carotid artery was ripped open. The crewman staggered back to the rail, where he teetered unfeelingly for a moment before pitching over the side and into the ocean.

J.B. had almost throttled the life from his opponent, and as the crewman dropped, the MP-5 fell to one side, leaving J.B. exposed if he wished to drop the unconscious man and grab the SMG. The Armorer knew he couldn't safely get the blaster if he kept hold of his shield, and it seemed as though the man opposite knew this, grinning with relish as he raised his harpoon gun and waited for J.B. to make his move. The grin suddenly turned into an expression of mute astonishment. He looked down at his side and noticed that the end of a harpoon was sticking out from just beneath his armpit. He turned his gaze back to J.B. with something approaching bemusement before falling sideways to the deck. The Armorer looked over and saw Jak holding the harpoon gun he had taken from his own opponent.

But there was no time for thanks. They had taken out the crew, but Mildred, Krysty and Doc were still in the water, and the predatory sharks were closing in…

Ryan was at the stern rail. He could see that the women had Doc free of his bonds, but the old man was still barely conscious, and it was all they could do to keep him on the rope. There was no way that they could get him up by themselves, and time was running short: the sharks were sniffing around, getting closer with every passing moment.

Except for a few that were clustered around a foaming pool of water some 150 yards back…

Of course—Ryan realized what had happened. Some of the predators had latched onto the crewman who had pitched over the side, and they were too preoccupied with his corpse to bother with Mildred, Krysty and Doc.

"Grab the crew," he yelled over the sound of the ocean. "Look..."

J.B. and Jak both followed the direction of Ryan's arm and could see the frothing, bloody pool in the middle of the sea. They knew immediately what he meant, and moved to gather the chilled crewmen. Taking them one at a time and swinging the bodies so that they sailed over the rail and into the sea, they worked their way through the seven chilled.

The eighth member was the woman who had chilled one of her own with a flare gun; it still sat uselessly in her hand as she sat staring into space. Ryan went across to her, crouched in front and took the flare gun from her unresisting grip. He said nothing; he could see that she was a million miles away. He couldn't throw her to the sharks when she was alive, in spite of the fact it was what she and her fellow crew members had been doing to the companions. She was no threat now; they would wait and deal with her later.

There were more important matters to attend to: with the seven corpses now in the sea, the blood and meat was attracting the predators away from where Mildred, Krysty and Doc were huddled on the pole. Ryan leaned over the stern as far as he dared and yelled down at them.

"Hang on, we're gonna pull you up," he yelled.

As they looked up, Mildred and Krysty wondered how the hell the three exhausted men were going to haul up three people and a wooden pole. They were still wondering when Ryan disappeared from view. At least the sharks had gone for the moment. The bait of the chilled fishermen had worked, and sections of the sea were now frothing pools of blood, salt water and entrails.

Back on deck, Ryan and J.B. had located where the ropes for the trailing poles were tied. They were knotted through metal loops at the base of a sail mast.

"Jak, think we can do this?" Ryan asked, indicating the individual loops.

The albino youth grinned. "Not get up any other way."

But all three of them knew that it wouldn't be easy, and they had little time before the predators finished with the corpses tossed to them, and came in search of more meat.

The first step was to untie the rope attached to the pole with Mildred, Krysty and Doc. As this was also the heaviest, it was the most risky to handle. But there was no other way. Ryan and J.B. took as much slack as they could and braced themselves while Jak unpicked the reef knot tying the rope to the loop. He yelled when the knot was loose, and the two men strained every muscle to try to keep the rope stable as Jak fed it from the loop, then played the slack around the sail mast before reknotting it to one of the other ropes.

"Done," he yelled when he was finished.

Ryan and J.B. tentatively let loose the rope, testing if it would hold steady. It did.

Then, while they kept a wary hand on the rope, Jak untied from its loops the rope to another three of the poles, attaching them also to the one rope. There were now four poles attached to one that was still looped. One of these poles—the occupied and heaviest—was wound around the mast.

There was one independent rope, and as Jak took it and attached it to the others, the ropes began to groan.

None of them had been sure if this would work in theory, let alone in practice. If it went wrong, they would lose their three companions to the ocean…and the predators who were lurking in the depths.

Jak looked up at Ryan and J.B., who were still keeping a wary hand on the rope attached to the pole with Doc, Krysty and Mildred. Their silence bade him to continue. Jak began to unpick the knot that kept the final pole—the one to which all the others were now attached—secured.

Ryan and J.B. tensed as they felt the shift in weight on the rope, and then released their grip as they felt the rope begin to move between their palms.

It was a slow movement at first, but began to pick up impetus as the ratio of the weights shifted. And it was movement in the right direction.

The idea had been simple. The weight of the unoccupied poles, if left free and unattached, would drag the occupied pole up onto the deck using the mast as a pivot. The unknown variable had been this: did the weight of five unoccupied poles add up to more than the single pole with three occupants? If it hadn't, then the operation would have worked in reverse and they would have lost their friends to the sea.

But now, as Mildred and Krysty, clinging to Doc, found themselves being hauled upward, there were other problems for the three men on deck. As the momentum of the pole increased, it would be whipped across the deck and around the mast, and would cause considerable damage to the vessel on the way—damage they couldn't afford, as the vessel was their only way of attaining land.

Ryan—who had located their belongings—had found his panga, and stood ready. "Climb! Hand up, Doc," he yelled as they closed on the boat. Hurriedly, J.B. and Jak reached over the side and helped drag the old man, now coming around and able to assist a little in his own rescue, up onto deck. As Mildred and Krysty made to leap aboard, they were aware that the pole, suddenly decreasing in weight and leaping incrementally in momentum, was ready to unleash itself like a coiled spring.

Ryan was ready to slash at the taut rope with his panga, his eyes fixed on Mildred and Krysty. He yelled at them, "Now!"

As they leaped, he brought the sharp blade down in a slashing motion at the rope, hoping he could cut it that fraction of a second before the pole crested the rail and whipped across the deck.

He had no idea if he had succeeded. The end of the rope jumped up violently and caught him across the face, driving him backward across the deck in a mist of blinding red pain. He felt his head crack against the deck, and then nothing.

When he came around, he was aware that Krysty was leaning over him.

"Hey, lover, you should learn to duck," she said softly.

Ryan winced as he moved his head. His skull felt as though it were made of crystal, ringing and ready to shatter at the first opportunity. "What's happening?" he asked in a hushed voice.

"We're heading toward the swamps. There's hardly any food and water aboard. Guess they weren't planning to be out that long, and we can't go back that way, can we? Jak figures we're near where we first found him, so mebbe we'll land, get our bearings, see if we can find the people he left behind. Mebbe they got together the kind of ville they were looking for. Leastways, at least we know there's a redoubt near there where we can jump."

Ryan grinned. "Seems like you got it all worked out."

A worried frown creased Krysty's brow. "It's not us I'm worried about. It's really hard to catch the wind to take us the right way—too many changes out there. I'm worried we're sailing into a storm, and it's gonna take us way off course."

"What about our guest?"

Krysty looked puzzled. "What about her? She's a bit more coherent than she was. Shit scared we'll chill her like the others, even though I've told her we would have done that already if it was our intent, but—"

"She was on crew, right?" Ryan interrupted. "She must know these waters. Mebbe she could help."

"Why should she?"

"Because if she doesn't, she's liable to get chilled, as well," Ryan answered simply. He groaned as he got to his feet. "Now where the hell is she?"

Krysty took him over to where the woman was sitting on the deck, huddled against the mast, looking sullen and withdrawn.

"Lady, I haven't got time to fuck about with niceties," Ryan said simply, squatting before her. "We're all in shit unless you help. If you do, then we'll let you go when we reach land. If not, then you'll probably buy the farm with us because we're not sailors. Can't be plainer than that. Do we have a deal?"

The woman hadn't been looking at Ryan as he spoke; she had been too concerned with the skies, which were glowering with low and ominous cloud banks, moving swiftly in the winds. She was also aware of the increasing pitch and yawl of the boat.

She looked Ryan in the eye, as if trying to see if there was any indication of truth or lies in that ice-blue orb. Finally she spoke.

"Guess I would be fishbait by now. Guess I may be if you're really that shit at sea. Where you heading?"

"The swamps," Ryan stated, opting to be straight with her.

She snorted. "Never do it unless I help. Storm's blowing up, and it'll drive northwest when you want to go south."

"Then, lady, you'd better get off your ass and help right now," Ryan said softly.

"Mebbe I will. Least I'll stay alive a little longer, if nothing else…"

Chapter Six

"Hope you know what the fuck doing—this not respond," Jak yelled at the woman over the roar of the ocean, which was growing louder as the storm clouds gathered overhead and the first heavy drops of rain were carried on the strengthening breezes.

"Stupe boy," she muttered by way of reply, wrestling the wheel of the boat from his hands. "You people listen to me, perhaps we'll get through this. But you gotta do exactly what I say, or we're fucked."

J.B. shot a glance at Ryan. Could they trust her? Ryan shrugged. Right now, they had little choice.

The middle-aged woman, whose wide hips and seemingly fat physique belied a strength apparent in the way she handled the wheel, began to bark out a series of orders for the companions to change the tack of the sails and move the masts so that they could catch the crosswinds that would carry them in the right direction. Ryan and J.B. had worked on ships in their time, having once been stranded in a whaling port and left at the mercy of the insane and sexually voracious female ship's captain Pyra Quadd, but Mildred, Jak and Krysty had less experience, and had to follow the woman's orders to the letter. Doc was excluded from working, despite his willingness to lend a hand. The old man had tried to raise himself and assist, but was still too weak, and was persuaded that he should rest.

If rest were possible in such a place. The storm came upon them rapidly as they sailed straight into the heart of it, unable to alter their course quickly as the sails were re-rigged, taken up by the air currents swirling around the cloud systems.

The rain started to beat heavily on the deck, huge fat drops that physically hurt as they pounded the companions' raw and exposed skin. Drops hit them like hurled stones as they were picked up by the crosscurrents of wind and driven almost horizontally across the deck. Crosscurrents of wind battered at them, almost sweeping them off their feet and down from the mast as they clambered around, desperately keeping a handhold as they sought to redirect the sails and pilot the boat out of the storm.

The deck rose and fell around them, making it hard to keep upright and to move with any degree of safety. At any moment, they could be pitched forward by a sudden roll of the water beneath, sent skittering toward the rail and over into the choppy waters beneath, where disturbed sea life either went deep to avoid the foam, or tried to take advantage of anything that was beaten down by the storm.

Still the woman yelled—they didn't even know her name, but she treated them as though they had sailed with her a thousand times. It was hard for any of the companions to tell if the boat was turning and making progress, as all around seemed to be a solid wall of rain and cloud, a permanent gray backdrop, illuminated occasionally only by sudden flashes of lightning as the clouds cracked together, the distant rumble of thunder buried beneath the whine of the wind and the roaring of the sea.

She seemed to be pleased with what was happening, and whenever Ryan could spare a second from the work to look over in her direction, it seemed as though she might just be doing it. Her expression was determined, but there was a light in her eyes that showed triumph. It was hard for him to grasp, as all he could feel was an immense weariness that crept over him as the rain beat down, hard and cold, seeming to freeze him to the bone, his eye aching and sore from the salt spray that mixed with the rain. His vision was a constant blur, no matter no much he tried to wipe clear his eye. What was the point? His arm was soaked, water running off his skin and matting his hair as though he were standing beneath a waterfall.

The deck beneath their feet—treacherous enough with the pitch and yawl of the sea—was made worse by the water that slopped over the sides and poured from the skies, making the planking slippery enough to land them on their backs, to slide them over the side. As if the work wasn't hard and urgent enough, they now had to move slowly to try to keep some kind of balance lest they lose their lives in the irony of trying to save them.

Concentration on the work needed to turn the boat around and pilot it out of danger was so intense and absorbing that they didn't at first notice that the storm was beginning to abate.

Mildred suddenly looked up, realizing that she was no longer being battered by raindrops like stones, even though the winds were still blowing strong. It was lighter than the gloom in which they had toiled for so long, and as she looked up she could see that although the clouds were skittering across the sky, they had broken, allowing the blue above to shine through.

"Shit, I think we're through it…" Mildred said softly, staring up at the sky with bemusement.

Ryan paused, noticing that the deck beneath his feet was no longer pitching with such fury, and—as he looked across—he could see that the sea around them was starting to settle.

"Fireblast, you might actually have done it," he yelled to the woman at the helm.

She looked back at him with a wry amusement. "Y'shouldn't have doubted, One-eye. Save my own skin, then I've gotta save yours."

"Friendly gal, isn't she," Mildred murmured to Krysty. "Better watch her."

"Look!" Jak yelled, pointing out over the stern. "Not safe yet."

"Shit shit shit…" screamed the woman at the wheel. "No way are we out of it yet."

Staring out over the stern at the dark shapes closing on them, it became clear why their helmsman was suddenly so terrified.

"What the hell are those?" J.B. asked slowly, not really expecting an answer. The shapes were sleeker than the sharks that had trailed them when they had first been dragged into the ocean, and they were moving at a greater speed. Somehow, they looked more menacing, more purposeful, as they sped toward the boat.

"Get back from the stern," the woman yelled at them.

"Seen those fuckers before, and they'll have you over the side if you give them the chance."

Doc glared at her. "Madam, I feel you are overstating the case and being a little too presumptuous. The mere thought that these creatures could—" he swept his arm out over the side as he spoke and was silenced as one of the shapes broke the waters and lunged up the rear of the boat.

They were dolphins, but unlike any kind of porpoise that any of the companions had ever seen before. Sleek and bottle-nosed, this particular mammal had twin rows of sharp teeth that were awesomely visible as its powerful tail propelled it out of the water and into the air. It hung over the rear of the boat, mouth open for what appeared to be an eternity, the twin rows of teeth looking razor-sharp and deadly, its fetid breath blowing back Doc's hair as he stared into the maw.

It made a noise—not the high-pitched intelligent squeak of dolphins they had seen before, but a lower, more menacing growl. Doc could almost swear he saw the creature's uvula vibrate as the sound emitted from its cavernous mouth. And then it snapped shut its jaws with a sharp crack, like a whip with more than a hint of wood being chopped. Doc had just had the presence of mind to snatch back his arm, and the creature's jaws closed on nothing but air. It hung there, disappointment almost obvious in the bright, intelligent eyes, before falling back into the wake of the vessel.

"Good heavens, I fear I should take it all back," Doc murmured in an awed, hushed whisper.

"Storm's brought them to the surface, scavenging," the

helmsman said swiftly, "and they won't go back unless they've got something to chew on. Seen it all before."

"What can they do?" Ryan asked, trying to work out where the danger would come from. He was answered as the boat began to be buffeted from side to side by a series of hard bangs, the deck resounding as the porpoises threw their weight against the sides of the craft, hoping to turn it over. The impact threw the vessel from side to side, pitching almost as much as when the storm was at its height, making it hard for the companions to keep their feet.

The helmsman clung grimly to the wheel, trying to keep the course straight. She indicated ahead of them. "Just need to outrun these bastards. Look up there..."

Land was within view—swamplands, with inlets of rivers running from the edge of the sea through the densely vegetated land, which seemed to be almost melting into the water.

"Try to turn the mast," she continued. "If we can get some more speed then we can get into the fresh water and run this fucker into the swamp. Just need to get far enough in for the lack of salt to drive them back before they smash us."

Following her barked orders, the six companions—Doc now fit enough to help, and determined so to do after nearly losing his arm to one of the creatures—began to trim the sails to catch the winds behind them, the helmsman using the wheel to guide the vessel closer to the freshwater inlets.

It was hard for them to keep their feet on the still rainsoaked deck as the dolphins hammered the sides of the boat. Each blow altered the course a little, making the steering almost impossible. Yet despite this, the helmsman was managing to guide them closer, closer... They just needed enough speed to outrun the ravening porpoises.

As if they could sense this, the mammals assaulting the craft increased the vehemence of their attack. The blows grew harder, and as Mildred lost her footing and skittered across the deck, looking for something to arrest her slide before she tumbled through the rail, a dolphin loomed up the side of the boat, hanging in the air and darting its head as far over the side of the rail as it could manage to reach, snapping its jaws in an impotent fury as she managed to keep out of reach.

After one series of blows, the vessel suddenly shuddered and lurched violently to one side, causing them to cling to the mast lest they be thrown to the mutie mammals. The helmsman swore heavily and loudly as the wheel was wrenched from her grip, spinning wildly, hammering hard and painful on her hands as she tried desperately to regain her grip. Gritting her teeth and hissing abuse at the pain, she grasped the wheel and tried to wrench them back on course.

The boat stayed at a forty-five-degree angle in the water as it moved.

"Dark night, the fuckers have managed to put a hole in us," J.B. yelled.

"Aye, that they have, but I figure we can just about make it. Only a thousand yards or so and the waters will change."

A thousand yards: not that much of a distance, especially at the speed that they had attained as the sails caught a sudden gust of wind, the current taking them in the direction they wanted.

But a thousand yards was a long way when a boat was shipping water and the craft was vulnerable. The mutie mammals knew this by some dark instinct, and redoubled their efforts to wreck the vessel.

Another crack from the left, where they were already listing, caused the vessel to suddenly slow as it began to ship more water. They had less than five hundred yards, and some of the porpoises had already begun to fall back, the mingling fresh and salt water at the mouth of the swamp proving too much for them to take. But there was still a core of mutie mammals who were inflamed with bloodlust and hunger, determined to finish the job they had set in motion.

"For fuck's sake, use your blasters on them," the helmsman yelled, pulling herself over so that she stood at a sharp angle to the deck, hauling at the wheel with all her strength to try to compensate for the drag caused by the sudden shipping of water.

It was, in a sense, incredible that they had got this far without firing on the mammals. Yet it had been hard enough to keep the sails tacked and to keep on the deck without even thinking about attacking the creatures.

Their weapons and belongings were still on the deck, their movement curtailed by the rocks that had been intended to weigh down and sink them when they were dumped over the side. They had moved a little in the chaos, but had come to rest against the small bulkhead, lodged in a safe position.

But getting to them wouldn't be simple. The bulkhead

was situated near the side of the boat, and in their desper-
ation, the mutie mammals who were sticking with the attack to the bitter end were hurling themselves up into the
air and hanging over the deck, heads moving, jaws snapping in an attempt to take some tasty morsel back into the
depths with them.

Snapping jaws that were dangerously close to where
the rock-bound blasters were stranded.

Ryan and J.B. exchanged glances. With the briefest of
nods, the two men set out across the deck, desperately trying to keep their footing as the vessel pitched and yawed
violently as the dolphins hammered against the sides, tip-
ping at more and more of an acute angle as the water
shipped in through the hole under the waterline. The
planking of the whole vessel groaned with the threat of
tearing apart under the stress.

And the swamps were in plain view, so close that they
could easily swim in if the boat sunk—except for the
predators that would have been glad of the opportunity to
attack them.

Ryan and J.B. thudded into the bulkhead almost simultaneously, reaching into the pile to try to extricate
their blasters.

J.B. pulled out his M-4000 and chambered a shell.
"Ryan, use my Uzi. It's no time for sharpshooting," he
yelled over the noises around them.

The one-eyed man gave him a wry grin. Ryan's own
blasters were more for single-shot firefighting, and he
was glad of the Armorer's offer.

The two men readied themselves for the next sighting
of the mutie mammals, yet no amount of wariness or prep-

aration could truly prepare a person for the moment when the giant predator burst from the deep, appearing suddenly in front of them with an awesome violence. The gaping maw opened, foul breath hitting them in a wave, the teeth standing sentry like a thousand soldiers poised to attack.

For the merest fraction of a second, both men were stunned. How could any blaster hope to make an impression on such a creature?

It lasted as long as it took their combat instincts to kick in. Both men fired simultaneously, the load of barbed metal fléchettes from the M-4000 ripping a hole through the upper jaw and snout of the creature, pulping the brain and splattering the glittering eyes, which now seemed to dull suddenly before disappearing into a mass of viscous fluid.

Ryan and J.B. were covered in a sticky, stinking spray of blood and eye fluid, the hot liquid sticking to them and running down their clothes, mixing with their own recently shed blood.

Realizing that there was no need for him to fire on the creature, Ryan moved the Uzi in an arc as he depressed the trigger, the shots weaving wide of the chilled mutie as it fell, but catching another of the dolphins as it broke the surface to join the attack. The creature squealed in a high-pitched tone, almost a human cry of pain. The Uzi fire wasn't concentrated enough to chill the creature, but it took enough lumps of flesh from its body to make it retreat in agony and confusion.

Scrambling to their feet, both men tried to attain the far side of the deck, almost having to climb uphill as the vessel yawed dangerously. As one of the creatures reared up out of the surf, J.B. racked another shell and fired into its snout, the impact spreading a rain of flesh and blood over the deck.

Ryan directed his Uzi fire to the stern, clipping another of the mammals as it came up and loomed over the decking. One of the shots exploded its left eye, the others stitching a line of holes down its snout and onto its exposed underbelly. It flipped back, squealing in pain, hitting the water on its back, flailing as it tried to extinguish the fires of pain that the Uzi shells had left inside its body.

"Hold on to something, this is gonna be rough," their helmsman yelled as she took the sinking boat into one of the channels leading into the swamps.

To their rear, the mutie mammals finally began to retreat, the combination of blasterfire and the freshwater into which the boat had now sailed too much for them. Not that the companions had a chance to see them retreat. Their world was now suddenly bounded by the overhanging trees and grasses of the swamp, looming up out of the waters as the land and rivers merged into a sludge that was sometimes more fluid, sometimes more solid.

The last-chance gasp of the boat had caught a gust that had whipped it in at too great a speed to negotiate the sudden turns and narrowness of the channels in the swamps, and they were thrown across the wildly pitching deck as the boat hit land, then water, then land, then water, throwing itself from side to side despite the attempts of the helmsman to keep some kind of course and bring the vessel in safely.

"Oh, fuck."

It was the last thing they heard for some time. The boat groaned, the air was filled with the sound of splintering wood, and the craft came to a violent, shuddering halt, throwing them forward and into the air as it hit a bank too wide and solid to plough through or bounce off.

The swamp turned upside down around them and then went black.

IT WAS DARK when Ryan opened his eye, a pain shooting through his skull. A clear night, with a three-quarter moon that was bright enough to illumine the swamplands around. He tried to move, tentatively, feeling for any damage on his body. Apart from the protestations of sore and aching muscles, there was no major damage. He hoped the others had been as lucky.

In the clear light of the moon, he was able to see that the boat had careened into a mudbank and finally broken up, the internal stresses taking their toll on its superstructure and forcing the wooden hull apart. Pieces of hull and deck were scattered around, and Ryan felt lucky that no part of it had impaled him and hopefully, others had been spared.

Moving carefully—partly to save his aching limbs and partly so that he didn't fall into the quicksand-like swamp in the semidarkness—Ryan tried to locate the others. In the thick undergrowth, he could see very little. Yet it was this undergrowth that had saved him from serious injury. The lushness of the foliage had acted as a cushion to his impact.

After some fruitless searching, he heard movement. Reaching for the panga usually strapped to his thigh, he realized that their weapons were still tied up in a bundle ready for dumping. He hoped that he would be able to find the bundle before he was in dire need; and for that he would certainly need daylight.

Dropping into a combat stance, Ryan crouched to hug the cover of the swamp, ready for the noise to be a source of danger. His relief when Jak Lauren emerged from the swamp grass was almost palpable.

"Ryan, found three others and our stuff," Jak said swiftly, with no pretence at ceremony. "Krysty and Doc still out, J.B. coming to. Here." He tossed Ryan the SIG-Sauer and the Steyr, then pulled the panga from his belt and handed it hilt-first to the one-eyed man. "Left stuff by them. No sign of Mildred or woman," he stated.

Ryan nodded. "I've seen no one except you...and I was wondering how I'd find these," he added with a grin, indicating the weapons. "Figured I might need them when I heard you coming."

"If enemy, then not hear me till buy farm," Jak said without a trace of humor. "Same for most around here," he added, making it clear that it was a warning for Ryan to stay triple frosty.

Ryan could remember his last time in the swamps, and readily agreed. The two fighters agreed to divide the area, search, and meet back in half an hour. "Told J.B. stay put until feeling okay and I come back," Jak added.

Ryan could see the logic: keep all those whose locations he knew in one place, then collect everyone together when they were fully conscious. Should, ideally, make it easier to find the missing pair...

Or maybe not. Almost half an hour later Ryan had nothing but insect bites and a mounting sense of frustration to show for his searches. The swamp area he had searched was empty—at least, devoid of human life. He made his way back to the meeting point, where he was astounded to see Jak standing with Mildred: between them they were carrying the woman who had helmed the boat. She was unconscious.

"Hey, Ryan, how's things?" Mildred said brightly, as though she had only seen him a second ago and they were crossing paths on the street of a friendly ville.

"Mildred, what—"

"I figure I got lucky and didn't land too badly...and I landed near her," she added, indicating the unconscious woman she was helping carry. "It was a real struggle trying to drag her around with me until Jak found us."

"But why were you trying to do that? Why—" Ryan began to ask, but was cut short.

"I'm not sure, but I think I've got a mild concussion that's making me do some stupid things," Mildred interrupted. "Good thing Jak found me, or no knowing where I would have wandered. It should pass—weird kind of knowing it, to tell the truth—but I figure one of you should stay with me while you round up the others."

Ryan sent Jak. It was obvious, as the albino knew where the others were situated. While Ryan waited for him to come back with them, he had to sit and listen to Mildred ramble on about anything that came into her head. Truth to tell, he had no idea what she was talking about, and he seriously doubted that she did, either. Eventually she fell asleep. The other woman was still out cold.

It became a long wait. Jak, having picked up J.B., was

obviously trying to rouse the others rather than have to carry them, and so by the time they appeared, the sun had risen in the early morning sky, and it was set to be another humid, misty day in the swamps. The marsh gases began to rise, moisture pulled from the swamp by the heat, and the sounds of swamp life began to echo around Ryan, Mildred and the woman. Strange to think that she had saved their lives—albeit to save her own—and yet they didn't know her name.

Ryan heard the procession through the swamp before he saw them, and when Jak led them to where he was waiting, he was glad to see that J.B., Krysty and Doc were showing nothing more than a few knocks and bruises for their ordeal. In fact, he hadn't seen Doc looking so strong since they had left the redoubt—fireblast, how many days had that been?—and the old man looked able to take on whatever faced them ahead.

Their approach stirred both Mildred and the woman lying beside her.

"Shit, my head feels like someone's used it for target practice with a baseball bat," Mildred moaned.

"You remember what you were saying before?" Ryan asked. She shook her head, giving him a blank, uncomprehending stare. "Dammit, that's a pity—thought you might be able to explain what the hell it was all about," he said wryly, before explaining what he meant.

Mildred whistled softly. "Man, I was gone. Can't remember a damn thing…"

They gathered together and Jak divided the bundle of belongings he had rescued. There was little left, as most he had distributed as he searched, but J.B. was glad to be reunited with his ammo and explosives stores. And, searching one of the bags, his eyes lit up when he unearthed his battered fedora. "Thought I'd lost it," he muttered, carefully placing it on his head as though it were some kind of talisman.

They ate some of the self-heats that had been stored in their belongings, and used the remains of the bottled water that had survived the journey. They were surrounded by water, but the brackish liquid of the swamp was an unknown quantity, and they were unwilling to risk drinking it until it was strictly necessary.

Over their unpalatable but necessary meal, they introduced themselves to the woman. She wasn't hostile, but by the same token she found it hard to be too friendly.

"Remember, I was ready to chill you all, and I don't think that I'd be too kindly disposed to me after that," she said warily.

Ryan shrugged. "That was a ville thing. You saved our hides after."

"To save my own," she pointed out.

"But that's the point," Krysty interjected. "We're on the same road now, so we need to look for each other's backs. No one else to do it. What happened before doesn't matter. Things were different then."

The woman shrugged. "Guess so, if you want to see it that way. Name's Coral, and I've never really done anything except fish. Don't know anything about surviving in swamps like this," she said with a shiver as she looked around.

"Figure you stay with us, it'll be okay until you find somewhere you want to stop." Ryan shrugged.

"Yeah, but where's here in the first place?" Coral asked with an answering shrug.

J.B. was on his feet, the minisextant in his hand, trying to get a fix on the position of the sun. "That's what I'm hoping I can tell you in a moment," he murmured. "Yeah," he said finally, looking down at the others, "I figure that if we head off to the northeast, we're about twenty miles or so from where we met Jak."

"West Lowellton," Krysty mused. "Wonder if they managed to build the kind of place they wanted?"

"Had chance when we left," Jak said. "Mebbe we'll see."

"What are they talking about?" Coral whispered to Mildred.

The physician shrugged. "It was before they, uh, found me. But around here is where Jak comes from," she added.

Krysty looked at the albino with an appraising eye. "Yeah, kinda figures. He looks like some of the swampies we used to deal with. That stopped awhile back, though."

"Any idea why?" Mildred asked.

Krysty shook her head. "No idea. Just like they weren't there, one day."

Mildred wondered if this was an ill omen, but there was no time to dwell on that as they prepared to head out.

Jak took the lead at Ryan's behest. The albino was at home in the swamps, and knew them intimately. Any dangers that may lurk from the native wildlife and from the treacherous ground beneath their feet were known as second nature to the hunter.

Yet, as they progressed, Ryan became aware that Jak

was moving with unease. When they stopped to rest, Ryan questioned Jak about that. The answer he got was unsettling.

"Feels weird. Not good, like something bad hangs over us...over all of this," Jak added, sweeping his arm to indicate the swamp around them.

Ryan frowned, then looked at Krysty. Her doomie sense was usually a good indicator of when trouble was around the corner. He noticed that her sentient hair was waving in tendrils that suggested a sense of unease.

"I can feel it, but I don't know what it is. It's...it's almost like an emptiness," she began, groping for words. "It's not the swamp or the animals—"

"Nothing wrong there, but no people," Jak cut in. "Where are hunt parties?"

Ryan tried to get an angle on these feelings, translate them into something concrete. Whatever was causing the atmosphere was also responsible for the lack of human population. However he looked at it, there was no way it could be good; but beyond that, he had little notion at present of what that could mean.

"Just stay triple red. Be ready for anything," was all that he could counsel. It wasn't enough to keep him happy.

They continued on for over an hour, with nothing to break the monotony of the march until Jak suddenly halted.

"Swampies...coming straight for us."

"What the fuck are swampies?" Coral asked.

"Met them before—muties that just won't lie down and die," Krysty snapped, drawing her Smith & Wesson.

"Can't we skirt around them?" Mildred asked. Like Coral, she had no previous experience of the creatures.

J.B. shook his head. "Tricky fuckers. They've got good hunting instincts, and if the swamps are as deserted as we think, then they'll sniff us out as the only fresh meat in town."

"Great," Mildred said dryly. "Just what we need."

With their weapons drawn, they continued on their way. Coral was unarmed, so Jak gave her a couple of his leaf-bladed throwing knives to use for defense. "Though not much good with these fuckers," he added less than help-fully. "Just use as last hope, and pray we blow the fuckers away."

There was no chance they could avoid the swampies. The mutie creatures would have scented them and would be closing in; it was merely a matter of hoping that the hunters wouldn't be able to surround and surprise them.

Slowly, they made their way through the swamps, every bird call, animal cry or sound of moving water holding the possibility of heralding attack. Their mouths dried, their nerves itched… The not knowing was the worst of it.

And yet, when the attack did come, it still took them by surprise.

Crossing a narrow strip of marshy grass that weaved an erratic path between two landmasses, surrounded on either side by rush-strewed waters, they could see clearly for several hundred yards in each direction, and felt relatively safe.

The one thing they didn't expect was to see a half-dozen swampies emerge suddenly and shockingly from the water on either side of them, waves of stagnant, stinking swamp water sweeping over them, blinding the companions. The muties had to have been laying in wait, using their enhanced respiratory capacities to stay hidden.

The swampies were uncannily silent as they attacked, the only sounds being the movement of their limbs through water. The dwellers in the bayou had called them *les morts vivants*—the living dead—and indeed they closely resembled the voodoo zombies of legend. But these were very much alive and had only one thing on their minds: chilling their prey.

J.B. let fly with a burst of fire from the mini-Uzi, catching a thin, rangy man across the chest and shoulders, flinging him back into the water. But it wasn't enough to chill him, and Coral screamed as he rose again. A well-aimed shot from Mildred's ZKR through the forehead took him out. She figured that if they had enough strength to keep getting up, maybe they could be chilled like traditional zombies, with a shot through the head.

"Never thought all those late-night movies would turn out to be educational," she muttered to herself as she took aim on a squat, fat woman who was wading purposefully through the water toward them.

The swampies were carrying machetes and knives rather than blasters—even the dumb muties had enough sense to know a water-logged blaster didn't work—so the companions had some advantage. But the blinding wash of swamp water had given the muties valuable seconds in which to draw close.

Two of them zeroed in on Coral, one from each side of the path, realizing that she had no blaster. They were waxy, their skins covered in sores, and as they reached for her, she was frozen with fear. One was short and skinny, the other tall with a huge gut. Both had immense strength, and, taking one arm each, began to tug at her. She screamed from pain as much as fear. Their combined strength was ripping the muscles in her arms, pulling her shoulders out of their sockets. The knives plunged uselessly to the path.

There was little help for her. Krysty, Jak and Ryan were using their handblasters to fire on the swampies, trying to get them in the head each time, other shots proving little more than a delaying action. The swampies were on the path, grabbing at the companions, who kicked out, trying to stop them closing their vicelike grips about their arms and legs, dragging them into the water.

J.B. took the M-4000 from his back and let loose a load of barbed metal fléchettes that took out one swampie by severing the top half of his body almost cleanly from the bottom. Doc, too, had dealt with one swampie in this manner, using the LeMat's shot chamber to equally lacerate a swampie who bore down. But the ancient percussion pistol had only one load of shot. Before Doc could reload, he had been dragged down by a swampie. The creature couldn't wait to take a bite from him, and he felt its fetid breath as its head came toward him, the dull eyes showing nothing of its imminent triumph. The old man twisted his arm and wrist so that the LeMat was against the swampie's temple, then loosed the ball round into its skull. The exit wound took half of the skull with the brain matter, splattering it with soft sounds into the waters beyond.

Coral was down, her arms useless. She screamed one last time as the swampie with the huge gut decided to end his tussle with his compatriot by using his machete to hack her in two. Her screams were drowned in her own blood as he hacked around her neck, chest and shoulders to try to cleave her in two. He was stopped only by a round from the M-4000 which reduced his own neck and shoulders to bloodied ribbons of flesh and splinters of bone. He was joined in oblivion by his compatriot, whose focus on his prey meant that he didn't even see Krysty fire into the back of his head with her Smith & Wesson, the .38 slug exiting through an eye socket, draining his head of all gray matter.

The last echoes of the last shots rang out over the swamp. The companions stood, panting heavily, exhausted by the struggle. They were covered in blood that was both theirs, their opponents' and Coral's. The woman was chilled meat, and there had been little they could do in the battle to save her. The corpses of some of the swampies lay on the path, while others had sunk into the swamp, claimed by the waters from which they had sprung.

"Dark night, we didn't repay her too well," J.B. breathed heavily.

"If you can't take care of yourself, you shouldn't be out here," Ryan said in reply, though his tone belied the words.

Pausing only to clean the blood from them as best as possible, and slipping the corpses into the water to cover their tracks for any other swampies, they continued on in subdued silence. What else was there to say?

When the sun began to fall, they were still some distance from Lafayette and West Lowellton—farther than they could make in the daylight left. There had been no sign of any other life; nothing to suggest that the swampie hunt party had been little more than a bunch of rogue scavengers. The random nature of the confrontation did little to improve their collective mood.

They set watch for the night as they pitched camp. There was still that oppressive air hanging over the swamp, as though it were bereft of human life, and this was amplified by their anger and sorrow at the outcome of the battle.

It was a fitful night's sleep for all. The following day they would reach West Lowellton and then they might have a better idea of just what was happening in the bayou.

Chapter Seven

"Far be it from me to be the one who wishes to cast a pall of gloom over the proceedings, but I have a feeling that all is not well… Indeed, there is something rotten in the state of Denmark."

"Where the hell is Denmark?" J.B. queried, his brow furrowed.

"Forgive me, John Barrymore, I quote from an old, old play, something from the days before the nukecaust, and something that I forget you would have little or no knowledge of. It merely means that I feel a distinct chill in the air, and one that has little to do with the weather." Doc smiled sadly, unable to suppress a little shiver as he spoke, almost as if to emphasize his point.

For now it was morning, and the sun blazed in a sky momentarily free of chem clouds or skittering rain, dappling through the leaves of the trees and swamp plants that grew taller and provided a canopy to the swamp. It was already warm, despite the fact that the sun had only been up for a couple of hours, and before midday it would be sweltering.

But, as Doc said, the chill had little to do with the weather. He and J.B. had drawn last watch, which had enabled them to get an unbroken rest before having to rise

and stand guard over their companions. Ryan had wanted
it that way. He knew that the old man had suffered more
than the others from the depredations of the journey, and
was in dire need of an uninterrupted sleep. J.B. was the
obvious choice to stand sentry with Doc, and so the Armorer had lucked out and also gained an unbroken rest.

However, as the two men stood a little distance from
the camp, watching the less nocturnal reptile, bird and
mammal life of the swamp begin to stir and go about the
business of staying alive, J.B. was regretting standing sentry with the scholar. The old man was inclined to go off
on strange tangents, and say bizarre things, as his life had
left his mind fragile and apt to wander from sense; yet
there was nothing wrong with his intelligence, and a Doc
Tanner in full possession of his faculties was a fearsomely
intelligent and sharp man, with an ability to put his finger
on the nub of any problem. Even if his words sometimes
made that completely incomprehensible.

"If you're saying what I think you're saying, Doc, then
I agree with you."

"And what, pray tell, do you think I may be saying?"
the old man asked with a mischievous twinkle in his eye.

"Doc, this isn't the time to be funny," J.B. muttered, not
wanting their exchange overheard until he was sure he
knew what Doc meant—as much to avoid his own embar-
rassment as anything else.

"Very well, John Barrymore, if you wish me to articulate in a more concise—and, indeed, a less verbose,
though one would take umbrage at the very notion that one
was as such—manner, then I shall. There is an air of
gloom that hangs like a shroud over this swamp. It weighs

down upon us, and has since we landed. It has nothing to do with the manner in which we arrived, and nothing to do with the chilling of our newfound companion, though, to be truthful, that was regrettable. No," he emphasized with a wagging finger and a brief nod of the head, "it has nothing to do with our own experiences, though I would wager that they have not helped. It's all around us. The creatures seem subdued and afraid, scuttling in shadows. Tell me, the last time we were in such a land, did we not fall prey to attack from hunting animals? Where are they now? And as for people… Swampies you would expect to be oblivious. They are little more that brainless muties who have only their basic motor functions. But where are the people? Not only have we seen nothing in the way of hunting parties, but we have seen little sign that there have been any around. Consider this—have we seen any signs of snares or traps? Have we seen any corpses or partial corpses that would indicate hunting? And those very creatures who have ignored us thus far, have they shown any sign of fear? No, sir, they have shown nothing. There is something very wrong and it ails my spirit as it ails theirs. I have nothing to prove this but a great sense of foreboding, but…" He trailed off, spreading his hands, palms up, and shrugged with a despairing inability to articulate his malaise.

J.B. had nothing to say to that. All the things that had been bothering him had been voiced by Doc. The lack of human habitation, or even signs of it, was something that was a temporary bonus. They were all exhausted, their journey from the redoubt being nothing but several days of constant, unrelenting hardship, so in many ways the lack of human opposition was some kind of respite. And yet, they knew from previous experience that this was an area of habitation, and so that very lack was also a sign that greater danger lay ahead. A greater danger into which they were marching, with no way of knowing what they might face.

"Doc, I reckon we're all thinking this," he said finally. "But we don't really have much choice but to go on."

Doc sighed. "My dear John Barrymore, I am only too well aware of this. And of the need for us to be ever more vigilant. But I am sorely worried by this one thing. If we have no knowledge of that for which we must be vigilant, how can we know that we have seen it? The dangers may not be apparent until we are already in the middle of them. For all we know—"

"We may be right now," J.B. finished for him.

Doc merely nodded. There was nothing more to say, and their watch was broken by the sounds of the others stirring in the early morning, as the warmth of the sun penetrated the depths of the swamp.

Returning to the main camp, Doc and J.B. elected by unspoken mutual consent to say nothing of their conversation at this juncture. They were both pretty sure that it was little more than what everyone else had been thinking, particularly now that they had the time to stop and consider. Prior to this, the constant drive to get out of trouble and attain a degree of safety had driven all else from their minds. But to say something and spark an unease that may not otherwise be at the surface could cause frazzled nerve endings to become even more stretched and liable to snap.

Best to see what would happen.

Besides which, it seemed as though Doc and J.B. hadn't been the only ones to voice their fears in the dark watches. There was a subdued atmosphere in the camp as they broke their fast on self-heats, taking advantage of the ease of the supplies rather than waste energy at this point by trying to hunt. The food tasted as foul as always, but it had nutrients, and although a rabbit or a lizard would have tasted better cooked over a naked flame, none had the in-clination to waste precious energy on trying to hunt down enough to fill their hunger.

They drank the last of the bottled water, and supplies from their own canteens, knowing that now they would have to find nonbrackish water in the swamp. To counter the hardship of the past few days, they also swallowed salt tablets that Mildred distributed among them. There were few left after their trek through the desert, but she gam-bled on the hope that they wouldn't be needing any for some time now that they were in the swamp.

The truth was that they were all being a little more reck-less with their supplies than was usual. In a sense, it was as though they no longer—at least, at this moment—cared.

Each one of them ached in body and mind. Since their mat-trans jump had landed them in an airless redoubt, they had done little except battle elements and people. There had been no respite, no chance to recoup energies or to rest up. No one could remember the last time they had been able to sleep relatively peacefully, and each had taken a battering in combat that hadn't been given the chance to heal. The cuts they had received from the fish-erfolk had also taken their toll. Mildred carried some antiseptic cream among her looted med supplies, but not enough to fully treat all the cuts on every one of the companions. Some had become infected, and not a single one of them wasn't carrying at least a low-level fever and infection.

Their reflexes had been blunted, and although they had still been strong enough to battle and win against the swampies, it had been harder than, in truth, it should have been. How much longer could they go without some kind of proper rest? How many more firefights before their fatigued reflexes and responses let them down?

That knowledge, combined with the atmosphere that hung over the swamp, was like a cloud that they carried with them. There was little discussion over their unsavory meal, as none wished to be the one who spread despondency. And yet they all knew how each other was feeling.

None more so than Jak. When he had joined the companions, longer ago than he could think of, he had never expected to see his homeland again. And yet here he was: with a sense of impending danger that was weighing heavily on his shoulders.

When they had finished, they broke camp and set off in the direction of West Lowellton, on the edge of Lafayette, not knowing what they would find.

Despite their weariness—something that now seemed to infuse every bone and muscle—they stayed triple red on their trek. Yet there was nothing to give shape or substance to the feeling that hung over the swamp. It was an uneventful journey through the swamp, hacking past the swamp plants and the trees, treading carefully to avoid the patches of treacherous quicksand and the foot-rotting puddles of stale and stinking water, trying to keep on solid and dry ground.

They made rapid progress through the swamp, finding nothing to impede their progress, and before the sun had reached its height in the still-clear sky above them, blazing through the cover of the foliage to raise mists of humid swamp water that hung in the still air around them like wreaths, they found that they had reached the area where the swamp had been hacked back by the developers of the twentieth century, and man had sought to conquer the elements and colonize.

Despite the gap between the nukecaust and the now, the swamp had been unable to gain back much of the ground. The survivors who still used the surviving shells of the preskydark world had made sure of that.

"Keep it close, and keep it frosty," Ryan muttered—as much for himself as for the others—as they broke the cover of the swamp and began to encroach on the remains of West Lowellton.

Keeping in formation, and moving slowly from the cover of one building to another, Ryan taking the lead and scouting a safe location before the others followed in single file, each waiting until the other was safe before continuing the movement, they made rapid progress.

From what they could recall of their previous visit, the outskirts of the suburb were mostly deserted, marked out into territory by graffiti tags. Back then, the main baron in these parts was named Tourment, and he ruled with an iron hand. A giant of a man, he had a sec force to match his own personality, and yet he had been unable to subdue the locals led by Jak's father, who the baron had chilled. It was perhaps this severing of ties that had led to Jak wanting to join them on their journey, and leave the remaining people to build their own ville.

West Lowellton was Cajun territory, and anything outside had been Tourment's, with this area the buffer zone, and a combat assault course.

But now it was silent. Like the grave, though none wanted to voice that. There was no sign of any life at all—even if the Cajuns had been able to move from their self-imposed exile and back toward the area where Tourment had previously held sway—the lands from which he had driven them—there should still be some signs of life here. There was the old movie house where they had avidly watched the few remnants of old celluloid that had survived the nuclear winter. Surely they wouldn't have deserted that?

As they became more and more sure that the area was deserted, so Ryan opted to abandon the formation they had used thus far.

"Jak, you know this better than anyone. Want to take a look around then report back?" the one-eyed man asked. He knew that Jak had an intimate knowledge of the suburb, and would be able to scout quickly and safely before reporting back. It would also give the others a chance to rest and calm frayed nerves. Jak was the hardest, the most difficult to rattle: that was another reason Ryan asked him. But he was aware that the albino had been through the same as the rest of the them, which was why he gave him the option to refuse.

Jak was quick to take up Ryan on his offer. He was frustrated at their rate of progress. It took time to get six people from the cover of one building to another. One man on his own could move with a much greater speed. Especially if that man had an intimate knowledge of the area. And he wanted to get on his own. Strange and conflicting feelings ran through the albino's mind and heart. Part of him wanted the people he had left behind to have made something of the dreams he and his father had shared with them, yet Jak had known so much darkness and despair in his life that he very much doubted this to be the case.

The atmosphere hanging over the swamp had extended into the suburb. Something was amiss. And the buildings and streets had the feel of a place that had been empty for a long time. Jak knew what emptiness felt like, had known it since his wife and daughter, and the homestead he had fought so hard to establish, had been snatched from him by the fates. Something had happened here that had emptied the suburb, and emptied the swamp.

What it could be, he had no idea: equally, he had no idea if it was something that the companions would be up to fighting right now.

Even if it came for them, rather than the other way around.

All these thoughts passed through Jak's mind while he made his recce. Not on a conscious level, but lurking beneath the surface. Consciously he was taking in what had happened to the suburb—something pretty big.

The most obvious sign was the old Holiday Inn that the companions had first scouted on their previous visit. That was before they had met Jak, and he knew the old hotel as something that his people had avoided. There was nothing much to loot there, and the rooms had been filled with preskydark corpses, some mummified and preserved as grim markers of history. But it had been standing, almost untouched by the nukecaust, a marker to the world that had been left behind.

Now, there was nothing more than rubble, heaped high in the middle of a couple of outer walls that stood precariously, crumbling slowly in the oppressive humidity of the suburb. Baron Tourment and his sec force had never considered this building a target, knowing that the locals stayed clear of it; but someone else obviously had it marked down as a target. Or perhaps, more ominously, it had been the scene of a desperate last stand.

Taking care to check for any signs of the ruined building being watched, Jak made his way across to the rubble. It had been this way for some time, and as he searched he became aware of one odd fact—there was no sign of any corpses ever having lain here. They had either been carefully extracted or the building had been empty when it was razed. Which only led to more questions. Why shoot the hell out of an empty building? And if it hadn't been empty, then for what sinister purpose would the corpses be removed?

The atmosphere around the suburb took on a sharper, more dangerous air. Jak's sense of danger, honed by his hunting skills, was screaming at him. Not right here, right now, but close by…something they could easily stumble into if they weren't careful.

Moving with more speed and urgency than before, Jak completed his recce and returned to the area where the companions waited for him. As he expected, there were no people—living or dead—but plenty of indication that this had been a combat zone to a far greater degree than in his time. The farther he went in, the more evidence of blasterfire pitting the walls of the buildings, the more of those walls had been demolished by high-explosive shells or grens. The air was dead, with no remaining scent of cordite, plas ex, or the stench of blood and death. This hadn't happened recently, but whatever had caused it had won the conflict, and wouldn't be far away.

Jak paused, controlling his breathing so that it was slow and shallow, cutting out as much extraneous noise and distraction as he could: the rest was silence. No one had been in this suburb for a very long time

Jak slipped back through the rubble toward the point where he had left the others. He took little care, knowing that he was unobserved and that speed was now the key. There was a kind of decay about the area. To stay here too long would be bad for the soul. Jak had never been a great believer in such concepts, and had never held them paramount, yet he could feel something—a kind of sloth and despair—gnawing at him. It was as though everyone here had given up hope. Did he feel this because it was that tangible? Or was it partly because these had been his kin, and the thought of them simply giving up and being blasted to oblivion was too hurtful?

It didn't matter, not in the end. What mattered was that Jak get back to his companions, give them the lowdown, then get the hell out. Maybe it was time to head for the secret redoubt, see if they could land somewhere other than this empty shell. Anywhere would be better than this...

J.B. WAS KEEPING WATCH, and he was surprised to see Jak moving freely and swiftly in the open.

"Ryan, Jak's coming. This place must be more chilled than a bunch of stickies after we've been through them."

Ryan joined the Armorer. "Guess we can relax a little," he said to the others. "Looks like the place is empty."

His suspicions were confirmed when Jak briefed them about the state of the buildings and the complete lack of life that he had found. "Must be big firefight, then everyone buy farm or move on," he finished.

"Yeah, or got moved on," Mildred mused. "Something with that much firepower wouldn't just leave them alone."

"Not our problem," Ryan cut in quickly. "Sounds like it was some time back. Just putting the pieces together over what happened could be hard enough, let alone chasing it down."

"I wasn't thinking about that," Mildred replied with a shake of the head. "Look at it this way—something with that much armory is gonna be a strong force in these parts. Some baron who wants to stamp his authority—"

"Never met one who didn't," J.B. interrupted.

"Yeah, exactly. So how come we haven't see anything of any wandering sec? How come there's no sign of life at all?"

"I hate to raise the notion, as it is fearful in the extreme, but I wonder that it has not occurred to you, dear Doctor," Doc began in his long-winded manner.

"Jeez, cut to the chase, Doc," Mildred muttered.

"Very well," the old man said with a wry smile. "I was thinking of it purely in this way. To cause so much damage suggests a good stock of preskydark weaponry. Correct?"

He waited for an answer.

J.B. nodded. "Yeah, sure—and the point is…?"

"The point, my dear John Barrymore, is that we are assuming this weaponry is purely in the form of blasters and explosives. But for such a firepower, the baron would have to have traded or discovered an extremely high-grade quality of armory. Would you not say so, my dear sir?"

Once again, J.B. agreed. "By the sound of it, Doc. And we know that's likely, if not usual."

"Exactly. Therefore, I find it not beyond the bounds of possibility that such a baron could also have chemical and germ warfare weaponry in that armory…a bunch of bugs, my dear friends, that could wipe out all human life in the area."

"Great, cheer us up why don't you, Doc?" Krysty muttered. "Are you saying that we could be in line for the big chill ourselves, just by being here? And what about the swampies, and the other wildlife that we've seen and heard?"

Doc shook his head sadly. "The whitecoats were swine of an extremely high order, though I do fear that such a comment is a slur on the noble swine. Do you so soon forget the minions of Bob and Enid?

"Swampies are muties, and as such their systems may in some way be immune. I know for a fact that the whitecoats had developed many strains of virus that would attack only human beings, leaving all else alone. Perhaps that is what has happened here. And it may have been long enough ago for it to have no effect on us… Indeed, it could be that those swampies we encountered were the first to venture into this land after being driven out by the chilling. I am, of course, merely speculating."

"You are, of course, scaring the living crap out of us." Mildred spit. "You could be right, but we don't know. Looking at us, we've been walking through this for a couple of days, more or less, and we don't seem to be any the worse for it. What problems we do have are down to fatigue and infection from cuts. It's a hypothesis, but one we shouldn't take too much notice of…"

Doc's brow furrowed. "My dear Doctor, the last thing I would wish to do was spread alarm and despondency. That was not my aim, I merely—"

Mildred stayed him with a raised hand. "Can it, Doc. I guess we all know that, but it doesn't make it any better."

The old man lapsed into silence, and Ryan took a look at his people. Doc's words had caused some doubts among them, he could see that in their faces. There was only one course of action.

"Fuck this, people. We're about as much use here as dickless man in a gaudy house. We need to move out and make our way to that old redoubt. Sooner we get away from here, the better."

The ghost of a smile flickered across Jak's scarred white visage. Ryan had echoed his own thoughts, and the albino had his own reasons for wanting to move on.

J.B. took a reading from his minisextant and that, combined with their recollections from their previous visit to West Lowellton, determined the direction in which they would strike out for the redoubt.

They began their march, knowing also from their last visit that they had a good distance to cover. It was past the middle of the day, well into the afternoon, and it seemed to Ryan that they would have another three or four hours before the dusk fell and made setting up camp necessary.

Each of them was wrapped in his or her own thoughts as they traveled, and there was little discussion. They fell into the usual pattern, with Ryan taking lead, J.B. covering the rear, and Doc sandwiched between Krysty and Jak. As the most vulnerable, he as always centered for his own safety. It was also the least vulnerable position for the rest of the chain should there be an attack. Not that they were expecting anything: the swamp seemed dead of all except the smallest of wildlife.

Ryan suddenly threw up his hand to halt them.

"Incoming," he whispered. "Over to the left."

"Swampies," Jak muttered. 'Can smell 'em."

In the midst of the swamp, it was hard to find cover that didn't entail getting bogged down in mud and stagnant pools. And there was no time for them to take the high ground of trees. They had to stand their ground and fight as soon as they saw the enemy.

In truth, they could hear them long before they became visible. A distant crashing through the everglades became louder as the swampies drew near.

"Holy shit," Mildred breathed, "how many of the fuckers are there?"

It was a good question. The amount of noise they were making suggested that there might be an army of the muties making their way through the swamp. Blasters were leveled. Ryan held the Steyr as his main option, and J.B.

opted for the M-4000 over the mini-Uzi, figuring that a scattergun approach would be of more immediate benefit than the tight arc of SMG fire. As for the others, they held their handblasters, knowing that they would have to make every shot count.

The first of the creatures crashed through the undergrowth, flattening the plants, splashing sprays of pungent water from long undisturbed puddles of mud. They were dull, blank-eyed, and seemed to be operating on a kind of blind instinct that was guiding them to the companions. The first of the swampies were male, and of varying heights and weights. The things they all had in common were their pockmarked and sore-covered skin, their tattered and stained clothing, and the antique and badly maintained blasters they carried, mostly old rifles that were Lee Enfield .303s stolen from a trader's stock before he and his crew had been eaten.

They were moving quickly for swampies, but it was still slow enough for the companions to take a good aim to try to hit them with shots that would matter. Every shell would count in this instance, where there were no second chances and the majority of the hardware consisted of single-shot pistols.

They fired in relay, leaving space to cover one another when the time came to reload their blasters, some having to reload more than others. Doc was able to cause some real damage and take out two swampies with the shot chamber of the LeMat, and then to hit another—this one a squat, fat woman with darkly curling hair and an evil leer helped by a scar across her top lip—square in the forehead with the ball chamber. Yet he had to take longer out of the firing line to reload, no matter how quickly he moved, because of the very nature of the LeMat.

Mildred, Krysty and Jak took careful aim for the head, as that was the only sure way of halting the swampies with one shot. A miss risked that creature gaining ground on them. Mildred's ZKR drilled neat holes in the foreheads of her targets, not a single of her shots going astray as she clicked into the kind of target-shooting mode that had won her medals in competition before she was cryogenically frozen. These were just a different kind of target, and she found that if she stopped thinking of the danger, and approached them solely as targets, it helped to ice her nerve and her trigger finger.

Jak's .357 Magnum Colt Python wasn't as accurate, but then it didn't have to be. The handblaster was heavy enough to rip open the skulls of its victims and spread their gray matter across the foliage and the other swampies that came behind, even if the shot wasn't dead center. Krysty's Smith & Wesson Model 640 was a .38, and not as powerful. Nonetheless, at that kind of range it was enough to work even if she failed to get every single shot dead center.

Ryan's Steyr was picking them off at long distance, leaving those nearer for his compatriots to blast, specifically J.B. The M-4000 was ripping through the swampies, the Armorer opting for body shots as he knew that the rounds of barbed metal fléchettes from the Smith & Wesson blaster would shred any internal organs they hit—whether they were single, double, or even treble. There would be little left but blood and jellied flesh by the time his blaster had finished with them.

The swampies tried to return fire, but the carnage around them made it hard for them to fire accurately. They were easily confused, and as the air was filled with deafening blasts, piercing screams, and the stench of charred and chilled flesh, it was hard for them to focus enough to really mount any kind of blaster attack. Instead, in their confusion, they kept coming, wave after wave.

Although the companions had been under no return fire, they were still being forced back. The gaps in firing where reloading had to take place gave the swampies moments of time to move forward, and the waves of muties began to drive them back by sheer force.

It was impossible to tell how many there were. They had to have found themselves close to a swampie settlement, for there were far too many of them for a hunting party. Whatever the reason, all that mattered was that they were being beaten back by sheer force of numbers, no matter how many they took out of the game. Gradually, they found themselves moving backward to try to get some space between themselves and the waves of swampies, stumbling and falling on the marshy ground, sinking into the soft mud of the swamp. It made firing harder, enabled the swampies to gain a little more ground.

Jak heard cursing in Cajun French—a girl's voice—and then a volley of blasterfire—blunderbuss and shotgun fire, pellets raining through the air and smacking into the oncoming swampies, slowing those it didn't take out of the game. The firing was staggered, and as he continued to fire, Jak counted three separate weapons. The woman—he couldn't think of her as a girl, even without seeing her—yelled instructions in Cajun, and the three fighters moved to join the companions.

With the extra blasters, the relays of fire began to take effect. The increase in pellets peppering their flesh began to make the swampies think twice, and the remaining muties began to retreat, some desultory rifle fire from them marking their retreat.

When they had vanished into the swamp, there was carnage laying before the assembled fighters. The mud was littered with corpses, the waters awash with blood.

Ryan turned to the woman. "Who the hell are you?"

Her eyes flashed and she snapped, "Some way to greet those who stopped you being stew for those fuckers." Then her eyes settled on Jak. "As for you—never thought see you again."

"Not know you," Jak replied, which was true. He didn't recognize her personally, but he knew where she and the two men accompanying her had come from. One of the men was small, with a barrel chest and a shaved head, a wispy beard tied in a knot hanging from his chin. The other was also short, but was whip-thin like Jak, with tattoos on his bare chest and arms. He was clean-shaved, but had a long ponytail flowing down his back. The woman was shorter than the men, with full breasts that strained at her shirt. Long black hair in ringlets framed a face that had full lips and flashing dark eyes. Flashing with anger.

Because these three people lived in West Lowellton— the ones Jak had left behind.

"So you come back when we're in shit, expect a welcome?" The barrel-chested man spit. "Lucky we didn't leave you to it, Jak fuckin' Lauren."

The woman held up a hand. "Shut fuck up, LaRue. No one gets eaten by swampies, no matter who."

"Lady, I don't want to interrupt this little family reunion, but can someone tell me what's going on here?" Mildred cut in.

The woman looked at her and smiled. "Hey, Blackie, don't remember you, Know One-eye, Red, Four-eyes and the old man. Where the others? Buy the farm somewhere? Don't matter," she added quickly. "What matters is that Jak go with you, leave us after chilling Baron Tourment. Only work not done. Someone else come and stir shit up—and where the man then? Gone."

"How supposed to know that?" Jak asked.

"Supposed to stay, help us," LaRue spat back.

"Leave it!" the woman snapped. "Mebbe this mean something, yeah? We pray for miracle, the Lord send Jak Lauren back. Mebbe to settle old score, mebbe to put things right. C'mon," she added, turning to go, "we go get dry, eat. Then stir some shit up ourselves."

The companions fell in behind the trio of fighters.

"So what do we call you—other than big mouth," Mildred questioned.

The woman laughed. "Like it… Marissa. Him LaRue," she added, indicating the barrel-chested man. "And him Prideaux," she continued, indicating the ponytailed man. Both glared at the companions. Marissa laughed again. "And guess what—they don't like you. Me? I ain't made my mind up yet."

Chapter Eight

The three swamp dwellers took them farther and farther into the heart of the bayou, and farther away from both West Lowellton and the area that housed the swampie settlement. The path was labyrinthine, snaking between deep pools of stagnant water, covered with weeds and swamp plants that emitted an even more foul stench than the waters themselves. They crossed tracks of relatively hard earth, covered in moss and grass, and squelched through mud puddles that sucked at the soles of the boots.

Overhead, the sun was beginning to fade into the dusk of early evening, and as they traversed deeper into the swamps, so the thick cover of the trees made the light less and less amenable to ease of travel. They had to stay close on the heels of the three natives in order not to fall into the treacherous quicksand that surrounded them on all sides, ready to claim another victim.

The foliage on the drier sections of the swamp was tightly packed with lobster grass that caught at their ankles, and taller plants that loomed over them, making it hard to cut through the path forged by the natives. It was a path that had been used before. There was enough of the foliage cut back to make it possible for the smaller members of the party to make a rapid progress, but not enough for it to be immediately obvious to the naked eye.

Marissa, LaRue and Prideaux moved quickly and with ease. The companions, exhausted and having to cope with a path that they didn't know, in darkness, found it hard to match their speed. Only Jak was able to keep pace, and even the albino was finding that it stretched his energy level.

There was no discussion but they were all thinking the same thought: could they trust these three, and whoever else was waiting back at their settlement? True, they had stepped in and helped them drive back the swampies. But they had been ambivalent about Jak's presence, and even Marissa's comments about him being sent to them in a time of trial had an edge of suspicion about them...almost as if she couldn't tell whether this was a good thing.

But in the final analysis, there was little else they could do. If they wanted to move on, they might have had to fight the three and risk being hunted by their compatriots from the settlement; and even if they did manage to part amicably, there was still the matter of having no idea where they could safely camp for the night. If nothing else, these people offered them food, bed and rest.

And right now, that was important—more so than anything else.

Still they continued. It seemed to most of the companions that they were going in circles, seemingly passing the same stagnant pools several times. But Jak knew differently. His childhood and youth had been spent hunting in the swamps, and there were few who knew the land as well as he; right now, he could see that they were headed for a

section that was almost dead center. It was the most treacherous area of the swamps, and one that had no settlements
of old predark villes anywhere near it. It was a dangerous
place to live, but a perfect place to hide.

So what—or who—were these people hiding from?

They arrived at the settlement before they even knew
it: a collection of huts and tree houses that clustered
around a pool that was about 150 yards in diameter. The
pool was fed by a small river that ran in a trickle, and sup-
plied the settlement with as much fresh water as it
needed—or, at least, water that they could boil and purify.
As they closed in on the settlement, they could see that
there were some lamps and small fires going, but these
were shielded by opaque materials to make detection from
outside almost impossible. Unless you were on top of the
settlement, all you would see was darkness by the pool.

There was some noise—voices, some singing, a few
babies cries—but it, too, was masked, this time by the natural screen of foliage in which the huts and tree houses
were nestled, acting as a natural cushion to soak up the
sounds.

"It's Marissa," Jak heard one voice announce a little
more loudly than the others. It came from off to the left,
and as the albino looked around to its source he saw a potbellied man of about fifty step forward. He was holding a
Sharps rifle, and it looked highly polished and cared for.
He held it casually, barrel pointing down, with both hands.
It seemed to be careless, but from the set of his hands Jak
could tell that it would take him a fraction of a second to
bring it up ready to fire. And his eyes were slits, taking in

the procession carefully, assessing any danger that might be present.

"Hey, okay, you put weapons away," Melissa said to the assembled throng. "They okay—found 'em blasting swampies, gave 'em some help. Fuck, man, they tired and pissed off, and so would you be. Give 'em some slack, let 'em rest up. 'Sides, seen who they got with 'em?"

The companions were now by the side of the pool—lake would be a better description, as its depths were dark and unimaginable, and even though it wasn't fully dark the far side was now lost in gloom—and it didn't escape their notice that LaRue and Prideaux had moved surreptitiously into position so that they now flanked the group. With Marissa in front, and the lake behind, that left them fully surrounded.

Not that it would matter too much. The dwellers who were still descending from their tree houses and coming out of their huts were clustering around, and they were all armed. A rough estimate showed that there were around a hundred of them, and all looked less than friendly, if not outright hostile.

"Shit, recognize that little fucker," one of them said, coming out of the throng. She was a woman a little older than Marissa, and perhaps an inch or two taller, with perhaps an inch or two more on the hips. Other than that, the women looked very similar. Jak recognized her, though it took a second for her name to come back. Luella, that was it. She had been the wife of one of his old hunting companions—Luke, a man he couldn't see among the others.

"Recognize you," Jak said blankly. "Where Luke?"

"Bought the farm 'bout two years back. Same as most

around here. Not many of us left didn't get the big chill or go over to the old ways."

"Old ways?"

"Voodoo, sweetie, or something like it," she said with a bitter laugh.

"Only ain't really voodoo, not like we learn it used to be," Marissa cut in quickly. There was something in her tone that suggested this wasn't just for Jak's benefit. "Ain't no such thing as the old ways, just ways of making the new look like it."

"Don't matter whatever you call it, still works," Prideaux growled.

Marissa shot him a black look. "Only 'cause he feeds them full of shit so they don't know what they're thinking," she snapped back impatiently. "How many times have to tell you that?"

Ryan held up his hands, partly to stop them and partly to show to the twitchy settlement dwellers that he was unarmed. "Hey, c'mon… Listen, we don't even know why we're here, let alone what you're talking about. Mebbe if you started at the beginning, then—"

"Ask Jak," Luella butted in, "ask him what. But he won't be able to tell you 'cause he don't know. Don't know 'cause he fucked off with you and left us to it," she spit out angrily. There was a mumble of agreement from the crowd.

"Shit, you people so stupe," Marissa said in an exasperated tone. "Don't you see that him coming back is a sign?"

"Two things that are bothering me, John," Mildred whispered to J.B. as Marissa spoke. "First is that I don't

know what they're so wound up about, and the second is
that Jak isn't exactly Mr. Popularity around here."

Before the Armorer had a chance to reply, Marissa's
voice cut across everything.

"Listen—least we can do is give 'em food and shelter,
then tell 'em what's happened. Mebbe Jak'll want to help."

"Yeah and mebbe he'll fuck off like before," Prideaux
growled, glowering at the albino.

But the tattooed man's warning was ignored by the
people. After a brief discussion among those who were the
elders of the settlement, including the man with the Sharps
who had first spotted their arrival, they were shown to one
of the tree houses, which was vacated by the woman and
child who were living there. Before they were taken to
their billet, they were stripped of their blasters by LaRue
and Prideaux. They also took J.B.'s canvas bags with the
ammo and plas ex, his Tekna and Ryan's panga. They
overlooked the scarf wrapped around his neck, which was
weighted at the ends to form a garotte if wielded cor-
rectly. They also left Jak with his patched jacket, failing
to remember or to recognize that it contained his leaf-
bladed throwing knives.

"You stay here. Zena and Kyle will stay with me," Marissa said as she led them up the rope ladder and into the
rickety construction. Inside, there were a few sticks of fur-
niture, but the house—only fourteen by fourteen—was
sparse, with only the doorway, covered by an old screen
door taken from a suburban house, and a small chimney
hole in the ceiling for ventilation and light. The light itself was provided by a small tallow lamp in one corner,
which cast long shadows over the far wall and ceiling.

It was going to be a tight squeeze to fit all six of them in, and as the tree house was really only built for three or four at most, all of the companions were worried about the structure taking their weight. Mildred voiced this.

Marissa response was to laugh. "Shit, you lucky if that's all you get. Some of 'em down there want to chill you now, in case you come from him. So you lucky you got somewhere. Don't argue 'bout it. Up here, you easy to guard. Wait now, and I get you when it's time to eat."

"One thing, my dear," Doc said hurriedly as she turned to go. "You keep talking about 'him' as though it should be someone we know. But I, for one, have no idea what you mean by this."

"I believe you," she said softly, "and mebbe a lot of others. But hard to trust anyone from outside since it started. Long, long story. You hear it when you eat, okay?"

"Great. Why do I get the feeling it might just give me heartburn?" Mildred muttered as Marissa disappeared out the tree house door and down the rope ladder. "And another thing—what the hell do they have against Jak?"

The albino smiled wryly. He knew only too well why he was resented by many of these people, and while they waited he told Mildred about his previous life in the bayou, and how he had met Ryan, J.B., Krysty and Doc. He continued by detailing how his father, who had led the resistance against Baron Tourment, had been tortured and chilled before they'd had a chance to eradicate the sick baron and his regime. He also told her why he felt they resented him. With his father gone, in many ways he was the next natural leader: certainly, he had the necessary combat and hunt-honed skills to be a baron. But instead of taking the reins, he had opted to leave the bayou and travel.

Without him, this—whatever it may be—had happened. Maybe it would have with him still around. Who knew? But obviously some of the residents of the settlement felt that he could have made a difference, and that he had betrayed them by leaving.

"Well, that's gonna make dinner a whole lot of fun, isn't it?" Mildred said dryly when he had finished.

They didn't have to wait long to find out. Just long enough for them to begin to settle and for Doc to fall off to sleep. They were discussing what options they had open to them—whichever way they looked at it, it always added up to wait and see—when LaRue pulled his barrel-chested frame over the lip of the doorway.

"Hey, stop making stupe plans you got no hope of carrying out and come down," he said roughly. "Marissa made sure you get to eat, and get to hear what's going down. Then you get to decide."

"Decide what?" Ryan bristled, having already decided that he and LaRue would come to blows—regardless of the rest of the settlement—if the sec man continued in this way. Even as he thought it, Ryan realized that it wasn't like him to be so hair-trigger. Had to be the fatigue. He'd have to watch that carefully.

Oblivious to Ryan's train of thought, LaRue continued. "You gotta decide whether you with us, or we find some way of getting rid of you." He leered at them then disappeared from view.

"Guess we'd better make our way down. Pity we

couldn't dress for dinner," Mildred remarked, continuing her own private joke, even if it was lost on the others.

Except perhaps for Doc. "Hardly the right standard for white tie and tails, I would have said," he murmured, tapping on the floor with his silver lion's-head cane. As with Jak's patched jacket and Ryan's scarf, he had been left with the seemingly innocuous cane, the settlement dwellers not realizing that nestling within was a blade of the finest honed Toledo steel. Therefore, they could muster some blades between them, and maybe the scarf would be useful for swiftly and silently eliminating a guard whose blaster could be taken. But in truth, they didn't have enough weapons to really mount an escape.

Not a feasible one, not until they were sure it was necessary.

One after the other they descended the rope ladder until they were all under the watchful eye of LaRue, Prideaux and another pair of sec men. One of these had one eye, like Ryan, except that his scar ran across the bridge of his nose and down, dragging his lip into a permanent sneer beneath his eyepatch. At least it distracted from his protruding gut and drooping chest, which were covered in thick, coarse black hair.

The other guard looked a little like Prideaux. He, too, had tattoos and a ponytail, except that he was less lithe, more muscular across the chest and shoulders. Both men were carrying remade Sharps rifles, and both in that deceptive manner, with the blaster pointing down but the grip right for a quick aim and fire.

"C'mon, let's go," Prideaux grunted, leading them across the shore of the lake, past a couple of huts, until they came to one that was larger than the others. Sounds of discussion crept out through the half-open door, a thin sliver of light cast across the shore toward the water.

"In," Prideaux snapped, moving around them, keeping his blaster down and pulling the door open to allow them entry.

Inside, the room was hot, lit by tallow lamps and filled with steam rising from the wooden platters that were lined up on the table that centered the room. Fillets gumbo, black-eyed peas, some kind of pumpkin that had a strange pink tint to it, sweet potatoes, and hunks of meat that looked like it might be pork were piled high on the platters. Despite the severity and uncertainty of their situation, the smell of the food reminded them that they had eaten little else but self-heats for several days, and it was all they could do, in this relatively relaxed situation, to concentrate on what was about to happen.

Because, much to their surprise, the atmosphere from the people within the shack was far more congenial than they had expected. Certainly, it was a giant leap on from the hostility they had encountered on their first arrival.

Marissa was there, as was the man Jak had seen on their way in. He was reserved when he was introduced, but certainly less hostile. His name was Beausoleil, which Jak recognized. The man had known his father back in West Lowellton, and they had worked together to try to build the resistance. Jak could see why Beausoleil would see his leaving as a betrayal, no matter what his true reasons.

Marissa bade them to eat, and they did so. It wasn't until they began to pile their plates with the steaming food that they realized how long it had been since real food—

not self-heat chem-processed garbage—had passed their lips. They noticed that the settlement dwellers also ate hungrily. It was puzzling, a sign that all was not as it seemed. Doc stopped, a quizzical expression crossing his face, and watched for a while before speaking.

"I can understand why we are so hungry, and yet you, too, eat as though you had been starving."

Beausoleil stopped, openmouthed, for a moment, and shot a venomous glance at Marissa before answering. "Some say that we should use a lot of stocks to impress you. Some say that you help us fight Dr. Jean if you think we have much to offer. Some do not realize that if we lie to you like this, we cannot lie to our own stomachs."

"You mean to say that you've been rationing your food to make it last, and now you're blowing it on making yourselves look good to us?" Mildred asked in amazement. "Are you people crazy?"

Marissa threw her plate at Beausoleil and turned her dark eyes, flashing fury, on Mildred. "Crazy? It crazy to want to live free and not hide? It crazy to risk a few less days with food or get a sec force that can smash Jean and his stupe ville? That can free everyone so we can go back to what was before, mebbe even make something better? Yeah, then crazy it is. But stupe old bastards like him more crazy if they want to die like rats slinking in the mud," she added, directing her glare now to Beausoleil.

"Things not that bad," Prideaux said, spitting onto the floor of the hut. "Could be worse. We free, we hunt and so if we don't catch we make do. How many of us? How can we go up against Jean? Mebbe some people think slinking in mud better than throwing ourselves into firefight we can't win. Better a live rat than a chilled hero. Or is that what you want, Rissa? You want to be like your pa and be a chilled hero that no one remembers?"

"You stinking bastard…" The woman threw herself at Prideaux, a left haymaker coming around as she landed. It caught him at the temple, and despite the fact that he was heavier than her, she took him down. They rolled on the floor, fighting and yelling curses at each other until two of the other dwellers pulled them apart. Prideaux dusted himself down and smiled slyly.

"Hey, baby, think I could smell your pussy, there… That what it is? Fighting get you hot?"

"Scumfucker. You'll never find out," she hissed. It seemed that there was history between the two of them that had colored their spat. And yet to the watching companions, who had been almost forgotten in the exchanges, it seemed as though this kind of infighting would make any kind of action to break out of their hiding place a fruitless task.

Beausoleil had been thinking on similar lines, as he turned to them, raising his voice to be heard above the arguments that had broken out among the others. Eventually, his louder tones—and what he had to say—quieted the arguments around.

"You see why this is pointless? Jak Lauren left the swamp for a good reason—because he knew we were too stupe to survive for long, and weak enough to let some other dipshit baron come in and take over. And that's exactly what happened. So we waste food trying to persuade him and the ones who took him away to come back and do our shit-clearing for us, 'cause half of us don't want to do it and the other half are so hotheaded that they would buy the farm as soon as a firefight started.

"Face it, people, we're fucked whatever way up. We fight among ourselves, and soon Dr. Jean is gonna find where we are and come for us. And when he does, some of us are gonna buy the farm and some of us are gonna get in line and worship his ugly fat ass. Just gotta make your minds up which."

He walked up to Jak so that he was staring him in the face, so close that Jak could feel his hot breath. The albino stayed impassive and unblinking.

"You should never have come back, son," Beausoleil said softly.

Then, turning to the rest of the now silent room, he added, "We'd be better off giving up or chilling. This isn't any way to live."

Slowly, and with no sign of the pent-up anger that had spurred him, he turned and walked out of the hut, pulling the door closed behind him.

He left a room that was silent. The settlement dwellers didn't know what to make of his outburst—particularly, in the case of Marissa, as it blew any chance she had of showing a united front to the companions; and the companions were left to digest the implications of what he had said.

They were in a small settlement that had little food, and seemed to be in disarray, with a split over whether they should fight the new baron, and even if they should request the help of the strangers. Come to that, the companions knew nothing about this new baron and his far-reaching powers beyond the fact that he used some kind of voo-doo—or something that traded on the old ways—and that he seemed to have had little trouble in sweeping his way through the Bayou.

Which made him a formidable enemy to watch out for whether they stayed to fight, or decided to move on and find the redoubt.

The first thing they had to do, though, was to stop the dwellers arguing among themselves and get some answers that made sense.

"Fireblast! Will you people shut the fuck up?" Ryan yelled over the swell of argument. It worked; they all turned to the companions. Some were just dumbstruck that an outsider had yelled at them in this way. Others were prepared to do something about it. Prideaux raised his blaster.

"Just who the fuck you think you are, telling us what to do?" Prideaux gritted, his temper barely contained.

Jak stepped forward. More than that, he moved across the room with a speed that was startling. Before Prideaux had time to move, Jak had snatched the blaster from his hands and had it turned on him. It sat well in his grasp. It was an M-4000 like J.B.'s, and so Jak was familiar with its weight and workings. Then, with a grin breaking across the otherwise blank features as he saw the sweat begin to spangle the ponytailed warrior's forehead, Jak emptied the shotgun and let it fall to the floor, useless.

"Think quicker, move faster, know out there better than you. That's who I am," he said quietly. He stepped back to let Prideaux bend and retrieve the blaster and its cartridges.

"That's why you're the one who can help us," Marissa said softly. "The only one who can, mebbe."

"And mebbe we can all help you, if we know what the hell we're supposed to be up against," Ryan countered. "So far, you haven't told us anything that makes any sense."

Marissa looked around at the four other settlement dwellers in the room. Impressed by Jak's speed—and the fact that he hadn't taken out Prideaux when he had the chance—they agreed to her unspoken request. She indicated that the companions should be seated, and then began to speak. While she told them her story, the other dwellers remained silent. It meant either that she had included every detail, or that the others thought her best equipped to speak.

Ryan kind of hoped it was the former. Otherwise they might get a few unwelcome surprises at a later date.

But for now, they listened without questioning her. Her story was long, at times rambling, but answered a lot of the questions they had wanted to ask.

It seemed that soon after Baron Tourment had been routed by the companions on their first trip to the bayou, the entire swampland had descended into internecine warfare. The peoples who had been ruled by Tourment couldn't come to terms with the different way of living that the rebels from West Lowellton had wanted. It seemed to them too soft after the iron fist of Tourment. The irony being that it took more strength to try to live in a fair society than it did to knuckle down to an oppressor.

So small groups appeared within the populace, all vying for some power over the others. But none of them had a man of the physical and mental stature of Tourment to lead them. Despite the fact that he was a perverted and sadistic lunatic as well as being a giant of a man, he had a great intelligence and an instinctive grasp of gaining and holding on to power. There had never been anyone like him in the bayou before…or, so they thought, since.

But there had been one man biding his time. A man named Dr. Jean. There had been rumors that he had been one of Tourment's sec men, and had watched and learned from the master. Other rumors suggested that he had come from out of the bayou. If that was the case, then he had picked up the ways and superstitions of the bayou with ease. Whatever the truth, the only thing known about him for certain was that he had suddenly appeared deep in the swamps with this name that no one had heard before, and he soon started to attract followers with his use of voodoo ceremony, and talk of going back to the old ways to go forward into the new—a better world where there would be more of everything.

The old ways were still spoken of, but no one had taken them seriously for generations. The fact of the matter was, when the old world had been eradicated by the old tech of skydark, then the idea of spirits and ghosts vanished. But it meant a chance to dress up and go wild. Perverse sexual rites and blood sacrifice were all part of the "old ways" espoused by Dr. Jean. Rumors also spread that ghosts and demons had been seen at his rites, conjured up by his hand. Perhaps, after all, there was something in the old ways?

It soon became apparent that these were hallucinations caused by the powerful drugs he was giving to his followers. They had the same high and addictive kick of jolt, but were cut with some kind of hallucinogen—like licking a toad's back or eating the right mushrooms, as Marissa put it.

Even when the secret of the "spirits" became known, people no longer cared. Those who were addicted followed him blindly; others wanted to be part of his ville because he offered them something—no matter what—other than the existence they already had.

As if that weren't enough, he had another weapon in his armory. Somehow, the reinvented man who became the baron known as Dr. Jean had access to old tech resources. He had comps and other items that were indescribable, but had the effect of subjugating any who may prove "difficult" in his quest to rule the bayou. To the companions, this sounded like some of the brainwashing weaponry developed by the whitecoats of the Totality Concept, which they had encountered along the way. The real worry for the companions was the question of where he had obtained this equipment: did it mean the redoubt they had been headed for was now under the jurisdiction of Dr. Jean, crammed with sec forces? And had he worked out how to operate the mattrans unit?

But that would have to wait. For now, Marissa still had more to tell. For Dr. Jean had a master plan: once he had gathered together the people of the bayou and had them under his control, he planned to use them as an army to spread out and take over the Deathlands, ruling it according to his own ideas of preserving regional purity and building races in each sector that could be used as his tools as his plans grew larger and more ornate.

He sounded insane. But dangerous, for he had power to go with that madness.

"So we have to stop him, 'cause he won't let us be. If he get more powerful, then we chilled meat anyway. "Least if we go trying to stop him, we go free. No matter what Prideaux say, we not be free for long," she concluded.

None of the settlement dwellers contradicted her. Instead, they were focused on the companions.

"You expect us to answer without discussing it among ourselves?" Ryan asked in amazement.

Marissa shrugged. "Easy answer."

"To you, mebbe. No, we talk first among ourselves, then we come back to you."

He led the companions out of the hut. They didn't go back to their tree house, but instead walked down to the edge of the lake, where curious eyes followed them from the huts and tree houses around.

"So what d'you reckon, Ryan?" Mildred asked. "It's a crappy call no matter which way we go."

"Got that right," Ryan agreed. "I figure that this Dr. Jean is nowhere near as powerful as Marissa says. Even if he is, he won't have the manpower once he gets beyond the swamps to do anything. But at the same time, we're gonna have to get past him to get to the redoubt and get out of here. So mebbe it'll be better if we have some help—make it of mutual benefit to us all."

"While I agree with your reasoning on broad lines, my dear Ryan," Doc mused at length, "I feel we should turn to the good Mr. Lauren for guidance. He knows this area and the people far better than we ever will. So what do you say?" Doc asked, turning to Jak.

The albino shrugged, as unreadable as ever. "Ryan leader. Let him decide."

With which, Jak turned and walked away into the darkness.

"What's he really thinking?" Ryan wondered out loud. He felt Krysty's arm on his shoulder.

"Mebbe he doesn't know himself, yet. Leave him for a while."

They let Jak wander off into the darkness. A darkness that was inside him as well as all around. Was this all that was left? The rebels that had fought so hard to defeat Tourment now reduced to a bunch of starving people, fighting among themselves and wallowing in the mud to survive.

JAK KEPT WALKING until he was sure that the settlement was far behind him, then he sat on the rocks by the lakeside, looking out over the featureless darkness of the water. He was trying to reconcile his thoughts and feelings when he heard a noise behind him. In an instant he was on his feet, one of his knives in his hand, balanced for attack.

He only halted himself when he saw that it was Marissa emerging from the darkness.

"Figured you'd find this spot. Only one around here that's away from the other fuckers, and dry enough to sit and think," she said, pointedly ignoring the knife, coming up beside him and settling herself on the rocks.

Jak sank down beside her. She was cool enough to be a good fighter when it counted, he figured.

"So what you thinking about?" she asked after a long pause, knowing that he wouldn't be the one to break the silence. "About how you alone now?"

Jak gave her a sharp glare. "How you figure that?"

She shrugged. "Lost my family to Dr. Jean. Lost my dreams, too. Got nothing except those miserable bastards back there."

Jak spoke without looking at her, his eyes focused somewhere out in the dark. "Yeah. Figure everything gone. Nothing left inside now. Pa chilled by Tourment, didn't want to stay. Knew others keep fighting. Knew they carried on. Went, made new life, had family of own. Taken away from me. Bastards pay for it, but not bring back wife, not see daughter grow up...but still had something. Still belonged here, even if not live anywhere near. But now that gone, like tree roots ripped up and tossed aside."

The words came slowly. Jak couldn't remember the last time he'd talked that much in one speech, and when he'd let something of what went on inside come out for someone else. But he figured Marissa would understand better than Ryan or the others. She was from here, too.

"So what you gonna do about it?" she pressed. "Walk away 'cause there's nothing there for you? Or try to get some of it back in some way?"

Jak looked at her, his unblinking red eyes a match for her own dark, fiery orbs in their intensity. "Inside like fire that not stop burning until something done...vengeance not bring back, but it feels good, stops the bastard doing any more shit."

A sly grin crossed Marissa's face. "Fuck it, Jak Lauren, I knew you were sent to save us. How else, why else would you be here right now?"

And to Jak's surprise, she grabbed him and kissed him. It was long and hard. It had been a long time since he had felt a woman this close to him.

"Hey, Jak Lauren—we don't have to go back and tell the good news right away, do we?" she said as she pulled away from him, lifting her dress over her head. "Shit, can't do anything else till sun up, anyway."

Chapter Nine

A ray of sun creeping across the rocks, penetrating the cloud and foliage cover, woke Jak with a start. The albino blinked, turning his face away from the light, and found himself looking into the face of Marissa.

"Hey," she said sleepily, "you ready to go?"

"Mebbe. You?"

She nodded. "If you were serious last night, then the sooner we get going, the better."

Jak merely nodded in return, hauling himself to his feet and dressing. Despite the warmth of the sun, he felt chilled to the bone through having spent half the night asleep and naked in the open. He had to take his patched jacket from over Marissa, where the woman had dragged it when half asleep.

Without exchanging words, they both dressed and set off through the swampland, heading back to the settlement. At some time during the night, he had asked her why the place had no name, and she had told him that they had always felt it been a temporary settlement, and so had never named it in any way. But as time had gone on, and the likelihood of breaking free of Dr. Jean's tyranny had receded further into the distance, they had just thought of it as home.

It took little time to reach the area around the lake where the huts and tree houses were clustered, and they found that people were going about their everyday business as though they hadn't been missed. Ryan and Krysty were washing clothes by the shore, while J.B. was checking the inventory from all their blasters and his canvas bags, which had obviously been returned to them at some point the previous evening. Marissa took this as a sign that the companions had, independently of Jak, agreed to fight, and could hardly contain her excitement. Jak, on the other hand, preferred to hold his own counsel until he found out more.

There was no sign of Mildred or Doc, but as soon as they saw Jak, the other three expressed their relief in seeing him.

"Thought you might have walked out on us for good, that time," Krysty said, eyeing Marissa as she spoke. "But mebbe you were just otherwise occupied."

"Lot to think about," Jak said flatly.

"I'm sure…" Krysty murmured.

"We need to talk," the albino said to Ryan.

Ryan ran his gaze over the dark-eyed woman at Jak's side. "That we do," he agreed, "but I think we should do it alone."

For a moment a flicker of anger and suspicion crossed Marissa's face, but after a glance at Jak, she agreed. "That's only right. I've got some talking of my own to do," she added as an afterthought before leaving them.

"When you get those back?" Jak asked with a frown, indicating the blasters J.B. had been working on.

The Armorer shrugged. "Last night. All I had to do was

ask nicely. I reckon after that little performance they gave us, they figured they had to try to keep us on their side somehow."

"Good. Trust rare, but needed," Jak murmured, almost thinking out loud. Then he added, "Where Doc and Mildred?"

"Probably be with us in a moment," Krysty said, eyeing the main body of huts and tree houses. She had little doubt that Marissa would be firing up the community, and that Doc and Mildred would soon hear of Jak's return. "They've been taking a look at some of the sick here, seeing if there's anything they can do. Just looking to be useful—or be seen to be useful," she added by way of an explanation.

"Lots ways to be useful," Jak said slowly. "Some better than others."

Ryan was about to ask him what he meant when he saw Doc and Mildred descending from one of the tree houses. They made their way over to where the others were gathered by the lakeside.

Ryan waited for them to arrive, then began before they had a chance to ask where Jak had been. "We need to make decisions here. They want us to fight with them, but I'm not so sure about that—"

"Have to," Jak interrupted. "If anything in the bayou ever the same again, then we need to take out Jean. 'Sides, if we try to go on, we come up against his sec anyway— bet your life they got the redoubt."

"That's not certain," Ryan said slowly, "but it is something we've got to consider. I know this place means a lot to you—"

"This land, these people, all there is left," Jak said slowly and with an edge to his voice that bespoke of the depths of his feeling, a depth he had rarely, if ever, let them see before. "Nothing else. If this goes, then mebbe me, as well. No choice for me, no matter what you want."

As he stopped speaking, with a shrug, it sank into the others exactly what he meant—he would stay, regardless of their decision.

Ryan chose his words carefully. "The bayou can never mean to us what it does to you, but mebbe you don't know what *you* mean to us—what we mean to each other. I'm not convinced that we've got the firepower or people power—even with these behind us—to take on Dr. Jean. Could be a one-way ticket to buying the farm, right? But one thing I do know is that we won't just go without you."

"We recce where Jean is, see what he's got, see if we can do it," Jak said quickly. "You, me, a couple others—small party to recce."

"Sounds fair. We need to know what we're up against regardless of our eventual action, so I figure we do it this way and even if we leave the fight, at least we know what we have to scout around."

Jak nodded. He didn't want to commit himself with words, as at the back of his mind he had the notion that whatever happened, he would be compelled to fight.

The companions turned to find Marissa and most of the settlement descending on them.

"So you gonna do it, like Jak says?" she asked without preamble.

"Mebbe," the one-eyed warrior said cautiously. "We've got a plan. We don't know where Jean's main base is, and what his strengths are. If we're going to mount an attack, then we need to know that, or else his superior numbers are just gonna blow us away."

"But you are gonna help us?" she pressed, sniffing around the fact that he hadn't been direct.

"Mebbe," Ryan said slowly. "No point chilling ourselves in an all-out attack if he's too strong."

"But Jak said—"

"I'm not talking for Jak, and he wasn't talking for us. Nothing's settled," Ryan cut in quickly. "What I'm saying is this—some of us form a recce party and take a good look at what Jean's got, and how he operates. Not until then will I say anything else."

Marissa was about to speak, her eyes searching Jak for signs of betrayal, when Beausoleil spoke up.

"Marissa, shut your damn mouth for a moment," he barked, silencing her with a gesture. "You know what I think about this idea," he continued, addressing the assembled settlement dwellers, "but I tell you one thing—I can see exactly why they want to do this. Think about it. For all your talk of fighting Dr. Jean, what do any of you actually know about his sec force, his defenses, his armory? Nothing. Do this recce mission, and even if they decide they don't want to stand with you, then at least you know what you have to do for yourselves."

"Talks sense," Jak said quietly, directing this at Marissa.

"Mebbe I don't want sense, mebbe I just want some action at last," she said softly. "Okay, you do it this way. I guess it makes sense. Who d'you want to come with me?"

"No, lady, no way are you coming with us," Ryan said in a tone that would brook no argument. "I don't trust you not to blow up at the wrong moment. Me, Jak and J.B. will go, and I want two of your people."

The settlement dwellers looked at one another. Talking about facing up to Jean's might was one thing, but being part of a small party at the mercy of his roving sec force was another altogether. There was a mumble of hushed discussion among them.

Jak spoke over them. "Want the two with Marissa yesterday," he said, pointing to LaRue and Prideaux. "Know how we fight, and we know a bit about them. Know we can trust their balls."

"Fuck it, I should be pleased you think that of me, but I wish you hadn't," LaRue muttered, running his hands over his bald head. "Fucker to go up against all that firepower with just five."

"We're not facing them off," J.B. told him. "It's a recce mission, the whole point is to stay out of the way. See and not be seen."

"Easier said than done," the bald man muttered again, shaking his head.

"Shut up, stupe, you're going," Marissa snapped. "Say no and you won't have no balls no more—I'll see to that. What about you, Prideaux, you wanna argue, too?"

The ponytailed man gave her a lazy smile. "Never argue with you, belle princess. Though I'd like to see you get your hands on my balls."

"Dream on," Marissa spit back at him.

"Okay, okay, so I'll go—dunno why, though. You know I don't think we've got a chance."

"Mebbe you're right," Ryan cut across him, "and mebbe you won't know until we do this."

Prideaux shrugged. "Okay, I'm in."

The settlement was abuzz with the realization that suddenly, after nothing but talk for so long, something was actually going to happen. The dwellers dispersed and went about their everyday business, leaving the companions alone with Marissa, LaRue and Prideaux. The two men looked uneasy now that it had come to action, but Marissa was their superior when it came to settlement sec, so they were obliged to follow her lead.

"We gonna sort this out here, or what?" Prideaux asked, barely keeping the nervousness from his voice.

"It's simple," Ryan said softly. "You get your weapons together, and then we go. We're more or less prepared." He exchanged glances with J.B., who had been doing a weapons check. The Armorer gave the briefest of nods. "Then we set off. After all, you know where we're going."

WITHIN HALF AN HOUR they were ready to go. While the two sec men gathered their weapons and prepared themselves, Marissa filled in the companions on their route. Jak knew where she was sending them, and to his amazement it was back beyond West Lowellton, in the heart of old Lafayette.

"But everything so dead—no signs of life being so near," he said, shaking his head.

"That's the bastard Jean all over. That old ville is sewn up tighter than a virgin mosquito pussy. Nothing and no one gets in or out, and only the sec patrols go over those dead lands now."

"Then how come we didn't come across one?" Ryan asked.

"Mebbe the time of day. Jean's ville works mostly by night, and that's when his sec patrols ride. During the day, they sleep."

"And he just leaves the surrounding lands unpatrolled?" Krysty asked, bemusement shot through her voice. "The bastard must be so arrogant."

"Dunno what that means," Marissa said, "but Jean thinks everyone with him, and we hide like frightened rabbits. Who else is there in the bayou now he owns it?"

"That may just be his weakness." Ryan grinned mirthlessly. "We'll see. Where are your men?"

Prideaux and LaRue arrived, ready but reluctant. Marissa briefed them on what she had just told the companions, and then outlined to them the route she wanted them to take.

"You don't trust them to get it right themselves?" Ryan questioned.

"It's not that. I've been nearer than anyone, and I know better than anyone. That's why I should be going," she couldn't resist adding.

Ryan and Jak ignored her, and making their goodbyes to Doc, Mildred and Krysty, they—along with J.B., LaRue and Prideaux—began the journey back to West Lowellton.

It took less time to get there than it had for the companions to make the first journey. This time they had guides who knew where they were going, and knew the quickest routes to take. They traveled in silence for most of the time; LaRue and Prideaux had little to say, neither did Jak. For J.B. and Ryan, it was a matter of saving their breath so that they could keep pace with the swamp dwellers, who dealt easily and naturally with the conditions.

They skirted around the area where they had encountered the swampies, and managed to avoid any roving groups of the muties. One of the few times he spoke was when LaRue told them that he and Prideaux knew the habits of the muties as they had hunted in this area, and had learned the best times to miss them. The dull-witted swampies were very much creatures of habit, and if you knew their patterns, you could easily avoid having to fight them.

It wasn't long before the five-man party had reached the suburb of West Lowellton. They made their way rapidly through the debris of the battered buildings.

"Haven't been here for years," LaRue said with a tinge of sadness as they slipped through shell-damaged ruins to avoid the main drags, which were empty and a little too devoid of cover to be comfortable. "Kinda forgot what it was like," he added with an edge to his voice, suggesting that he may be remembering that some things are worth fighting for.

It was now dusk, and the recce party had to slow its pace as it moved toward the heart of the old city. The sec patrols would be coming out of the main ville, and it was imperative that they keep clear of them. Not only did they wish to avoid a firefight, they also wished to remain undetected so that any subsequent attack would come as a complete surprise to Dr. Jean.

They were about a mile from the main ville when the noises began. Where there had been silence, now they could hear the distant sound of chanting and drums, along with a low-level electronic hum. Perhaps it was one or the other, or mebbe it was both. Whatever it was, the feeling of oppression and gloom that hung over the ruined city suddenly grew sharper and more defined, eating into them and tugging at their nerves.

"What the hell is that?" J.B. asked.

Prideaux smiled without humor. "That, my friend, is Dr. Jean getting his people hyped up. I suggest we take cover now. We're in the wrong place to be out in the open."

Ryan, J.B. and Jak had no idea what he meant by that, but followed his and LaRue's lead by taking cover in an old building that had kept most of its structure.

"First floor if it'll hold, just to be sure," the ponytailed man added, leading them to a position where they could observe the road below without being seen themselves. "Now wait, and you'll see some of what we're up against," he whispered hoarsely. "That old road down there leads from the main gates of Jean's stronghold and out into the lands beyond. Just watch."

They crouched in silence in the shadows. After a short while, an ominous rumbling began to sound in the distance, growing louder and more distinct with every second.

"Wags," J.B. breathed. "Powerful ones, too, by the sound of them."

"Where would Jean get them from, and the fuel to power them?"

"Bayou's pretty big. That's a whole lot of ground, whole lot of villes that he's ridden over during the last few years," LaRue replied quietly.

The lights on the wags began to illuminate the road and the surrounding buildings. They drew back into the shadows, moving farther back so that they couldn't be caught by any stray beams. At the same time, they wanted to stay close enough to see what was going on.

When they did catch sight of the sec patrols as they rolled down the main drag before splitting off into their patrol routes, it was truly something to see.

There were a dozen wags in all, each of them painted a strange combination of yellow, purple and red. Even with the lack of daylight, the colors seemed to jump off the sides of the wags and loom ominously into the darkness with a life of their own. The wags themselves were of at least three different models, but they all had one thing in common—they were open behind the driver's cab, with wooden seating arranged along the sides and metal frames suggesting they could be covered with canvas if that was required. The fact that they weren't was useful for the recce party, particularly Jak, J.B. and Ryan, as it gave them their first glimpse of the sec patrols.

There were a dozen men in each wag. All sat upright, unnaturally stiff, and all wore dark goggles, even though it was night. They were dressed in fatigues dyed the same color as the wags, and they held a variety of blasters— some had AK-47s, others had M-16s, and there were a couple that weren't quite clear enough for J.B. to identify from this range and in this light. But they were all heavy-duty.

"The shades make 'em see in the dark—don't ask me how," Prideaux murmured to Ryan.

But the one-eyed man knew how, and wondered how Dr. Jean had got hold of a cache of infrared goggles.

The sec men looked at each other—directly ahead— across the rear of each wag, without moving at all. It was as though they were under some kind of drug or hypnotic influence.

"What happens next?" Ryan asked.

"The wags branch off to cover a certain area. When they reach a central point, the sec men get out of the wag and mount a foot patrol. And believe me, they're vicious fuckers if you cross them."

"That I can believe…" J.B. stated. "Thing that's weird is that we never saw them in the swamp."

"Not so weird," LaRue replied in an undertone. "They move like fuckin' ghosts, they're so quiet. Never talk, never make a sound. Unless you ran straight into 'em, they could probably walk real close and you wouldn't spot 'em."

"Something else," Jak muttered. "No smell. Like they had all their body scent taken off."

"Mebbe they have," Ryan pondered. "If Dr. Jean has got hold of some old whitecoat tech, then mebbe there's some old sec thing in there that does that." If nothing else, it would account for why there had been no indication of the sec patrols when they had traveled through the swamp. Ryan thanked their luck that they, themselves, hadn't been taken by surprise.

"Yeah, seen enough weird shit from back then to make it possible," J.B. put in, scratching under the band of his fedora. "Thing is, if he has all that shit, then we need to find out exactly what before we go up against it."

Prideaux and LaRue exchanged puzzled and worried glances. "What the fuck are you guys talking about?" the ponytailed man asked, a slight tremor in his voice. "What do you know about this?"

"Nothing yet," Ryan answered firmly, staring the man down with his one good eye, "but we've seen old tech that's been dragged out on our travels, and we know enough to know we don't know shit until we've had a better look."

"I was afraid you'd say that," Prideaux muttered. LaRue kissed his teeth and shook his head. He knew what was ahead, and knew that no matter what he felt, he was outvoted and would have to roll with it.

By now the procession of wags had receded into the distance, the noise having dropped to a low rumble. The street below was empty, and Ryan led the recce party to street level, pausing at the blown-off doors of the old block.

"LaRue, Prideaux, you know the sec layout and the boundaries on this ville, right?" Ryan asked. He waited for their replies, before continuing. "So you take lead. We want the weakest point, right?"

"No such thing, Ryan," LaRue said with a sorry shake of the head. "The whole place is walled and guarded."

"Bullshit. There's always one weak point, you just have to find it," Ryan retorted.

Prideaux scratched his chin, as though this would aid in the deep thought his expression implied. Finally he said, "There is one thing, if you don't mind wading through shit…"

"Better to wade through shit than get sprayed by blaster fire." J.B. grinned. "Take us there."

Prideaux led the recce party off the main drag and through the deserted side streets and squares of the old city. The sound of the ville walled and fenced off within grew louder, suggesting they approach. But there was no eye contact as yet.

"Need to get around to the west side, that's where we can do it," Prideaux explained. "Need to make some torches, too. We'll be in the dark for about half a mile."

They paused to scavenge in the ruins for wood they could use as poles for their torches, and tore off strips of their clothing that they wrapped and bound around the end.

"This'll do it. Waste of good liquor, but what the hell," LaRue shrugged, unstoppering a flask and pouring it over the two bundles of rags they had made on the poles. The spirit smelled strong and potent; it should burn easily. Both Ryan and J.B. had lighters that still had flints in them, so lighting the torches should be easy when the time came.

"Carry 'em, but don't light 'em till I say," Prideaux whispered. "This is the tricky part…"

They turned a corner and came face-to-face with the walls of the ville. The noise was still muffled, and it was no surprise, for although they were now only a few hundred yards from Jean's stronghold, the walls his people had built were thick and strong enough to muffle any sounds within.

"Dark night, am I glad you've got a way in," J.B. breathed as he viewed the defenses. Rightly so. The walls were forty feet high, made of rubble and concrete and stacked like a dam, so that they were thick at the bottom and narrowing to a point at the top. Although they were uneven enough, and angled enough, to provide footholds for a good climber, the top was strung with barbed wire, decorated with human body parts and the occasional head.

Spaced at roughly five-hundred-yard intervals were blaster ports, with what looked like drum-operated blasters—Thompsons? J.B. guessed, unable to see clearly—mounted under canopied awnings to shield the daylight. Each post had two men on it, though both could have been dummies for all the sound and movement they made.

"Pretty difficult to get past, eh?" Prideaux whispered to the Armorer. "Stupe thing is, where they've got the old buildings inside there repaired and running, they still shit in the old way, which means it uses the old sewers, which means that Jean should have them guarded 'cause he knows they're there. But he don't."

"Arrogant bastard probably thinks that no one is as smart as him, and wouldn't think of it," Ryan mused. "Seen that kind of attitude before. You certain about this?" He fixed Prideaux with a searching glare.

"Yeah, sure as I can be. Wasn't me that found it, it was Marissa. She was keen for us to go under, but we weren't having any of it, y'know?"

"That sound about right," Jak muttered.

"So you haven't actually been into the ville?" Ryan asked.

Prideaux shook his head. "Been into the end of the old sewer, but never came up in the ville. Know how to, though. Saw that much."

Ryan looked up at the imposing walls and the sec posts from his position in the shadows. It was risky, but at least it gave them a chance.

"Let's do it," he said simply.

Giving no more than a backward glance to the imposing walls of the ville, Ryan and the others followed

Prideaux and LaRue as they scouted around the ruined buildings on the edge of the ville. Dr. Jean hadn't bothered to clear a defensive open space between his entrenchments and the old city, so they were able to move easily within the shadow of the wall and still keep in cover. Yet again, it was a sign of the man's arrogance.

They moved out, away from the ville, for about a quarter mile, before Prideaux halted them. "Down here," he whispered, moving through a narrow alleyway until their sense of smell told them they were near their goal.

At the end of the alley, the asphalt had been broken and the ruptured sewer had risen up in a land movement, the broken concrete pipe breaking surface, the tip of it visible above street level.

"Fireblast, there must be one hell of a buildup of shit at the bottom of that," Ryan said, not without a little trepidation.

LaRue's face creased into a grin. "Don't worry, my friend. It's not as bad as that. It runs back from here and into another pipe at a junction about fifty yards thataway." He pointed to the wall of another ruined building. "So it goes under there."

"That's some kind of consolation, I guess," J.B. stated. "So who goes first?"

Prideaux and LaRue, holding the torches, squeezed themselves into the narrow channel between the top of the pipe and the road surface, half falling, half scrambling down the length of the pipe until they reached the bottom. Ryan went next, followed by J.B., and finally by Jak. They descended into darkness, desperately feeling under hands and feet for something to slow their descent, trying to keep balance when it became hard to know which way was up.

At the bottom of the pipe, with the illumination of the torches, it was easy to see what their route would be. The concrete pipes had a five-and-a-half-foot circumference, requiring J.B. and Ryan to stoop as they progressed. For the smaller swamp dwellers and Jak, it was an easy avenue of progress.

The sewer stank: not as badly as might have been expected, as it was built for a larger ville—the old city of Lafayette—than even Dr. Jean had managed to amass, but still enough to cause them to breathe shallowly, and through their mouths when possible, to avoid a gag reaction to the stench. It wasn't until they'd walked a hundred yards, past the first junction of the pipe, and the incline they had entered through leveled out fully, that they hit the flow of sewage, and the rats.

The light from the torches, hissing and spluttering from the alcohol poured on them, was enough to drive all but the most adventurous of the rodents into the farthest reaches of the gloom, squealing and seeking relief for their suddenly tortured eyes. Those that came near to investigate the intruders into their realm were driven away by a well-placed kick. The smell of the alcohol, as the torches burned brighter, also served to mask some of the smell.

Wordlessly, using only gestures, Prideaux and LaRue guided the three companions through the maze of concrete tunnels, following the flow of sewage that came from the enclosed ville. It was easy to see the point at which they moved under the wall, as the concrete suddenly came alive with a flow of stinking water and solids, whereas before they had seen empty and long dry pipes, with just the one main flow out from the enclosed ville.

"Okay, now that we're in the ville, how do we get up there?" Ryan whispered to the two swamp dwellers, jerking his thumb upward and keeping his voice down, noting how sound traveled in the pipes.

"Along here," LaRue replied, beckoning them on. They walked through the flow for another fifty yards until they came to a ladder set into a narrow tunnel that shot upward from the pipe.

Ryan looked up. There was a metal cover over the top of the tunnel.

"What's past that?" he whispered.

"Most of 'em along here you can't trust, but this one comes up in a yard behind one of the buildings. Dunno what they do in there, but Marissa said it was empty at night, so no one can see you come out."

"How d'you know it's the right one?" Ryan asked suspiciously. Prideaux grinned and pointed to the rounded wall of the pipe, by the side of the ladder's bottom rungs. An X was scratched into the concrete, a dull rusty color in the indent made by a blade of some kind.

"Marissa did that. Even put her own blood in to colour it," the ponytailed man said with an evil grin.

Ryan decided to take first crack at the ladder, but Jak stopped him. The albino knew that his eyes were better adjusted to the lack of light, and he also knew that his reflexes were quicker. Ryan was fast, but Jak's were honed to an almost preternatural state. And that might just make all the difference between getting out alive and being chilled.

Jak estimated that the sewers were sunk to about fifteen feet below the surface, counting it off as he ascended the ladder, feeling the cold concrete closing around him, the light from the torches receding. The air got close and stale as he reached the iron covering at the head of the ladder. Reaching up experimentally, he put a hand to it, testing the weight. It was heavy, but it gave easily. He drew his Colt Python with his free hand, leaning his back against the cold concrete, using his balance as a lever to push against the metal. It moved, and as he slid it back, he cautiously raised his head, taking a look around for as near to 360 degrees as he could manage in this position.

Marissa had been right. The tunnel brought them up into the courtyard of a building that was currently empty. The remaining three sides were walled to a height of about twelve feet. There was noise coming from beyond these walls, but inside—and in the building—all was quiet. The atmosphere of dread oppression was, however, worse than Jak had felt before. It was like a physical force, hitting him in the chest.

They would have to watch how that made them feel and react. Jak pulled the metal cover back and slid down the ladder. He rapidly filled in the details for the others, then ascended once more, this time dragging himself out into the yard, and standing cover for the other four as they lifted themselves out of the sewer. Prideaux and LaRue came last, extinguishing their torches in the effluent flow and wedging them in the bottom of the ladder for their return.

When all five of the recce party were above ground, and the sewer cover was back in place, they made their way across the yard to the building. It was a four-story construction, with a metal fire escape up the rear and double doors that were unlocked.

"Feels empty," Jak whispered. "Not hear anything inside. Move slow, frosty."

Ryan nodded, and let Jak lead the way into the building. It was used a dormitory by the look of it. Beds were arranged neatly across the floor, and all were empty. Otherwise, it was Spartan, with no signs of any individuality to break up the uniform monotony of the bare walls and beds. A glass storefront, whitewashed, led onto the street beyond.

"Workers quarters?" J.B. questioned.

"Yeah, but what are they working on?" Ryan replied.

There was only one way to find out. They made their way to the front of the building, and Jak opened the door a crack.

"Man, I should be back in that sewer, I shake so bad," Prideaux murmured. "Nerves, man, nerves."

"Yeah, I'm fuckin' scared, too, but there ain't no way back right now," LaRue growled at him.

Ryan and J.B. exchanged looks. They didn't want the swamp dwellers giving out on them. It would be an extra worry they could do without.

"Lot of people out there, and not look like sec," Jak whispered. "Figure we keep blasters hidden, be triple red, we could get by."

Ryan was relieved. He, too, had wondered if the strange colors worn by the sec were a uniform maintained across the ville. If so, they would have real problems. Thankfully, it didn't seem to be the case. He could feel the atmosphere, like a pounding in his gut. It welled up in him, but he suppressed the urge to panic.

"Okay, let's do this. Just be casual, keep clear of any sec patrols, move with the crowds, and don't talk unless we have to. Stick close, and ignore that gnawing in your gut. Guess we've all got it, and it's something to do with Jean. But keep it calm, and we can do this."

He nodded to Jak, who pulled open the door enough for them to slip out onto the sidewalk.

And into a strange world that seemed to operate in the night as though it were day.

The enclosed ville had obviously been built at a time when Dr. Jean had a smaller population. The streets were now teeming with people, all of whom had a slightly distant look in their eyes, and moved as though floating. The streets were lit by the old streetlamps, restored and powered by a powerful generator. It was almost bright enough to be day on the sidewalk.

All the traffic was pedestrian, and despite their distant look and languid movements, all the pedestrians seemed to be moving with a sense of purpose. There were a few traders who had wares for sale, but as the recce party walked the streets, adopting the same pace as those around them, they could see that Dr. Jean had, for the most part, established some kind of centralized system whereby food, clothing and weapons were dealt out from large storefront concerns staffed by people in the distinctive colors of the sec force. There was evidence of the use of electrical devices from predark ages, and he had a primitive vid system operating, with screen on street corners preaching his message of coming together against the out-

sider, the different, and crushing them if they didn't want
to conform.

It all confirmed the notion that he had a strong supply
of old tech spirited in from somewhere.

He also had one hell of an ego on him. The walls were
covered with paintings and murals, and the street corners
adorned with statues, all of the same man. Without asking, it was obvious that this was Dr. Jean. A tall, light-
skinned black man, he was broad across the shoulders
and had a wide girth. He was a man mountain. And even
in representations of him, the authority in his strong,
square jaw and piercing round eyes was obvious. He was
depicted in a number of heroic poses, routing his enemies.

Drifting with the mass of the population, they found
themselves moved into a central square. Here, at one end,
a number of banners with Jean's image hung over fires that
burned incense and spices that filled the air with a seduc-
tive yet insidious smell—the smell of incipient evil. The
oppressive atmosphere, heightened by the chanting of the
acolytes who drifted in, made prayers and obeisance to the
altar, and then moved out, was almost tangible. Fear, hatred, evil…all of these. The feeling of absolute power, and
absolute corruption.

The recce party had so far felt that they had moved unobserved among the ville dwellers. But now it was different. It was like an animal instinct in the square: if you were
apart from the pack, then they could sniff you out.

Jak and Ryan noticed that they were getting more and
more glances from those who watched them pass, and the
glances grew more and more hostile. It was as though they
stood out more here, where the atmosphere of the ville was

heightened and the senses of the ville dwellers were like-wise sharpened. Their hands tightened on their hidden blasters. Ryan had left the Steyr back at the swamp set-tlement, choosing only the SIG-Sauer and panga because they could be easily concealed. Jak's Magnum revolver was always as well-concealed as his knives.

J.B. had his mini-Uzi, and his M-4000 was concealed by the long coat he wore for this trip. The two swamp dwellers carried handblasters for ease of concealment, es-chewing their regular shotguns.

But even with their hidden hardware, they were out-numbered to such a degree that it would only be a matter of taking some with them rather than escaping in a fire-fight.

"Trouble at four o'clock," J.B. whispered.

Looking over to where the Armorer indicated, Jak and Ryan could see a sec party—noticeable by its distinctive colors—making its way through the crowd, heading straight for them.

Chapter Ten

"Fireblast! We need to get the hell out here. That way," Ryan commanded, taking in what was happening with a single scan of the area. The sec party making its way toward them was coming from one direction, and from all around they were starting to attract more and more hostile looks—but there was no sign of any other sec. If Ryan took them in the opposite direction, forging their way through the crowd, they could reach one of the exits from the square and try to lose themselves in the side streets—assuming, of course, that there were no other sec parties making their way toward the square from any of the other exits.

Only one way to find out. The recce party forged its way through the crowd, picking up its pace as the sec party located them by sight and began to increase the speed of its own progress. It wasn't hard for them to locate the recce party, as they were pushing their way past people who looked at them with blank eyes that were turning to hatred and even confusion as they were barged out of the way. The wake they created of jostling, shouting people could be easily seen in the otherwise calm and hypnotized environment of the shrine. But at least the disturbed people were less easy in giving way to the next force trying to part them, even though it was their own sec.

All members of the recce party now had their blasters to hand and were waving them to part the crowd. The people, despite their hostility, seemed reluctant to draw and fire in the square—if it was some kind of shrine to Dr. Jean, as seemed likely, then by the same token this could be a kind of sacrilege—and parted as the handblasters were made visible. Ryan hoped that they wouldn't have to fire yet—no knowing when and how often they would have to fire once they were in the streets, and they didn't have an infinite amount of ammo or time to reload at leisure.

Riding their luck, they reached one of the side streets, charged out of the square and into the thoroughfare. Once again the people parted, despite having blasters of their own, and there seemed to be an air of shock about them. Perhaps it was unusual for such dissent to be shown inside the walls.

Ryan had two great concerns: first, they were in a different street to the one they had used to enter the square, so they had no idea where they were in relation to their escape route. Second, if there were vid screens on the street corners broadcasting the glories of Dr. Jean, then it was also possible that among his old tech he had vid cameras that could be used to spy the streets. In which case, they were in trouble, as the sec force would be able to trace their movements and close on them.

"Where the fuck are we going?" LaRue yelled breathlessly. The potbellied swamp dweller was having trouble keeping up.

"Away," Ryan answered shortly. "Worry about it later."

In truth, things looked bleak. They were five men alone

in enemy territory, with the possibility that they could be easily tracked. Certainly, if the sec party had fought its way through the confused crowd and into the streets, they could follow the recce party by the trail of angry residents left in its wake. And yet, despite the fact that everyone seemed to be armed, they had encountered no blasterfire.

That, allied to the attitude in the square, got J.B. thinking.

"Jak, know where we've got to go?" he yelled as they pounded along the road, scattering the confused residents.

"Come in due east, go out northwest—yeah, can figure it," the albino rapped back. Unlike the others, he wasn't even short of breath.

"You do it, we'll follow," the Armorer gasped, feeling his heart pounding in time with his footsteps.

"Got an idea?" Ryan asked, drawing breath into his aching lungs.

"Mebbe," the Armorer replied enigmatically. That wasn't his intent, but he had no wish to waste valuable breath on talk.

And with good reason. The commotion and noise behind them grew louder as the sec force gained ground, the crowd parting more readily for the men in the distinctive uniforms. They were gaining ground—enough for them to risk shots over the heads of the scattering crowd.

It was the last thing the recce party needed. There was no way they would be hit by the first volley, but as it forced the crowd to part, it gave the sec party chasing them an easier path...and a clearer shot.

"Jak, find a side street soon," J.B. gritted.

The albino hunter had an inkling that he understood

what the Armorer had planned—it was no more than he
would have done himself—so he complied as soon as possible. A narrow street on the right would start to double
them back toward the dormitory building that concealed
their escape. Jak took the right turn, and the others followed.

The street was almost empty, the human traffic being
confined mostly to the main drag, and it was lit by five
electric lamps spaced the length of the street. J.B. raised
his mini-Uzi as he ran, with the blaster set to short bursts,
and hit the lamps with chattering SMG fire that shattered
them. For good measure, he took out the vid unit that
stood on one lamppost, silencing the flow of drivel about
the mightiness of Dr. Jean.

Ryan grinned. The darkness marked their path, but
would make it harder for the sec party to draw a bead on
them.

But J.B. hadn't finished. Jak led them onto another
thoroughfare, cutting across to a side street almost diag-
onally opposite. As they ran across, cutting through the
crowd and pushing people out of their way, J.B. dropped
back so that he brought up the rear of the recce party. He
turned on his heel and fired above the heads of the crowd,
taking out some of the lights and plunging a portion of the
street into darkness. Lowering his arc of fire, he also took
out some of the startled pedestrians. Whether he chilled
or merely injured them was of no significance to him.
What mattered was that, as they went down, the street
erupted into panicked chaos.

J.B. turned once more on his heel and raced to catch
up with the others. As he suspected, there was no return

fire from the street behind him. From the behavior of those in the square, he had deduced that they were unused to any blasters being used in the ville except by the sec force, and as Dr. Jean's mind-control techniques worked so well, that was probably a rarity. So to actually fire into them would cause panic and confusion rather elicit return fire, and the more panic and confusion, the harder it would be for the sec to follow them.

Now all they had to worry about was another sec force intersecting them…and the small matter of finding their way back to their own way out of the ville.

The vid screens on the street corners were now filled with images other than those relating to Dr. Jean: they were filled with images of the recce party running through the streets. A voice exhorted the people to help the sec force stop these intruders, who were already responsible for chilling innocent citizens—with which the screens lit up, repeating images of J.B.'s spray 'n' pray fire into the crowd a few moment before.

So everyone in the ville would now be on their tails, and it certainly answered the question about whether Dr. Jean had surveillance camera tech. In turn, this would make attaining their exit safely all the more difficult.

They had no time to take in any more of their surroundings. The streets became a blur of artificial light, people and moving buildings. No time now to make a proper recce, they had seen enough before this, anyhow. Now all they had to do was get the hell out. Ryan had no idea where they were headed, he could only trust to Jak's instinct.

The albino cut across more streets, this time firing to

left and right of him with the Colt Python, clearing a path before him. The recce party was now using its handblasters to clear a path, zigzagging the sporadic and random bursts of fire that spit past them. Some of the residents were alert enough to react when the recce party burst past them, and drew their blasters to fire on them, but the fire from the running men was enough to deflect their aim. And now, after seeing the vid broadcasts as they took flight, they had no illusions that they could proceed without being noticed.

All that mattered now was to get back to the exit tunnel down the sewer. And only Jak could guide them.

Ryan wondered where the hell they were going. They had headed off the main drag and were running hell-for-leather down a series of back alleys that ran behind the old buildings that faced onto the main roads.

Suddenly, Jak stopped and halted them with a hand. They pulled up short, all gasping for breath, LaRue and Prideaux almost sobbing as they gulped the air into their lungs, every breath catching painfully in their throats. They had run down at least four intersecting alleyways, and they had no idea where they were. In the distance, they could hear shouts and the sounds of commotion. They could also hear wags rumbling in the ville, transporting sec men to the last known locations to mount a search of the area.

So much for keeping the recce mission low key.

"Why stopped?" Ryan gasped.

"Lost them for while, and no cameras. Look." Jak gestured upward, and Ryan could see that there were no vid screens and no posts on which cameras could be mounted.

"That's okay so far," Ryan panted, "but what—"

"Ryan, we left the screens behind a while back. And I'll tell you something else…" The Armorer indicated to one side of the alleyway. It was a brick wall, with a four-story building behind it.

Ryan allowed himself a laugh. "Fuckin' A—you did it, Jak. And they won't be able to find our escape route. Let's get to it."

In their exhausted state, the twelve-foot wall was more daunting than it would have been ordinarily. Jak went up first, given a lift by Ryan and J.B. Once up, he laid himself down and extended an arm to LaRue while Ryan and J.B. assisted him to scramble up. After a struggle, he was on the wall.

"Shit—weak link, Jak. Get started on the cover," he gasped heavily and almost incoherently. Jak slapped the bald man on the shoulder to acknowledge what he was saying, and leaned down to help Prideaux up while LaRue lowered himself to the ground on the other side and ran across to the cover over the sewer access.

Prideaux was able to ascend with greater ease, and was soon over by his fellow fighter, helping him to remove the cover. The fat man dropped into the sewer, sliding down the ladder.

Back by the wall, Ryan had lifted himself up and clapped Jak on the shoulder. "Go—I'll help J.B."

The albino nodded and slipped down onto the ground, moving like a silent white shadow over the ground to the open sewer access.

Ryan reached down for J.B., and the Armorer grabbed at his hand and tried to scramble up the wall. His feet lost their purchase on the wall, and with a curse he fell to the ground on the wrong side of the wall. Looking to his left and right, he could see nothing, but the sounds of pursuit were closing in.

"Dark night, why do I always have to take it last," he hissed at Ryan, pulling himself to his feet and taking a running jump at the wall. He gained enough height, and grabbed at the top of the wall. He felt Ryan's iron grip on his wrists, and the one-eyed man hauled up his old friend.

"Because I know I can trust you to get it right," Ryan grinned as J.B. made the top of the wall safely.

"Well, thanks," J.B. replied, not bothering to keep the sarcasm from his voice. "I'll bear that in mind next time I'm being shot in the ass."

The two men dropped down and ran across the yard in a crouch. Ryan waved J.B. down first, ignoring the sly grin the Armorer gave him as he entered the tunnel. Ryan paused and took a good look around before he followed. The yard was quiet, there was no sign of any cameras or anyone who could catch sight of them. At least they wouldn't be followed from this end.

He lowered himself into the tunnel, feet groping for the ladder, and pulled the metal access cover over the hole as he retreated into the dark of the narrow ladder shaft.

By the time he had secured the cover and descended the ladder to the bottom, the concrete pipe was lit by the two torches, which the swamp dwellers had retrieved from where they had safely stashed them on the way out. They had waited in the dark until J.B. had reached bottom, then used his flint lighter to fire up the torches. They were giving off a strange hybrid smell, where the sewage water they had used to extinguish them mixed with the alcohol that had soaked into the rags. The burning effluent and the alcohol produced a roasted smell of indefinable unpleasantness, and also reduced the flame from its previous bright yellow and orange to a purple-blue.

"Fireblast, what are those people eating and drinking to make it like that?" Ryan said, pointing to the torches.

"Who knows, but we need a better light than that," J.B. said, shaking his head. "You got any more of that alcohol?"

LaRue frowned. "Aw, man, you gotta be kidding. I'm gonna need that to get me back home."

"We don't get a good light, then we're not gonna get home," the Armorer replied, gesturing for the bald swamp fighter to hand over his canteen.

LaRue looked at Prideaux, who indicated his agreement with a brief nod. Sighing heavily, LaRue got out his canteen, took one last swig and poured the remains over the burning torches, which Prideaux held at arm's length. Both flared brightly, causing the recce party to wince at the sudden brightness, and then settled into an orange-and-yellow flame that was possibly brighter than before. Gobbets of flaming alcohol hissed and whooshed as they dropped from the torches into the effluent.

"More like it. Let's haul out as fast as we can," Ryan said.

They trawled their way through the sewer, back the way they had come, until they reached the point where the broken pipe began to slope up. As they reached it, Ryan stayed them with a gesture.

"So far, so good. Now we need to check this out."

"Let me," Jak murmured. "Fresher than you."

Ryan nodded. Certainly, the albino hunter looked less tired than the rest of them, and was moving with much more ease. But more than that, he had the hunting instincts to know if there was anyone watching at the top of the pipe, or a sec patrol roaming nearby, he would be able to hear and track it. The last thing they wanted was to give away their position before they were clear of the ruined city.

Having arranged to signal his return with a bird call he sometimes used on such operations, Jak left them waiting at the bottom of the pipe. LaRue and Prideaux waited anxiously, barely able to control their nerves. They were exhausted and strung out, could hardly wait to put as much distance between themselves and the Lafayette stronghold of Dr. Jean as possible. By contrast, although they were also exhausted, Ryan and J.B. felt strangely calm. They had seen what the mad baron had to offer, and they had trust in Jak to find them a safe passage back into the bayou.

They didn't have to wait long. The call sounded softly, but still jarring in the total silence of the pipe, before the albino picked his way down.

"No sec outside. If got radio, then outside patrols not tracking back. Can hear noise inside ville walls, but figure still looking for us there."

Ryan gave a short laugh and shook his head. "Same old shit. So arrogant in their position that they can't figure how we could get out. Fuck 'em, let's use that time they've given us."

The recce party climbed out of the broken sewer pipe,

squeezing themselves out into the narrow alleyway where the access was hidden. Moving swiftly and silently, realizing that they were, to all intents and purposes, alone in the ruined city but not wishing to make their presence obvious, they made their way by the shortest route to the outskirts of old Lafayette, passing through the ruins of West Lowellton.

They paused at the point were the swamps began to reclaim the ruined suburb.

"Okay, we need to keep it real cool and look for the sec patrols," Prideaux muttered, still keeping his voice low, even though the surrounding area seemed deserted. "If we're lucky, we can make it through without encountering any of them."

"Do you know the routes they take, and how regular their passes are?" Ryan questioned.

Prideaux shrugged. "Not really. We don't go near enough to make notes, you know what I'm saying? How about you, LaRue? Ever noticed anything like that?"

The bald fighter tugged on his beard and thought about it for a moment. "Dunno. Tell you one thing, though, they all seem to move out from their wags in a clockwise direction, spiraling, and they keep quiet the whole time. Ain't no help, I know, but all I'm saying is that we've got to be real careful."

Jak frowned. "No noise and no scent. Got to be ready to blast anything moves out there."

There was a moment's silence as the problem hit them in its entirety. There was no way they could plan to move around the worst of the patrols. All they could do was to quite literally trust to blind luck.

It wasn't the greatest of prospects.

J.B. looked up at the night sky. It was starting to lighten with the encroaching dawn. "Mebbe we'll be all right," he murmured. "Sun should be up in about an hour, and if they come back during the day, then as long as we avoid the main paths, we should be okay. We can hear the wags, if nothing else. Other thing we need to watch is if they've got a radio system working in those wags."

Ryan understood immediately, even though Prideaux and LaRue looked a little confused. "Let's hope that they think we're still in the ville," he said with a mirthless grin. "Otherwise we're gonna be running an obstacle course in a blindfold."

"Given the choice, I think I'd rather take that right now," J.B. replied wryly. "Let's haul ass."

Ryan agreed, and the recce party headed out into the swamplands, keeping close and moving in single file. They kept to the lesser used and little known paths that had been cut by the swamp dwellers during Dr. Jean's rule. These were disguised and ran in oblique patterns to lead anyone who may stumble upon them away from the hidden settlement. Only rebels like Prideaux and LaRue knew when to diverge from them and hit other paths that had been cut.

If the sec from the walled ville of Lafayette ever stumbled across these paths, it would be by accident, and they would have little idea of their true use. However, the recce party still proceeded with triple-red caution, knowing that at any moment they could cross paths with the undetectable sec patrols.

They moved swiftly and in silence, as they had on the

outward leg. There was no sign of any life on the return leg, no clue as to where the sec patrols may be, and so everyone felt the tension build on them, exacerbated by the still-oppressive atmosphere that hung like a tangible fog over the bayou. Nerve-endings jangled and heart rates exceeded the exertion of the trek.

They were well into the swamp, and skirting around the area where the swampies had gathered, when Jak stayed them with a gesture.

"Listen—in distance," he whispered in reply to Ryan's questioning glance.

They could hear the rumble of a wag and the whine of its engine as the gears ground to cover the uneven turf and mud of the swamp. Listening closer, there were other wags whose engine notes were farther away, but could be heard blending into the overall sound.

"Guess that settles that—they're on their way back. About time, too," J.B. added, looking up at the lightening skies above the canopy cover of the trees.

"Yeah. It'll make getting home just that bit easier," LaRue said with an audible relief in his tone.

They relaxed, but not that much, as there were still other dangers that could spring at them, they resumed their journey through the swamp. With the sec patrols safely on their way back to the walled ville of Lafayette, there were only natural hazards that stood in their way.

By the time the sun had broken over the horizon, they had skirted the treacherous quicksands and bogs within the swamp, moved past any wildlife that could have posed a threat, and avoided any roving hunt parties of swampies. They were almost home.

Home… Jak found himself thinking of the settlement in that way. Not because of the actual place, but because of the people in it: not just Marissa—although she was a part of it—but all of them. They were bayou people like himself, and ones who had opted to take the rough path rather than give in to the mad Baron Dr. Jean.

Yeah, home sounded good.

They reached the settlement and were escorted in by scouts who patrolled the area at all hours, protecting the hidden position of the ville. Waiting for them were the elders of the settlement, including Marissa and Beausoleil, as well as Krysty, Doc and Mildred. Marissa was eager for them to make an immediate report, but Beausoleil could see that they were exhausted after their mission. He overruled her, asking Mildred and Krysty to take them away and make sure they were fed and rested before any further action was taken.

All five of the recce party were grateful for that. It would give them time to recover, and also to think about what they had seen in the ville. For all of them had very different ideas about what should be done.

"NO! I CAN'T BELIEVE you're saying that. What are you, some kind of fuckin' stupe coward? You… Ah, I can't believe that Jak would have anything to do with you!"

Almost spitting out the last sentence with disgust, Marissa turned on her heel and stormed toward the door of the hut. Prideaux rose and cut off her retreat, grabbing her by the shoulders.

"Hey, princess, wait and hear what everyone has to say. You can't go around saying shit like that about people just 'cause you don't like what they say," he added as she pulled herself away, eyes flashing.

"I'll say what the fuck I like," she shouted, aware suddenly of how stupe she was making herself sound, like a petulant child. "Shit, Ryan, I didn't mean—"

Ryan dismissed her apology with a gesture. "Doesn't matter. It's only words in the heat of the moment. Doesn't change what I think."

"Didn't think it would," she snapped back, eyes suddenly afire once more.

Her anger had been caused by Ryan's considered conclusions about attacking the walled ville within the ruins of old Lafayette. After the recce party had slept for a few hours, eaten and bathed so that they felt more awake, they had convened with the elders of the settlement for a debriefing. The whole population knew what the recce party had been for, but were to be told the details after the five-man party had been able to put their views individually in counsel.

As leader of the recce party, Ryan had been the first to speak. He had detailed as accurately as he could how they had entered the ville, and what they had seen within the walls. He spoke of the square, the way in which it had been converted into a shrine to Dr. Jean, and of the attitudes of the people, and the way in which they seemed to be in a trance.

Discussing the sec cameras and the vid screens on the street corners was more difficult. The companions had a greater knowledge of the old tech than the swamp dwellers, and it was sometimes hard to make them understand just what the old tech meant in terms of attack.

Judging from the hardware he and J.B. had seen the sec patrol toting, the ville also had a good armory. With old tech surveillance and a strong sec force, plus the sheer size of the population within the ville, it would be a suicide mission to mount an attack.

"In the end, I agree with you—Dr. Jean is evil scum, and dangerous scum. If he spreads out beyond the swamp, then it could be bad news, and make things worse than they already are out there. But there'll be more fighters out there to oppose him. Here, he's a shark in a lake. Out there, he's a fish in the sea. I've looked around here, and I'm telling you, there's no way you have enough hardware or enough fighters to take him on in his own territory. If you could fight and run, then mebbe—just mebbe—you could make inroads on depleting his forces. But even if you could get all your people inside without being spotted on the way, you'd still get wiped out.

"Face a few facts, here. You might be against him, but you're going to need more than that. You're going to need hardware—where's that coming from? And half the people here are either children or too old, like Beausoleil. Shit, he'll tell you that himself. You need people old enough to have some fighting smarts, but young enough to still move at speed. You haven't got that.

"Truth—it's not our fight, and I don't want to send my people in to buy the farm because of someone else's fight."

There had been a moment of silence after Ryan's speech before Marissa exploded. Now she had calmed a little and returned to the table.

"Let's hear what the others have to say," she said through gritted teeth. "Mebbe they'll have more balls."

J.B. spoke next. In many ways he echoed what Ryan had said about the capabilities of the sec force, and the difficulties the old tech presented to any force attempting to gain access to the ville and fight. He finished up, "Have to agree with Ryan on this. There isn't the armory here, or anywhere near enough fighters to make it anything other than surefire way of buying the farm. If I was in his position, I wouldn't want to commit us to this." He took off his spectacles and polished them, expecting another explosion from Marissa. It didn't come.

Instead she asked, "LaRue, Prideaux—what have you got to say about this?"

The bald fighter screwed up his face, scratched his head and tugged at his beard. Slowly he said, "Y'know, Rissa, everything about me wants to fight them, but they scare the living crap out of me. They've got it nailed down tight, and even with these guys, me 'n' Prideaux nearly got ourselves iced in there. We could mebbe take out some of them, cause some damage, but we wouldn't stop them." He stumbled as he saw the expression on her face. He had been her ally in the camp, as she saw it—one of her own— and now he was letting her down.

"Fuck it, Rissa, I'd say let's go for it if there was any chance. But at the very least we'd have to spend a lot of time training up, mebbe try to get some more hardware. It'd take a shitload of time."

"Time's something we've had a lot of, still got a lot of," she murmured bitterly. "I suppose you're gonna back everyone on this," she added, turning to Prideaux.

The ponytailed fighter shrugged. "Princess, you got me all wrong. You think like I'm some kind of coward who doesn't want to fight. You really think that after we've stood together and blasted fuck out of whoever was against us? Shit, babe, it's not about that. If I'd thought we had a chance of taking on Jean and a realistic chance of kicking some ass and ending his reign, then I'd be with you. But you weren't there, you didn't see it. It was like Ryan said. All of it. Shit like we've never seen. Shit we couldn't do anything against. It's like I've said all along. There ain't enough of us, and we don't have the firepower. I wish we did. No matter what you think of me, that's true."

For once, he dropped his sardonic exterior and allowed his true self to show to Marissa. That made his words hit harder than any of the others, who she had expected to be on her side.

"Figure it's not really worth going any further," Beausoleil sniffed, "but I'd still be interested in what young Lauren has to say."

All eyes were on Jak. What he had to say surprised them all.

"Figure we can take them. Not easy, but it can be done."

There was a stunned silence. Then Krysty said, "Jak, you can't be serious, not after everything else that's been said. Not after what you must have seen."

Jak fixed her with an impassive stare. It was impossible to tell what was going on behind those immobile features, but it was some moments before he answered.

"Wouldn't understand. Not about what and what not possible. About what you make happen. Figure can take these people, work with them, make them better fighters. Take time, but what else we got but time? Mebbe even get some better blasters. Jean not going anywhere, and neither are we."

"Jak, there's no way you could take these people and make an army out of them—not one that could beat Jean," Ryan said. "Fireblast man, you've seen what it's like in there."

"And you not seen what it's like in here," Jak replied vehemently, thumping his chest with a fist. "Can't leave again. Once was enough. Stay and fight this time."

Ryan said nothing. Suddenly it made sense. Jak felt he owed these people because he'd walked out on them before, back in West Lowellton. They were his history, his home. This was the place where he was raised. It was his history, his self that was being eradicated by Dr. Jean. What else could he do? How would Ryan have felt if it was Front Royal they were talking about? It didn't take him more than a second to realize that this had nothing to do with rational thought. It was something your conscience would make you do, regardless of the consequences.

But he couldn't let Jak's imperative dictate what the rest of the companions should do. To stay and fight would be to buy the farm. He couldn't agree to that.

Jak had to realize that this was going through Ryan's mind, for he said, "Want you to stay and fight. Can do this without you, but don't want to."

Ryan looked at the others around the hut. J.B. shrugged. Like Ryan, he knew what a thankless and futile gesture it would be. Krysty, Mildred and Doc looked as though they couldn't make up their minds what they wanted to do, which wasn't surprising, as this had been sprung on them and they had all realized what it would mean if they said no.

Ryan spoke slowly, considering every word. "We've been together a long time, and done a lot of things that looked triple stupe at the time. But we've always stuck together, and not put each other knowingly in danger. But what you're asking now is for us to stay because you want to, and do something that's almost certain to buy the farm. I realize why you have to do this, but I'd rather you stayed with us."

"Means you won't stay," Jak said flatly. It was statement, not a question.

Ryan shook his head.

"We can't just do it like that," Mildred exploded. "We can't just desert Jak."

"You didn't see it in there, Millie," J.B. said softly. "Jak's doing what he has to do, but Ryan's right. We can't follow on to what's a certain chill, because we don't have the same reasons Jak does."

"John, I wouldn't have thought you'd give it up that easily," Mildred said, looking at him in puzzlement.

"It's not about that, it's about what's best for all of us," J.B. replied.

"But surely it is not best for all of us if we have to leave one behind," Doc mused. "Certainly not for that one," he added, casting a glance toward Jak.

"That's what they used to call democracy, isn't it?" Krysty asked him. "Back in the day, the greatest good for the greatest number?"

"Not quite." The old man smiled. "Democracy was about everyone having a say in how things were done, which I venture to suggest—"

"This isn't a democracy," Ryan interrupted. "It never

has been. Trader taught me and J.B. that years ago—unity is strength, you get a leader who you can trust, and you act on what he says. Sometimes it isn't that easy to ask everyone's opinion. You need a fast decision, and so you have a leader to carry the can for that shit. And don't think that this was easy."

"My dear sir, that is the last thing I wished to suggest," Doc said quietly. "The responsibilities of such leadership weigh heavily, and I would not wish to criticize the manner in which you have handled anything. It's just that to leave Jak behind seems, somehow…" He shrugged.

"I know, but Jak wants to do this, and he'll do it anyway. I have to think about the rest of us. And this would be bad for us as a group. I can't see it any other way. And I doubt if any of you can, in truth. But if you accept me as leader, then you have to accept my decisions. That's part of the deal. Otherwise you get a new leader, and we don't stay together at all."

The swamp dwellers had been watching this silently, wondering what would happen. It was Jak who broke the tension.

"Ryan right. I stay, can't accept his decision. But the rest of you need to be strong together. No matter how much it hurt."

"Yeah, no matter how much…and, believe me, it does," Ryan said with a sad shake of his head.

Chapter Eleven

Ryan rested his people for a couple more days before wanting to move them out. There were still traces of fever and infections in the old cuts and sores that needed treatment. Mildred had the medications, she just needed the time to apply them. By the same token, the companions paid for their keep by helping to hunt for the slim pickings that could be found in the swamp. Ryan was mindful of the fact that the settlement dwellers were letting them stay because of Jak, and that they were using valuable supplies. There was little enough food in the settlement at the best of times, without it being used on five people who wouldn't fight.

Marissa was unhappy at their staying, but Jak convinced her. The other elders understood Ryan's position—even those who didn't agree with him—but the hotheaded Marissa was in no mood to listen to reason until Jak managed to turn her around.

It made for an uneasy truce.

But it did give the companions a chance to see what the settlement had to offer in the way of fighting forces, and exactly what Jak had to work with. Prior to that, they had seen only a few of the swamp warriors out in the field, hunting and running sec patrols. Now it seemed that the entire ville was galvanized to action.

Almost immediately after his decision to stay, Jak had faced the mass of settlement folk who were waiting for word from their elders. At the behest of Beausoleil, who wanted his people to know exactly what they faced, Ryan spoke first. He outlined everything he had told the elders in the hut, and explained why he couldn't commit his people to the fight. Behind him, the other companions were ready for the tension to break into a firefight. In many ways, they wouldn't have blamed the swamp dwellers for this.

And yet the atmosphere wasn't as they expected. Many of the dwellers had their own skepticisms about the chances of taking on Dr. Jean, and their fears were confirmed by what the one-eyed man told them. But despite this, they were fired up by Jak's words. Never one to demonstrate with speech, Jak simply told them it could be done, and he, for one, would rather buy the farm trying than walk away.

This faith—the faith that they could win, the faith that he could mold them into a force that would be capable of overcoming the odds and taking the enemy to the wire— was enough to fire even the most skeptical. All those who were fit enough—and not too young or too old to be of some use—were willing to undergo combat training to prepare themselves. Those who couldn't fight would be the backup, gathering what weapons there were, venturing onto trade routes to either trade for or steal weapons, perhaps even taking on some of the sec parties. Enthusiasm outstripped practicality, and it took some time for the euphoric atmosphere to descend from the heights to a more practical level once more.

"I don't get it. They were real down when we arrived, and now they think they can take on the whole Deathlands," J.B. muttered.

"Morale, my dear John Barrymore," Doc whispered by way of reply. "There is nothing like hope to fire the human spirit. Better to live one day as a lion than a thousand years as a lamb…or something like that, I forget exactly," he stated.

"Doc, the meaning…?" J.B. asked, trying to figure out the sense of the old man's words.

Doc smiled. "It means better to die free than live a slave, or in fear," he said simply.

J.B. thought about this. "Yeah. If this was our fight, I guess I could see that…"

And so the preparations began.

"Y'KNOW, IT'S GONNA TAKE a hell of a lot more than this to get past the kind of armory that sec force has got," J.B. said, shaking his head as he surveyed the paltry stock of arms and ammo that the swamp dwellers had amassed.

Jak, by the Armorer's side, tried to keep his disappointment hidden. The settlement had very little in the way of hardware. They had handblasters, a few rifles, two SMGs, a couple of shotguns, and some of the old blunderbuss-style weapons Marissa, LaRue and Prideaux had used when the friends had first encountered them.

"Most hunting done with snare and knife," Jak commented shortly. "Guess no real need for blasters this deep."

"Yeah, that figures, but this…" J.B. shook his head once more. "Jak, you're gonna have to go out and get hold of some more blasters somehow."

"Can loot from sec as we go—if take it in series of surprise attacks, then take out small parties and get their
weapons," the albino mused.

J.B. blew out his cheeks in an expression of exasperation. "That's a slim chance, no matter how well you get
these people trained. You're talking about making no ripples until you've taken out a series of sec, and then using
their own blasters—ones that your people have had no
chance to learn to use."

"You think of anything better?" Jak asked him bluntly.
"How deep this place? How far from trade routes?"

"Wish I could think of something else, but there isn't,
is there?" J.B. said quietly.

The Armorer dropped to his haunches and examined
the blasters. The handblasters consisted of a number of
Smith & Wesson .38 Police Specials, some 9 mm Wal-
thers, a couple of Glocks, and some even older Colt
.44's—Peacemakers, which J.B. suspected had been
looted from a museum. The store of ammo to go with these
was erratic, with some of them having no more than fifty
or sixty rounds apiece.

The rifles were old Lee Enfield .303s and Sharps—
again, looted from some kind of museum. There was nothing more contemporary than this. The SMGs were a couple of Uzis, and half a dozen H&K MP-5s. Again, the
ammo for these amounted to very little when doled out
among the individual blasters. There were two Smith &
Wesson M-4000s, like the one favored by the Armorer, but
again there was little ammo for a long-term firefight. The
five old blunderbuss-style blasters were like nothing he'd
seen before—parts of them were identifiable as being

from the original blasters, but new stocks had been added
to some, and the trigger mechanisms had been repaired
with wire over the years. If they didn't explode in the
faces of whoever used them, it was a plus by his reckoning. There was plentiful shot for these, but their condition
was a grave cause for concern.

"Jak, there's no way—even if we work on these—that
they're gonna be up to taking the ville on their own.
Mebbe you need to rethink what you're really hitting."

"What?"

"Yeah... I mean, Dr. Jean has a stronghold on that ville,
right? He controls the people with either drugs, hypnosis
or old tech...mebbe all three. But that's why they follow
him. Not 'cause they really believe in him, or they're in
fear of him."

"So mebbe... if take out Jean, there is no other enemy?"

J.B. nodded slowly. "Could be the only way unless you
get a miracle of some kind and a wagful of hardware lands
on your damn head."

WHILE JAK MULLED OVER the possibility of forming such
a plan, he was faced with the task of shaping the settlement dwellers into a fighting force. For some of them,
such as LaRue and Prideaux, this was easier than for others. Those in the settlement who had been hunting already had the skills needed for a guerrilla attack, and they
had accuracy with a blaster and ability with a knife. Their
problems were related to their attitude. As for the others,
it was a conundrum for the albino hunter. To improve
their blaster skills, he would need to use precious ammo,

yet without some kind of practice, they would be unreliable in a firefight. Asking the likes of Prideaux, who regularly used a blaster, where the settlement got their ammo, was of little use. It did nothing other than bring the man's resentment and antipathy to the fore.

"Listen, Lauren, we've always had to make the ammo last for a long time. You think we get many traders in these parts? Sometimes we get ships washed up on the edge of the bayou—same way you got here—and sometimes we can mebbe trade or raid a stray wag. But there ain't no regular port of call around here, and we've always had to scrimp and save, and be careful. You think that's gonna change now, just 'cause you want us all to go out in a blaze of glory?"

"So that'll be a no, then," Krysty remarked to Ryan as they overheard the exchange.

"Dammit, Jak's taken on more than you could wish on your worst enemy," Ryan replied.

"So you want us to stay, help out?"

Ryan sighed. "All it does is make me sure it was the right decision for the group—doesn't mean that I don't feel for Jak, though."

The albino would have been unconcerned if he had caught this. He had other things to worry about. Training the settlement dwellers in unarmed combat, and the art of using knives, wasn't without its own problems. Some of the people were used to fighting, and others weren't. And those that had scores to settle used the practice sessions to try to even these instead of working to the common good. As Jak found out as soon as the second day.

Down by the lake, in front of the land-built huts of the

settlement, was a patch of land that the albino had decided would be useful as a practice ground. He gathered groups, ten at a time, to attempt to instruct them in what was needed for the fight ahead. Demonstrating holds that would cut blood and air supplies to their enemies when approached from behind, he used other settlement dwellers as "victims," then paired off the remainder, according to what he perceived as their ability and experience, changing the pairings as he observed their skills and capacities. His notion was to bring together a front-line force from within the settlement that he could use as a guerrilla troop in the plan that was beginning to form in his mind.

But that sometimes meant that those with deep-seated antipathies went up against each other. Such was the situation when he paired Marissa and Prideaux in knife combat.

Knives were something that the settlement had in abundance. Sometimes their origins were unidentifiable, but they were sharp enough to do the job.

And as Marissa and Prideaux began to circle each other, it became apparent that despite the nature of the session, there was to be no quarter given.

"So, princess, you gonna show off your skills in front of your new man, are you?" he taunted her, feinting as he hoped to distract her attention.

"Have to do lot better than that, little man," she said, thrusting at him. He parried her easily and tripped her. She rolled as she fell, away from the arc of his blade that sliced the air around her dark mane.

"Bitch—you never gave me a chance, and now you and that stupe white asshole of yours are gonna get us all chilled," he hissed at her, whirling to parry an overhand strike, kicking out at her and landing a foot in the middle of her stomach. She grunted as the air was forced from her body, her diaphragm contracting under the force of the blow. She doubled up as he came in to strike with an underhand blow, but caught enough of a sight of him to realize his intent.

Throwing herself backward, gasping air back into her lungs, forcing herself to breathe, she flipped and landed awkwardly, stumbling to one side. But it was enough, as his upward thrust into thin air had unbalanced him and he stumbled as he tried to halt his momentum and stay his forward movement…a movement that would bring him directly in line with her knife hand.

"You don't believe in us, you can never be one of us," she gritted, making ready to place a blow between shoulders, aiming for the juncture of his throat and chest cavity. His stance was completely open and there was nothing he could do to prevent her from chilling him.

Jak stepped in. Moving with the preternatural speed he had developed over years of hunting, he came between the two of them, forcing Prideaux to one side so that he stumbled and fell harmlessly. His left arm shot up in a straight-arm blow that pushed Marissa's hand to one side, the force of the blow numbing her fingers and making her drop the blade. His right hand, bunched into a fist, hit her with a sharp jab at the point of the jaw. She crumpled to the ground, unconscious.

Jak whirled to where Prideaux was just regaining his balance. The ponytailed man looked confused. He had thought he was about to buy the farm, and hadn't expected

Jak to save him. Moreover, he hadn't expected the albino to treat Marissa in such a fashion.

"Look, all are same now," Jak yelled, as much to the assembled crowd as to Prideaux. "No one better than others. All in this together. All stand or fall together. All the same," he reiterated, fixing his stare on the confused Prideaux. Then, before the man had a chance to work out what was happening, Jak hit him with an uppercut that took him off his feet, depositing him on the ground with a thud.

"We all learn from this, or we try to fight each other instead of Jean?" he asked the assembled throng, scanning their faces for signs of dissent. He could see some sullen expressions that bespoke of unease, but there was no audible dissent.

"Okay, now we learn, okay?"

There was no indication that the settlement dwellers were now anything other than rapt, ready to prepare for combat. But just maybe they were too scared to face down Jak Lauren. Maybe they still weren't convinced.

And if they weren't convinced of their own power, how could they fight effectively?

ON THE MORNING of the third day, it was time for the five companions to move on.

"You could always stay a little longer," Beausoleil said as they gathered to go. "With the training for the raid going down, we're short of hunters. Someone has to bring in the food."

"Yeah, but we eat as much as we catch—mebbe more," Ryan replied with a smile, "so it doesn't really figure."

"Mebbe not," the old man agreed. "But mebbe I was figurin' you could come in useful around here. Face it, we need all the help we can get. Young Lauren's good, but he can't do it all alone."

"And he can't do it with us," Ryan stated firmly. "There's no changing that."

Nonetheless, the others caught the note in his voice, it was a note of regret that it should end like this, that they should have to walk away from Jak.

The albino caught it, too. He came out to see them off, with Marissa in his wake. Never one for goodbyes, he stood apart from the group as they gathered their baggage for the haul ahead. J.B. had taken a reading with his mini-sextant, and they had worked out the direction of the re-doubt. Perhaps it would be in the hands of Dr. Jean and his sec, perhaps not. If it proved to be impregnable, they would just strike on past it until they found the next ville on their route.

"Jak, been a long time. We're going to miss you," Ryan said, fixing the albino with his single, ice-blue orb.

"Miss you—but know why you go," Jak replied simply.

The companions struck out for the heart of the swamp. LaRue would go with them part of the way, to guide them to nearest clear-cut path that would put them on course.

Doc could feel tears of sadness and nostalgia well up as they left the albino behind. No one looked back except the old man. The others kept their eyes fixed on the path ahead, not trusting themselves, and knowing that Jak wouldn't want it any other way. But Doc cast a glance over his shoulder. Jak stood watching them as they melted into the foliage, his scarred white face as inscrutable as ever. Marissa stood by his side. Despite having someone so near, Doc had never seen Jak look so alone.

A single tear trickled slowly down his cheek. In truth, he couldn't tell if it was for leaving Jak behind or for himself, as if this incident had brought home to him the losses they had suffered as a group over the years, and going back farther, the losses that he had suffered over a life that had spanned centuries.

Ashes to ashes, dust to dust. Another one bites the dust. From the earth we come and to the earth we return, and in between is naught but suffering…

Doc looked away, eyes now fixed firmly ahead.

LARUE LED THEM out of the maze of paths that linked the settlement to the main tracks leading through the swamp. It was a long and arduous haul, with the bald man setting a fast pace. No one wanted to speak; there were mixed emotions among the companions. All agreed with Ryan's decision on an intellectual level, and yet all of them—even the one-eyed man himself—felt that in some way they were letting Jak down by leaving in this manner.

There was nothing about LaRue's bearing that suggested that he felt any differently. As the swamp dweller detailed to guide them, he set a fearsome pace, hacking his way through thick undergrowth and crossing treacherous stretches of quicksand without a chance of the companions following his footsteps with anything other than blind faith. It was obvious that he wanted to get this task out of the way as soon as possible, and get back to the settlement.

Eventually, after several hours without a break, they reached a plateau where the land stretched ahead in a winding, natural path. LaRue stopped dead and turned to them.

"This is as far as I go. You know your direction from here, and you're back on the trails that you were using before we found you."

"Thanks. Thought we weren't gonna get that far, the pace you were setting," Ryan commented.

LaRue sniffed. "Yeah, well, figure the sooner get rid of you and get back to training, the better."

"You that keen to go and fight?" Krysty asked, sensing that the man wanted to say more, but would need prompting.

LaRue fixed her with a penetrating stare and tugged at his beard. "Y'mean, am I keen to buy the farm? No, I like living, even if it is hard. It's better than the other way. But I figure if we got any kind of a chance, then it needs all the fighters like me and Prideaux and Rissa to pull together, 'cause little Whitey ain't had much chance to pull us together, and if you wanna know what I really think, he ain't got much to work with. Some of us can fight, and others farm and hunt, and others ain't really up to much. We can stick together 'cause we ain't got jackshit but each other. Only now we all got to fight, and some don't want to and some can't. If you'd helped us, things would have been better."

"You think we're taking the easy way out?" Krysty asked.

A smile twisted across his face. "Mebbe…mebbe it ain't so easy to leave Whitey behind after so long. Fighting together gets you kinda close, so I ain't gonna say. See, me 'n' Prideaux don't like each other, but I know I'll always back the fucker in a firefight 'cause it's bigger than us. Mebbe it ain't so easy for you—" he shook his head sadly "—but, y'know, we coulda done with you along for the ride."

"Not our fight," Ryan said simply. "And we've got our own way to go."

LaRue sniffed. "Yeah, well, you know your way from here, so that's all I care about. I gotta go. Mebbe see you one day on that place where fighters go when they buy the farm."

The bald man turned on his heel and struck back into the undergrowth, being swallowed up by the foliage and leaving the companions standing by the open track. They stayed still and silent for some moments.

"Think he's right?" Mildred asked finally, if only to break the silence.

"Mebbe he is," Ryan mused. "Wasn't a right or wrong in this." He looked up at the sky, noting the position of the sun. "Got a few hours before the darkness falls. Let's try to make some progress…"

They set out in the direction of the redoubt, which was still a two-day trek, by their reckonings. If they could make some headway on the distance by nightfall, then they could set up camp out of the way of any main paths, hopefully avoiding the sec patrols from Lafayette. In the meantime, they had to keep an eye out for swampies in search of food.

Avoiding the places where the muties could hide themselves with ease, they made a swift progress. And yet an

air of depression hung over them. Without Jak, they felt
incomplete. Leaving him had been one of the toughest decisions they had made.

As the sun began to fall and the twilight turned the
swamp into a land of shadows, they deviated from the
open spaces to find a dry, secluded place into which to set
up camp. They carried with them nothing but the self-heats
and some water they had taken from the wells in the settlement. There was so little food in the rebel ville that they
would have felt wrong taking any of it, even if it did con-
demn them to the chem-soaked gruel until they could hunt
once more.

The camp was well-hidden as night came, and they settled in to rest for the night, with a rotating watch. Ryan
took first watch, with Mildred relieving him after a couple of hours. As used as they were to sleeping for short
periods, the medic found herself coming awake in the
darkness almost on cue. She looked at her wrist chron, the
light from the moon penetrating the cloud cover just
enough to show that she was only a few minutes away
from her shift.

She shook the sleep from her muzzy head and rose
slowly, creeping through the undergrowth to where Ryan
had established a watch post.

He turned as he heard her making her way toward him.
She was quiet, but he was still able to pick her out. As he
became visible in the gloom, she could see that he was indicating that she be quieter.

Her brow furrowed. Beyond the one-eyed man she
could hear some movement. She went triple-red as she
drew nearer, taking each step carefully. As she reached

Ryan, he gestured with an inclination of the head that she look beyond, but with caution. Now that she was close, she could hear more movement beyond the sentry post.

Ryan had chosen to make his post behind a group of swamp plants that gave off a noxious odor, and were clumped so thickly that they suggested they extended back for a depth of several feet. In fact, the shallow-rooted plants extended in a horse-shoe shape, needing muddy soil to root and finding a rock shelf barring their progress. It was perfect for Ryan to use as cover.

As Mildred joined him, she could see a group of three sec men on patrol. In a cluster, they moved as though on an assigned route from which they never deviated. Dressed in the orange-and-purple dyed camou that signified Dr. Jean's men, two of them carried AK47s, while the third had an Uzi. All carried their blasters with the barrels down, and all were wearing infrared goggles. They turned their heads as though on strings, moving almost exactly in unison. They were well-programmed machines, but seemed to have no independent senses.

Mildred and Ryan exchanged glances. The sec men were making no attempt to do anything other than follow this route. They had to do this every night, exactly the same.

Exactly.

If they were this inflexible, then they should be easy to slip past. Maybe Jak should know this. Maybe it would be possible. What was it J.B. had said? The people were so brainwashed by Dr. Jean that they couldn't adjust to sudden changes, to sudden explosions of action. And Ryan had seen the arrogance of the oppressor at work. So unused to opposition that there were gaping holes in the defenses that had never been tested, both physically and psychologically.

But it was something else that made up their minds. As the sec trio passed so close to Ryan and Mildred that they could almost have reached out and touched them, in the silence of the swamp night they could hear the faint hiss and crackle of static, and the high, tinny murmur a voice that seemed to emanate from the heads of the trio. Looking closely, Mildred and Ryan could see that the headsets that held the infrared goggles to the heads of the trio also had earpieces attached that were plugged into the right ear of each man.

So Dr. Jean did have radio-transmitter old tech that was working. Ryan realized how lucky they had been on their recce mission to Lafayette.

As the trio receded into the swamps, Ryan beckoned Mildred to follow him, and he broke cover, moving quickly and silently back in the direction the sec patrol had come. Mildred followed, half guessing Ryan's intent.

The one-eyed man gestured her off the path when he caught sight of the wag that had brought the patrol to this point. Mildred understood what he was seeking. As they approached, she could hear the whine of static and the distinct tones of a distorted human voice. The driver of the wag sat in the cab, an M-16 across his lap, looking blankly ahead through the infrared goggles, and listening to the voice on a small loudspeaker that was set in the wag's dash.

"...glory of the great Dr. Jean. The next sacrifice to the old gods will be three nights from now, and those honored with the task of taking the lord's blessings into the next realm will be those who are ranged against us in the swamps. The military detachments leave in two nights to round up these heathens who have rejected the glories of Jean. They will be blessed and sent into the next realm to realize their mistakes and bring Jean's requests for glory to the gods. Dr. Jean wants you to redouble efforts and bring your own sacrifice to the shrine during this night and the next, so that the gods will look kindly upon our sec force."

Ryan gestured to Mildred that they should pull back into cover. They retreated the way they had come, then took refuge in the cover of the noxious plants.

"That screws everything," Ryan stated. "I know what I said before, but this is different. There's no way that I can let these bastards pour into the swamp and take Jak's people by surprise. There's no way they've got the numbers to withstand it unless they're warned. We're going to have to go back, warn him, and stand and fight. We can't let him face this alone."

Mildred raised an eyebrow. "You think I'm not going to agree with you, Ryan? Hell, this is one time I'd gladly follow orders. Let's get back to camp and the others. I don't think even Doc's going to mind being roused from his beauty sleep over this one."

"SICK YOU FUCKERS. You want fight Jean or each other?" Jak yelled at the assembled force. "You want fight, okay, we go fight that fucker now, ready or not. Leave longer, then all do is kick fuck out each other."

The albino hunter turned his back in disgust and

walked off toward the shadows where the edge of the settlement bled into the swamps, and the light of the lamps
grew dim.

Marissa cast flashing, dark eyes over the swamp dwellers who stood mute, frozen in astonishment at Jak's outburst. It was the most they had heard him speak in the time
he had been at the settlement. The normally taciturn
fighter had been spurred into the outburst by yet more dissent among the ranks of the settlement rebels who were
of the right age to fight.

"You stupe bastards," Marissa hissed at them. "This is
our chance to fight back against that scum Jean, and yet
you want to fight among yourselves. Don't you realize that
fate sent Jak here, now, so that we could unite and do this?
What about all your families who died or are now zombies under Jean's control? Doesn't that hurt you in here?"
she asked, thumping her chest. "Doesn't that chill you just
to think about it? You want to end up like this or hiding
like a stupe beaten dog in the middle of swamp, hoping
that you don't get caught, for the rest of your life?"

As if Jak's outburst had not been enough, now Marissa's equal explosion left them even more speechless. They
all knew her history, which she hadn't told Jak. Marissa's
brother and her husband, one chilled and the other now a
sec man zombie, moving with those glasses that hide the
dead eyes; her child, just a babe in arms, lost when West
Lowellton fell to Jean's advancing forces.

Maybe she felt that she had a bigger ax to grind with
Dr. Jean—to bury in his sick skull—than any of the others in the settlement. And maybe she was right. It had
seemed to affect her much more deeply than the other sur-

vivors, who had accepted the vagaries of fate and had tried to just carry on living without thinking too deeply about what had happened to them.

As Marissa disappeared into the shadows in search of Jak, the crowd of rebels began to slowly emerge from their cocoon of shock, and move once more. Looking at one another, the ragtag army of men and women couldn't for the life of them see what hope they had against Dr. Jean. Those who had been unwilling to fight, but had been pressed into training by the majority rule of the settlement, had always felt this hopelessness, and their constant harping on the matter had caused dissent and internal friction with those who had wanted to train, and believed that they could be wielded into a force that could penetrate the heart of the Lafayette ville. Fights had broken out when practice on combat moves had turned into genuine, no-holds-barred skirmishes. And now even those who had agreed the most vociferously with Marissa in backing Jak began to feel the black despair creep over them, defeated before they even started out.

"Shit, even l'il Lauren's gonna have to pull something out of the bag to get this together," Prideaux remarked to no one in particular, looking around him at the tired and beaten expressions on the faces of the rebel force.

In the shadows, Marissa had caught up to Jak, who was staring out over the dark water.

"Fuck 'em, babe. They don't know what they can do till they try, and we ain't got any other way but to go ahead and go for it."

"Mebbe. If people not want fight, then what point?" he asked her quietly, turning so his piercing red eyes penetrated her own dark orbs.

"The only point is that we can't go on like this—you or me. Or them, though mebbe they don't know it."

Jak was silent for some time. His gaze remained unwavering, and she found it impossible to work out what was going on in his head. Eventually he spoke. "If they want to fight each other, guess not give 'em a chance. Go now."

Marissa was taken aback and found it hard to disguise her shock. "Now?"

"Yeah. Prepare tonight, move tomorrow. Not give 'em time to think about it, just do it."

Fired up, the albino rose and began to move back toward the settlement, leaving a stunned Marissa momentarily frozen. Shaking herself, not believing that she was finally going to get the action she had craved for so long, she scurried after him.

When Jak reached the area at the edge of the settlement and the lake where the fighters had been training, the rebel group was beginning to disperse.

"Wait—back here," Jak yelled. There was an edge to his voice that made the even the most antipathetic of them turn back.

He waited until they had gathered, and Marissa had caught up with him, before beginning.

"Want fight each other, waste time and energy and blood? Or want to fuck over Dr. Jean. We can do it if we hit hard and soon. Tomorrow." He paused, letting the speed of his action sink in, listening to the mumblings of surprise from the rebels. He allowed himself a grin before continuing. "Only one way can do this. Don't mount full-scale attack. Go straight for Jean. Chill him and take out the brain of the ville. Rest of it like a chicken with head cut off."

Prideaux grinned. "Y'mean to say that if we can find a way to take out the boss man, then the rest of 'em won't know what to do, and the whole thing'll tumble down?"

Jak nodded. "Jean control 'em, tell 'em what to do. No one tells "em what to do, not know what to do."

Prideaux nodded slowly, then turned to the rest of the rebels. "Y'know, that one might just work, if'n there's a way to get to him."

"Is—but have to move fast, and remember everything told," Jak affirmed. He outlined his plan with as few words as possible. It was a simple idea, making advantage of their small numbers, and it began to win over even the most sckeptical of the rebels. By the time he had finished, the atmosphere around the lake had changed.

Jak grinned. "Get ready—move at sunup to be in position by tomorrow night."

"Sounds good to me, and I never thought I'd say that to you," Prideaux said, shaking his head and laughing.

Marissa looked at Jak, disbelievingly. It seemed so simple the way he put it. Maybe the fates were, for once, on her side.

Chapter Twelve

"Necessity, my dear sir, is the mother of many things, it would seem…not merely invention."

"Doc, what the hell are you talking about now?" J.B. asked, a puzzled expression crossing his face at Doc's proclamation.

"I think he's just kind of saying that, hey, we lucked out because we've got a great excuse for actually turning back after all," Mildred replied, filling in the blanks.

"Dark night, why doesn't he just say that?" J.B. muttered, shaking his head.

Mildred and Ryan had made their way swiftly back to the camp. Waking his friends, the one-eyed man had outlined the broadcast he and Mildred had overheard, and also informed them of his change of plans. As he suspected, it met with nothing but approval. Doc, J.B. and Krysty were soon ready to leave.

"Triple red on this," Ryan cautioned. "I reckon that the sec patrols run until dawn, and that's still a couple of hours off. We need to make sure we don't run across them."

"Then perhaps, if I should make so bold, it would be better if we wait for the dawn to break before beginning our journey?" Doc posed.

"I did consider it, Doc," Ryan replied, "but I really don't think we've got the time to do that. If they're mobilizing to attack the lake, then it means they know where the ville is, and they've just been leaving it alone. They can move triple fast, which means we have to move even faster if we're going to give Jak any kind of warning."

Doc thought it was a reasonable point, and one with which there was little argument. Time was of the essence.

Retracing their path was easy, even in the moonlight that filtered erratically through the canopy of foliage that hung over the swamp. They moved in single file, with Ryan and J.B. at each end, Doc sequestered in the center of the formation. It was important to move swiftly and silently, keeping careful watch for any sec patrols.

Despite this, there was a lighter air to the group as they marched. The pall of gloom that hung over them as it hung over the swamps had lifted, they had a purpose, and they wouldn't be deserting Jak. This sense of purpose pumped them with adrenaline, allowing them to maintain a high level of alertness despite the paucity of rest.

They retraced their previous path. There was no sign of any sec patrols as the sky began to lighten with the coming of the new day. Ryan felt that this only confirmed his suspicions about the sec from Lafayette. They moved in a rigid, regimented and long-established pattern. They were used to being the lords of the swamp, with no opposition to test them or to sharpen their reflexes. They were slack, and paid no real attention to their surroundings. And they moved only at night.

This could only help the odds of taking them on with such a depleted force as the rebels possessed. It would still be a tough task, but one that had a slim chance rather than none.

As the day broke, they knew that they were on safer ground. The sec patrols would have returned to Lafayette. It seemed that they posed little threat if you could work out their routes and avoid them. And yet, they were well-armed, and to take them on in the confines of their own walled-in ville would be a different matter.

A thousand possibilities for attack and defense ran through the one-eyed man's mind as they made progress through the swamp. He would have plenty to discuss with Jak when they met up. In the meantime, they were able to move with ease now that it was light, and the memory of the path they had taken was fresh enough to make retracing their steps simple. With their quicker pace, they hoped to get to the rebel ville before sundown, even eschewing the chance to stop and rest along the way other than for the briefest of pauses.

At least, that was the idea until they hit the area where they had parted company with LaRue. Although, up until this point, they had been certain of their route, now some doubt crept in.

Faced with a wall of swamp grass, lobster grass and bizarrely flowering shrubs of orange and purple that carried a sickly sweet scent, Ryan paused. He knew this was where the bearded fighter had left them, but beyond that…

"Fireblast, where do we go from here?" he breathed.

Doc sighed. "A dilemma. Friend LaRue adopted an admirable policy in leading us a merry dance back and forth to disguise location, but…"

"It doesn't give us a direct route, even if we can trace

it... and any attempt at a direct route might take us straight into quicksand."

Mildred grinned. "So when has anything like that ever stopped us, then?"

J.B. returned the grin. "Not really any choice, is there?" He took out his minisextant from within his capacious pockets and took note of the sun's position, estimating how long it had been since it had risen. He knew where the rebel settlement was in relation to their position as he had taken a reading before leaving, and from the two he worked out which direction they should take.

"Think we'll be able to follow any of their trails when we come across them?" he asked. "That'd make things easier."

"They're damn good at disguising them," Ryan mused, "but as we used them, we might. Just have to hope so."

They struck out in the direction of the lake and the rebel settlement, hoping that they would be able to shortcut without running across any of the swamp's natural hazards.

They got lucky. After fifteen minutes of floundering through densely packed foliage, the ground beneath their feet treacherously muddy, water seeping from the earth with each step, sucking at their boots, they came upon a trail they recognized. It was faint, but it was there if someone knew what to look for. With a palpable sense of relief, they hit the trail, and had made a rapid progress when they became aware of a rustling—faint, but there—in the bushes and weeds to their left.

Ignoring the wet and muddy conditions underfoot, each of them hit the ground, searching for cover in the low-level grasses as they did so, blasters to hand and ready to fire.

They heard the cocking of a rifle, and then a familiar voice coming from somewhere within the lobster grasses.

"Hell, unless you've got some kind of purpose, I'd have to say that you've got the worst sense of direction I've ever come across. I hope you can control your trigger fingers better."

Emerging from cover, almost seeming to melt and re-form, so subtle was his exit, they saw the old man Beausoleil. He was holding a Sharps rifle, as he had been the first time they had seen him, only this time he held it one-handed, with the barrel pointing up into the sky, a definite gesture of nonaggression.

The companions got to their feet, Doc attempting with little success to brush the mud from his frock coat. Ryan moved toward the old man, but stopped suddenly when Beausoleil raised his free hand.

"Watch," he said quietly, picking up a rock and tossing it into the empty grass between them. Ryan watched it part the blades and land with a dull thunk. The earth seemed to open around the rock and swallow it in a matter of a second or two. Beausoleil grinned at Ryan across the divide. "Good thing you stuck to the path we made, eh?"

Before Ryan had a chance to answer, he had skipped across the divide, years of living in the swamp having given him a knowledge of where his feet could land safely.

"So why are you back? Not that I'm miserable to see your face again, but I figured you were on your way. So I'm guessing that it ain't good news brings you back."

Ryan quickly outlined everything that he and Mildred had heard from the sec wag, and why they had returned. As he spoke, he became aware that the old man's face adopted a more serious mien with almost every word. Even before he had finished, Ryan knew that there was trouble ahead.

Beausoleil told them about the internal schisms within the fighters, and how Jak's solution had been to lead his ragtag army out on the attack.

"Ain't that long since they left, for fuck's sake," he spit.

"This could be really good," Ryan mused.

"In what way?" the old man asked. "How can it be good if they're walking into a firefight and we've got hardly any defenses for when Jean's men come down on us?"

"Think about it," Ryan said urgently. "Dr. Jean isn't sending his sec in for a couple of nights. Before then, Jak's forces will have mounted their attack. If it works, then you don't have anything to worry about."

"And if it don't?"

"Then you're fucked anyway, face it," J.B. put in.

"Thanks for reminding me of that—like I needed reminding," the old man said bitterly.

"Take us back to the ville," Ryan said quickly, not wanting things to degenerate into a round of recriminations. Action would have to be swift if it was to have any effect. "If your people don't have much of a start on us, we might be able to catch up with them, bring Jak up to speed on what's going on. And if we tell the people you have left with you, then at least you can get them prepared to put up some kind of defense if the attack does come."

Beausoleil sighed. "It ain't perfect, but I guess it'll have to do," he said. "C'mon, follow me—and I mean follow. I'm taking you on a short cut."

The companions followed the old man across the swamp. Having seen the speed with which the mud had claimed the rock the old man had tossed into it, they made sure that they followed his footsteps with extreme caution. He was following no path they had ever seen before, and it was a matter of minutes before they found themselves on the outskirts of the settlement. Word of their arrival spread quickly, and the old and children—the only ones left—gathered to hear what they had to say.

Considering they were down to the bare bones, and they were facing annihilation unless the companions could reach Jak's force and assist them in achieving their goal, the few remaining settlement dwellers took the news with considerable fortitude and stoicism. Under Beausoleil's command, they immediately began to make plans for the defense of their settlement, should it come to that. The old weren't afraid to buy the farm, and the young were perhaps too young to really comprehend what might happen, but the phlegmatic manner in which they began to work said everything about why they had stuck out against Jean's regime for so long.

In the meantime, Beausoleil left his people to their tasks and took the companions to the point were the rebel force had begun its journey to Lafayette. He led them some way into the swamp and away from the settlement.

"They came this way. They were gonna cut across the usual trails and make a more direct route. The idea was that by moving during the day they wouldn't have to worry about the sec patrols until they were actually into West Lowellton. Moving quick enough, they should do that by sundown."

Having identified the trail taken by the rebel force, the old man left them to it, opting to return quickly to the settlement and assist in mounting a defense in case of the attack taking place.

With no words other than a swift farewell, he was gone, leaving them to take the trail on their own. It soon became apparent why he felt that his tracking skills weren't necessary—the trail was easy to follow. On his own, Jak would have left no trace, and they would have had no chance of following in his wake. Even with the swamp dwellers, they would have expected things to be difficult. Those who acted as sec, like LaRue and Prideaux, were adept at leaving little trace of the trails and paths that they used. But the force that had set out for Lafayette had left a trail that was obvious. It was as though Jak had opted for speed over stealth.

That wasn't like him. It suggested the speed was as much to keep the force together as to surprise the enemy. That he hadn't bothered about the trail they left in their wake suggested that he was having enough trouble controlling a force that was undisciplined and moving in many different directions.

An army like that was never going to be easy to control.

Much less to direct successfully.

It looked like Jak was having problems.

HIS TACTIC HAD BEEN simple. They had to move swiftly and attack with an equal speed. That would prevent the members of the army arguing among themselves. And yet he couldn't afford to risk splitting them up into small groups that could travel without being detected. With the fighters out of his earshot, there was no knowing what kind of arguments they might fall into. If the plan had any chance of working at all, then he had to keep them together.

To move such a mass of people without leaving a trace was an immense risk, and one that he wouldn't have wished to undertake in the normal course of things. But he couldn't see that he had any choice. It rankled that they were leaving an easily traceable trail in their wake, but he could see no other way of getting them into position without any more internal factions forming.

Jak didn't realize that the only people following his trail were the companions. Even if he had, he wouldn't have had the time to stop and wait. His plan—such as it was—demanded swift movement with no time to rest or for the fighters to stop and think… and worry—about what they were doing.

By the time the sun had begun to sink, they had spent all day trekking through the swamp. The army marched in an almost silence, only a few daring to voice any thoughts, and these being almost whispers that died quickly for being ignored by the others.

As the darkness began to fall, an air of nervousness began to sweep through sections of the army. They knew that the sec patrols would be out before long, and they knew that a large force such as theirs was easy to spot.

Jak could feel the tension as it began to spread. By his reckoning, they were less than five hundred yards from the edge of West Lowellton. Once they reached the old sub-urb, there would be plenty of places to hide from the out-going patrols.

"Keep alert," he whispered, spreading the message

back through the ranks. "Nearly at edge of old ville. Safe there."

"Man, easy for him to say. Wish I could feel the same way," LaRue said uneasily, some five yards back in a phalanx of fighters.

Prideaux grinned at him, a smile that held no humor, only contempt. "You starting to get a little nervous, mebbe? Wish you'd stayed at home with the women and children?"

"Listen, stupe, there's a lot of women here who'd have your balls for that," LaRue growled by way of reply. "And I figure you'd have to be some kind of crazy not to get a little nervous. This ain't gonna be easy."

"Sure, ass-boy, you say what you want," Prideaux replied with a knowing wink.

LaRue was infuriated. He hated Prideaux anyway, but hated him even more when the bastard seemed able to see inside his head and know that, for all the bravado, he was shitting himself with fright. As far as he was concerned, a person would have to be a fool not to be frightened of the odds. But he couldn't let Prideaux know this.

The rebel force had now reached the edge of the old city, and had the stretch of barren ground that led from the swamp to the first crumbling remains of the old suburb. A few hundred yards of lobster grass and a few vines that crawled along the ground—the swamp was beginning to encroach upon the predark remains, but not with enough fervor to provide them with cover.

Jak divided the force into small groups of six and seven, sending them across to scuttle into the shadows of the ruined buildings, providing cover while they ran. He sent

Marissa with the first group trusting her to keep them together until all the rebel army had gained the city.

Jak moved in the last group, outpacing the other guerrillas as he sprinted across the open ground. He turned and
watched the last of his group make the safety of darkness.
In the distance, over the chanting that always sounded
from the walled ville at night, he could hear the rumble
of the sec wags as they left the enclosure to take the old
road out of the city and on to their regular patrol routes.

Ushering them into the cover of the shadows surrounding the building debris, Jak waited while the sec wags
drew near. The rumble grew louder and the tension he
could feel rippling among the rebel army grew more and
more taut.

The wags rumbled past, their cargo of sec men oblivious to the fighters waiting in the darkness. The last of the
convoy went past and beyond them into the darkness of the
swamp. There was an almost palpable release of tension
among those who were hiding in the rubble, and some even
exchanged a few whispered words of encouragement.

"C'mon, let's get moving," Marissa whispered, her
voice carrying back over the assembled army. The relieved swamp dwellers stirred from their positions and
began to move toward the old road, feeling safe now that
the sec convoy had passed.

Jak strained his hearing, trying to pinpoint something
over the hubbub of the rebel force. He wanted to quiet
them while he tried to work out what was disturbing him,
making him feel uneasy, but it was too late for that: under
Marissa's direction they had started to move out.

Jak moved through the mass of the guerrilla army, catching up to Marissa. "Wait," he said, "go triple red."

"Why?" she asked, her face clouding. "What's the matter?"

"Dunno—just…"

Jak never got to finish. His words were broken by the chatter of SMG fire and the scream of one of the rebels, who had been hit in the shoulder and upper arm by the spray.

"Cover, now!" Jak yelled, hoping that his shout would galvanize the guerrillas. The sudden fire had shocked them into staying frozen, easy targets out in the open.

Scrambling into the burned-out shell of an old shop-front, Jak headed for the rear immediately, skirting around the back of the old building until he came to an alley. Down the far end, out in the street but just around a bend—and so unsighted—from where the rebels had been walking, he could see a sec wag. It had been part of the convoy, but had been delayed by a mechanical problem. It was obvious from the way that the hood of the vehicle was raised, as though the driver had been working on it. The sec men who had been sitting in back had heard the rebels as they had come out of hiding, and were now trying to pin them down with fire from their AK-47s and MP-5s.

There were six sec men, and they had positioned themselves in cover behind groupings of rubble or half-demolished walls. However, because of the angle they needed to get a clear shot, dictated by the bend in the road, they were leaving themselves exposed to an attack from the rear.

Six was too many for Jak to take on alone without driving some of them deeper into cover. There was already some returned fire from the guerrillas to keep them pinned into position. Now he needed to go back and get a couple of other fighters to come with him and pick them off from a position behind their lines.

Running, picking his way over the rubble at the rear of the old row of shopfronts, Jak returned to where the guerrillas were clustered. There were some on each side of the road, with a no-man's-land between. Marissa was on the far side with about half the rebels. Prideaux was on this side, and Jak went to him.

"Need you and LaRue come with me. Go around back of these stupes, hit 'em in the ass quick. None of "em covering each other."

Prideaux nodded. "I'm with you. Dunno where LaRue is, though."

"Shit——mebbe he's on other side."

"I'll do it," one of the other rebels volunteered. She was Marissa's age, perhaps a little younger, and wielding a Lee Enfield like she knew what to do with it.

"You sure, Claudine?" Prideaux asked.

"Rather do that than stay here and get shot or die of fuckin' boredom waiting for them to run out of ammo," she said with a grim smile.

Jak nodded. "Good—we go now." He looked across to where the other group of fighters was pinned down. He could see Marissa in the dim light, and gestured to her that he was headed around the back of their opponents. She nodded, and directed her soldiers to keep up a suppressing fire. If she could pin down the sec men as they had tried to pin her people, then it would make Jak's task easier.

Jak took Prideaux and Claudine out through the back of the old shopfront and along to the alley. Silently, he led them as far toward the street as he dared, and indicated the positions of the sec men. There were the six who had been in back of the wag, and the driver, who was huddled in his cab. He was frantically scrabbling with some wiring in the dash, clearly visible through the open door, and Jak hoped that meant that any radio contact he might have had with the ville had been broken.

Jak indicated which of the sec men he wanted the fighters to take out and began to move forward. They had to get as close to the mouth of the alley as they could before acting. Surprise was the key.

The sec men were concentrating on the rebels they had pinned, almost without realizing that they, too, had been pinned. Jak led his small force to the lip of the alley, then indicated that they should attack.

The driver was the only one to realize what was happening. He looked up from his dash and saw the three rebels in the alley. He opened his mouth to yell a warning, but got no further than a death rattle as Jak's Magnum round ripped a hole where his nose used to be, the exit wound splattering his brains against the far door of the cab.

The direction of the shot made the sec men whirl, almost as one. But again, their reflexes were just that little too slow. Claudine took the two nearest, sinking to one knee and ignoring her own lack of cover, concentrating instead on rattling off two accurate shots that drilled holes in their foreheads. Prideaux took two who were at the edge of the bend, running and going into a forward roll to avoid the shots that kicked up dust around his feet, coming up firing. The Smith & Wesson he was using was in a two-handed grip to steady it, the volley of four shots striking home three times, the fourth hitting a block of concrete where his chilled target had already slipped down.

Jak went for the two who were farthest away. He figured that as leader he should take the biggest chances. And in having already taken out the driver, he gave himself a bit more to do. It was a fraction of a second spent readjusting his position, but it was enough for the two sec men to turn and open fire on him.

He used the side of the wag as cover, diving beneath and wriggling across the tarmac, Colt Python raised enough to snap off a shot as soon as he could sight one of his opponents. It didn't hit home, but it did deflect the man's fire, his own shot smacking into the boards on the side of the wag. Before he had a chance to aim again, Jak took him out with a shot that hit him in the gut, the soft nose of the Magnum shell spreading inside him, the percussion waves turning his internal organs to jelly.

Before the man was even chilled, Jak had switched to the remaining sec man, who was lining him up. It was a question of whose reflexes were quicker. The sec man's fire went high and wide as he fell back, a single slug from Jak's Magnum pistol tearing a hole in his throat and neck, rupturing the carotid and throwing him off balance.

There should have been silence, but now they were being fired on by their own people, who were unaware that the danger was being eradicated and that they could cease their suppressing fire.

Jak and Prideaux were in no mood to appreciate the

irony as they squirmed back into the cover of the alley, avoiding their own force's fire to join Claudine in the cover of the alley.

"Let's get back and shut them the fuck up," she said. "They're wasting ammo."

As they regained their original position, and the realization that they had been successful spread through the guerrilla force, Jak felt something that was, if not a sense of optimism, then at least a glimmer of hope. The rebels had stuck together and achieved their first victory. This had lightened the atmosphere among them. Moreover, in Claudine he had found at least one more fighter in whom he could have some faith.

The two groups came out of cover and came together again in the middle of the road.

"Got keep it triple alert now," Jak warned. "Mebbe others like that sec patrol out there."

"Hell, we'll trash the fuckers if there are," Marissa said with a grin, ignoring Jak's pointed stare. He was concerned that the rebels would get too cocksure and careless unless he kept hammering the point home.

"Jak's right," Prideaux cautioned. "We need to keep it cool and keep ourselves covered. We got caught too easily there. If it had been more than one wag, then we would have been fucked."

He turned to Jak. "Mebbe we should have a scout party go on ahead, just two or three of us, to check the way's clear."

Jak grinned. "Good idea. You want go?"

"Yeah, me an' that stupe bastard LaRue can do that sort of shit in our sleep. Not much difference doing it in the ville as opposed to the swamp."

"Okay," Jak agreed. "You and LaRue. Where is he?"

Marissa frowned. "He was with us until the blasting started. Now he's gone. Fuck it, I wouldn't have had him figured as running scared."

LaRue was triple stupe. He knew he was. In fact, he didn't know what the hell had come over him. He'd been fighting all his life in the swamps, and a little bit of blasterfire had never disturbed him before. But here, in the old ville, where you didn't know the layout and where that feeling was so intense that it took you over.

He'd run. He didn't know why or where, but he'd just taken off like a hare being chased by a mangy old cur. And now he had no idea where he was. Could he go back and find the others? They had to have noticed that he was gone by now. What would they have to say to him? Or would they just chill him there and then as a liability?

Fuck it, he didn't know what to do. And he didn't know anything about this damn ville. He was completely lost, stumbling blindly from building to building, across roads littered with rubble and those that were completely clear, until he had no notion of where he was, where the walled ville was, or where the guerrillas were.

He could hear nothing but the blood pounding in his ears, the sound of his own terror. Perhaps this was why he didn't hear the sec wag as it approached. Before his radio had shorted in the same electrical burn-out that had killed his engine, the wag driver who had just been chilled had got off a message to the walled section of Lafayette to send a replacement wag for the sec patrol, and a mechanic.

This wag was now on its way, and its path was about

to intersect with that of LaRue as he stumbled around a blind corner, no longer knowing where he was going.

Above the sound of his own blood pumping it was the high-pitched squeal of the brakes that he heard, not the dull roar of the engine that meant the wag was on top of him before he had a chance to see it. He yelled, stumbled backward, and felt a jarring run through his body from head to foot as the near-side fender of the wag caught him. His backward momentum saved him from being chilled as it meant he rolled with the force of the blow.

He was saved further pain from the impact by a blow on the back of the head as he struck a piece of raised concrete on the old sidewalk.

All became blissful, oblivious black.

"HE'S COMING TO, now."

LaRue heard the voice rather than saw anything, as his eyes were still closed, and the voice sounded as though it came from a distance, through a fog. Distorted, and not real.

He opened his eyes and it was real enough. He was lying on the floor in a room lit only by candles that were placed on ornate holders around the room. The floor was soft, covered by thick carpets and rugs. Everything was muted, in oranges and purples that were dull in the dim lighting. Huge chairs and sofas were scattered about, and an oak table covered in papers took the center of the room.

The speaker had been a sec man, dressed in the dyed camou. He was about fifty, with a slightly protruding gut and an MP-5 holstered on his left side. He had scars on his chin and across his forehead, and his eyes were dark with pinprick pupils. They bore into LaRue.

"Good, let me talk to him." A huge man hove into view. He was dark and leonine, with immensely powerful shoulders, dragging one leg with a limp. He was wearing a cloak and tunic, with dark leggings that disappeared into highly polished leather boots. His face was dark with anger, and his eyes, too, bore the pinprick pupils of a heavy jolt user.

LaRue lost control, soiling himself as he realized where he had seen the man: he was in the presence of Dr. Jean himself.

The big man laughed as he sniffed the air. "I see you've realized where you are, fool," he commented. "Now I want to know just who the hell you scum think you are? Taking out a few of my men isn't gonna do anything more than make me mad as hell. See—oooh, I'm scared," he added mockingly, putting his face up close to LaRue's and enjoying seeing the man back away, wincing.

"You must be one of the disbelievers who hides in the swamp," he continued. "But you've got brave all of a sudden, haven't you? Still, it'll save me a task rooting you all out if you're coming to me to be chilled. Oh, yes," he continued, enjoying the look of shock on LaRue's face, "I was sending my boys in two nights from now, so you've done me a little favor."

His tone had been mocking, almost gentle. But now it changed as he suddenly grasped LaRue, pulling him to his feet and then up off them, using his height and reach to dangle the smaller man. Now his voice had a harsh, unforgiving edge.

"Now listen to me, you sniveling, pathetic piece of turd. There must be a reason you people have gotten brave and decided to attack now, and I want to know why. And I want to know how many of you there are. And I want to know just how the hell you intend to get in, 'cause I doubt you're gonna come knocking on the door, asking nicely. And I guess there's only one way to find out."

Still holding the man at arm's length, Dr. Jean strode from the room, preceded by the sec man. They walked down a corridor and ascended three flights of stairs, lit by neon light. There was a sec man at a door on each level, but not one even acknowledged that the baron had passed, standing impassive.

Dr. Jean carried LaRue, weeping and gibbering to himself, with his own mess running down his leg, into a room whose door had been opened by the sec man. Inside was an array of electrical equipment, and in the center of the room stood a chair with leather wrist and ankle straps. Dr. Jean flung LaRue into the chair, and the sec man deftly strapped the man's wrists and ankles before he had a chance to even register what had happened to him.

At a gesture from the baron, the sec man then took a knife and ripped LaRue's shirt and pants, pulling the material away so that he sat naked. Meanwhile, the baron switched on a generator and fiddled with an amp meter. This would have struck terror into his own people, who would have known what was coming. LaRue was scared, but also confused. Red-hot pokers and blades he understood, but he had no experience of electricity.

However, he wasn't so stupid as to hazard a guess when Dr. Jean connected electrode clips to his genitals and nipples. These hurt enough on their own, and he had a notion that it would be nothing compared to the main event.

"No, you don't have to do that," he cried. "Look, I'll tell you. It's a stupe idea and it was never going to work anyway." Pleading for his life, he poured out all he knew, hoping it would be enough to save him. He told Dr. Jean about Jak, and about the old sewer the recce party had used, and that the guerrillas would be using. "That's all it is. Now please, I beg of you, don't chill me. I could join you. I can see how wrong I was before."

Dr. Jean smiled mirthlessly. "Nice try. But y'see, all you've done here is spoil my fun, and that just pisses me off." He held out his hand and the sec man handed him a machete. "I do so hate to have my fun spoiled," Jean said mildly before hacking into LaRue's head and chest with the blade, repeatedly stabbing and hacking around his neck until the blade was slick with blood and the man's cries were drowned in his own gore. He was chilled after the first halfdozen blows, but the baron continued, hacking until he had nearly managed to sever the head, and he was soaked in the chilled man's blood.

He blew heavily as he stepped back, handing the machete to the watching sec man.

"Thank you, Diamond," he said mildly. "I appear to have made a terrible mess. Get it cleaned up, will you? But first, I think we have something to attend to."

Chapter Thirteen

"Dark night! Sounds like there's already a full-scale fire-fight going on," J.B. breathed as they sunk farther into the cover of the ruined buildings on the edge of West Lowell-ton.

"If there is, then who the hell are they fighting?" Mildred questioned. "I don't know about you, but I counted them all out."

"Only one way we're going to find out," Ryan said decisively. "We've got to follow the sound of the firefight."

"Follow the drum," Doc mused. "How appropriate for the way we live."

"Think I see what you mean, Doc, but now really isn't the time for any philosophy," Krysty told him.

At an indication from Ryan, they moved out of cover and began to progress stealthily along the roads that criss-crossed the old suburb, cutting across ruined buildings to keep cover and save time as they sought the source of the blasterfire.

They hadn't let up their pace since leaving the swamp settlement that morning. Keeping close on the obvious trail left by the guerrilla army, they had soon worked out that speed and not stealth was Jak's aim. He had taken a direct route and hadn't rested along the way. Their own

momentum had carried them toward the old ville of Lafayette, and in the same way the companions had marched
without respite to keep within distance of the main army.
It was imperative that they try to catch them before they
entered the walled ville. After that, who could tell what
would happen.

They had still been in the swamp when an ominous
rumble in the distance had warned them that the sec patrol
wags were emerging in their nightly convoy. They had
taken shelter in the undergrowth and watched as the wags
rolled past, silently waiting for the moment when they
would dismount and begin their nightly circuits of the
swamp.

After the last of the wags had rolled past, they had
waited still, the notion that there may be some stragglers
among the vehicles a possibility, albeit an unlikely one.
After a nerve-stretching interval, Ryan had signaled
that they should proceed. They had made their way
through to the edge of the bayou and across into the remains of the old suburb with no problems, and had
paused only when they heard the sounds of a distant
firefight.

"Which way?" Ryan asked J.B. as they moved once
more.

The Armorer indicated to the north west, across a row
of half-demolished apartments and past the remains of the
old hotel they had searched during their first visit to the
suburb, some years before.

"I'd say it's coming from over there, which makes it
certain that it must be Jak's people."

"Why certain?" Mildred asked.

"Because it's on the way to the walled part of Lafayette and is probably the route they would take," Krysty said. "Am I right?"

J.B. agreed. "That's the way I figure it."

"Then perhaps we should make some speed and attempt to assist our friend and his little band of angels in their struggle," Doc said, directing this to Ryan.

The one-eyed warrior grinned. "I was just about to say that, Doc. Keep in cover. They might not think to ask who we are before firing on us if we sneak up on them too quickly," he added.

Using the cover of the buildings, they headed toward the source of the noise. It had also occurred to them that there had to be another party in the firefight, and if the sec convoy had already left the old ville, then it meant that there was at least one sec party roaming free within the ruins. If there was more than that one party, then they had no wish to confront them.

The trouble was, they knew that Jak's plan would be to hit fast and with stealth. That surprise element was almost certain to be removed now that this firefight had broken out. So he'd probably need all the tactical and combat experience he could get beside him. They had to balance keeping out of sight of any patrols with getting to Jak before he reached the walled ville.

As suddenly as the firefight had begun, silence fell over the ruined suburb. Not even an echo of a blaster shot hung in the air.

"Shit, why has it gone quiet?" Ryan asked.

"Mebbe they've overcome the sec patrol. They probably had the numbers," J.B. mused.

"The problem is, we need them firing to pinpoint where they are. How the hell are we going to find them now?"

"We know where they're headed," Krysty said. "If we head off that way, then we should be able to head them off before they reach that sewer outlet you mentioned."

"Yeah, that should— What's that?" he asked suddenly, his tone changing as he caught the faintest of sounds carried on the air.

"Take cover—it's at eight o'clock," J.B. snapped, his ears attuning to the sound quicker than anyone else.

They were close enough to the opening of an apartment building to use the lobby as shelter. A few wrecked couches and a torn and stained carpet were all that remained of its previous existence, the elevator doors showing a permanent out-of-order sign.

The sound resolved itself into footsteps—running—and a heavy, panicked breathing. As they watched, LaRue ran past them.

Doc stepped forward to leave the shelter of the lobby and hail the man. Ryan held out a restraining hand.

"My dear boy—" Doc began, bewildered.

Ryan shook his head. "Why's he running? Who's chasing him?"

A look of understanding spread across Doc's features and he drew back into the shadows of the lobby.

Yet there was no other sound than that of the bald swamp rebel as he ran, his footsteps and labored breathing getting farther away with each second. There were no other footsteps, no sounds of a wag in pursuit.

"I don't get it," Krysty said. "If there's no one chasing him, then why is he running like that?"

"Yeah, and is he running to find the others, or away from where they were?" Mildred asked with a raised eyebrow. "Either way, it can't be good to have him running around loose."

Ryan agreed. "Let's get after him, and try to find out what the hell is going on."

Keeping close to the walls of the ruined buildings, with an escape route to cover only a few steps away at any given moment, they slipped out of the ruined lobby and chased after LaRue. He had turned left at the corner, and J.B. hoped that the left turn didn't lead to a junction with five separate roads leading off. He wanted to keep the swamp dweller in sight and not have to split their own force to find him. That could be self-defeating. It kept nagging at him: what had made LaRue run? Some problem within the rebel army, some kind of infighting breaking out? Or were there extra sec patrols because of Dr. Jean's intention to strike out for the rebel ville?

Either way, it could cause an immense problem for them now they were here and looking for Jak. Furthermore, if there were extra sec patrols and LaRue was to run into one of them on his own, there was no way he could neutralize them all—and so the rebel presence would be widely known. He would never have said it out loud, but he knew that the others thought it, too.

The road that turned left was straight for about four hundred yards: yet there was no sign of LaRue along its length.

"Where the fuck has he gone?" Ryan whispered, bewildered.

Krysty silenced him with a gesture. "Listen…" she whispered.

It was there, faint, but still audible—La Rue's footsteps echoing through the mouth of a ruined building about a hundred yards ahead and to their right. He was breaking through the rubble wherever possible, as though he had a definite goal.

Maybe he did—they'd have to catch him to find out.

The companions set off after the fleeing man, trying to keep to speed with him. It was difficult, as the building he had chosen was littered with treacherous debris that moved underfoot, threatening to twist and disable feet and ankles with one wrong step. Some of the upper floors had also caved in, leaving great hills of rubble that extended up through a hole in the ceiling. They had to move around it, and work out where LaRue had run to. The enclosed space acted like an echo chamber, making his footsteps more audible, but also bouncing echoes of the walls, making direction hard to determine.

It was only when he became briefly visible exiting the ruins that they were able to determine his direction. Setting off in his wake, they came to the rear of the building as LaRue was breaking for the far corner of the street, heading toward the walled ville.

That they didn't follow was determined by the sound they heard in the distance. Lingering in the well of the ruined building, Ryan stayed the others with an arm.

"Listen—" he whispered.

"Sounds like a wag, and coming fast," J.B. added.

It was: a sec wag responding to the radio call of the malfunctioning wag that the rebels had attacked. As the companions watched, they could see LaRue run blindly toward it, some two hundred yards from them. He cut across the corner of the road and ran directly in front of the wag.

"What in the name of the Three Kennedys is he doing?" Doc breathed. "The fool, he is bound to be caught."

"If he isn't chilled first," Mildred said. She could see that he was about to be hit by the wag, and figured that a direct impact might just buy the farm for him.

She was wrong. At the last minute, the man's instincts—blunted for so many minutes by his fear—took over, and he noticed the wag racing toward him. He tried to pull back, stumbled and fell backward. The wing of the sec wag clipped him, and he hit the ruptured tarmac and broken concrete with a sickening thug. The sec crew were out of the wag in an instant, surrounding him.

"We can take them," Mildred said calmly. "There's only four of them, and we've got surprise—"

"No, it's too late for that," Ryan said. "Why are there only four of them? Where are the others? Besides, by the time we reach them they could already have raised a warning."

"But we can't let them take him," Mildred said.

"We'll have to. Mebbe they'll torture him for information, but I figure he'll hold long enough. We've got to think of the bigger picture."

"Which is, exactly?" Mildred said angrily.

"Which is that we let Jak and his army know that Dr. Jean now knows about them. And then we help him get another plan," J.B. said calmly. "We go after LaRue, then mebbe we lose more lives in the long run," he added.

Mildred glared at him, then at Ryan. She looked to Krysty and Doc for support, but she already knew they would back Ryan. In truth, she knew that he was right. But the thought of losing one man was as painful to her as losing many. Sometimes there were no easy choices.

THE VID SCREENS on the street corners stopped pumping out their bland eulogies to the glories of Dr. Jean, and what sounded like Klaxon erupted. The noise cut through the hubbub of the neon-lit city and caused the people on the streets to look up, penetrating even their jolt-induced stupor. In every building that was inhabited during the hours of darkness—the factories in which the workers toiled on the weapons and old tech that Dr. Jean was seeking to develop, the brothels that serviced the workforce, the bars that fed them liquor laced with powerful narcotics, the trading posts that sold clothing, blasters and food—there were vid screens that were permanently broadcasting, as on the streets. These, too, saw the people react to the sudden alarm. Work ceased, transactions were stopped halfway through, drinks were put down, couples stopped screwing in midhump. All responded to the frequency of the alarm as it cut through to some part of their brain unclouded by the drugs or hypnosis, and tuned to respond to the signal.

The face of the baron appeared on the screen.

"In two nights' time I planned to mount a raid on the last remaining scum that stood between ourselves and the complete domination of the bayou. A small, insignificant number of people, they had nonetheless succeeded in hiding themselves away like canker that festers in a sore. In much the same way, they had made themselves an irritant on the skin of our glorious regime. So, much as you would lance a boil, squeeze the pus from a spot, or clean out the festering pus in a wound, I had decided to rid us of this irritation. Having located the sickness, it was time to burn it out.

"But, with an audacity that I find breathtaking and, at the same time, incredibly stupe, they have decided to attack our ville this very night. They have a childishly and cretinously simple plan, which involves using the sewers to gain access under the walls. An appropriate manner in which to enter when you consider the shit that these people are. Why, you may wonder, do I not just send a force into the area beyond the walls and wipe them from the face of the earth?"

Dr. Jean paused and smiled. To anyone under his spell, it would have seemed the mark of a benevolent leader. For anyone else, there was a cold malice in the smile that would have chilled the blood. He continued.

"Because, my people, I feel that it would be a good way for you to show your love and loyalty by dealing with this yourselves. I shall tell you where they will enter our ville, and I want you to mobilize so that you have your own quarters defended in case of attack. Look on it as an exercise in how well you can work together. Strength through unity, my friends. That is the key. That is our strength.

"Defend your own quarters and be ready. Those of you who live on Fifth and Vine will be aware now that in the backyard of dormitory seven there is a cover over the sewer. It is in this yard that the intruders shall emerge. I will be sending you a detail of sec to assist you in the eradication of the rebel army. I want most of them chilled straight away. Do not waste time on them. But there are those who I wish to be made an example of, and offered as a sacrifice to the gods who guide us.

"We must work together on this. I have faith in my people, for they are as one. That is all."

The screens went blank for a second before the regular broadcasts returned. But the atmosphere in the ville had changed. It was now more highly charged than it had been a few minutes before, with an edge of anticipation for the fight ahead.

DR. JEAN LAUGHED as he sat back in his chair. It was an old leather-covered swivel chair set behind what had once been the newsdesk of the local Lafayette cable news channel. The equipment within had somehow survived the nukecaust relatively unscathed, and had been ignored by looters as it held no interest for them. But it had held an immense interest for Dr. Jean when he had first established his ville. He had enough knowledge of old tech, and access to equipment in enclaves he had discovered during his time in the wilderness, hiding from those who sought revenge against anyone associated with the old Baron Tourment, to know that he could get this old tech studio working again, and use the cable lines to set up vid screens in every building and on every street corner. There would no escape, no solitude safe from the word of Dr. Jean.

And it was at times like this that he felt the most proud of his achievements. That had been Tourment's trouble, and something from which Jean had learned—keeping a population in its place by terror was a useful means of control, but it was a sure way of building a long-term resentment as well as using a vast amount of sec resources. He had no plans for making such a mistake. He used propaganda, used the old tech to feed them a constant diet that told them how lucky they were to live in Lafayette, how they could only prosper with such a leader at the helm. How much he did for them, and, indeed, in many ways he could be said to have furnished them with a relatively comfortable life within the walls of his Lafayette.

But at a cost. There was always a cost.

Time for action. Dr. Jean hauled himself out of the chair, ignoring the lackeys who operated his equipment, and beckoned to the sec man who had been with him when he chilled LaRue. The scarred man approached him cautiously. He was Dr. Jean's sec chief, and had worked closely with him since he had established the walled ville within the old Lafayette; and yet, he still knew next to nothing about the baron and his plans. And, if truth be told, he was scared to find out; scared of the power and hate that this giant held within his frame.

"Sir," he said as he approached, trying to keep the tremor from out of his voice.

"Walk with me, Diamond, I have something to tell you," Dr. Jean said mildly. He was always at his most dangerous when his tone was that mild, and as the stocky sec chief fell in beside the baron he felt the apprehension grow within his breast.

The two men set out for the baron's chambers, which were two blocks from the old studio. As they walked through the streets, those they passed fell to their knees and sang praises for the ebony giant, who barely acknowledged their presence. Some came up to him, seemingly just for the privilege of touching his cloak. He pushed them away and they fell to the ground, writhing in an ecstasy that would, in predark days, have been called evangelical. Even to be manhandled by the baron was a joy: he had touched them. That was enough.

It always sent a ripple of fear through Diamond, the sec chief, to see this happen. Everyone was armed, and the baron took no precautions. Before he could have had a chance to draw his own blaster, the baron could have been chilled from anywhere, by anyone. Yet the people were totally in thrall to him. He could do anything. Probably would. That was what seemed so scary.

Dr. Jean didn't speak to Diamond for the whole of the two blocks. They covered the distance in a short time. Despite his limp, the baron moved swiftly, with long strides that had a rolling, irregular rhythm to them. Perhaps he was just concentrating on this, or perhaps he had something to impart that he wanted no one else to hear.

Diamond was soon to find out. They ascended the stairs in the block where the baron had his throne room, past the sec guards on each level, and past the torture room—the body of LaRue had been removed—and three women with buckets and brushes were scrubbing the blood from the floor and walls, chanting along to the messages and imprecations that came out of the vid screen as they worked.

In fact, Dr. Jean didn't speak until they were in the throne room, alone. He slumped into the large wooden chair he used as a throne and rested his forehead in one vast palm.

"They have played into my hands, perhaps made it eas-

ier for me, and yet I will not be happy until the task is completed," he muttered. Diamond said nothing, knowing
from past experience that all speech from the baron was
rhetorical. Raising his face to look at the sec chief, and
raising his voice to a proportionate level, he continued.
"Hidden away in the swamp, they've been a bastard to
find, and thorn in my paw for too long. This way, they've
made it easy to take them by coming right out into the
open. At the same time, they've given me a chance to
show the people what they can do if they pull together, if
they follow me. That much is good."

He lapsed into silence. Diamond waited, knowing that
his role was to be silent, and act when he was ordered...when the order finally came. Eventually, Dr. Jean.
continued.

"I want you to send our best fighters to the location the
scumsucker swamp rat told us about. I want twenty men,
with enough blasters to take out five times that many. I
want whoever is leading this arrogant little party to be
spared if possible—I have plans for them. Remember,
Diamond, I want them to take no chances. I want them to
be there ahead of the people that live on that block and in
that dorm building."

"Sir," Diamond said simply. It was one word alone, but
there had to have been something in his tone that made
the baron look up sharply. He could see the confusion
written large in the sec chief's face, and yet the unwill-
ingness to face his wrath by asking the questions that
strained at the leash. This pleased Dr. Jean, and he decided
to grant Diamond an answer to his unspoken query.

"You are wondering, are you not, why I want a sec

force to get there first and not allow the people to do the job, especially as I made great play of telling them that this was to be their chance to prove themselves."

Diamond, not quite knowing what to do, settled for a halfhearted and nervous shrug. It made the Baron erupt into gales of laughter. He rose from his throne, put his arm around the sec chief's shoulder, and guided him to the window looking out over the walled ville, pulling back a heavy purple-velvet drape so that the electrically lit night intruded on the candlelight of the throne room.

"Look at them, Diamond. They love me. Because I tell them to, because I give them jolt and guide their thoughts and actions. Because I give them food and shelter. Yes, I work them hard, but they are rewarded for it. The problem, my friend, is that they do not fight. And the food they eat is diseased. No matter how much we try, this accursed bayou is full of disease that eats at their strength and bodies. And there is the pox brought in by those gaudy shirts we have traded for; they do their jobs, but they spread drip-dick and pox sores with every fuck. The people we have here are debilitated by their lives. When I get beyond the bayou, I will have strong people—sluts without disease, food that is healthy. And yes, these people will come with me. Some of them. Those that survive.

"But not yet. And not now. I tell you, Diamond, I know these people would chill each other if I asked them. They would try to chill the swamp scum. But I cannot be sure of them, because the food and sex that helps bind them to me also makes them weak. You do not send children to do a man's job. They are children. Your sec are the men.

"Now do you understand?"

Diamond looked into the face of his baron. There was a darkness in the deep pits of his eyes that chilled the sec chief to the bone. He hadn't understood more than every other word, and yet he nodded eagerly, not wanting to anger the man who terrified him.

Dr. Jean sighed. "Of course you don't. Just go and do as I say, Diamond."

The sec chief scuttled from the throne room, leaving the baron to look out over the ville. Dr. Jean heard the door shut behind him, knew his orders would be obeyed. He sighed once more, and let the drape cover the window, leaving him alone in the candlelit throne room.

Alone as ever.

Shaking his head, he limped across the room to where he kept his ceremonial sword. When the leaders were brought to him, there was work to be done.

Beside the sword was a bow of off-white powder, streaked with yellow. It was a refined version of the drug he fed to his people, more pure and powerful than anything they had known. He laid out two lines and sniffed them, gasping as they hit his sinuses and, shortly after, his frontal lobes.

Shaking his head, he began to finger the razor-honed blade of the ceremonial sword, smiling to himself.

There was work to be done...but work he would now enjoy.

THE GUERRILLA ARMY had made rapid progress from the site of their firefight to the point where they would gain access to the sewers, and thus into the walled ville. With nothing to stop them, they had been unimpeded. The failure to locate LaRue had given some cause for concern, but Jak had opted to ignore his disappearance and press on. It was likely that the man just took fright and was still running. Time was too tight to worry about such things.

The sounds of the walled ville grew louder and more oppressive as they drew closer, until they were at the point where they were almost directly beneath the walls and one of the SMG posts mounted along its length. Keeping an army this big under wraps so close to the enemy was one of Jak's worries, but their own fears served them well in this. The atmosphere was so frightening that it kept them triple cautious and in cover.

Jak reached the pipe first, and under his direction they made enough torches to keep the tunnel well lighted for all of them. They would have to string out and take their time getting down into the sewer itself. There wasn't enough space for a force this big to attain access with the speed Jak would have liked.

At the bottom of the incline he directed the swamp dwellers as they descended. He had decided to send some of them forward while the others descended, in order to keep the bottom end of the pipe clear. He would catch the leaders when the tail end of the army had descended. They set off, following his directions, with torches blazing. Talk was kept to a minimum, in case some noise travel upward.

All the while, Jak mused on the one problem that still bothered him—try as he might, he still couldn't find a truly satisfying solution.

It was simply this: the narrow service shaft that led up into the walled yard behind the dormitory building would only allow for one fighter at a time to ascend. So it would take some time for all his guerrillas to make it up to surface level. Time: that was the problem. He could mount guards and send sentries to warn of anyone who came close to the building, perhaps even take out with stealth those that stumbled upon them. But he could do nothing to cut down that long stretch of time: time for an alarm to be raised, time for a sec force to come and wipe them out.

The plan was thin enough as it was: this just made it seem like a suicide mission.

As Marissa descended—the last of the army, having stayed up top to see the others down safely—Jak gave her the briefest of nods before picking his way through the rebel force to the point where the first fighters were now wading through the effluent from the ville. As Jak had directed, Prideaux was at the head, making sure they took the correct turns at sewer pipe junctions. The alcohol with which they had doused their torches was taking the edge off the stench in the sewer, but the smell of fear was still all pervasive.

To be truthful, Jak didn't blame them for being scared. In fact, part of him hoped that it would give them that adrenaline edge that would power them through the mission.

Prideaux greeted the albino hunter with an inclination of the head. They were only a few hundred yards from the service shaft, marked by the faint rusty streaks of Marissa's blood smeared into the concrete. When they reached the shaft, Jak and Prideaux halted the first wave.

"I'll go first, scout area, then signal," Jak said softly. Prideaux nodded, and watched as Jak scaled the ladder into the dark, claustrophobic tunnel. He pushed against the metal cover, felt it give under the pressure. Gently, he moved it so that he could squeeze out.

The yard was empty, the building beyond in darkness. It seemed to be clear: he scanned the walls, listened carefully to try to pick out anything other than the usual sounds of activity beyond their brick confines. It seemed clear…and yet he was aware of some instinct gnawing at the pit of his stomach telling him there was something very wrong.

Without referring to those beneath him, Jak eased himself out of the service tunnel and stretched aching muscles as he scanned the yard. There was no time to crawl back down and tell them that he was making a recce of the area: Prideaux would know this.

Jak didn't realize how flawed his judgment had been in this case. For while the albino began to move swiftly and silently to the walls, searching for a quick and quiet way in which he could scale them and check out what was going on beyond the confines of the yard, Prideaux was down the bottom of the shaft. He could see the night sky framed by the circle of the service hatch, the darkness seeming light against the black that surrounded it, the few stars shining through the scudding clouds. He felt an overwhelming desire to escape the shit and smell of the sewer.

Jak had disappeared from view. He hadn't turned back and told them there was some kind of problem. Prideaux made a decision that he had no right to make: he decided to get up the ladder and take a look himself. Scooting up the metal rungs, greedily gulping down the cold night air as it hit him, he poked his head out of the service hatch, looking around for Jak. He could see the albino, over by the far wall. Prideaux rightly guessed that he was recce'ing the area, but not that he wanted the guerrillas to wait until he had finished.

To eager to get out of the sewer, Prideaux darted out of sight, slipping down the ladder so that he reached the bottom quickly. Jak heard something and turned quickly, but Prideaux was already out of sight. The albino resumed his careful recce, feeling even more uneasy.

At the bottom of the shaft, Prideaux started to send up the army. Fifty people would take some time to move if he sent them one at a time, so he didn't bother. Knowing Jak was up there, and throwing caution to the winds, he sent them up on the heels of each other, so there were four on the ladder at any given time.

Up in the yard, Jak had found a foothold on the back wall and had lifted himself up, searching for a handhold. Two such holds and he would be at the top, looking over at the alley beyond.

He was only halfway up when he heard the mass exodus from the service tunnel. Momentarily stunned by the stupid action, he froze on the wall, turning his head to see the guerrillas pouring out of the service tunnel. They were easy meat if anyone was watching, as they milled around without a clue as to what to do next.

Why the hell should he think that?

Suddenly, Jak realized what had been bothering him. The sense of oppression that hung over the ville had blunted and distorted his instincts, but they had been nagging at him all the while. Why had he felt the need to look over the back wall? Why would he think that there may be something there?

Because there was. All his preternaturally developed instincts had told him this, and yet, like a stupe, he hadn't been listening to them, as he was too concerned with acting like a brood mother with the guerrilla army.

And now it was too late.

"Cover!" Jak yelled, dropping down the wall and flattening himself to it. The rebels turned at his yell, and then started to scatter as the tops of the walls began to explode into light and sound as blasterfire rent the air.

The members of the sec force sent by Diamond had positioned themselves at the foot of each of the three walls, spread out, and with ladders they could use to scale the walls with speed. They had waited for the first indication of a presence on the far side, and had heard Jak emerge and start to recce the territory. Hearing just one man, and knowing that there were more waiting in the sewers, each section had held its fire. Only when the emergence of the rest of the army became apparent had they decided to act.

Ladders hit the walls, and sec men were scaling them before they had even struck the brick at the crest of the wall. AK-47s and MP-5s were the blaster of choice, with a few Uzis thrown in: anything that could lay down a good, suppressing SMG fire. They wanted to prevent the rebels from making a break for the dormitory building and finding cover. There were sec men waiting in the street beyond, but attaining the cover of the building would give the rebels a stronghold and prolong the firefight. Dr. Jean didn't want that. He wanted the rebel army annihilated, and those leading it to be captured alive—if possible—with a view to sacrifice. That wouldn't be easy if the guerrillas could hole up in the dorm. It wouldn't be what the baron wanted.

And the baron always got exactly what he wanted.

Chapter Fourteen

As the companions drew near to the walled ville, it became apparent that something was occurring within. The atmosphere that hung like a pall over the old city changed—not just in the kind of imperceptible way that could be detected by a doomie like Krysty, but in an almost physical sense that could be felt by J.B., Doc and Ryan. It was as though the monotone note of the chanting and endless devotions to Dr. Jean had suddenly become infused with a sense of purpose unlike anything they had felt before in that region.

"What's going on in there? Why have they suddenly changed?" Doc muttered. "Could it be the swamp army?"

Krysty shook her head. It looked odd, as her normally free-flowing Titian hair was now clamped so tight with the encroaching danger that it didn't ripple with the movement; rather, it stayed close to her skull, moving as though part of the bone.

"It's not that," she said. "It's a different kind of feeling—anticipatory, like they were on the verge of something…like they know the rebels are coming, even though they're not there yet."

"Dark night, that treacherous fuck LaRue has dumped Jak right in the shit," J.B. said, either unmindful of, or ignoring, the irony in his choice of words.

"Yeah, but at least it means that they haven't got their hands on them yet, and they won't be expecting someone else to try to get into their vile another way," Ryan said.

Mildred screwed up her face in exasperation. "Easy to say, Ryan, but just how exactly do we do that?"

On their way toward the walled ville, they had talked on the run about how best to tackle both the ville and the rebel army. The problem was that Jak and the swamp dwellers had thought them long since departed, and if they attempted to catch up with them while they were in the sewers, then the rebels would assume they were being attacked, a firefight would ensue, and at the very least there would be unnecessary casualties. At the worst, they would also alert the sec within the ville of their presence. Nothing could successfully disguise the sound of a firefight underground, and it would easily be traced.

From the looks of things, this last argument no longer mattered. But the problems of approaching the fighters without sparking a firefight still existed.

Now their task was laid bare—to follow the guerrillas would be pointless, as they would risk being fired on, and they would only be walking straight into the same trap—whatever that may be—that was being set for Jak's people. They had a twofold task: to gain access to the walled ville without being observed, and to get themselves into a position where they would be able to support the swamp dwellers when the firefight kicked off.

The second part was considerably easier to achieve than the first. They now stood in the shelter of some ruined buildings that were overlooked by the wall, and were exactly halfway between two SMG posts. Both were manned by two impassive sec men in infrared goggles. The wall was of a uniform height all round, and although its ragged construction meant that there were foot- and handholds all the way around, the problem was that to use any of these brought a person right out into the open and made him or her easy meat for the blasters mounted on their turrets.

There was only one gate in and out of the ville as far as they could see. To try to circle the entire compound looking for any other egress would be too time-consuming, even assuming that one could be found. They had to find a way in quickly to be of any use.

In the state of agitation that Dr. Jean's announcement over the vid monitors had caused, the people had begun to prepare themselves for battle. The sec force had also heard the announcement, and knew that they would soon be receiving their own orders from Diamond. The sec chief had called all sentries off the walls: they knew how the guerrillas were gaining access, and they were required to take part in the annihilation of the rebel army.

"Ryan, I don't believe what I'm seeing," J.B. whispered, indicating as first one, and then both of the sec posts along the wall were vacated by their sentries. "What the fuck is going on?"

"The bastard's preparing a hell of a welcoming party for Jak, that's what," Mildred murmured. "He doesn't know about us—LaRue didn't know about us—and so he's going to use all his men where he thinks the danger's coming from."

Ryan grinned. "Then he doesn't know shit, does he?"

he said softly. "Cover me, just in case one of those fuckers comes back when we least expect it."

Leaving the cover of the ruins, shouldering the Steyr so that he had both hands free, Ryan sprinted across the small open area between the ruined old city and the walled ville of Lafayette. He kept low and zigzagged to make himself a harder target, even though he was pretty sure that no one was watching him. Once he was by the wall, he looked up and around, raking his glance along the top of the wall. It was still deserted.

Finding his handholds, and clamping one combat boot to a jutting piece of concrete, he began his ascent. Moving hand over hand, drawing deep and regular breaths as he hauled his body weight upward, the foothold being mostly for balance, he made it to the top in less than a minute. Raising his head slowly above the level at the top of the wall, he could see the ville spread out beyond him.

There was a no-man's-land of cleared and trampled earth that extended for ten yards before the ville really began. Some of the higher-level buildings had been visible from outside, poking up over the level of the sec wall; but most were two or three stories at most and were protected from view by the wall.

Ryan didn't like the look of the strip of bare earth. They would have to move pretty swiftly to avoid being spotted. On the other hand, the streets and sidewalks he could see were in a state of agitation, so if they could traverse that unseen, then once they were into the throng, they'd be safe.

Anyway, there was no choice. They had to tackle it that way.

Ryan turned, still managing to hug the wall, and beckoned the others. They came out en masse and started to scale the wall. Krysty and J.B. were quickest; Mildred found it more of a problem, and Doc lagged behind. But that was okay. Ryan stayed in position but sent them over the wall, J.B. taking first run, until he was left on the outside with Doc, who—by this time—had just managed to drag himself level with the one-eyed warrior.

"I fear, my dear sir, that I am no longer cut out for some of these physical endeavors," the old man grunted as he attained the crest of the wall.

"Bullshit, Doc. You're here, aren't you?" Ryan replied, giving him assistance by hauling on his arm.

Doc gave Ryan a wry look. "And that, of course, is why you felt it incumbent upon yourself to tarry and assist me, is it not?"

"Just go, Doc," Ryan said, pushing the old man over the top of the wall. He watched him scramble down and run in a crouch across the bare expanse. From his vantage point, he could see the others waiting for him, and he could see that no one seemed to be paying much attention to the wall and to the protective band of empty ground between. Their focus was much more inward, directed to where they knew the swamp dwellers would be exiting.

Ryan dropped from the wall, landing heavily and using the momentum to power his run across the empty space. When he reached the others, they all moved as one from the boundary of the ville and the sec area, slipping into the busy streets. They hadn't exchanged any words about this maneuver, nor had they needed to. They knew one another well enough to read this as the right course of action.

They hadn't been spotted as intruders. If anyone had taken notice as they'd scaled the wall, they hadn't raised an alarm. If they had seen them on the edge of the no-man's land, they had assumed they were involved in some sort of preparation for the defense of the ville.

"You figure you can find our way from here to where we came up before?" Ryan asked the Armorer.

J.B. nodded. "Just follow me."

As he led them through the streets, they could see that the people were moving with a sense of purpose. They seemed to be forming phalanxes that would protect their own piece of territory, as though they had been organized into neighborhood gangs, protecting their turf. Another thing that Ryan and J.B. hadn't noticed before, in their haste during the earlier recce mission, was that these people weren't just detached in the manner of joltheads and those who were under some kind of hypnosis. They were detached because they were dying and diseased. For the first time, they could see the sores and scabs of pox and malnutrition, could see how spindly some of these people were, their flesh wasted by the diseases that ravaged them.

Their apparent insularity from one another was as much a byproduct of just coping with the delirium of their diseases as it was their brainwashed state.

Without having to speak to one another, the companions felt heartened about that. It meant that, although they and the swamp dwellers army were outnumbered, they were probably fitter and faster. These people weren't used to combat, they were not healthy, and their reflexes would be slow, their combat skills—if they had any to begin with—would be rusty.

If they could get to the place where Jak's team would emerge into the ville before the sec force had a chance to cut it off, then they would be able to perhaps mount a counteroffensive from the rear and divide the fire from the Lafayette sec force.

It wasn't much of a plan, but then there wasn't much time or information with which to formulate anything approaching a comprehensive scheme.

But even this strand of hope was whipped from their grasp by the sudden sound of blasterfire emanating from the direction in which they were headed—not just the random fire of a brief skirmish or mistaken identity, but the full-blown sound of an all-out firefight.

"Fuck it," Ryan gritted. "No point trying to slip by unnoticed now. Let's do this fast."

As one, they increased their pace, preparing their blasters and themselves for imminent battle. They had tried to blend in with their surroundings before, but now they were beyond caring. They attracted a few confused glances from the citizens who were preparing their defenses, but they were only five, and they were headed toward the firefight, not away from it. How could they be part of the enemy force?

The insularity of the brainwashed citizens allowed them this swift and unimpeded path with J.B. leading the way. The incessant and unceasing chatter of blasterfire rent the air and grew louder with every second, with every yard covered.

"Dark night," J.B. cursed as they turned the final corner and found themselves faced with an army of sec men mounted along three walls, blasting down into the yard. "It's like a blasted bear pit."

"Still might save the bear," Ryan yelled, bracing himself against a wall for cover and starting to pump out rounds from the Steyr, firing from the hip into the sec men gathered on the nearest wall.

Choosing whatever cover they could find, the other four companions started to fire on the sec force, who were suddenly torn by the activity to their rear. Some tried to turn and fire on the attackers to their rear, falling off the wall and into a hail of fire as they did so. Others tried to ignore the fire behind them, hoping or assuming that someone else would cover them as they continued their assault on the swamp dwellers.

Mildred and J.B. moved behind Ryan, Krysty and Doc, coming out of cover and running back so that they could double around the maze of alley that ran behind the buildings. Each block in the ville was made up of four streets forming a square, with alleyways behind linking the sidewalks on the front of each building. From their initial position, they could fire on two of the three walls that were swarming with Lafayette sec men. But this still left one wall from which the sec force could fire on the swamp dwellers with impunity.

It was this problem that J.B. and Mildred sought to address. By moving around the alley, they intended to attain a position from which they could hit that wall, one from which an uninterrupted stream of fire was raining down into the yard and onto the rebels.

"Hope you know where we're going, John," Mildred panted as they pounded the concrete.

"Trust me," he said, "and hold back when I say."

She was about to ask him why, but saved her breath for

running when she saw him dip into the canvas hardware bag he carried. He took out two grens, both of which were shrapnel grens. As well as their explosive power, they would spread white-hot and razor-sharp shards of metal in a large radius.

It was a gamble. Tossing the grens into the alley would give the pair little or no time to escape, and the enclosed space would ensure a maximum chill from the explosions. But the force would also take out part of the wall, and the danger was that some of the shrapnel would chill some of the rebels.

Not that much of a gamble. The way things were right now, the fighters would soon be wiped out anyway.

"Back!" J.B. yelled to Mildred as he pulled the pins on both grens and tossed them underhand into the alley, so that they would keep a low trajectory, centering their impact at around three-quarter height on the wall.

She hugged the wall, shutting her eyes from the light of the blast, opening her mouth to stop the pressure of the sound wave, blocking her ears.

"Okay," J.B. yelled, coming around with the mini-Uzi in his hands. He fired in short, choppy bursts, aiming for groups of sec men as they staggered out of the clouds of brick dust. Some of them were ripped to shred, bleeding from wounds caused by the shrapnel, screaming incoherently as pain and blood blinded them. Some had missing limbs, others were crawling since their legs had been torn by shrapnel. Loss of blood would make many buy the farm, as the white-hot metal had ripped holes in them that had ruptured arteries, their lifeblood pouring from them too quickly to staunch. Those that could remain in some way mobile now found themselves walking into the fire from the Uzi, and the carefully chosen shots from the ZKR as Mildred stood behind J.B., choosing her targets as befitted a handblaster.

Her concentration was broken by the sound of wags behind them. She left J.B. and ran back to the corner of the alley. She could see three wags, each carrying a contingent of sec, speeding toward them.

If they stayed in position, they would be trapped.

"John, pull back," she yelled as she ran toward him. "Backup's arrived—too many for us."

Still firing to prevent any stragglers advancing on them, he followed her backward, turning and twisting along the maze of alleys that would take them back to the others. He suddenly held up the Uzi and stopped firing, sure that he had spotted a familiar face among the dust and debris. Was that Prideaux? Were some of the rebels using the gap blasted in the wall to make good their escape?

It was too late to do anything about that now. He could hear the wags screech to a halt and the sec forces start to pound the sidewalk and hurtle into the alley, still uncannily silent.

"Millie, I—"

"Yeah, I saw him, too…I think," she said breathlessly. "We need to regroup with the others before we make another move."

WHEN THE ATTACK had started, Jak had cursed Prideaux for being a stupe and taking the army out of the sewer before he had completed a full recce. Then he had cursed the sec force for knowing that they would be here. But most of all he had cursed himself for not thinking of the possibility that this could happen.

The thoughts took a fraction of a second to cross his mind, and didn't even impinge on his true consciousness. His drive for survival had kicked in with his first shout, rendering everything else secondary.

Jak could see the battle begin in front of him as though it was in slow motion. Perhaps it was only the speed of his own reflexes as he watched and assessed that made it seem that way, but nonetheless he urged his ragged army to move faster. They were all clear of the maintenance hatch by now, and for any of them to attempt to scramble back down would be tantamount to buying the farm. The only thing they could do was stand and fight—but where could there be cover, here in this completely open yard?

Jak had found some himself, and in many ways there only two obvious answers: hug the walls or head for the dormitory building. Casting an appraising glance, Jak could see that the sec forces were using all three walls to fire over with SMGs. That meant that to fire at a downward angle of 180 degrees, the men on the crest of the wall would have to lean right over to sight and fire, making themselves obvious targets. It gave anyone up against the wall a slight respite, and the opportunity to fire up and along, catching sec men before they had a chance to realign.

Also, there seemed to be no one coming through the dormitory building to either storm the yard or to establish it as another command point from which to fire on the rebels. Did that mean that Dr. Jean didn't trust his men to meet the rebels face-to-face, without the protection of the wall? Or was it just an oversight?

Either way, it didn't matter. If they could get out of the yard and into the dormitory building, then they could either use that to mount a siege, or be through it and out into the streets before the sec force had a chance to move on them.

But right now, there were more pressing concerns. The walls were lined with sec men mounted on ladders, who were firing into the yard. The area itself was a mass of screaming, heaving people as the rebel army tried to keep moving, avoid being hit and fire back.

It was still in semidarkness. That was the thing that prevented it being a massacre. For some reason, the sec force hadn't thought to bring spots to light the area and make every target clear. The fact that the sec men had infrared goggles was something he forgot in the heat of the moment. Jak counted about eight rebels down and probably chilled. Others may be injured, but they were still moving, and they were returning fire. It was impossible to see if they were hitting any of the sec force, but if nothing else they were distracting its fire.

Considering the sec force had the rebels more or less trapped, they were poor tactics, and Jak began to wonder if Dr. Jean's men were going to be the problem he had suspected after all. But right now, he had to act.

"Walls—fire up—move to building shelter," he yelled, straining to make his voice heard above the noise. He knew he had no hope of being heard by all of them, but he prayed that his words would be picked up and passed on.

In some way, it had to have been working. The area in the center of the yard began to thin out as the rebel army moved to the edges.

He heard shattering glass—the frequency high and cutting through the dull roar of blasterfire—as some of the rebels broke into the dormitory building.

Looking up, Jak could see the muzzle of an SMG and the hands holding it. The torso of the sec man edged over tentatively, searching for more prey. He became that prey himself, as Jak twisted his body, angled the Colt Python and fired. The Magnum slug ripped into the area where chest and throat came together, rending them apart with its force, the exit wound shattering the man's vertebrae at the base of his neck, his head lolling limp and useless as he fell backward, driven up and out by the momentum of the slug.

One down, who knew how many more to go…but it was a start.

The firefight continued, the rebels adopting the tactics of firing from what little cover they could find, and making the sec men reveal themselves a little more to become targets themselves.

Marissa skipped around the rebels lining the walls, looking for Jak.

"Hey, babe," she said when she found him, fighting for breath and shouting to make herself heard above the roar of blasterfire, "we're gettin' back at 'em."

Jak shook his head. "Still pinned here."

"Yeah, but the guys in the building over there may be able to do something about that." She grinned. "Some of 'em are clear in there, and they're thinking about making a charge around the side, hitting the sec as they're perched on the walls. Cool, eh?"

Jak looked at her. His face was seemingly as impassive

as ever, but behind the white mask he was agog. How stupe were these people? With no notion of how many sec there were, and no recce of the position beyond the dormitory building, they were going to risk running into a certain chilling.

He was just about to voice his doubts, or make a run for the dormitory himself to stop them, when the wall to his left imploded, the sound of two grens going off close enough to meld into one momentarily deafening him so that he saw the wall fall in, spilling chilled and wounded sec. Some of the rebels were trapped by falling masonry, others fled from the carnage into the center of the yard, not caring that they might be fired upon, hoping that the clouds of dust would cover them.

It was hard to see what was going on with the noise and the clouds of dust, and why the wall had exploded was a complete mystery. All that Jak knew was that the battle had increased suddenly in intensity.

Sec men—those not directly in the line of gren impact and the line of blasterfire that chattered from beyond the wall—began to pour into the yard, running and yelling through the clouds of dust, all caution abandoned. In the distance Jak was sure he recognized the firing patterns of one of the SMGs, and could hear the crack of a target pistol. Could it be possible that… There was no time to develop the thought. All concept of keeping battle lines and formations were lost as the yard became a melee of bodies, blasting at one another and coming up together in hand-to-hand combat.

It was almost impossible to see what was going on in the confusion. Most of the rebels were chilled by now, of that Jak was sure. Hopefully, some had managed to get away. If they could get out of the dorm building, in this confusion it might be possible to run. Despite their infrared goggles making it easier for them to see men in the confusion, many of the sec had also bought the farm, and this would do little more than piss off Dr. Jean in a big way. It seemed as though the whole attack had been futile.

Yet how had they known that the rebels would use the sewers?

No time to think of that now. Jak and Marissa stood back to back, pinned by the wall farthest from the dorm building, with little hope of an avenue of escape. It looked as though their only hope was to go down fighting and take some of the sec force with them.

"Been nice knowing you, babe. Pity it never worked," Marissa said.

Jak didn't bother to reply. The whole thing felt hollow to him.

They picked at sec men with their shots as they came out of the confusion, but even using his Colt Python with care, there came a point where Jak had to reload.

As he did so, a stocky sec man with infrared goggles and a scarred face to match his own loomed out of the dust clouds. He was holding an AK-7, but not in a shooting grip; rather, he was holding it as a club.

Jak, still fumbling with his blaster, noted this with an almost detached curiosity before the sec man swung the blaster, the stock taking him under the chin. He tried to move, to roll with the blow, but for once his reflexes—dulled by the realization that they had blown the attack, perhaps—were just a little too slow, and he felt the world spin sickeningly, bile rising in his throat almost as quickly as the darkness closed in from the corners of his vision...

"OH GOOD, I WAS HOPING YOU wouldn't take too long to come around. Otherwise I would have had to try to rouse you myself, and that would have made me terribly angry."

The voice was sibilant and soft, too much so for the man from which it emanated. Jak knew this as soon as he forced his eyes open, ignoring the pain that coursed through his skull as the light hit his retinas. He recognized him as Dr. Jean from the statues and murals they had seen during their recce mission. Beside him, standing slightly back in an attitude of respect, was the sec man who had hit him back in the yard. He recognized him even without the goggles by the scars on his face. His eyes were better hidden: small, piglike and shifty, not resting on anything for any length of time. Perhaps he was nervous. Certainly, the baron made Jak cautious, if nothing else. He was too calm, too quiet.

Jak flexed his muscles. He was bound hand and foot to a rack, standing upright. He was still fully clothed, and he was pulled tightly to the rack, but not so tight that it was painful. He could just feel the edge of strain in his muscles, but no more. He moved his head to the left and right. It was free to turn, and he could see Marissa bound to a similar rack over to his left. She was conscious, and her face was white, her dark eyes large and round. She was obviously terrified.

The rest of the room was filled with electrical equipment and some pieces of metal that reminded Jak of ancient predark torture implements he had seen. There was a chair with leather restraints in the center of the room.

"You show a curiosity, which is good," Jean remarked mildly, watching Jak with his head cocked to one side. "Marshaling that swamp scum into something even approaching an army was a feat of which you should be proud. I know what many of these people are like, and I congratulate you. It's a great shame that fate has placed us on separate sides of the divide, for in another time and place I think we may have been allies."

He paused, as though waiting for Jak to answer. The albino stayed silent, his gaze now fixed on the giant before him.

Dr. Jean chuckled. It was strange to hear such a benign sound from someone who was the iron-fisted dictator of the area. "Very well," he said between his laughter, "play it that way if you wish. It is no matter to me. Soon you shall buy the farm, and go to meet the gods. You will carry with you a message from me, and from the people. Your pathetic force was the last thing to be arraigned against me. Now I have control. The next step is to build my force and extend beyond. I have the old tech, I have the numbers, and I shall use my methods to build other villes, with even greater power. Eventually, my power shall be limitless. But I need the assistance of the gods if I am to succeed. So you shall be my messengers, aided by the words of the people."

"You really believe that shit?" Marissa asked him, her voice trembling despite her best efforts.

Dr. Jean walked over to her and caressed her long, dark hair. "I do, now. Not when I began, but perhaps I was just being used as a channel then, and needed to discover the truth for myself. It was a tool to begin with, but just late-

ly… Yes, I have seen the gods, and they are guiding me.
I will feed them, and they will guide me. To this end, I have
evolved a better ritual than those I have used before. It's
an interesting one. Perhaps you may have heard of it."

He left them attached to the racks and began to walk
back toward the door, which Diamond had already opened
for him.

"It's not actually a voodoo ceremony, it's something that
comes from even farther south and even further back. I read
about it in some old texts that I found, and it seemed suitable as a symbol of ultimate power. Basically, I wait until
sunup and then I offer the gods your hearts. But the catch
is that they have to still be beating. So I've got to cut them
from your bodies and hold them aloft quite quickly. It'll
be interesting to see how I manage with that, won't it?"

He turned and left them alone, Diamond closing the
door behind him, to ponder on their upcoming fate.

THE COMPANIONS HAD PULLED BACK into cover when the
sec force had burst through the wall. J.B. cursed himself
for the counterproductive effect of his gren attack, but it
had been a chance he had to take. The rebels would have
been easy meat. At least in the confusion they had seen
some be able to effect an escape.

It meant, however, that the sec force was able to regroup and attack.

"We should be in there," J.B. said bitterly, regretting his
actions.

"No, that'd be triple stupe. They've got infrared, and
we wouldn't be able to see who the hell we were blasting," Ryan stated.

"He's right, John. Let's see what happens when the dust settles," Mildred said quietly, trying to reassure the angered Armorer.

In truth, it was almost impossible to see what was going on. Using the confusion as a cover, they moved out of the shadows and the alley, and onto the main streets. The ville dwellers were still going about establishing their own posts, and took little notice of the companions as they moved along the street. They had their weapons combat ready, but so did everyone else. Added to this, a small crowd was gathering on the street near the old building that housed the dormitory. The front had been broken in, and some sec men had spilled through.

"Figure some of 'em got away through there." J.B. smiled, feeling better about his gren attack.

"Yeah, at least you bought them that opportunity, John," Mildred murmured.

The companions tried to melt into the milling crowd outside the building. Beyond the broken glass of the old shopfront, they could tell that the blasterfire had almost decreased to nothing.

"Reckon Jak's one of those who got away?" Krysty asked.

Ryan shrugged. "Mebbe. I don't know how we're supposed to find him if he has, though."

"I think we may not have far to look," Doc commented dryly. "I fear that the good Dr. Jean knew only too well for whom he was searching."

As the companions watched, Diamond led out four sec men, each pair of whom had a body strung out between them. Both were easily recognizable: one was Jak, the other Marissa. Both were obviously breathing.

"Friend LaRue did have a large mouth, did he not?" Doc commented.

"Mebbe that's saved them," Ryan muttered. "At least they're alive, and we've got a chance to snatch them back."

At their leader's urging, they began to move through the crowd as the sec force started to disperse it. Moving to the margins, they could see that Jak and Marissa were loaded up onto a sec wag, which started to roll down the street.

In the space of less than an hour, their objectives had completely changed. From seeking to aid the insurrection and warn the rebel force of attack, they had been forced by circumstance to change their focus. Now, rescuing Jak and Marissa and getting out in one piece was the primary objective.

They kept on the track of the sec wag as it rumbled through the ville. It was relatively easy. Its appearance heralded a swarm of armed dwellers, eager to see what was happening, and their attention impeded its progress. The companions were able to disappear into the crowd. As long as they could keep the wag in sight, then they could plan a rescue bid when they found its final destination.

It was no surprise to J.B. and Ryan when the wag drove across the square that housed the shrine to Dr. Jean, pulling up by the building that housed the altar on what would once have been courthouse steps. As they held back and watched, Jak and Marissa were unloaded and carried into the building. Looking up, they could see it was about eleven stories high.

"Well, that's really simple, then," Krysty said sighing. "They're in there somewhere and we don't know the layout or what the security's like."

"We've got one advantage," Ryan said. And in reply to Krysty's raised eyebrow, he added, "They're not expecting us. We're ready for them, but no way are they ready for us."

Chapter Fifteen

The square was a lot emptier than it had been when J.B. and Ryan had taken part on the recce mission. Back then, making your way across it without being spotted would have been easier. Now was going to be harder. The baron's call to arms had left the ville dwellers with tasks of their own to undertake and their pilgrimages to the shrine much curtailed.

The companions held back after watching Jak and Marissa being carried in. A sec guard manned the doors around the side of the building where the wag had stopped, and as it pulled away they could see there were two sec men on guard, each with what appeared to be an MP-5.

"Five on two is good odds," Mildred murmured.

"Yeah, but what are the odds on us alerting a whole shitload of others on our way?" Krysty returned.

In truth, this was their problem. They had to get across the square without attracting attention, and then overpower the sec men—the easy part—and get into the building without being noticed—the not-so-easy part.

Dr. Jean inadvertently gave them a helping hand. As they lurked in the shadows, the vid screen around them blared a fanfare, followed by the face of the baron, broadcasting once again.

"My people, we have secured a great victory. The swampland scum have failed in their pitiful attempts at insurrection. With your help, our sec forces have captured those who led this sacrilegious attempt to defile our ville. As I planned to take them and offer them as messengers to the gods after we had raided their hovels, so now they have come to me. Truly, my friends, this is a sign from those who seek to guide our hand. In honor to them, I will still send forth these wretched souls as our messengers, but I will do it tonight. In just one half of a passing hour, they shall be sent on their way to the gods with our blessings and wishes for our greater victories."

The fanfare blared once more and the burble of regular broadcasts continued.

"Our friend does not believe in leaving any loose ends, does he?" Doc mused. "It doesn't give us a wealth of time with which to plan."

"Mebbe that's for the best, Doc," Ryan said grimly. "Besides which, it's going to give us a little cover."

"You can say that again," Krysty said, looking over her shoulder. Already, those ville dwellers living nearest to the square were beginning to leave the streets and buildings they had been defending, and were flocking into the square in preparation for the night's ceremony. All were still armed, and it seemed that this would give the companions clear cover.

"Follow me, keep close," Ryan whispered from the corner of his mouth as he slipped into the crowd that was beginning to congregate. The others followed him, keeping close as commanded. It was easy to keep each other in sight as the square was still quite sparsely populated, the crowd naturally drifting to the shrine that was built on the steps of the old courthouse building. As they neared the front, where people were headed, they peeled off toward the side. The attention of those in the square was so firmly fixed on the shrine, in their drugged haze, that they didn't really notice the deviation of five people.

The sec guards on the side door did, however. Both turned to face the companions as they approached. All had their blasters holstered or shouldered, so that they presented no obvious threat. The sec men nonetheless raised their own weapons cautiously.

As they drew nearer, Ryan took the scarf from around his neck and started to mop his perspiring brow, shifting the weight of the loaded material in his palm. Doc appeared to lean more heavily on his cane with each step.

The sec men said nothing, eyes unreadable behind the infrared goggles. They stood their ground, waiting for the companions to make the first move, utter the first words.

"Hey, any chance we can get a look at these scum before anyone else?" Ryan asked, adopting what he hoped was an innocent tone. "They were taken right by where we were defending, so we kinda feel like we've got our name on them."

The sec men said nothing for a moment, exchanging glances from behind their goggles. They might not have been able to see each other's eyes, but it was easily understandable when one of them shook his head.

"No, you know no one comes in here except the chosen ones who work for the baron. You'll get your chance soon enough, so why don't you just go and wait around the front like everyone else."

While the sec man had been speaking, J.B. and Mildred had been checking out the crowds behind them. No one was looking in their direction, and with Krysty they moved closer together to block the angle from the square, so that anyone looking would see five people who had approached the sec men cluster around them. Nothing more.

"Okay," J.B. murmured, only loud enough for Ryan to hear.

"That's a real pity," Ryan continued, addressing the sec men, "because would have made things a lot easier for you."

Without warning, the scarf snaked out from his fist, flung with a flick of his strongly tendoned wrist. The weights sewn into the end of the scarf affected its angle of flight, and it coiled around the neck of the nearest sec man, choking him as Ryan pulled it. The one-eyed man pulled it tight, and the force tugged the sec man to his knees, tightening the scarf even more. Forgetting his blaster in the desire to draw breath, he put both hands to the scarf and tried to free it.

Behind him, the second sec man had reacted at Ryan's action, but not quite quickly enough. As he raised his blaster, leveling it on Ryan and tightening his finger on the trigger, Doc took action. In the blink of an eye, he had withdrawn his sword from the sheath of the swordstick and, in one fluid motion, brought the blade up, proscribing an arc in the air that caused the honed Toledo steel blade to cut through the wrist of the sec man wielding the blaster. Nerves and tendons cut, blood pouring down useless fingers as he attempted to adjust his aim and still fire, the switchback of the arc sliced across his throat, ripping through the purple-and-orange camou shirt and scoring across his shoulders before opening a red maw across his throat. He stumbled forward, not knowing whether to staunch the flow at his throat or at his wrist, fumbling for the MP-5, which he had dropped.

His stumble took him onto the tip of the sword, which Doc had thrust up and under, bringing it to a position that took it under the breastbone and up into his heart. His deadweight nearly toppled the old man as he sought to retrieve his blade. He was forced to turn the chilled sec man over with his foot and heave the blade from the corpse.

While he had been doing this, Ryan had chilled his own target. Increasing the pressure on the scarf, he had pulled tighter, the weights in the end acting as counterbalances to keep the scarf firm despite the attempts of the sec man to get his fingers underneath and gain himself—literally— some breathing space. As he choked more and more, so his color changed from a pale tan to a darker, blood-red hue, his tongue poking from his mouth and swelling as he tried to gasp for breath with small, stifled choking sounds. It was impossible to see behind his infrared goggles, but there was little doubt that by now his eyes would be bulging, clouding over as consciousness started to slip from him.

He was on his knees, slumping more and more with every second that passed, every second that was precious if they were to evade detection and get into the building.

Ryan pulled tighter, not relinquishing his grip until the sec man had stopped moving. Unraveling the scarf, he could see the deep indentations and weals in the sec man's neck where the scarf had bitten into the flesh.

J.B. looked over his shoulder. "Clear so far. Let's get these bastards out of the way before someone wanders over here."

Mildred and Krysty took one sec man between them, while Ryan and J.B. took the other. Doc covered them, keeping an eye on the crowd beyond the side of the building, which seemed oblivious to all except the shrine at the front of the old courthouse.

Inside, the companions found themselves in the well of a staircase that led upward, with glass-inset doors leading through to corridors beyond. Ryan looked around for a camera, but couldn't see one. He hoped that the reconditioned old tech didn't extend to an interior vid sec system. Opposite the glass-inset doors was a plain wooden door. It was open, and inside was a darkened cupboard, used possibly for storage...if not before, it certainly was now, as they bundled the chilled sec men into the space before shutting the door.

"Okay, where would you suppose they keep prisoners in a place like this?" Ryan asked. He was rewarded by a series of thoughtful expressions, but little input. "Yeah, that's kind of the way I figured it," he said with a wry grin. "We're just going to have to work it out as we go along."

This part of the building was obviously a service stairwell for the entire block, and was used only for the removal of large objects and for use in an emergency. That was the only conclusion to draw, as on each level there were glass-inset doors on each side of the mezzanine, with corridors leading off that were occupied by active ville dwellers. It didn't take long for them to realize that not only was this where Dr. Jean lived and kept his captives, it was also the nerve center of his empire. They could see that this was where the broadcasts to the vid screen emanated from—one floor in particular seemed to lead straight onto a studio floor from one set of doors— and as they climbed higher, they were aware that they were entering the more private areas of the baron's domain. Here there was less activity, but there was also a higher quotient of sec men. They walked freely along the corridors and moved from room to room.

By the time they had reached the eighth floor, it was starting to look as though they would need some kind of a miracle to locate where Jak and Marissa were being held.

As they recced through the glass insets on the eighth floor, Ryan and J.B. taking one side, Doc and Mildred taking the other, Krysty peered over Ryan's shoulder and gasped.

Ryan turned to her, puzzled. He had seen what she had, but had failed to grasp the significance: two sec men wheeled a clothes stand on which were arrayed a half dozen costumes of colorful design, complete with headdresses. They turned left into a room, then came out minus the pole and headed on down the corridor, talking inaudibly to each other.

"Jak and Marissa are to be a sacrifice, right? That implies ritual. People will be needed to assist Dr. Jean, and they'll wear those costumes."

"And those masks," Ryan finished. "Good. The least ripples we cause now, the easier it'll be to snatch them back later."

"You mean, you want us to take Jak and Marissa in

front of the whole ville?" Mildred asked, coming over. "And that's not causing ripples?"

"We fuck it up now by getting into a firefight before we've found them, and what are our chances of saving them at all?" Ryan queried.

Mildred had to concede. "Okay, guess you're right."

They moved through the glass-inset doors and toward the room where the sec men had left the costumes, checking each room as they passed. They weren't the only ones on this floor, but those working in the other rooms were too engrossed in their tasks to notice them pass, and too sure of their own security to suspect intruders.

The companions made it with ease to the room where the costumes were housed, and found that the room was empty. J.B. kept watch while Ryan inspected the costumes. It might be a tight fit for himself and Doc—who was considerably taller than the average ville dweller—to get into the costumes, but the others should be able to manage easily.

"Hey, there are six of these and only five of us," Mildred said. "We're going to have to take one of them with us."

"Could be a good thing," Ryan replied. "We won't know what to do, so one of them could be a useful guide, 'specially if they know they're chilled meat for one wrong move."

They settled back to wait for the occupants of the costumes to enter. As they waited, they could feel the pitch and hum of activity and tension build outside in the square. Somewhere in this building, they knew that Jak and Marissa could hear it, too.

J.B. kept watch on the corridor, making sure that although he could note all the comings and goings, he himself wasn't noticed. It seemed as though these stupes were leaving it until the last moment until they dressed for the ritual, and he was starting to get edgy. So it was with a palpable sense of relief that he saw six people enter the corridor through a set of double doors at the far end. They were talking among themselves, and an armed sec man trailed behind them. They, too, were armed, but their blasters were holstered, which meant they could be taken by surprise. The Armorer relayed this to the others.

Ryan nodded, and quickly climbed onto a table to take out one of the bulbs illuminating the room. It was small, lit by two sockets, and Krysty followed his lead, rapidly unscrewing the other and blowing on her burning fingers. To knock the bulbs out would cause too much noise, and stealth was their greatest ally.

"Shit, Frank, the fucking lights are out again," said the woman in lead of the party as she entered the room and flicked the switch. "Power's on, as well. Don't maintenance do anything around here?"

"All right, all right, I'll see to it," the sec man replied wearily, turning to move away from the threshold of the room.

This was the biggest risk. He was outside in the corridor, and anyone looking would have seen Ryan's scarf snake out around his neck, lock with the weighted ends and pull him back. The one-eyed man kicked the door closed as the sec man fell back into the room, and all was plunged into darkness.

Ryan drew the panga from his thigh and wasted no time

in chilling the sec man with one swift stroke. "Krysty, light," he said hoarsely. The Titian-haired woman screwed back the bulb in its socket, and the room was once more illuminated. The stunned ville dwellers took in the four companions with blasters trained on them, and the fifth, who was standing over the chilled corpse of the sec man, Frank. They knew that they had no chance of reaching their own weapons.

"Okay, we can do this the easy way, or the hard way," Ryan said simply. "Easy way is that you let us knock you out and leave you for later while we take your place. Hard way is we chill you all like Frank, here."

The woman who had been berating Frank as she'd entered the room went for her blaster. "Dr. Jean'd chill us all anyway," she muttered, a sentence she hardly had a chance to finish as J.B.'s Tekna streaked through the air and took her in the side of the neck. The force knocked her sideways, the blade penetrating skin, tendon and her carotid. The shock rendered her immobile as she began to drown in her own blood, which flowed thick and free down her throat and into her lungs and stomach.

"Who wants to be next?" Ryan asked. The remaining four backed off, hands clear of blasters. "Rather take a chance, eh? You," he added, pointing with the blood-dripping tip of the panga at the smallest of the group, "you're going to help us. The rest of you…" He nodded to the companions, and without warning they launched into four of the group of five. It was a swift, brutal assault using hand-to-hand skills. Before the group had a chance to respond, three of them were unconscious.

J.B. took the Tekna from the throat of the woman he

had chilled and sheathed it before joining the others in binding and gagging the three they had disabled. Ryan sheathed his panga and took the remaining ville dweller by the arm.

"What's your name?"

"Roisin," she said with a stammer and the hint of a cleft palate. Her eyes were wide with fear.

"Okay. You do this right, and you'll be okay. You try to fuck with us and you'll be joining them," he said, indicating the two corpses. "Is that clear?"

She nodded frantically, too frightened to trust her own voice.

"Good, then let's get started," he said, suddenly brisk and businesslike.

"OH DEAR. I DO HOPE YOU haven't gone and bought the farm before I've had a chance to give you my message to the gods. That would be very inconvenient, to say the least... Wake up, scum!"

The order was delivered in a harsher, louder tone, and accompanied by a backhand slap that made the teeth in Jak's jaw feel like they had been loosened. The albino opened his eyes and spoke lazily through a mouth filling with blood. His voice was mushy.

"You made point."

Dr. Jean stepped back and threw back his head, roaring with laughter. Both Jak and Marissa were in a state where nothing much registered: no pain, no sound, no sense of danger. A part of Jak, deep inside, was screaming at him that this was wrong, but there was nothing he could do to break out beyond the torpor. Shortly after Dr.

Jean had spoken to them before, the scar-faced sec man had come back into the room and injected them with something that had given an immediate rush. Mebbe it was because it was straight into the bloodstream, or mebbe it was because Jean's old tech labs had developed a more pure strain than had been known before, but this jolt had hit them straight between the eyes.

Jak had felt himself slump on the frame, knowing that the pull on his shoulders would strain his muscles, but not caring: he couldn't be bothered to lift himself up, and anyway his joints weren't giving him any grief. And if they did at some unspecified future point? Why the hell should he care about that?

The drug had washed any semblance of care from his mind, had numbed any pain that he might feel, and had left him feeling as if he were floating on a cloud. That part of his brain that was still the ever-alert hunter, sniffing out danger, told him that this was a dangerous way to feel. Some jolt induced speedy, hyperactivity, some gave you visions, some made you feel as though nothing mattered and just lie down and drift. It depended on how it was cut and how it was made. But this was something else entirely. Jak knew that the point was to make Marissa and himself completely subservient, to make them pliable and easy meat for Dr. Jean to sacrifice. And it was working well. He felt on one level as though he hadn't a care in the world, and that he could just stand there forever.

He had meant to look over at Marissa to see how she was doing, but somehow he hadn't been able to motivate himself into doing this, and before he knew what had happened he had drifted into a dreamless sleep, broken only by the soft, sibilant voice of the baron and the sharp blow of his hand.

Now Jak moved his head so that he could see Marissa off to the side. Her head was lolling uselessly, shaking slightly as she tried to clear it. Her head turned and her eyes met his. He hoped that his own eyes didn't look as wide and clouded as hers. Wherever she was, he doubted that it was in this room.

"Good, I'm so glad that you've awakened fully. I must admit, that was quite a powerful jolt—if you'll pardon my little joke—that I had Diamond administer to you. Necessary, as you could be a threat. You think I don't remember you, Jak Lauren? I was with Tourment when it all fucked up, I saw what you did to him with the help of those other bastards. Fortunately, they seem to have deserted you—or perhaps you parted company with them some time back. Who knows—and frankly, who cares? I know I don't, not now."

The baron was dressed in a costume covered with rags and feathers that had been dyed a variety of bright colors. Bones—some obviously chicken others just as obviously human—hung from the costume. He had a top hat perched on his head with a feather plume at the crown, and ribbons tied around. His face was painted a ghostly white, his cheekbones etched out in charcoal. It made his eyes seem larger than normal, the whites of them yellowed and shot with red veins. The pupils were like pinpricks.

He loomed up in front of Jak so that the albino could smell the crude spirit on his breath.

"You've done me a big favor, really. You've offered yourself up to me and taken away the threat of the swamp scum. Played right into my hands—" he clapped them loudly in front of Jak's face and laughed wildly "—and saved me the effort of clearing out the swamp for myself. And now you've come to me to be my messengers to the gods."

"You really believe that stupe shit?" Jak asked, aware of how mush-mouthed he sounded, how strung-out and distant the jolt had made him.

"An interesting point, my little man," Dr. Jean mused, waving a finger in Jak's face. Despite himself, the albino found he was following the finger as it moved, and he vaguely realized the suggestibility that had been fed to him by the drug in his system. Jean continued. "You know, at first I thought it was crap myself, just something I could use to control people, mold them to what I wanted. But the strange thing is that after a while I began to see that there were gods out there, and that somehow they were shaping my destiny. Driving me on so that I can move beyond the pest-ridden swamp and to the lands beyond, where I can accrue greater riches, and greater power. Where I can fulfil my destiny."

"Bullshit—just jolt talk," Jak said.

Dr. Jean brought his hand around in a swing, open-palmed as before. The hefty flesh of his palm slapped Jak on the side of the head, making him spin, opening more cuts in his cheek from his jarred teeth.

"Perhaps you're right," Dr. Jean mused mildly, in contrast to his action. "But does it matter, really? If you want something to be so much, then you make it so. Enough—time to go on with the show."

Jak spit out a glob of blood and phlegm. It was meant

to be a last defiant gesture at the baron as he limped away, but the albino was so weak that it landed almost at his feet, splattering on the concrete.

Dr. Jean hadn't noticed. He was already at the door, beckoning the sec men waiting outside and ordering them to take Jak and Marissa down from the racks and carry them out to the shrine in front of the building.

As his bonds were released and he flopped off the frame of the rack, Jak tried to move. Not too much. He knew he couldn't fight back right here and now, but he wanted to try to flex some muscles, see what kind of response he got from his drugged limbs. There was no response. No matter how much he tried to use his muscles, they failed to be anything other than jelly.

He had no choice. He had to let the sec men carry him. Even if he had been offered the chance to go on foot, he could barely have crawled or shuffled his way out of the room. He could see that they were doing the same with Marissa.

As he let himself be carried through the building, Jak got little more than a series of impressions. The corridors were lit like the redoubts, and the air hummed with the same kind of predark tech that he had witnessed before. There were people moving through the corridors who paid no attention to himself or Marissa, as though this was always happening; he did notice, however, that they were deferential to the baron, who followed a few steps behind.

They left the corridors and began to descend a staircase, turning right to come out into an airy lobby with a high ceiling. This had to be the front of the old building, before the steps that had been turned into the shrine facing the square. Jak had seen old buildings designed in this style before, and knew they would soon emerge into the night air.

But it was more than that idle impression. It was something he could feel, a palpable change in the atmosphere as they approached the exit onto the shrine. The chanting had grown louder, and seemed to carry with it a note of humming, vibrant excitement, an electricity that made the hairs on the back of his neck suddenly stand to attention, and made his spine buzz. It started to get adrenaline pumping as he rode the wave of energy coming off the crowd. Mebbe, just mebbe... He tried to flex his muscles, get some life flowing back into them. There was some response, but not enough to be of any use to him. Not yet.

As they left the lobby of the old building, he noticed that Dr. Jean held back, turning and muttering something to one of his sec men. Jak tried to catch it, but it was lost in the exultant roar that broke from the crowd as the sec men carried Marissa and himself out onto the platform of the shrine. It was a shrill, animal cry that oozed bloodlust and expectancy.

All else was lost in this consuming atmosphere of lust and hate. He felt himself be lifted onto a stone slab that was decorated with feathers and stones. He could feel the stones press into his back, causing him discomfort, but couldn't control his own muscles well enough as of yet to move from them. He looked up at the night sky beyond the electric lighting, which was augmented by blazing torches. The naked flames cast warmth into the cold air, streams of which flowed around the slab and contrasted with the occasional bursts of heat from the torches and

from the massed ranks of humanity that stood in front of
him.

Jak tried to look across at Marissa. Her slab was to his
right, some two yards away, and he could just about see
her lying there, inert. The angle was too acute for him to
see any more.

The cheers and exultant cries suddenly gained volume,
melding together into one mass chant, a voice of the crowd
that was so strong and vibrant that it was almost a physical force, hitting Jak in the stomach.

They were chanting Dr. Jean's name.

The baron had walked out onto the shrine, his arms held
aloft in recognition of his people.

"WHERE ARE THOSE STUPES?" Dr. Jean had asked Diamond, keeping back as his sacrificial victims were taken
out onto the steps of the old courthouse.

Diamond furrowed his scarred brow. "Should be down
by now, sir," he said. "I'll check 'em out. It's not like they
usually keeping you waiting."

"I should hope not. They know what the consequences
are," Dr. Jean said with a mildness that belied his meaning. "Ah, here they are," he added as another of the doors
onto the old lobby opened and six people in costume entered. Five of them were already masked, but the woman
in lead had her mask under her arm.

"Sorry," she mumbled, "costumes late in arriving." She
was hesitant, sounded terrified. Dr. Jean took this to be a
sign that they were worried about their slack performance.
After all, they were all masked already.

"These things happen. I will look into it later," the

baron said magnanimously, little realizing that her fear was caused by Ryan's SiG-Sauer, trained on the small of her back and concealed in the long sleeve of the costume. "Now get ready, like the others," he urged, almost avuncular, "we have a ceremony to conduct."

He turned and strode out onto the platform, where the sec men were tying down Jak and Marissa. The people cheered at his arrival, and began to chant his name as the sec men finished their task and pulled back into the old lobby.

Watching the crowd and also their backs, the companions found that their skin began to crawl and prickle with sweat that dripped down their backbones. There was a sense of power and menace in the air that was solid, and was almost like another presence up there on the platform with them.

Dr. Jean began to chant in a high, keening voice, his tone breaking on the highest notes as he tried to reach them. He held his arms aloft and then gestured at the two prone sacrificial victims with a sweep of his arms. He broke into a garbled chant that was in Cajun French. It was difficult for the companions to understand, as none of them had a firm grasp of the patois, but to Jak it became clear. As he lay there, he could hear Dr. Jean call on the gods to accept these messengers and the hopes of the people that they conveyed on their journey. He called on the gods to help him and the people in their search for a better land and a greater life. He began to sing again, setting up a call and response chant that was taken up by the crowd below, the sound swelling into a mighty roar as the people joined with him.

But it was more than that. Up on the platform of the shrine, and outside of the conditioning that Dr. Jean had placed on his people, it was obvious to see how his effects were achieved. Under the chanting of the crowd, a low humming sound was barely audible. It was unsettling and disturbing to the companions. But more than that, because they were free of the years of hypnosis and drugs, and because they had experienced similar phenomena before, they were able to identify the sound as something emanating from the vid screens around the square.

Ryan, Krysty and J.B. didn't know quite how it worked, only that it did. But Mildred and Doc, for differing reasons, knew exactly what was going on. The sound was a trigger to impulses that the old tech had planted in the people of the walled ville over a period of years, augmented by the jolt that they were fed. Even now, they could see people all across the crowd snorting powder. Those who didn't have their own were helping themselves from bowls of the drug the sec men were carrying.

All of this was designed to whip the crowd into the fervor and bloodlust frenzy for the ceremony, to spur them on to work harder for the baron and to help him extend his sphere of influence beyond the bayou.

So now they were five, standing on the platform in disguise, with an armed and frenzied crowd before them and a sec force behind them, hoping to save Jak and Marissa and somehow spirit them out of the square.

Behind their masks, they exchanged glances. Whatever else this was going to be, easy wasn't the word any of them would choose to describe it.

The only member of the ville who didn't seem to be

affected in any way by the events taking place was the woman who had led them onto the platform. She had gestured to them to take their places—three at each slab—as they would if they were the genuine sacrificial priests. Any influence the hypnosis or drugs of the past may have had on her, had been temporarily wiped clean by the rush of her own fear.

She looked out at the crowd as if seeing it for the first time, which, in a way, she was. Other times she had been as influenced by the baron as the rest of the population. Now, she was apart, and it seemed an alien and scary presence to her.

She looked around, eyes wide behind her mask, no longer knowing quite what was expected of her by anyone. Dr. Jean finished the chant and spoke to the crowd in the broken French of the bayou. He told them that the time to begin the sacrifice was nigh. He turned to the nearest slab, which was Marissa's, and held out his hands, chanting.

J.B. was nearest to the baron, with Mildred and Krysty around the slab. He cast a glance toward their captive, hoping that she would guide him. It was a vain hope, as her horrified and glazed glare spoke only of someone frozen in fear.

J.B. decided that now was the time to take matters into his own hands. As the baron drew near, J.B. pulled out his Tekna and stepped in toward Dr. Jean, using the folds of his costume to mask the thrust he made.

The baron's eyes, already exaggerated by his makeup, became almost absurdly wide as the Armorer's thrust took the knife up and into his stomach. Dr. Jean was a big man, sturdily built, with layers of fat and muscle that slowed the progress of the blade as it surged toward his intestines, intent on causing a massive internal hemorrhage.

The baron had the presence of mind and speed of reflex to push at J.B., thrusting him away. With a bellow that was part rage and part pain, Dr. Jean staggered backward as J.B. went sprawling, the bloodied knife still in his fist. The crowd began to hum with confusion, the people, in their trancelike state, not being sure of exactly what was going on.

But Mildred and Krysty knew. As soon as J.B. closed with the baron, they realized that they had little time in which to act. As quickly as they could, they released the bonds that kept Marissa on the slab. Because of her jolt-addled state, the sec men hadn't bothered to tighten the knots on the bonds. They were there merely to stop her struggling too much when her heart was torn from her body.

Mildred and Krysty pulled the woman off the slab. She stumbled and tried to keep her feet, but they couldn't assist her. They had to prepare themselves for the firefight that they knew would come. J.B. was already on his feet, Tekna sheathed and the mini-Uzi in his hands. He threw off his costume so that he would no longer be encumbered by it.

The revelation that something was very wrong sent a visible shiver through the crowd. The people could see Dr. Jean staggering across the platform, bent over and clutching at his stomach, blood staining the rags and feathers around his middle the same shade of red.

Ryan and Doc exchanged a quick glance. It was obvious what they had to do. The time for subterfuge had passed, and they needed to be ready for combat. Throwing off their costumes, they hastily untied Jak. The albino shook himself, stumbling as he attained his feet.

"Leave me. Okay," he yelled as Doc made to come to his assistance. He was far from okay, however. Despite the adrenaline rush that had started to feed life back into his limbs as he was being carried out by the sec men, he was still nowhere near fighting strength, and it was all he could do to stand unaided.

He had no idea how Ryan and Doc had suddenly appeared from nowhere—he was equally surprised to see J.B., Mildred and Krysty standing near a faltering Marissa—but he had no time or inclination to wonder about that right now. He could see the crowd, could see the sec men beginning to rush the platform, and most of all he could see the bellowing, wounded figure of Dr. Jean stagger along the lip of the shrine.

Total choas was about to envelop them, and if he was to stand any chance of getting himself and Marissa out of this in any kind of shape, then he had to look after her and make sure that his friends could fight without having to worry about him.

Lurching alarmingly as his weakened limbs tried to deal with the urgent message of flight that his brain was feeding them, Jak made his way over to Marissa. Watching them go, Ryan knew that he and the others could get on with the more serious business of staying alive.

Sec men were pouring out of the front of the old courthouse building and onto the platform of the shrine. Diamond was at the forefront, noticeable primarily because he was the only sec man without infrared goggles. Not that this helped him as he charged straight into a hail of fire from the Armorer's Uzi, which stitched a line of blood from his left shoulder down to his right hip, throwing him backward into a group of sec men who were on his heels, making them stumble. They were unable to aim and fire on the companions, and so were easy targets for the first wave of fire from Mildred, Ryan and Krysty.

To the left of the stricken Diamond, and coming from another set of doors, was another phalanx of sec men. Doc wasted no time in centering his LeMat on this group, and letting them feel the full force of the shot charge. The white-hot metal pellets ripped through them, tearing at flesh and bone, spreading a fine mist of blood across the group. The group were scattered, some chilled, others wounded too heavily to return fire.

Driven back by the hail of fire, and the flying bodies of those who were chilled and wounded, the sec force was temporarily pushed back into the old courthouse. But this was not the only source of problems for the companions.

An awareness of what was happening began to permeate the crowd in front of the shrine. They were hyped up, jolt-fueled, and in a state where they weren't sure what was real. It was what Dr. Jean relied upon, and it was what had slowed their reactions. But however much it had dulled them, it hadn't completely wiped them out. Down in the crowd, some of the ville dwellers were beginning to realize that something was wrong. The sight of their baron stumbling around the platform, blood dripping from his guts as he bellowed in agony, was a signal that those on the shrine weren't all there to help him complete his task.

As they had discarded their costumes, the companions hadn't revealed themselves to be swamp dwellers or part of the rebel army. But whoever they were, they were the enemy.

And they had to be destroyed.

One by one, increasing incrementally so that a volley of single shots became a hail of fire in a matter of minutes, the crowd in the square began to rain blasterfire onto the shrine.

Not thinking about who was in direct line of fire.

Dr. Jean straightened, outraged and shocked as the first of the fire began to hit him. "No—nononononono…" he bellowed, inaudible above the volleys of shells. Standing upright now, blood pouring from the wound in his guts, he was peppered by handblaster and rifle fire, his skin and flesh puckering as the bullets hit home all across his head and body, ripping chunks from him.

He was chilled long before he fell. His inclination was to fall forward, the direction of his weight, counterbalanced by the spread force of the fire that still ripped skin and flesh from his bones, his blood spraying over his people—the people whose bloodlust he had cultivated; the people whose bloodlust was now the cause of his own demise.

They didn't even notice, in their frenzy, when his corpse finally collapsed and fell from the platform.

Chapter Sixteen

Something happened the moment that Dr. Jean finally bought the farm. The companions, now clustered together in the center of the platform, between the two slabs from which they had plucked Jak and Marissa, could feel it. The atmosphere within the ville had changed. The baron may have used old tech and jolt to instil the hypnotic suggestion into his people, but it was himself that that they followed, his personality that controlled them. And they had just seen him chilled before their very eyes.

They had no leader. They had no lead. All they had was an uncontrollable bloodlust that had to be sated at any cost. So they began to turn on one another. Attention that had been focused on the platform was now turned on themselves. Day-to-day disagreements and rivalries now took on a much greater significance than heretofore. Instead of training their blasters on the platform and trying to take out those who had caused the downfall of the baron, they instead turned their blasters on one another. The square turned into a heaving mass of people indulging in a firefight and in hand-to-hand combat. At such close range, there were plenty of casualties from blasterfire, and it was beginning to look as though the walled ville would wipe itself out in an act of self-destruction.

The companions were stunned for a second by the sudden transformation in the crowd as soon as it was released from the grip of Dr. Jean. Unable to believe that they were no longer under attack themselves, they were transfixed by the carnage that was taking place before them, their own presence seemingly forgotten.

"Ryan, look," Jak yelled, throwing a wobbling arm in the direction of the old courthouse lobby. More sec men were making their way from the rear toward the sets of double doors, primed to repeat the attack that had seen the first wave wiped out.

"Fuck this," J.B. muttered, taking a gren from his munitions bag, pulling the pin and tossing the gren underhand into the lobby of the building. He signaled to the others to take cover, which they did by using the slabs on which the sacrifices were to have been made. The gren went off inside the building with a dull roar, almost drowned by the firefight that was taking part to their rear. The hot metal fragments from the detonating grenade decimated the sec force within, and a few of the fragments were flung clear of the doors and out over the platform. The woman who had been their unwilling guide to the ceremony, and who had stood rooted to the spot, unable to take in what was occurring around her, fell victim to one of these. The fragment hit her in the left eye as she watched openmouthed at the destruction within the building. It penetrated cleanly into the eyeball, frying the viscous fluid of the eyeball and cutting right through muscle tissue into the soft brain beyond. She slumped to the floor of the platform, still unable to comprehend the destruction around her, even as the life was extinguished from her body.

Coming out from cover, the five companions headed for the lobby, ignoring the carnage behind them. As long as the ville dwellers were intent on chilling one another, it meant that they weren't paying any attention to the companions or Jak and Marissa. Mildred and J.B. held back to cover the two jolt-addled ex-sacrifices as they staggered across the platform toward the ruined lobby.

"Shit, think you'll be okay moving?" the Armorer asked Jak, yelling to make himself heard over the sound of a firefight.

"Yeah, just as long as we not run too far," Jak replied with a wry grin. He could feel strength returning to him with every step as the adrenaline pumping around his system and sheer willpower fought off the effects of the drug; but Marissa wasn't doing as well. Perhaps because of her smaller frame, perhaps because she wasn't as strong, she was still weak on her feet, her eyes still pinpricked pupils and wide irises, staring in confusion at what was happening around her. She tried to run and halfstumbled, as though her limbs were lagging behind her brain. Mildred took her arm.

"You go, Jak. I'll take her," she said to the albino. In truth, he was glad to hear that, as he was still some way short of being up to speed himself, without having to carry Marissa along with him.

The group entered the lobby of the building. The shrine and the heavy masonry in front of the building acted as a shield for the noise in the square, and they seemed to be in an almost unnatural calm. The lobby was littered with bloodied corpses, some still barely alive and moaning, others long since having been chilled. The walls were damaged and blackened by the blast, and the floor and bodies were covered with debris from the explosion: brick, masonry, plaster, wood.

"Dammit, where do we go from here?" J.B. asked.

"I don't know," Ryan mused, "but at least that gren bought us some time."

The Armorer was gratified, feeling that this time his use of the gren had been justified. At the back of his mind had been the concern that—like back in the ville when he'd attacked the sec force besieging the rebels—he might have made matters worse.

But this wouldn't get them out of the walled ville. That had to be their number-one priority.

"Fireblast, I wish we knew the layout of this damn place a little better," Ryan ground out. "Feels really weird, as well."

Krysty shook her head. As a doomie, she could feel this more than any of them. "It is different…all that old tech shit is still pumping out those noises, and the jolt is still working, but there's no Dr. Jean to direct what they're feeling. Now they just want to chill."

"Let us look upon the brighter side of this," Doc said.

"There's a brighter side?" Mildred questioned.

Doc laughed. "Of course there is, my dear Doctor. At least they are not after us, for a start. If we attract fire, it is only because we happen to be in the wrong place at the wrong time—"

"You know, somehow I don't find that very reassuring, Doc," Mildred interrupted wryly.

"Perhaps, my dear Doctor, if you stopped trying to be humorous and let me finish, we may get somewhere. I realize that cheap jokes are your reaction to stress, but I fear we do not have the time for them right now. As I was saying," he continued, leaving Mildred openmouthed, "we are not a target as such. So may I suggest we adopt a policy of trying to keep to the shadows? Rather than rush, and make ourselves noticeable, would it not perhaps be better if we kept to the margins and let these people blast seven shades of hell from each other, moving only when we can be sure that we shall not be noticed?"

Ryan looked levelly at Doc. "You know what, Doc? That's a damn fine idea."

Forming into a line, with Jak and Marissa sheltered in the middle, aided by Mildred, Ryan and Krysty in the lead, Doc and J.B. covering the rear, they set off to canvas the building. The lower levels were deserted. With Dr. Jean gone, and the hypnotic effects of the drugs and old tech causing a desire to fight anyone over anything, the only occupants of the rooms they recce'd were corpses or those who were close to buying the farm—the victors in those particular fights having left the building to take up arms in the square.

Moving up the staircase, keeping tight formation with blasters ready to shoot the hell out of anyone who stepped into their path, they traversed the whole building. The story was the same on every floor. The only occupants of the building apart from themselves were those who were either already chilled, or were mortally wounded and well on the way. Those who had emerged victorious from these internal firefights had already made their way out into the square.

On the sixth floor they came across an open-plan office layout that housed a series of comps and tone and noise generators that were running and were linked by cables to the vid machines that were still pumping out the propaganda about the now deceased baron to a crowd that was no longer listening and no longer cared.

"This is where it's coming from," Krysty said, immediately going over to the comp consoles and seeing if she could make much sense of them. Dean had taught her what he had learned at the Nicolas Brody school. Mildred stood over her shoulder.

"Can you switch it off?" Doc asked.

"Sure we want to do that?" Ryan asked. "If they're not out for each other, would they come looking for us?"

"No more than if we stumble on them by accident while they're like that," Mildred replied. "You take this shit away from them, and they're going to see what they've done to one another. Hell, they're not going to know what to do," she theorized.

"Can't be any worse one way or another." Ryan shrugged. "It's convinced me. Can you turn this shit off?" he asked Krysty.

She shook her head, her long, sentient red hair flowing more freely than it had for some time. "Hard to tell. Some of this stuff is really complex, more so than anything I've seen before. If I screw with it and get it wrong, I could make things worse. You want my honest opinion?" she asked, grinning as she looked Ryan in the eye. "You really want to make sure about this, then I'd say blast the shit out of the fucker."

"That should work." Ryan laughed. He beckoned for them to pull back to the doorway, in case the shorting of the comp circuits caused a fire or small explosion in the room.

"J.B., you want to do this?" he asked, indicating the M-4000 that was slung over the Armorer's shoulder. The load of barbed metal fléchettes would certainly cause considerable damage to the delicate comp circuitry.

"No, let me," Marissa said, her voice sounding unusually loud and clear. "It's my people who suffered because of that shit, so I'm the one should finally end it." Her voice cracked under the strain of controlling herself while the jolt was still in her system. She held out her hands for the M-4000. J.B. eyed her appraisingly, trying to judge if she was up to the task. She still looked a little dizzy from the jolt, but her expression was set and firm. He could tell that she wouldn't take no for an answer, and so held out the blaster to her.

Steadying herself, she aimed for the main bank of comps and fired into them. The load from the shotgun spread and ripped through the metal casings of the comps, rupturing circuit boards and transistors, breaking delicate chips. The shattered comps fizzed and crackled, flames licking at them.

She turned her attention to the tone and noise generators that were feeding the hypnotic impulses. Firing at each of the three generators in turn, racking the blaster between each, she reduced them to shattered hulks of metal that now lay silent.

There was no danger of a fire spreading, as the few flames that had been produced flickered and died with nothing to feed them among the metal of the old tech.

"It's over…" she said before handing the M-4000 back to J.B.

THEY WAITED UNTIL DAYLIGHT, watching the ville destroy itself, from the top of the old courthouse building, resting in turn and feeding from Dr. Jean's kitchens. They were also able to stock up on their own supplies by looting the deserted building. Through the night the inhabitants of the walled ville of Lafayette waged war, sporadic bursts of blasterfire and outbreaks of actual fire occurring at random around the ville. From the roof they were able to get a panoramic view of the settlement, and could see the same patterns repeated all over.

For some reason, the old courthouse was left alone. Perhaps because it had the shrine in front of it, and even in their confused state, freed from the hypnotic bonds of the baron now that the vid screens were blank and silent, they still held a fear of the place where he had once dwelt.

No matter. It suited the companions well for this to be the circumstance. It gave them a chance to rest up and wait in the middle of all the mayhem, to have a chance to recuperate before attempting to leave the walled ville and return to the swamp.

By the middle of the following morning, a kind of calm had descended over the ville. A few fires still burned, and there was the occasional crackle of blasterfire, but for the most part the people had fallen into a kind of stupor, worn from the fighting of the previous night, and dazed about what to do next.

Ryan gathered his people in the baron's old chambers.

"Time for us to leave," he said simply. "I figure the best thing we can do is get hold of a sec wag and try to drive out as far as possible."

He turned to Marissa. "There's a chance that some of your people who managed to escape the battle last night may be trying to get back to your ville. Mebbe we can pick some of them up along the way, if they—and us——can avoid the sec patrols who are coming back. I figure it'd be good if you were there to meet them," he finished.

Leaving the old courthouse, keeping the same formation as the previous night, even though both Jak and Marissa seemed fully recovered from the drugs, they searched for a sec wag. It didn't take them long to find one. All the wags had been deserted, and some had been set ablaze.

Ryan and J.B. sat in the cab, with the others on the bench seats on the open back. Keeping triple red as they drove through the ville—as a precaution—they found that there was a defeated atmosphere about the walled ville, even though the only battle had been among the ville dwellers. People looked on blank-eyed as the wag passed them, unable even to register curiosity. When they reached the gates, they found that they had been left gaping wide, the SMG posts along the walls deserted. Wags were scattered around the entrance, left by returning sec patrols who had no orders and leadership anymore, and who had rushed into the ville to take part in the firefight within. Some of sec men sat by their wags now, returning to them as they had little idea what else they could do with themselves. They, too, sat and watched as the companions drove past.

Without his charismatic figurehead, the reign of Dr. Jean had ended within hours, the great empire he had planned to build little more than dust. Jak and Marissa looked on this, but neither considered their army to have been the cause. If anything, the catalyst had been the intervention of those who sought to save Jak and Marissa when their own campaign had crumbled. As the wag ground to a halt where the swamp became too impenetrable for a four-wheeled vehicle to proceed, they both considered—separately—that this had been a Phyrric victory: they had defeated Dr. Jean, but at the cost, it seemed, of all those who had remained united against him.

So it was with a weary tread and heavier hearts that they made their way through the hidden paths of the swamp to where the settlement lay hidden.

Scouts who kept watch on the paths sent ahead word of their arrival, so that they were greeted by Beausoleil when they entered the ville. Those who had been left behind gathered with the old man. To Marissa and Jak it seemed a pitifully small number of old men, old women and children.

"So you reached Lafayette in time to save them, if no one else," was his bleak greeting.

"There haven't been any others made it back yet?" Ryan countered. The old man shook his head.

The one-eyed man told the assembled throng what had happened. The others left it to him, and for her part Marissa was glad not to have to talk about the action she now saw as ripping the heart from her ville.

"I suppose you'll say you told me so," she said bitterly, addressing Beausoleil when Ryan had finished.

The old man shook his head. "Ain't no blame to put anywhere. Never forced no one to do nothing. Besides which, Dr. Jean is gone, so whatever comes next has got to be better. Sometimes it just costs more than jack to get things done."

"How can you say that? Nearly everyone is chilled," she countered, tears beginning to flow down her cheeks.

The old man shrugged. "Things is as they is. Don't expect me to feel bad to make you feel better."

He turned and walked away, leaving her to start sobbing on Jak's shoulder.

OVER THE NEXT FEW DAYS, some did come back. They had tales of how they had run through the streets of the walled ville, hiding while the firefights raged, then made their way out past blank-eyed and lost souls wandering the broken ville. Some carried injuries that had slowed them, others had stayed to try to loot before running for home, hoping to bring things back with them. Eventually, the stream trickled and dried. About sixteen of the rebel army had managed to stay alive and stay free, making it back to the hidden settlement. If nothing else, it made Marissa feel better. They now had a few more people back to band together and come out of hiding. There was nothing to hide from. Now they could start to build a new community, a new life.

And Marissa wanted to build it with Jak. But the albino hunter had no wish to stay.

"But why?" she asked him when he told her. "I thought we were your people, and you were one of us...and I thought that you and me..."

Jak shook his head. "Nothing here now. This your land, your people. Mebbe been away too long, and mebbe not really belong anywhere anymore. Except mebbe with them."

He looked over to where the companions were preparing to leave. J.B. and Mildred had been distributing ammo and med supplies as needed before they set out for the redoubt they had originally been headed for. They figured that Dr. Jean's sec force would have wandered away after his fall, and they could enter undisturbed. If nothing else, a few now-isolated sec men would present little problem. As he watched the companions, Jak knew that they were his people. When he had chosen to leave with them the first time, when he had returned to them after avenging the murder of his wife and child… They shared bonds that no one else could understand.

How could he explain that to her?

Jak took Marissa's hands in his and looked in her eyes. "Another time, another place, mebbe this was home. Mebbe always looking for home. Thought found it, but was wrong. Mebbe home is with them, wherever find together. Mebbe… But even with you here, this not it. Not know where it is."

"So how will you know?" she asked him tenderly. He could only shrug.

"Only know when find it. So until then, can't stop searching."

James Axler
Outlanders

LORDS OF THE DEEP
Outlanders #38

The turquoise utopia of the South Pacific belies the mammoth evil rising beneath the waves as Kane and his companions come to the aid of islanders under attack by a degenerate sea nation thriving within a massive dome on the ocean floor. Now the half-human inhabitants of Lemuria have become the violent henchmen of the one true lord of the deep, a creature whose tenacious grip on the stygian depths—and all sentient souls in his path—tightens with terrible power as he prepares to reclaim his world.

Available August 2006 wherever you buy books.